MIND'S EYE

F. Lynn Godfriaux

WolfSinger Publications ~ Security Colorado

In honor of Ray and Fran
May Peace be with you both.

"Beloved Pan, and all ye other gods who haunt this place,
give me beauty in the inward soul;
and may the outward and inward man be at one."

—Plato, *Phaedrus*

Acknowledgements

There are several people I would like to thank, without whose patience, support and expertise I would never have made it to the end of this manuscript.

To Elizabeth: Thank you for all the lunches, debates, challenges, ideas, and brain-storming during the long process of getting this manuscript completed. Your friendship and support are invaluable. I look forward to helping with your WIP.

To Steve and Brenda: Thank you for your honest, blunt challenges concerning police procedure, investigations, writing style, villain psychology, my single-minded color default tendency, and wayward alleys I inadvertently traversed in my organic writing approach. You both are close to my heart and my family's heart, and I could not have made it through this project without both of you, your support and your guidance.

To Gordon and Evelyn, Cristina, Paul, and Jody: Thank you for your friendship, your support, your professional expertise, and your notations on mistakes I made through ignorance and my impatience to get this thing finished. You saved the life of a Corvette.

To Carol and Tim Hightshoe and WolfSinger Publications: Thank you for your expertise, high expectations and publishing standards, your friendship, and your support. Without you this book would never escape cyberspace restrictions.

To Nancy and family at Mark Reyner Stables, and the therapists and volunteers with the Colorado Springs Therapeutic Riding Center: Thank you for your equine expertise and the loving care you give to horses and people. You all have hearts the size of the Grand Canyon, and I am very fortunate Pirate and I found you.

To Dad (12/17): Thank you for the brilliant idea involving the white van, and for your love and support over the years. I wish you were here.

To Mom (03/18): Thank you for your love of music throughout the years, for your care, and your love and support. I wish you were here, too.

To Joe, Erin, Josh and Tori: You all are my rock. Words are woefully insufficient. Thank you for being you, for being there for me even when I'm intolerable to be around. I am not whole without the four of you.

To Shelly, Bud, and Andrea: Cornhusk and jungle gym forts on crisp fall days; summers at the Holiday Inn pool; rainy Saturdays with popcorn and apple slices; glowing cigar ends on Halloween nights; excited whispers while waiting under the intercom on Christmas mornings; foggy school days as we ran to catch the bus; lava-filled living rooms and blanket forts under the piano. Priceless memories worth treasuring before adulthood, alcohol, and aging took us away.

Prologue

Brilliant orange glowed across the expansive southeastern Colorado evening sky. A gentle October breeze touched high desert vegetation, bringing with it a breath of cold air and promising a starkly clear night. The Milky Way would be especially brilliant once darkness fell. Even now, early stars peeped through the curtain of lingering light, securing their spot for the literal star-studded celestial show. In the emptiness below, a tall pole jutted upwards, it's small neon sign blinking against the darkening sky as flaming orange faded to a rosy glow. Yellow light washed through tiny windows of a squat gas station, recently rebuilt. A handful of slowly disintegrating wood-plank buildings dotted the surrounding landscape.

A frantic, high-pitched man's scream shattered the silence, echoed over the plains, caught the attention of the two humans occupying the small gas station.

Joe Healing Water's hand paused in the act of handing his customer his change.

"Hang on a sec," the seventy-year-old Ute Indian muttered, stepping around the counter and through the front door. His dark brown eyes squinted towards the one-room adobe hut hunched across a large field. A weathered barn leaned haphazardly, a gaping black hole indicating he had forgotten to close the barn doors. Not that he had any livestock to worry about. Joe narrowed his eyes against the residual light and grinned when a vague shadow flitted between the one-room adobe and the location of the outhouse. He spun on his heel and re-entered the station, made his way around the counter and faced the customer, who eyed him with a surprised and confused expression.

"No worries," Joe assured, retrieving a plastic grocery bag and filling it with the snacks and drinks the man had just purchased.

"What was that?" The middle-aged truck driver persisted, eyeing the Indian as he pulled at his long bristly brown beard. Heavy-set from years behind the wheel of his rig, he wore an obnoxiously orange Broncos T-shirt and blue overalls that stretched tight over his expanding belly. His small brown eyes narrowed. "Sounded to me like someone's in trouble."

Joe Healing Water shook his head. "Naw. Just our local Brit's first encounter with a tarantula."

Chapter One

"Do your own laundry. I'm not your frickin' maid." Riley's disgusted voice drifted from the upstairs bedrooms.

"You're one to talk. I can smell your stench from behind closed doors," Aiden snapped.

Great. Another argument to start the morning. I listened from downstairs as I made coffee for the three of us. I rolled my eyes and thought the siblings needed to move out soon.

Two sets of feet tramped down the hardwood staircase. Aiden appeared around the corner first, his dark brown hair in a crew cut that emphasized his high cheekbones and sharp jaw line. He stood six feet with a thick chest and shoulders and trim waist, none of which gave him any advantage over his sister, younger by two years. Riley rounded the corner, her five-foot six stature muscular and lean, same facial features and high cheekbones as her brother, her dark hair almost as short. They wore jeans with loose, baggy gray sweatshirts that concealed their service weapons. They worked on the local town police force and would change into their uniforms once they got to the station.

As though rehearsed, brother and sister turned as one and looked at me.

"Oh, no," I shook my head. "Don't either of you even think of asking." I motioned towards the coffee machine as gurgling noises filled the silence. "It'll be ready in a few minutes. It's cold outside this morning. Foggy, too."

Riley threw up a hand. "I know better. Dork Brain here will probably try to pull a fast one."

Aiden sauntered to the counter and picked up a black leather jacket. "We've been pulling a lot of extra shifts these last couple of weeks," he started.

I snorted. "Nice try." The coffee maker spluttered and fell silent. I poured myself a cup, then moved to one side and reached for the cream and sugar.

"Not going to fall for the con, eh, Aunt M.J.?" Riley crossed the kitchen, retrieved her favorite mug, and poured a cup. Her brown eyes avoided contact.

"You were going to try the same thing and you know it," I told her. I sipped my doctored coffee. Sugar and cream, with a little coffee taste. Perfect.

"And it's Mary Joe, Riley. MARY. JOE. *Not* M.J." I pressed my lips into a thin line. Riley was egging me, and she knew it.

Technically, I wasn't their aunt. In fact, I had no idea whether I was anybody's aunt, sister, daughter, or relative, since my lifetime memory expanded only over the last couple of years. I had woken up in a hospital bed with no memory and, apparently, no friends or family, since none had come to visit.

I had also woken up without a right leg. According to a very tall man claiming to be my attorney, I had lost my leg in a severe automobile crash that put me in a coma for months. He told me my family had died in the crash, which explained why no one came to visit. He had not offered an explanation why no friends, work acquaintances, or even religious figures visited during my recovery and extensive rehab.

With the help of a wooden cane I limped on my prosthesis until I stood between the two siblings. At five feet ten inches, I split the difference between their heights. I had shoulder length hair grayer than I thought I should have, especially since the tall thin man assured me I recently passed my thirtieth birthday. According to the bathroom mirror every morning, I had green eyes that were too big for my face and a Grand Canyon-sized nose.

I turned my head, locking eyes with each of them in turn. "Either the two of you get a handle on this constant bickering, or I will throw both of you out of MY house. I don't care what Stephen Campbell says about having you two here for security reasons. You got that?"

"You wouldn't throw us out, Aunt M.J. You'd be bored in no time." Aiden's expression seemed always about to burst into laughter. He was one of the most spontaneously happy people I'd ever met. Well, at least among the ones I remembered.

Aiden turned and poked his sister's left biceps with a finger. "Hear that? You need to stop picking on me."

Riley swatted his hand, then stood on her tiptoes and thrust her face into his. "Listen, Dork Brain. I'm not the one stinking up the entire house with locker room filth."

"We need to get going." Aiden crossed his eyes at his sister.

They checked their weapons and spare magazines. Aiden shrugged into his leather jacket, and Riley retrieved hers from the back of one of the counter chairs.

"No coffee?" I asked Aiden.

He shook his head. "Naw. We're running late already."

Early October brought damp, foggy weather to the Blue Ridge Mountains in southwest Virginia. Riley turned to me as Aiden headed for the door leading to the triple car garage. "Chief said he's gotten two sick calls for the swing shift, so we may end up pulling doubles again. Is Randy coming over today? Or are you meeting him at the barn?"

"I haven't heard from him," I told her. The view through the open garage revealed a Friday morning blanketed with fog so thick visibility extended only a few shifting gray yards.

"You planning on going out today?" Riley asked, her eyes scanning the thick, engulfing fog.

I shrugged. "Yeah, probably. I'll get bored if I stick around here."

"You could spend the time helping us with our laundry," Aiden interjected as he slid behind the wheel of his red Jeep Wrangler. Riley climbed into the passenger seat, balancing her mug on her thigh as she pulled her seat belt across.

"Use the indoor arena if you decide to ride," Riley commented, her eyes meeting mine.

I ignored Aiden's comment and shrugged. "I'll think about it."

"It'll be safer than riding in this," she persisted.

I bristled. "I'll ride where I want. The weather won't bother Twister." She opened her mouth to argue but I cut her off. "Go on. Get out of here."

I limped to the door and watched them pull out. A gray Ford Explorer custom-designed for my needs occupied the second bay. The third bay held a large green John Deere riding mower the siblings used on the six acres surrounding the property.

My home for the last two years, the three-story stone house stood on a knoll in the middle of rolling lush green pasture hemmed in by the surrounding mountains. The upstairs held bedrooms, one on either end and two in the middle. Riley and Aiden occupied the end rooms. The main floor contained an expansive kitchen, an enormous cathedral ceiling great room with glass windows that framed a stone fireplace. An office and a master bedroom occupied the back part of the house, and a broad wood-planked covered porch wrapped around three sides of the main floor, a screened-in portion opened off the master bedroom. The basement held two separate entertainment rooms and another bedroom. Broad oak staircases connected each floor, polished oak floors spread across the main floor and the upstairs hall and bedrooms. Warm, plush, forest-green carpeting kept the basement warm. Air conditioning cooled the inside during the summer when the mountain breeze wasn't enough to keep heat and humidity at bay. A large wood-burning stove generated enough heat to comfortably warm the place during winter months. The décor echoed the wood floors with earthy brown tones, forest greens, and light tan accents.

I closed the door, limped to the kitchen, and wiggled onto one of the six counter bar stools. Glancing at the clock on the wall, I debated whether to go back to bed. I was still in my pajamas. Things wouldn't get started at the stables for another couple of hours. I could use the sleep.

If I could sleep. I'd had major issues with insomnia ever since I'd moved into this house eighteen months ago. Stephen Campbell, calling himself my benefactor and friend, helped me settle into this remote location. He'd grown up here, knew most of the people in the small nearby town, had arranged for two police officers to move in with me for company and safety.

Safety from what? I'd asked. But Stephen had not explained. Nor had he offered any information where I originally was from, who I had been, or what I had done. It seemed odd at the time, and I'd asked him on several occasions why he was unwilling to tell me any-thing about my past. Every time, he shook his head, insisted he was looking after my best interests. Protecting me.

Which bothered the hell out of me. I mean, if my memory loss and injury had been because of an automobile accident, what in the world did I need protection from? He had not forbidden me to drive. But short of regaining lost memory, I had no way of finding out who I was or what had happened. I tried searching the Internet but had no name, date, or event to start with.

But I did have dreams. Lots of them. Vague images, threaten-ing, clutching, looming over me like the shadow of a giant monster. I would wake up streaming with sweat, crying for no reason, shaking with utter terror that gripped me with invisible, unexplainable talons. So, while I couldn't figure out why Stephen felt I needed protection from an outside source, I was painfully aware I desperately needed protection from something my subconscious was trying to tell me.

I warmed my coffee in the microwave, poured some more creamer in now that the siblings weren't around to harass me for drinking my coffee like a wimp. Then I limped across the hardwood floor to the massive fireplace and curled beneath a blanket on the large couch. I stared through the large cathedral windows at the moist, sifting gray cloud cover. Trying to relax, I closed my eyes and leaned my head against the deep cushions while my coffee turned cold on the end table.

Sleep remained annoyingly illusive. Sighing, I opened my eyes, noted the grayness outside had lightened ever so slightly, and threw off the blanket. I limped to the master bedroom and dressed in jeans, a long-sleeved green turtleneck and a black cotton sweatshirt, pulled on one thick sock and wiggled my left foot into a riding boot that zipped up the side. I had difficulty working the boot onto the prosthesis, but I really wanted to ride. I got the prosthesis into the empty jeans leg, then stood and felt my stump sink into the padded socket.

The whole one-leg thing still bothered me. A lot. I would be able to accept my handicap better if I knew more about the circumstances of the car accident and why I had ended up with amnesia. I kept nagging Stephen whenever we talked that I would progress further in my emotional rehab if he would fill in some blanks.

The man was a stubborn old coot, I thought, shaking my head as I stared at my wide-leg jeans. I'd practiced my gait until I walked with minimal limping, but still used a cane for security reasons, because at times I forgot about the prosthesis, lost my balance, and ended up in a face plant. I used a cane most of the day, crutches when I was at home, a wheelchair when I was too tired to maintain balance and coordination.

I returned to the kitchen, re-heated my coffee, sat at the counter and drank the soothing sweetness this time, then headed out. The stables were ten miles north along the Interstate and I had ten miles of twisting two-lane mountain road before I reached the highway.

Stephen introduced me to the owner of the stables when I first moved to Virginia. Kinsey Wells was about my age, had long, thick natural blonde hair she kept in a ponytail, and had ridden horses since she could walk. She owned a thirty-horse boarding set-up that included a large indoor arena and three outdoor arenas, the largest surrounded by a grandstand for annual county horse shows and fairs. She ran a therapeutic riding center and trained volunteers to work with riders suffering physical and emotional handicaps.

Eighteen months ago, I balked at Stephen's ludicrous idea of putting me on a horse. I asked him if I'd ever ridden and he admitted that, no, I had not grown up around horses. Then he and Kinsey proceeded to bully me on to a large black gelding. With a volunteer on each side and one leading the animal, I had started my thirty-minute riding lessons twice a week. The first couple of months left me physically exhausted and I ended up in my wheelchair or in bed the rest of the day. Slowly, though, I'd noticed improvement in my core strength and coordination. I fell in love with Twister, the gentle, aging Tennessee Walker I now rode almost every day.

Fog reduced visibility to a scant twenty yards along Interstate eighty-one. I took the first exit into town and turned onto the sloping dirt road that led to the stables. The outdoor arenas hid behind curtains of thick, undulating gray moisture. Buildings appeared as ghostly shadows. I pulled to a stop in the large parking area, retrieved my cane, and limped through the dense cloud cover. The unnatural silence created by lack of birdcalls and other chattering voices of nature sent a slight shiver along my spine. Pulling open a side entrance, I entered the indoor arena.

Kinsey stood in the center of the arena, working with one of her regular private lessons.

"Hey there! Wasn't sure you'd come out in this weather," she called. She turned her attention back to her student, a ten-year-old girl who beamed at me from the back of the black-and-white pony she rode.

Little Amy Wittmore was the daughter of Randy Wittmore, the man I'd been dating for the last several months. Amy was largely responsible for my own riding progress. She had lost her mother in a freak equestrian accident that instantly killed both rider and horse. Amy, eight years old at the time, had withdrawn into a world of her own, become non-verbal, even with her father. Soon after my arrival at the stables, Amy wandered over to sit beside me. To everyone's amazement she started talking to me, asking what had happened to my leg, if I liked horses, whether I wanted to ride. At the time, I hadn't known how to answer her. But we soon bonded through our horses—Twister for me, Fuzzy for her.

Brown pigtails poked from beneath her purple furry hat, blue jeans, little purple cowboy boots, and matching purple winter coat and gloves. She was a regular at the stables and looked forward to my arrival.

"Miss Mary Joe, watch this!" Her grin turning serious, Amy concentrated her attention on her pony. Gathering the reins in her left hand, she leaned forward, clucked, and kicked her heels into her mount's furry sides. Fuzzy broke into a trot, then briefly into a bouncy canter before slowing back down into his normal lazy walk.

"Wow, Amy. That's terrific!" I called as she rounded the far side of the arena.

"Remember not to lean so far forward," Kinsey said with a smile. She glanced at her watch. "I think we're done for the day. Go ahead and walk Fuzzy around before you put him away."

"Okay." Amy patted Fuzzy on the neck with a purple-gloved hand as he walked along. "Has Daddy talked to you yet, Miss Mary Joe?" she hollered across the arena.

I shook my head, puzzled. "Riley asked the same thing. I'm starting to get suspicious. Am I in trouble for something I don't know about?"

Amy's face beamed, her voicing echoing in the large, spacious interior. "He's got something for you. He made me promise not to tell you. It's really, really pretty. I can't wait for him to show it to you."

Hum, I thought, my curiosity getting the better of me. "New riding boots?" I glanced down at the ones I wore. "He's been after me to get a pair that will fit my prosthesis better."

"No, silly," Amy laughed as she stopped Fuzzy across the railing from me. "Boots are cool, but they aren't *pretty.*"

I liked Randy. A lot. And I struggled with wanting more than a friendship, and he had not pushed the intimacy. He was a wonderful guy and down deep I hoped that maybe the gift Amy was referring to meant commitment. My heart did a couple of very noticeable internal flops around my chest.

Yeah. I liked Randy. More than a lot.

"He's around here somewhere." Amy nodded, then turned her

attention back to Fuzzy. Kinsey joined us. She was in her usual jeans, boots, wool jacket and wool hat. Her thick blonde ponytail streamed like a horse's tail down her back.

"You're going to be quite a rider before long," she smiled at the girl. "No one else can get Fuzzy to do anything he doesn't want to do. You get on and he's a different pony."

Amy's flushed cheeks turned darker and she grinned. "I've asked Daddy if we can buy him."

Kinsey's eyebrows lifted. "Well, I can't promise anything. After all, he's one of our lesson horses. But we'll see," she added when Amy's expression faltered. "I said, we'll see. That means I haven't said 'no.'"

"Can I ride some more?" Amy grinned. Kinsey nodded, and she nudged Fuzzy into a walk.

"She's really come out of her shell," I murmured as horse and rider moved away.

Kinsey turned to me. "Because of you." She hesitated, then added, "So has Randy. You've been a Godsend to them both."

I shook my head. "I don't know who's a Godsend to whom."

We watched Amy and Fuzzy amble around the arena, then Amy pulled him to a stop in front of Kinsey.

"Will you check him, please, Miss Kinsey? I don't want him to get hot," Amy requested.

Kinsey laughed. "The day this pony works hard enough to break a sweat is the day I'll quit riding. He feels good." Kinsey smiled at the child, pressing her hand against the pony's chest. "Do you need help unsaddling him or putting him away?"

Amy shook her head. "No, ma'am."

"Okay. I'll open the door for you." Kinsey strode across the expansive dirt floor with the pair until they reached a large sliding double-door. She pulled it open and watched Amy guide Fuzzy through.

"Holler if you need help." She left the door ajar, crossed the arena, stopped at the railing separating us. Her clear blue eyes stared at me. "How's that contraption of yours working out?"

I shrugged. "Twister doesn't seem to mind it." Randy had carved a wooden prosthesis that buckled into the right stirrup of the Australian saddle I used. It was more for weight balance than leg signals, but I'd found my thigh strength improved enough that I could create a little bit of pressure, and Twister was sensitive enough to respond. "I still use mostly rein signals," I admitted.

"Whatever works," Kinsey nodded. "Going to ride today?"

I limped to one of the access gates, then accompanied Kinsey towards the sliding door.

"I'd like to, if the indoor arena is available. If not, do you think he'd mind the fog?"

Kinsey shook her head. "He's an old hat. He's cool with this weather."

Chapter Two

We made it outside in time to see Amy leading Fuzzy to his outdoor run. The pony looked as though he'd just been to a spa. His coat shone, his mane and tail combed until silky. He followed docilely beside Amy, his head relaxed, his tail swishing gently. I watched her lead him into his pen, remove his halter, then slip her hand into her jacket pocket and pull out a treat. I turned my head away from Kinsey to hide my grin.

Kinsey didn't like giving horse treats. And to be honest, she was right. Horses tended to start nipping when given treats. Kinsey frowned at the pandering, but Amy slipped an occasional treat to Fuzzy anyway. I told her to give him something only sparingly to keep Fuzzy from getting pushy, and to keep the two of us from getting into trouble with Kinsey.

Yes, I give my horse treats, too. And no, Kinsey doesn't know about that, either.

Kinsey shook her head, jerking my attention. For a moment, I thought she was about to reprimand Amy for her soft-heartedness.

"I'm afraid it's booked."

Booked…oh, right. The indoor arena.

Kinsey continued. "Randy's conducting horsemanship classes, then I think he wants to work with Norseman, that new Arab we got in last week."

"And he's not going to want to work that horse in these outdoor conditions," I added.

"Good Lord, no," Kinsey frowned. "I'm not sure that horse is worth the effort. Spooks at his own shadow, unreliable, high-strung, and not a brain in that beautiful head of his."

"Talking about me?" chuckled a deep baritone voice from behind us. We turned around.

A man appeared from the mist like a ghost from a Halloween horror movie. The image crept through me, sent a shudder of premonition down my spine. I shook my head to rid myself of the creepy feeling.

Randy, tall, lanky, with a runner's build, beamed at us from beneath his cowboy hat. "Howdy, girls." His deep voice floated across the mist like velvet, his manner as easy-going with people as it was with horses. He wore jeans, boots, and a padded dark-colored corduroy jacket. His black hair was tied back in a short ponytail. His broad face, strong nose, and dark eyes reminded me of American Indian, though I'd never asked, and he'd never volunteered his background. He spoke to horses and horses responded to him unlike any other trainer.

Horses are extremely sensitive. They pick up on a human's character and emotional state faster than a trained profiler. I've wondered whether they're actually telepathic and we humans lack their gift. It sounds crazy, but I swear Twister and I have exchanged emotional thoughts. And I'd seen the same type of communication between Randy and the horses he trained. "Weather's supposed to get really crappy tomorrow and Sunday." He spoke to Kinsey, but winked at me. "Wind and rain. I don't like conducting classes when the weather's like that. Too much strain on the horses."

"Yeah, I noticed you booked the arena for the whole day." Kinsey sounded mildly irritated.

Randy frowned. "I thought I remembered you saying Amy was your only Friday lesson this week."

"Yeah," Kinsey admitted. "Just double-check with me in the future in case I have a new student or one that's been re-scheduled."

Randy wiped a hand over his face. "Sorry, Kinsey. I heard the weather report yesterday evening and got tunnel vision. I'll check with you first next time." He turned to me. "I bet you were hoping to ride in the indoor arena this morning, weren't you?"

I shrugged. "I can use the back arena."

"Well, dang it. It's not fair to ask you to ride in these conditions when I'm not allowing my student riders to put up with it." He bent his head towards me. "How about you ride in one of the classes?"

I hesitated. His offer was appealing, and the indoor arena was a good deal warmer than the outside temperature.

But I really enjoyed the time alone with Twister. And I felt confident he would do fine despite the fog. He had been born and bred here. Fog was nothing new to him.

"Don't worry about it, Randy. There's no wind, it's not raining, and I sort of wanted to spend some time alone. I'll use the back arena. Don't worry about us." I grinned.

"Well, keep an eye out for wildlife. That'll be your biggest risk, especially deer jumping the fence," Randy advised.

I nodded. "I imagine he'll pick up on them way before I see them."

"And it's late enough in the day that I don't think that will be a problem anyway." Kinsey turned to Randy. "Do you need any of the equipment in the arena? The poles or activity items we use for therapeutic students?" She asked.

Randy shook his head. "I hate to be a pain, but the first class has a couple of pretty spooky horses participating, so the emptier the arena, the better."

"Okay, I'll start clearing stuff out." Kinsey turned towards the indoor arena, leaving Randy and me alone.

He walked with me as I limped along the outdoor runs. "Can you stay? I have a lunch break around noon, we can grab something to eat."

"Sure." I hesitated, and instinctively Randy leaned his head over, intuitively encouraging me to tell him what else was on my mind.

I spoke slowly. "Kinsey said you want to work Norseman today. I…don't think…well, it's none of my business, but she really doesn't like that horse very much. Maybe you could wait for better weather?"

"Hey, you guys! Wait up!" Amy's voice yelled from within the fog. We turned and saw her appear slowly, her purple outfit strangely muted into gray that blended almost exactly with the enveloping cloud cover. She looked like a small round spectral figure floating towards us.

"So, Daddy, have you shown it to her?" Amy panted, stopping abruptly.

"Amy, you and I talked about this," Randy slid his eyes to me, their twinkle no less bright despite the acute sense I got that Amy had just spoiled a surprise. I covered my mouth with my hand to hide a smile. Randy really was a very cool guy. And a very soft-hearted father.

"But you can't wait until tonight. You just *can't*," Amy flung her arms out. "I want to be there when you give it to her! I want to see the look on her face!"

Okay, it was becoming clear what this present seemed to be.

As if reading my thoughts, Randy slipped a hand into his jacket pocket and pulled out a small, royal blue velvet ring box. I felt my eyes widen and my jaw drop to China, followed by a beaming smile as happiness practically exploded in my chest.

"There, now. I showed it to her. Stop your nagging," he admonished gently. "But I don't really think kneeling here in the middle of all this fog and dirt and horse smell is the most romantic spot to pick, do you?"

Amy, bless her heart, jabbed her hands on her hips. "Well, why not, Daddy? It's where you met her, isn't it? And it's where you two are always together, right? Why does it have to happen in some fancy-pancy restaurant with just the two of you?"

Randy slipped the ring box back into his pocket. He winked at me, obviously seeing my delight and obvious answer to his yet unasked question. I couldn't wipe the beaming grin off my face. He turned again to his daughter. "Well if I'm the one who's going to do the kneeling, I want it to be in some nice, warm, cozy restaurant. What if I told you I've made reservations for the three of us?"

Amy's bravura evaporated so suddenly that I bent down.

"I don't mind," I reassured, peering intently into her large brown eyes. But Amy shook her head.

"Fancy-pancy restaurants are for grown-ups. I wouldn't fit in at a restaurant, and everyone would just stare at me wondering why I was spoiling a special date for the two of you." She thrust out her hand. "If you're not going to give it to her now, give me the box. You'll just lose it between now and tonight."

I straightened and couldn't suppress a laugh. Amy sounded like a fussy mother. Randy retrieved the box and started to hold it out towards me, but Amy reached over, grabbed it from his hand, and stuffed it into her coat pocket.

"Besides, I spoiled your surprise after you asked me to be quiet." Tears clung to her long eyelashes, pulling at my heartstrings. "And then I got mad about it in front of Miss Mary Joe, and now I'm all embarrassed." She spun on her heel and broke into a run. I started after her, but Randy caught my arm.

"I'll go talk with her. I shouldn't have expected her to keep a secret so important to her," he murmured. "You mean so much to her, and to me. You have no idea how much you've helped us over the last two years."

Tears slipped down my cheeks and I could not for the life of me think of anything to say. Randy's expression grew soft, supportive and gentle, the same manner that brought him so much success with horses. "If you want, I'll go retrieve your gift and kneel here, right now," he soothed.

I smiled, stepped close and wrapped my arms around his chest, hugging him tightly against me. The warmth through his clothes felt safe, comfortable. "How about some place kid-friendly later? Like a McDonalds?" I whispered.

A soft chuckle rumbled through his chest. "I love you." His finger touched my chin and I drew in a contented breath, then raised my face. He gave me a kiss on each cheek, then lingered on my lips. I hugged him tighter, then backed away.

"What time?" I asked.

"I'll let you know," he smiled. "I'll be all day with the horsemanship classes, and I really do need to fit in working Norseman somewhere." He grasped my shoulders and pulled me close until our noses touched.

"I appreciate your concern for me. Yes, he's high-strung, but he's an Arabian. And he needs to adjust to the climate out here, and the only way to do that is to take him out on days like this and show him there's nothing to be afraid of. He hasn't learned to trust his instincts yet, that's all. And I promise I'll be careful. I'm not riding, just doing some line work."

I smiled into his warm eyes. "Okay. That sounds great. Just be careful. Please."

He kissed my nose, stole another kiss on my lips. "I promise."

We turned to go our respective ways, and I limped to the run Twister occupied. He must have heard my voice through the fog because his black well-shaped head appeared at the gate, his ears pricked forward. He nickered when I got close.

"Hey there, fella." I rubbed his nose, and he dipped his head down for me to rub his ears. "You're spoiled, you know that?" I smiled, tears of pure joy dampening my face as I turned to the tack room that held my riding equipment. I thought about Randy and Amy, realized I was about to pick up someone else's saddle, and released laughter that bubbled through me, making me feel light as air. Better concentrate on tacking up my horse, or I'd end up with his bridle on the wrong end. So I concentrated on getting Twister ready to ride.

When I started riding unassisted, I settled on an Australian saddle because of the side pommels which I could grip with my thighs. The one I used had a saddle horn, which helped when I was mounting. I wasn't good enough to hop and catch the stirrup with my left foot. Not yet, anyway. I was working on it, though, and planned to show off to Kinsey one day. I left my cane in the tack room, retrieved Twister's halter and got him from his run. I spent a lot of time brushing him down, picking his feet out, talking to him about Randy and Amy. The happiness swelling in my chest must have reached Twister because he turned and nuzzled my backside, then the nape of my neck when I checked his front feet. I secured the saddle and pad beneath my left arm, used my cane for balance when I carried everything outside. It had taken time and a lot of strength building, but I could now swing pad and saddle up without help. I bridled him, limped back to the tack room to prop my cane against the empty saddletree, then led Twister towards the arena located at the back of the property. He walked calmly beside me, careful to maintain distance so I didn't trip. His non-verbal communication amazed me, and our mental conversations often took over my verbal ones.

Fog hid the woods crowding the enclosure, and I hoped Kinsey was right about it being too late in the day for deer to be a problem. Twister seemed calm and unconcerned, so I took heart that, at least for the moment, nothing was amiss. We passed through the gate, latched it behind us, and then I led Twister to the mounting block.

I'd tried several ways of working with the prosthesis, and the least awkward had proven to be removing the thing on the mounting block, then grabbing the saddle horn and swinging my stump across the saddle before securing the stirrup with my left foot. Twister always turned his head to watch me. I know he sensed my handicap because never in the time I'd been riding had he ever moved a muscle when I was trying to get on or off. I settled into the saddle, wrapped the empty right jeans leg around my thigh, then worked my stump into the leg extension thing. Then I took the reins and clucked to Twister. He raised his head and pricked his ears forward, and we set out into the vast empty whiteness shrouding the arena.

The morning was cool and damp and the warmth from Twister's body created vague washes of steam. I felt the same strength and warmth from him as when I hugged Randy. The image of the blue velvet ring box came back into my mind, my whole face broke into a colossal grin, and I began talking with Twister about what kind of ring Randy might have chosen.

"What do you think, bud?" My voice, despite the low tone, crashed against the intense, intimate silence engulfing us. Twister heaved a contented sigh.

"Yeah, I'm thinking it's not going to be the usual solitaire diamond, either." My grin widened until my face hurt. Knowing Randy, he'd found a farrier to create a ring from a horseshoe nail. I laughed; the happy sound muted by thick fog. "Matching horseshoe nail rings. What do you think about that?"

I didn't care if the ring he'd chosen came from a toy dispenser. I stretched and worked my thighs, gripping the side pommels and holding my backside off the saddle. 'Standing in the saddle' as Kinsey called it. It was hard work, and I still could not hold myself aloft more than a few seconds. But that was a few seconds more than I could when I started riding two years ago.

"Think of the trail rides with you and me, Amy and Fuzzy, and Randy and…" I trailed off and frowned. To my knowledge, Randy did not own a horse, even though he trained several. "Hum, I think we need to ask Kinsey about how to get Randy a horse of his own." Twister released a long snort.

I rubbed his neck affectionately. "Okay, I'll make sure Randy's horse isn't as pretty as you are, how's that?"

Another contented sigh. *Silly horse.* I grinned again. Always needing to show off he was the best-looking horse at the stables.

Well, okay, maybe I'm just a little biased.

It seemed Twister and I were the only beings on earth. Nothing stirred the vegetation crowding the railing, no currents rustled the surrounding foliage. Conditions were wonderfully serene as we followed the railing. I urged him into his gait, felt the smoothness of his powerful muscles beneath me as he broke into the classic run-walk that made his breed so famous. It felt like riding a magic carpet. My thighs gripped the side pommels, the extension gave me the extra feeling of balance, and during the time I was in the saddle, I could pretend I was whole again.

My happiness faltered. Darn it. Why did I have to think about that?

My lingering self-consciousness about my missing leg would not abate. I knew I shouldn't worry; I knew Randy didn't care. I had spent the last two years trying to come to terms with missing a leg and accepting Stephen's explanation.

And if it weren't for the frickin' recurring nightmares my subconscious seemed determined to bring to the surface, I would make progress in the self-image department.

I squeezed my eyes shut against the thought of us in bed together. I would get over that, I scolded myself. I would leave the nightmares behind me; Randy would make sure of that. And Amy. We would be a happy threesome.

Maybe even one day, a foursome.

I failed to notice when Twister and I were no longer alone. Twister warned me when his head came up and his ears perked forward, alert and tense. I slowed him to a walk, felt the tension through his body, and wondered what type of animal it was and whether it had joined us in the arena. I gripped the saddle horn just in case Twister decided to shy.

As we neared the gated end of the arena a dark shadow appeared hovering above the ground. Twister snorted and I thought he might take off.

It must be Randy, but his behavior didn't make sense. Randy would call out to help Twister recognize him. And anyway, Twister would have picked up his familiar scent. "Easy, there," I murmured, rubbing his neck with the hand that held the reins and re-securing my grip on the saddle horn. "Who are you?" I broke the silence, hoping my voice would help calm Twister.

"I should have called out. I did not mean to scare you," the shadow spoke. "The woman in the office told me where you were." The man sat on one of the gateposts.

I felt Twister relax. Hearing a human voice helped him recognize the unexpected image.

"Can't see a thing in this fog," I responded, guiding Twister closer. Something about the man's voice stirred deep-seated memories. We were within five yards before the fog parted and I got a good look at him. His black hair trailed in a shoulder-length ponytail. His cheekbones protruded sharply from beneath his eyes, his skin color dark against the white mist that swirled around us. He dressed in jeans and a denim jacket that hung open to reveal a black button-down shirt. Recognition began whirling through my head and the blood drained from my face. Vaguely, I felt Twister sense my shock because he shuffled his feet and moved away.

I didn't stop him. I needed the distance. Memory flooded back, fast, furious, like a gigantic tsunami wave. I opened my mouth, struggled to choke out my next words.

"Hello, Jeremiah."

Chapter Three

I hunkered into the saddle, thankful I was not standing on the ground because every muscle in my body began to tremble. My bones threatened to dissolve into a massive, tangled heap. We stared at each other for what seemed like a couple of years. Twister shifted sideways, jarring my attention and breaking the spell engulfing me. I circled him a couple of times until his head dropped and his ears twitched.

"You look good up there," Jeremiah commented from the gatepost.

I settled Twister a few feet away. "Why are you here?" My question came out curt, expressionless.

"Your memory has come back?" he asked.

Obviously, he was ignoring my question. "Why are you here?" I repeated.

"To see you. To see how you are recovering. To see whether your memory has returned." Jeremiah climbed from the gatepost but did not close the distance between us. I looked down at him from Twister's back and felt for the first time in my life I was the one in control, I was the one with power.

"Up until just now, I've been Mary Joe Majors and nothing else. Thanks to you showing up like a ghost, I know who I am and what happened two summers ago." I rested my hands on the saddle horn. "Why now?"

"It took me a while to locate you. Stephen Campbell was not helpful." Jeremiah broke eye contact and looked at his boots.

"Stephen Campbell was responsible for relocating me out here in the middle of nowhere, away from all the danger I now understand he was protecting me from." My eyes narrowed. "Including you."

No wonder Stephen refused to tell me the truth about the chain of events. A huge hole of loss and despair threatened to swallow me up, and tears stung my eyes as the list of dead scrolled through my mind. I closed my eyes and tried to push the list of names back into the shadows of my subconscious. I no longer questioned why I had woken up with amnesia. I swiped a hand at tears, then opened my eyes and glared at the man standing on the ground.

"My parents, my sister, Bill and Becky Parsons, Mud Rain, all dead because of a man who kidnapped me, shot me, ruined my leg." My voice, ugly and accusing, hung in the fog crowding round us.

Jeremiah's head snapped up. "Not quite. You are confusing some of the events," he corrected quietly, locking his eyes with mine, his voice so soft it seemed whispered from the fog itself. His hands slid into the pockets of his jacket. "Tell me what you remember."

I swiped my eyes again. "Death. A lot of it. Our friends, your brother, my parents, my sister. Explosions. Men who wanted me dead. Horrible men."

He shook his head and I met his eyes with a hard stare. "I also remember you weren't around to help me. At all." Twister sidled sideways again, and I walked him in a large circle around Jeremiah. Jeremiah's eyes followed my actions, but otherwise he did not move. I stopped Twister and rested my hands on my thighs, the reins hanging loosely from the saddle horn.

Jeremiah shifted his weight, lifted a hand to smooth his ponytail. I noticed his fingers shook slightly. "I made a mistake, trusting your safety to Hawk. But he did save lives. Bill and Becky Parsons and Mud Rain are alive and well. They have a new house."

Terror sizzled through me at the strange name, and a vague face loomed just beyond recall. Hideous pain and cold-blooded decisions swirled around the image. I squeezed my eyes shut to hide my reaction, felt stupid and angry that a name generated such a powerful, primal surge of fear. Twister tossed his head. His instincts were strong, and he was picking up on my distress. I opened my eyes and leaned forward to pat his neck and run my hands through his mane. Then I backed him away from Jeremiah.

"You should have been there. I needed you."

Jeremiah did not move. "I understand your anger. Joe Healing Water, Hawk, and I debated who should be with you."

"*Debated*, Jeremiah?" I snapped. "You were my husband. It should've been a no-brainer." I leaned forward. "Especially after I ran you down in the middle of those mountains."

Jeremiah dropped his gaze to his feet again. "Hawk convinced us he was the best choice. He had intimate connections with the Charlie Network."

"Ha!" I scoffed. "What you're really saying is you prioritized a mission over the safety of your *wife*. You didn't call, text, or email after you disappeared out of that hospital in Alamosa. Why the silence? Why weren't you there for Angela's funeral? Was I that unimportant to you?"

His black eyes snapped up and locked with mine. "I understand how events might make it seem that way."

"If you'd been there…" I started.

"If I had been there instead of Hawk, I would have been shot," Jeremiah declared flatly. "And then there would have been no one to stand between you and those killers."

I snorted. "Is that what Hawk did? Stood between me and those men?" I started walking Twister in a circle again, hoping the movement would vent the anger surging through me. "He was their leader. He was in charge of them. He told them to blow up my parents' house, then the Parsons' house. He told me in so many words just how much pain and suffering he was going to put me through." I stopped. Gray cloud crowded us, mute and moist, holding my words in the air until I could almost see the letters. "And my leg. You have no idea what he did. And because you put your trust in that killer, I'm…I'm…." I trailed off, unable to finish. Twister's powerful muscles moved beneath me, giving me strength and courage. I stopped between Jeremiah and the gate. Jeremiah turned to face me and shook his head. He opened his mouth, but I cut him off. "Are we still married?"

Jeremiah held up his left hand, and I saw the ring on his finger. His eyes fell to my bare hands. He sighed. "Stephen drew up divorce papers, told me to sign them. I did not want to, but he said it was for the best since you had amnesia. He did not sign for you. Said if your memory returned, you would make that decision yourself."

"I'll contact him and tell him to fax the papers." I gathered the reins. "Please open the gate."

"Mattie…," Jeremiah started.

"We're done here. Go back to Colorado, or Oklahoma, or wherever the hell you're living now. Leave me alone," I threw over my shoulder.

Jeremiah strode around us and paused when he reached the gate. He tilted his head back to look me straight in the eyes. "I will not leave you. Not again. You are angry with me. I understand that. I will devote whatever time you need to…."

"To nothing!" I shouted, causing Twister to jerk his head. "Leave me alone, Jeremiah! I don't want anything to do with you!" As Jeremiah pulled the gate open, I urged Twister forward into his walker gait, turned towards the dense woods and a path that disappeared into the mist.

"Mattie! Wait!" Jeremiah called after me, but I was already out of sight, the fog enveloping me, separating us. The arena blurred into a shadow, then faded as I urged Twister along the path. I realized Jeremiah might try to follow, so I increased our pace until Twister broke into a smooth canter. We reached a place where the path split into three directions. I slowed Twister and took the route furthest to the right, the one that led to the Blue Ridge Parkway. Twister settled into his walker gait, his breathing even, his movements smooth and relaxed. He and I could go like this almost all day.

And right now, that sounded like the most wonderful idea in the world.

The path was wide and easy to follow, so even with visibility down to a few yards I had no fear of running into anything or getting lost. And we were moving fast enough to scare off any wildlife despite the thick layer of wet, soggy leaves muffling Twister's hooves.

Recognizing Jeremiah and regaining my memory brought images to mind I desperately wanted to forget again. And the pain of knowing Jeremiah deliberately allowed a total stranger to take his place at my side made my insides boil until I thought I would explode. There was a blessed ignorance around the identity of being Mary Joe Majors and I desperately wanted to forget the poisonous past and concentrate on creating a new me. Things would be better if my recall returned to the obscurity of my subconscious.

Randy. The ring box. Amy. A new life. A new family.

I would make a new start with Randy. He and Amy already felt like family. And Riley and Aiden seemed more like family than acquaintances. Thanks to Stephen Campbell I had started building a new life. I did not need to cling to the past. I would let it go, and in time it would fade into deep memory recesses and I would slip back into my identity as Mary Joe.

The fog grew thicker as we worked our way up the mountainside. If the trail hadn't been so obvious, I would have turned around. I couldn't even see the trees bordering each side, could just make out the winding path beyond Twister's ears. I pulled him down to a walk and leaned forward until I could feel his chest. He was warm but not sweaty, and I thought it a good idea to walk him. I didn't want to reach the highway, the ribbon of two-lane paved road that wound its way through the heart of the Blue Ridge Mountains. On a clear day, scenery was spectacular. In current conditions, I worried we might accidentally end up on the pavement. With virtually zero visibility, a car would be upon us before either the driver or Twister could react.

Worse still, we might inadvertently come upon the tree stump nicknamed "Hunchback of the Ridge." The grotesque shape startled horses and more than one rider had ended up on the ground. Normally Twister only snorted at the sight, but in this fog, he might be fooled into a reaction that would unseat me.

Besides, Randy mentioned the weather would be deteriorating. There stood more than an even chance the system would move in early. I did not want to get stuck in a storm, didn't want Twister carrying me in a soaking rain all the way back to the stables.

But I didn't want to turn around too soon. Jeremiah might be hanging around hoping I would show up, and I desperately wanted him gone by the time I returned. I thought about Randy again, thought about him proposing to me. On his knee. In a McDonalds. And Amy, her eyes brighter than bright, watching me accept. Randy had the patience of a saint. I would get over my self-image issues. I didn't need Jeremiah or my memory. I could become whole again despite my missing leg.

I sighed. The day would smooth out. I thought about Riley and Aiden's constant arguing, Amy riding Fuzzy, Randy's warm, secure hug, and spending time with my horse. Already Jeremiah's image seemed to be fading.

Twister made no noise on the damp vegetation covering the trail. The air chilled and moisture blew from his nostrils like steam from a locomotive. Most of his winter coat had grown in so I didn't think the chilly conditions would bother him. I, on the other hand, shivered and pulled the sleeves of my sweatshirt over my fingers. But I did not turn around. Not yet. I wanted to stay away from the stables until Jeremiah left.

Surely, he would see the futility in lingering, especially after I explicitly told him I wanted nothing to do with him. I did not want to see that man again. I didn't care if I never saw him again for the rest of my life.

Despite my efforts, bits of our conversation intruded into my thoughts. I reined Twister to a stop, sat in the stillness to think.

How in the world had Jeremiah managed to track me down? Stephen had changed my name, had separated me from every known contact. What clues had Jeremiah found? And could those same clues lead killers from my past into my future?

Hawk.

The name sent a violent, uncontrollable jolt of terror through me. I could not recollect a face, but with the name phantom pains shot through my absent right leg. If Jeremiah had tracked me down, it stood to reason Hawk could do the same. He had almost killed me once.

Might he try again?

Male voices drifted through the thick white cloud cover, and my attention focused on my surroundings. Twister pricked his ears forward but didn't seem otherwise bothered by the disturbance. I thought about calling out.

"You better pay me a bundle," one of the men shouted angrily.

"You're hot as a jacket potato, laddie." A second man's voice held a faint lilt that sounded strangely familiar. Somewhere, at some time, I had heard that voice.

Terrific. Another ghost from my past. Just what I needed today.

"Ain't nobody looking for me, not clear out here," retorted the first man, his voice accented with a southern country drawl. "They be looking fer me in Richmond, up and down ninety-five and sixty-four."

"Precisely why I insisted on not stopping until we got here," the man with the lilt replied. The utter calm in his voice sent a chill down my spine. Something in his manner sounded wrong. I rubbed my hand along Twister's neck. I might be on a horse, but the glaring fact remained; I could put Twister and myself in a lot of danger being alone like this. Especially since I would have no way of walking if I were somehow forced off my horse. I rubbed Twister's neck again to keep him still. I would not move until the men had gone, did not dare risk breaking the silence around us for fear the men would hear our presence.

"I done stuck my neck out big time fer you. So, you just start thinkin' about increasing my share. It's thanks to me that thar is yers now. There should be more in it for me. You and that fancy car, you can afford it."

"I'm already paying you a very tidy sum." The man's voice vibrated with malice. My heart began thudding against my chest. The tone of their conversation alarmed me. "Yeah? Well, I done all the effort," the second man retorted. "The security firm will know I'm missing and put two and two together."

"We'll renegotiate your fee in a minute." There was a pause during which I worried whether one of them might hear Twister mouthing his bit.

"Ah." A lifetime of satisfaction sounded clearly through the second man's sigh.

"Seems awfully small to be worth so much effort," the first man grumbled. "They had them double eagles, and those others from some shipwreck. I would've thought you'd be after one of 'em."

"This, my friend, is the famous 1870-S three-dollar gold coin," the man with the lilt cooed. "There are no others in existence. Which makes this one priceless." Another pause.

Oh, my god. I was eavesdropping on a couple of thieves. I needed to get out of the area immediately but didn't dare move in the silence. I forced myself to breathe calmly, tried to slow my rapidly beating heart. Nervously, I waited for them to resume their conversation. Then I would put distance between us, hightail it down the trail and away from danger.

"Hey! What you doin' with that?" the southerner exclaimed. The alarm in his voice cut like a knife through the fog. "Put that away you damn fool!" The man's panic spiked my own. Silence or not, I needed to get the heck out of here. Now. I backed Twister, trying to keep our movements as quiet as possible. My heartrate pounded in my ears.

"I appreciate your efforts, Freddie. Truly, I do." The first man spaced his words. The tone of his voice brought Twister's head up, sent waves of panic through me. Our bodies tensed as one. At this point I didn't care if he suddenly bolted.

"Yeah, well, you got a lousy way of showin' it," the southerner sounded frantic. "You don't need no damn-fool gun to make yer point!"

"You wanted to renegotiate your part of the bargain. I'm renegotiating," the man with the lilt sounded so calm they might have been discussing the weather.

A suppressed *thwump* followed, and I saw the unmistakable flash of flame from a gun muzzle several yards directly in front of us. A surprised, painful gasp broke the hush, then another suppressed gunshot. Twister snorted and tossed his head, his bridle rattling and making all kinds of noise in the thick stillness as he dug his hooves into the soft ground cover.

"*Shit!*" I blurted, trying to regain control of my horse and get him turned around.

"Who's there?" the man with the lilt challenged, anger in his voice emphasizing his accent.

Shit. Shit, shit, *shit*.

In my haste, I dropped the reins. I leaned far over Twister's neck, trying to grab the dangling ends. I glimpsed the muzzle flash again, heard a strange whiz inches above my lowered head.

My outstretched fingers caught the slender leather and pulled Twister around as he jumped. The man with the gun had already guessed perilously close. My heart squeezed hard against my chest. Twister presented a far bigger target than I did. I had to get us out of here.

Another bullet whizzed past my ear as I kicked Twister with my left leg. He didn't need urging. With a spring that almost unseated me, he leapt into a dead run down the path, away from the danger. I managed to catch the right rein as it flapped upwards, then bunched both in my left hand and grabbed the saddle horn with my right. I leaned close to Twister's bobbing neck, buried my left hand with the reins into his mane, gripped the side pommel with my left thigh, and prayed hard I would not fall off.

Shadowy trunks flew by, the mist swirled and swam as Twister ran flat out, his neck stretched forward, his long mane flying into my face. I pressed my cheek against him, the saddle horn digging into my gut because I was so low in the saddle. I didn't try to guide him, didn't care where we ended up, just so long as we put distance between us and what I knew was a man who had just committed murder.

And I was a witness. Which meant I was in danger. Not only in danger, but a target. *Again.*

Twister didn't slow when we reached the place where the trail sloped down the side of the mountain. I felt his shoulders drop and almost went sailing straight over his head. Tears streamed. If I fell off, I would be alone and helpless facing a man with a gun and a very good reason to kill me.

I was terrified Twister would run into something and hurt himself, step into a hole, break a leg. I prayed the man did not have the means to follow us. The trail was too narrow for a vehicle.

But the trail was wide and easy to follow on foot and led straight to the stables. And the man knew it wasn't wildlife because he had shot at us. If he followed us all the way back to the stables, he would find Twister and me.

Twister flew in a full gallop as I clung to him for dear life. In the dense fog he could easily veer off the trail and into the woods, impale himself on a jagged limb or tree trunk, trip and fall and do all kinds of damage to himself.

Get a grip, I scolded. *Slow him down before you both end up head over heels.*

I untangled my left hand from Twister's mane and pulled on the reins, trying to ease him out of his panicked run. He strained hard against the bit and totally ignored my efforts to slow him down. His breathing sounded labored as he blew hard with every stride. I pulled again without results. I couldn't see anything in front of us or around us, didn't want to risk trying to pull him into a circle or a one-rein stop. He might break off the trail and plunge headlong into the heavy undergrowth. I hunkered down again, wove the fingers of my left hand into his mane, and held on.

The trail flattened out and I felt Twister slow. I sat up and pulled carefully, trying to regain control. He tossed his head and slowed to a bouncy, nervous lope. I still had a death grip on the saddle horn and my leg and stump hurt from gripping the side pommels. Lather coated his neck and withers, steam rose from him in thick clouds. His muscles began to tremble. I listened to him heaving and gasping, felt him slow more and tried to ease him into his gait. He broke out of that into a fast walk, his head dropping as he blew hard in labored, painful gasps. He was trembling violently, and I feared he might collapse. We had been going at a dead run for what seemed like forever. The distance, his fear, his age, and the mountainous terrain had wrecked him, and I really needed to get off.

But I couldn't walk if I got off. Tears streamed down my face when Twister stumbled.

The wooden prosthesis. The one Randy made.

Trying to sit as lightly as possible, I moved my stump from the wooden leg, unwound my jeans leg, then awkwardly worked the material over the prosthesis. Randy had not made it with the idea that I could actually wear it, so my stump fit loosely into the cupped end. I would have to hold it on. But it was an option. I leaned over and unbuckled the straps holding the wooden leg in place. Twister tripped again, almost lost his balance. I had to get off.

"Easy, boy," I murmured, pulling gently on the reins. Twister stumbled to a stop, his head so low I could have slid down his neck to the ground. I grabbed the wooden leg, swung it carefully across his withers, then felt myself slip off the saddle.

I hit the ground too hard, lost my balance, and toppled onto my face. The artificial leg jarred lose from my stump. Twister groaned and acted like he was about to collapse.

"No!" I jerked his reins, and his front legs straightened. He was shaking abominably, heavy lather soaked him. I did not want to add any strain on Twister, but I had no choice. I grabbed the stirrup and hauled myself to my foot. He swayed, and frantically, I tried to reposition the wooden leg enough to walk on. Holding it against my stump, I limped forward, tugging at the reins until Twister took unsteady, unwilling steps behind me.

Shadows appeared in front of us and the vague shape of the back arena became visible. I thought about my prosthesis on the mounting block but didn't dare ask Twister to walk the extra distance to retrieve it. I needed to find Kinsey and get Twister some help. Fast.

The rear sliding entrance to the indoor arena stood ajar and I guided Twister through, not caring whether I interrupted Randy's class.

"Kinsey!" My voice cracked. The indoor arena was deserted, which surprised me, because I thought Randy said he had classes going all morning.

"KINSEY!!" I shouted again. I thought I heard a muffled reply.

"KINN-SSEY!! N-O-W!!"

I heard a toilet flush, then Kinsey appeared around the far

corner where her office, a small snack bar, and bathroom facilities were located. She stopped dead in her tracks, her expression shocked. "What in the world…!"

She vaulted the railing and ran towards us. I kept Twister walking until she reached us and caught one of his reins, then I slumped into a heap in the dirt, the wooden prosthesis dislodged at a bizarre angle in my jeans leg.

"Please help him," I begged. "Please help him. Please don't let him collapse."

Kinsey ignored me, her full attention on the distressed animal. In a heartbeat she had stripped off his saddle, raised his upper lip and pressed his gums, which looked really awful to me. His nostrils flared wide as he heaved breath after breath, his head so low his nose almost touched the ground.

Kinsey scowled at me, her unspoken anger clear. "I need to cool him down, dry him off, get a blanket on him. His hindquarters are all cramped up and he's about to go down from exhaustion."

I looked at her from my position on the ground. There was no way I could be any assistance at all unless I had my cane or my prosthesis. I balled my fists in the dirt and stamped down the urge to scream at my helplessness.

"Good Lord Almighty," Randy's voice boomed from the rear entrance. I swung my head around and watched him run towards us.

Chapter Four

Randy locked eyes with me, hesitated, then changed direction and jogged over to kneel, his face close to mine. "Are you hurt?"

I shook my head and waved frantically towards Kinsey and my horse. "Help her with Twister."

Instead, he scooped me up, carried me out of the arena, and settled me into one of several white plastic chairs around tables spectators used for concessions. Gently he removed the wooden leg he'd made and laid it under my chair. My empty right jeans leg dangled. I tucked it beneath my thigh, then stared at Twister and felt tears stream down my face again.

Kinsey's voice rang out. "Randy, get me a blanket, one of the light ones. They're hanging in the office." Even from here I could tell Twister was only half-conscious, his head drooping, his body teetering, his eyes dull and unfocused as he heaved and heaved. His hindquarters were alarmingly rigid, the muscles taut against his furry hide.

Randy disappeared through the office door, reappeared moments later with a light-weight green horse blanket. He vaulted one-handed over the railing and jogged to Kinsey and the horse. The two of them got the blanket on Twister, who was still trembling horribly and looking like he might fall over any minute. I sat utterly still and prayed.

"I'll stay with him. Go get towels and cool water," Randy ordered urgently.

Kinsey ran to the end of the arena, through the gate, and into the office. She came back with two buckets, both of which she took to the utility room. I heard her turn on the water faucet. She reappeared carrying both buckets and several white terrycloth towels slung over her shoulders. Backing through the arena gate, she made her way to Randy and Twister, set both buckets down in front of the horse, dropped the towels into the buckets, and removed a red rope halter and lead slung over her arm. While Randy removed Twister's bridle and eased the halter on, Kinsey began rubbing him down beneath the blanket with the cool, wet towels.

"Come on, boy," she coaxed, using one of the soaked towels to sponge Twister's mouth and tongue.

"I don't think we'd better try to walk him," Randy advised.

"Let me get some Banamine." Kinsey ran to the office and came back minutes later with a thermometer, a stethoscope, and a syringe. She worked the horse's mouth open and slid in the syringe. Then she listened to his chest with the stethoscope before taking a rectal temperature. She shook her head as she studied the result.

"His heart rate is high, and he's hot. We need to cool him off, but I'm afraid that'll aggravate the muscle cramps." She whipped out her cell phone and paced back and forth in front of Twister as she waited for an answer. "Hey, Jen. I've got a horse about to collapse from exhaustion. He's gone into Monday Morning so bad I don't want to risk walking him. I've given him some oral Banamine, but I'm afraid to wait to see whether he responds. How fast can you get out here?" Kinsey listened, then cut the call. "What do you mean by Monday Morning?" I called out. "Today is Friday."

Keeping her eyes on the horse, Kinsey explained. "An older term for tying up. Comes from handlers who use draft horses and other heavy work horses. They don't work their horses on Sundays and sometimes on Monday mornings they get tied up like this. Normally it's best to walk them, get the muscles to loosen up. But Twister's hindquarters are so rigid where his muscles have cramped, I'm afraid of more muscle damage if I try to move him." She glanced swiftly around the empty arena.

"How long 'til Jen gets here? He's not drinking anything. We're going to have to tube him to get some fluids into him." Randy wrung out another towel and began rubbing Twister's soaked neck and legs. Kinsey continued to talk to Twister, running her hands over his head and lathered neck. Randy worked his way around the groaning horse, wiping him down underneath the blanket, changing to a fresh wet towel every few minutes.

I jerked my head around when the front doors opened, and two teenaged girls walked in. One of them had long straight brown hair woven into a French braid. She was tall and thin, wore old jeans, boots, and a heavy coat several sizes too big. Her friend appeared average in height and weight, had on jeans, sparkly blue cowboy boots and a matching rhinestone studded jacket that wouldn't keep her warm on a sunny summer day. I thought the tall skinny girl was one of the volunteers who worked with the special-needs kids. I had no idea who the second girl was.

"Hey, Susan," Kinsey called out. "Go into the office and pull up the list of Randy's horsemanship classes. I need you to call and cancel classes for him."

Susan ran to the railing. "Miss Kinsey, what happened?" Her concern echoed plainly across the expanse. She turned to me. "Oh, Mary Joe. What happened?" She crossed the concrete area to where I sat, her friend trailing behind. I watched their eyes drop to the empty space beside my left leg, watched their automatic jerks of surprise. Susan's frank brown eyes met mine and I saw embarrassed curiosity. "Are you okay?"

Kinsey interrupted her. "Dr. Jen's on her way. If anyone asks, just tell them we had an emergency with one of the boarders."

"Yes, ma'am." Susan turned to the office, her friend following at her heels, her blonde head still swiveled in my direction as she blatantly stared at my missing leg.

"Susan!" Randy called out. Susan stopped and turned around. "Have your friend find Amy for me, will you?"

"Yes, sir," Susan answered. Her friend's expression showed plainly she didn't appreciate being sent on an errand.

"Please, keep Amy away from the indoor arena," Randy called out. The blonde teenager threw a careless wave over her shoulder as she stalked through the front doors.

After what seemed like an eon, I heard the powerful growl of a diesel engine outside and moments later a middle-aged woman appeared through the rear entrance. She had a stocky build and short gray hair that stuck out beneath her ball cap. She wore utilitarian overalls and a heavy blue sweatshirt. A stethoscope hung around her neck and her arms held what looked like half a ton of medical supplies and buckets. Randy ran over and took equipment as the vet went through the same motions Kinsey conducted earlier, then slipped the stethoscope into her ears and listened to Twister's chest and belly.

"Sounds like a full-blown asthma attack in addition to everything else. Does he have a history of asthma that you know of?" she asked, stepping back to study Twister.

Kinsey shook her head. "He's one of our older horses, Jen, but he's never been pushed this hard before. His previous owner never mentioned anything about a lung condition."

Jen ran her hands beneath the blanket. "Wow, he's tight. Have you tried to walk him at all?"

Kinsey shook her head.

"How long since you gave him the Banamine?"

Kinsey winced. "Long enough that he should have started loosening up by now. He hasn't improved at all since I called you. Honestly, I keep waiting for him to collapse."

The vet looked around, spotted me sitting outside the arena. "Is he your horse?" she called out.

I nodded.

"What the heck were you thinking, running your horse like this?" She turned towards Kinsey and Randy. "Let's get him tubed and get some fluids into him. See if he perks up a bit." She began opening plastic-encased medical supplies.

Randy gathered the wet towels lying about on the ground, crossed the arena and through the gate, then walked to where I sat. He dropped the towels into a pile on the table, then frowned down at me.

"You look terrible." He knelt and pressed his fingers beneath my jaw, then against my forehead. "You're cold as ice, Mary Joe." He pressed a hand against my clothes. "And you're soaking wet."

I was shaking uncontrollably. He strode to the office, returned a moment later with a blue horse blanket which he wrapped around me until I felt like a caterpillar in a cocoon.

"Where's your prosthesis?" he asked.

I hesitated. I didn't want him messing with the artificial leg even though the glaringly empty space beside my left leg said it all.

Randy frowned. "Quit being self-conscious and tell me where to find your leg."

I relented. "The back arena on the mounting block. I took it off before I got on Twister." He nodded, then trotted through a side door. I turned my attention back to my horse.

The vet lubed one of Twister's nostrils, then inserted a large, incredibly long tube. Kinsey had to support Twister's head because he seemed too weak or too out of it to hold it up by himself. His sides heaved, his nostrils still flared. I didn't know enough about horses to be able to tell whether he would be okay. I knew just enough to understand he'd almost killed himself getting us to safety.

I swiped at the tears running down my face. Sounds of suppressed gunshots echoed through my memory along with sounds of bullets narrowly missing my horse and me.

I needed to report the incident immediately to the police. There was a body lying somewhere on the Blue Ridge Parkway.

But I couldn't take my attention off Twister. I should have slowed him sooner, should have gotten him under control before he became so winded. The man with the gun would not have followed us. He had a body to deal with, for crying out loud, unless he planned on just leaving it for someone to find. Somehow, his demeanor struck me as more calculating than that. He wasn't the type to take off and leave a dead body on the trail.

I shook my head again. Stupid, stupid idea, riding out of the arena. I should have ridden to the indoor arena and called the police when Jeremiah showed up, then found Randy and told him who Jeremiah was. He managed half-ton animals all day, he would have managed Jeremiah without a problem, had him ready to hand over when local law enforcement arrived.

Randy returned with my prosthesis. I didn't realize how weak I was until I tried to stand. I thought about my cane still in the tack room, decided not to ask Randy to retrieve it.

"Easy," he murmured, catching me before I face-planted on the concrete floor. "You need an ambulance."

I shook my head. I tried swatting his hands away, but he ignored my gestures and worked the artificial device into the right leg of my jeans. I settled my stump into the socket, then sat down and pulled the horse blanket around me until everything was hidden but my eyeballs.

"Stay here." He disappeared into the office again, came back moments later with a steaming Styrofoam cup. "Drink this."

The horse blanket helped warm up my outsides, but my insides were still freezing cold. I nodded and took the cup, blew gently then sipped on what turned out to be really good hot chocolate. The warmth of the blanket and the hot liquid together went a long way to help me feel better.

"If your color doesn't improve soon, I'm calling that ambulance." Randy pulled a white plastic chair over and sat down. I ignored him and watched the activity around my horse, which wasn't much since Kinsey and the vet both were standing around waiting for Twister to show signs of improvement.

Miss Blondie appeared through the front doors and wandered

over to our table, Amy following behind her.

"Hi, can I join you?" She looked at Randy and smiled, displaying a set of beautiful teeth her parents no doubt spent a lot of money on. Her long blonde hair hung around her face in soft curls that must have taken a couple of hours to perfect.

Randy turned his attention to Amy, and he couldn't control a grimace of irritation. "Hello, Sweetie."

I remembered his request to keep Amy away from the indoor arena.

Amy ran over to hug Randy. Her young curious eyes looked first at me, then towards the activity around Twister in the arena.

"What's wrong with Twister?" she asked, alarmed.

"He just got a little excited and ran too much," Randy told her, hugging her close.

"Is Twister going to die?" She turned wide, fearful brown eyes towards me. Mine filled with tears. Fortunately, Randy interceded.

"No, Amy." He hugged her tightly. "Twister got scared in the fog and ran a little too long, that's all." His eyes met mine over the child's head. *You will tell me later what happened*, his expression clearly implied.

Randy dug around his pockets. "Left my cell phone in the truck." He helped Amy into a chair between us, studied the activity around Twister, then looked at me. "You don't happen to have your cell with you, do you?"

"Sorry." I shook my head.

Either disregarding or oblivious of Randy's irritation with her for bringing Amy into the arena area, I couldn't tell, but the teenager wrinkled her nose at the wet towels and sat down. "I'm Linda." She batted her eyelashes at Randy. I stared at her blatant disrespect regarding the emergency surrounding my horse, realized my jaw had dropped, clamped my lips shut and turned my attention back to Twister. He didn't look like he was getting better, and I felt a large wave of fear ooze through me.

Randy ignored the teenager and turned to me. "What happened?"

I shook my head. "Later. After I find out whether Twister's going to be okay."

Randy's lips thinned in irritation at my answer.

Amy slid from her chair to stand beside me. Her hand gripped mine. "Twister will be fine." She squeezed my hand and I squeezed back.

Linda wriggled in her chair, rhinestones on her electric-blue jacket flashing in the corner of my eye. After way too long, she stood. "I'm going to saddle Golden Boy. Maybe the arena will be empty by the time I get back."

Startled, I stared at her. "You have a horse here?" I blurted. I knew most boarders at the stables because I came out almost every day, and most everyone had introduced her/himself to me at one time or another. I had assumed Linda was a friend of Susan's and had come with her to the stables today.

"Yeah," Linda acknowledged.

"Golden Boy," Amy turned her attention to the teenager. "He's that new palomino. He's really cool."

Linda looked at her and shrugged. "Yeah, he's mine."

"I love his mane and tail," Amy said.

Linda turned to me, her azure blue eyes incredibly clear and beautifully accented by very long dark lashes. "We just moved from Oklahoma. I haven't ridden much because Miss Kinsey told me to wait for him to get over the trip."

Admittedly, I was only half-listening to the girl. Commotion in the arena caught my attention and I watched Jen infuse more fluid through the tube, listening frequently to Twister's belly, then checking his gums. Twister's head had drifted up until his neck was level with his withers, but his eyes still appeared only half open. He continued to heave, but his nostrils seemed less flared.

"Should I try walking him?" Kinsey asked the vet.

Jen shook her head. "No, I don't think so. He's still too rigid."

Standing beside my table, Linda glanced at the activity in the arena. "You rode him too hard," she observed bluntly, then went on before I could reply. "Miss Kinsey gets on my case for doing that. But it's *fun*. And I love Golden Boy's canter."

"Yeah, you ride him until he's all wet," Amy piped in, frowning. "That's not a smart thing to do to your horse."

Linda's eyes narrowed at the young girl before turning to me. "Hope he's okay. See you later." She turned and sauntered through the front doors.

"I need to call your Aunt Jilly, tell her to come pick you up," Randy told Amy. Amy shook her head. "Please, Daddy, can I stay here with you? I want to make sure Miss Mary Joe and Twister are going to be okay."

"We'll see," Randy stalled. "If it starts to rain, you're going to Aunt Jilly's house."

"Aw, rain isn't going to hurt me," Amy argued. "You work in the rain all the time."

I thought Randy wanted Amy out of the arena in case Twister collapsed, felt another ugly ball of fear curdle my insides, and turned my attention to the arena. I saw Jen shake her head and felt a hysterical surge of emotion leap into my throat. Randy must have seen my reaction because he reached a hand out to squeeze my shoulder.

"He'll be okay," he murmured, which I ignored when the vet walked over. She leaned her arms on the railing and looked at me, her brown eyes tired and concerned.

"Honey, you need to learn fast when to quit riding. You rode that poor horse almost to death."

Tears gushed and I gulped several times before I could get any words out. Randy's strong fingers gripped my shoulder, Amy's small fingers tightened on my own. "I'm so sorry. He...." As bad as Twister was, I did not want to admit in front of Amy the real reason for our wild ride. "He...spooked, and...I couldn't control him."

The vet looked me straight in the eyes, and I knew she knew I was leaving out a lot of the story. Or maybe she thought I was trying to cover deliberately running my horse too hard.

"It wasn't intentional, Dr. Jen," I added, trying to soften her opinion of me. "I swear I haven't ever ridden him like this."

"Miss Mary Joe is a really good horse owner," Amy asserted, nodding her head until her braids bounced around her small face.

"What spooked him?" the vet asked.

I shook my head. "I...don't know. We were on the trail heading up the ridge. Twister took off and I couldn't get him to slow down."

Jen's expression did not soften. "He would have slowed down when he started feeling tired. Something not only spooked him, it scared the life out of him. Next time, think twice before you go out in these conditions."

I nodded, clamped my mouth shut and refused to look at Randy, whose fingers began massaging the back of my neck. I felt Amy wince and realized I had a death grip on her hand.

"I'm not happy with his response," Jen continued. "And as bad as he is, he could colic."

I wiped my free hand across my wet face and wished the tears would slow down.

"With that said, I think he's stable enough to transport. I'd like to haul him to the clinic hospital so I can put in an IV." Jen paused and I nodded to indicate I understood her lingo. My hand covered my mouth, muffling a sob.

Beside me, Amy sat rigidly upright in her chair.

Jen shook her head, sensing both my own and the young girl's distress. "Don't go thinking the worst, you two. I think he'll respond better to IV fluids and medication, but I can't do any of that here." She paused. "While he's there, I'd like to take some x-rays, make sure he hasn't suffered leg or hoof damage. It's not necessary, but as hard as he ran, we may be looking at a crack cannon bone or injured stifle, or damage to his naviculars." She studied me, then added, "Although I don't want to run up a huge vet bill on you. We could wait here another couple of hours, see how he does." "I don't care about the money," I cut in. "Do whatever you have to do."

Jen nodded, then looked at Randy. "Keep an eye on her. She looks almost as bad as her horse." She studied me for several moments. "Do you need an ambulance? It wouldn't hurt to get you checked out at the ER."

I shook my head. "No, I'm fine."

"Well, I'd argue you're not, since I've seen corpses with better color than yours right now. You look like you're about to topple over."

"I'm scared about Twister," I admitted, feeling tears leak again.

She turned and crossed the arena. Kinsey obviously had heard our conversation because she handed the vet Twister's lead and disappeared through the sliding double doors. Dr. Jen removed the tube from Twister's nose. A few minutes later Kinsey's truck and large covered horse trailer crept through the entrance. Jen ran another assessment on Twister, then ran her hands up and down his legs.

"I think he's stable enough to transport," she told Kinsey. "Find a dry blanket, will you?"

Randy heard the vet's request and disappeared into the office again. He came out with another blanket, which he carried across the arena. Jen removed the blanket on Twister and replaced it with the fresh one. Then, Kinsey led Twister towards the back of the trailer. He stumbled along, his hindquarters stiff and slow. She closed the section panel, then jumped from the trailer and secured the back.

"I'll follow you," Jen called as she began gathering her equipment.

Randy helped collect empty plastic bags and returned equipment to the vet's truck. Kinsey climbed into the cab, leaned through the window and waved at me. "I'll be gone for a couple of hours at least. I want to talk to you when I get back."

I nodded. "I'll be here."

Carefully, to avoid unnecessary jarring, she guided the rig in a large circle, then through the double doors. The vet hurried through the entrance and moments later the growl of her diesel truck ground to life, then faded.

Silence settled over the indoor arena. I stared at Twister's saddle and pad, which lay in a heap in the arena where Kinsey had dropped them. I stood and shrugged off the blanket, left the hot chocolate on the table. Amy followed, and Randy walked over, but I waved him away and limped into the arena to retrieve my tack. The saddle and pad were far enough off the ground I wouldn't have to bend over far to grab them.

"I'll get them," Amy offered, beating me to the spot and retrieving the tack. Sweat soaked the sheep's wool pad and most of the saddle leather. She carried everything to the mounting block. I looked around for Twister's bridle, which I spotted at the other end of the arena. I waved at Amy when she started to retrieve it.

"I'll get it. Thanks," I told her. I felt Randy's eyes on me as I limped across the expanse. Wishing I had my cane, I bent over awkwardly and got the bridle, then re-crossed the arena and lay the bridle beside the rest of the tack.

"Mary Joe, how can I help?" Randy walked over.

I sighed, felt my leg turn to water, and almost collapsed. Randy caught me, guided me to the mounting block, sat me down.

I shook my head and tried to focus on him in order to force the picture of my distressed horse from my mind. I needed to think about what I had seen and heard on top of the ridge. I needed to tell him about it. "I witnessed something up on the ridge. I think someone was murdered up there," I told him.

A long silence followed.

"Are you sure?" Randy sat beside me, his eyes studying mine.

I clamped my hands against the sides of my head. "That's the problem. No, I'm not sure. It was really foggy, and I heard these two men arguing, then what I think were gun shots. But they sounded funny. That's what spooked Twister. I think one of the men tried to shoot at us. That's when I got really scared and Twister ran all the way down the mountain."

Amy sat down on my other side. "Oh, my gosh, Miss Mary Jo. No wonder Twister ran so hard. That's really scary." I felt her small body begin to tremble.

So much for not saying anything about the incident in front of the child.

Randy studied me. "You need to call the police."

"You sure do," Amy agreed.

"And tell them what, exactly?" I balked. "I don't have a location, or a description, or even a clear idea of what happened. It all seemed like a nightmare." I rubbed my face with shaking hands. "Maybe it was. A nightmare, I mean. Maybe I'm confusing reality with something I've dreamed about."

"You can't be serious," Randy countered.

"You couldn't make something like that up." Amy's commentary was not helping my state of mind, but I didn't have the heart to ask her to stay out of the conversation.

I met his warm, brown eyes. "Yes, I am being serious. My nightmares are vivid. Maybe Twister just spooked, and I couldn't control him."

"You're too good of a rider for something like that," Amy declared. She hunched into her winter coat and shivered. "Boy, what a scary thing to watch."

"You should still call the police," he repeated.

"No," I told both of them. "I don't have anything to report. I need to go home and take a shower, then call the vet clinic for an update on Twister." I tried unsuccessfully to stand. Randy pressed a hand on my arm.

"I'll drive you home. You need a hot shower. Maybe that will help clear things up in your head." He looked at Amy. "Why don't you stay with Miss Mary Joe here while I go get the car?"

Amy nodded, but I cut in.

"Randy, I'm fine. I need to dry this stuff off, then call Kinsey, see if Twister made it okay to the clinic." I needed him to quit hovering over me. "Go work Norseman."

Amy dug her heels in. "Miss Mary Joe, you need help. I'll carry these for you," she argued, waving at Twister's tack, "and then keep you company until Daddy takes you home."

"Norseman can wait," Randy agreed. "My classes are cancelled, so I have plenty of time."

I wanted to be left alone. I wanted Twister to miraculously recover.

I didn't want anyone around to watch my reaction if Twister didn't make it to the clinic.

"You're supposed to be getting Norseman ready to show," I snapped. "There is no reason to pamper me. I'm fine." I searched for a reason for both of them to leave me alone. "I'll wait for you in the office. You'll be done before long. I can wait."

Randy hesitated for several long minutes. I mustered strength I didn't have and stood.

"I'm fine," I insisted. "The best thing you can do to help me stay calm is to go about your normal schedule. I'd come out back and watch, but I admit I'm more wet than dry, so I'll stay in the office."

A shadow at the edge of the rear entrance caught my eye, and suddenly I had a very good reason to convince Amy to stay with her father. I turned my attention to the child.

"I promise I'm okay," I told her. "Go with your Daddy and make sure he doesn't get hurt while he's working Norseman. I won't mess with any of this until you and your Daddy are done. I'll stay in the office and warm up." I was tired of repeating myself. I looked up at Randy. "Susan's in the office." I waved at them. "Go. I'm fine."

"What about the police?" Randy was not ready to concede. I blew out an irritated sigh.

"Let me get my thoughts together, and I'll call them from the office, if that makes you feel better."

"Okay." He agreed after a long hesitation. "See you sooner than later." He held his hand out towards his daughter. "Come on, Sweet Pea. Help me keep Norseman from pulling all those tricks he keeps coming up with."

Amy hopped off the mounting block and threw me a concerned look as I watched father and daughter cross the arena and disappear through the rear doors. I turned my attention to Twister's gear. I needed to dry everything off, which meant rummaging through Kinsey's office for something to treat the leather.

From the corner of my eye I watched Jeremiah enter the building. Damn. I'd hoped my earlier glimpse of him had been my imagination. My heart jolted, and I knew he had witnessed the entire chain of events. His timing was too perfect.

Susan appeared from the office and crossed to where the horse blanket lay in a heap on the concrete floor. The towels still lay piled on the table.

"Mary Joe, do you need the blanket anymore?" she called out.

I shook my head. "No."

"Can I put it away?" she asked as she gathered the large blanket into her arms. Jeremiah ambled around her and through the far entry gate into the arena.

"Sure. Thanks," I answered, my eyes on him.

"What about these towels?" She asked, apparently oblivious of Jeremiah's presence and sudden tension that filled the entire building.

I tried hard to keep my voice neutral as Jeremiah crossed the arena. "They'll need to be washed." She nodded and returned the horse blanket to the office, then gathered up the towels. Jeremiah stopped a few feet away from me. With a sinking heart, I watched Susan leave the building with an armful of wet towels. I swung my attention to the man standing beside me.

"Look. I don't need your help. I don't want you around. If I need help, I have people here I can call. What you really need to do is leave. Now." I kept my voice low, kept my tone civil because I wasn't sure whether Susan might still be within earshot.

To my irritation and dismay, Jeremiah shook his head. "I want to know what happened," he demanded in an undertone.

"That's none of your business." I stepped away because I did not want him towering over me.

Jeremiah looked me up and down. "You would not ride a horse that hard without good reason," he persisted. "I want to know what spooked the two of you. Your condition was almost as bad as your horse."

I glowered at him. "Drop it, Jeremiah."

He slid his hands into the pockets of his jeans. "For the time being I am staying with you. First on the list is to get you home and into dry clothes. Second is to get you something to eat while you tell me what scared you and your horse into running like that."

"I don't remember you being this nosy or this stubborn," I objected, leaning against the mounting block for support.

He took a step back and glanced around. "There are quite a few things I have changed about me during the last couple of years," he murmured.

"I've been managing just fine by myself. Randy and his daughter will be back soon, and they will give me a ride," I shot back.

Jeremiah fell silent and stood still for so long I had to fight to keep from fidgeting.

"What?" I demanded.

"Whatever happened today is at least partly my fault," he admitted slowly. "If I had not wanted to see you, you would not have ridden off. And whatever occurred would not have happened."

I rolled my eyes. "Jeremiah, get off it. I could've ridden out anyway. In fact, I probably would have."

Jeremiah shook his head. "No. You have better sense than that. I need to find out what I instigated."

I decided right then that come hell or high water, I was not going to tell Jeremiah what I had witnessed. Susan appeared through the front doors providing a welcome distraction. "Hey, Susan," I called out, "Are you going to be around all day?"

Susan turned towards me. "Yes, ma'am," she answered. "I still need to contact some of the class participants." She hesitated, then came through the arena gate and walked over to us. She was taller than my five foot ten but not quite Jeremiah's six foot plus. She motioned towards the tack lying on the mounting block. "I can put that away for you if you want."

I managed a smile. "Thanks. That would be helpful. And, well, would you bring my cane back? It's next to the saddletree I use. In the middle tack room."

"Sure, no problem." She picked up the tack. "This is such a cool saddle," she commented. "I've never seen an Australian saddle before. All I've ever known about are English and your basic Western."

I watched her leave the arena. Jeremiah stood beside me. An eon of stubborn silence passed before Susan returned with my wooden cane.

"Thanks." I took the cane and leaned on it gratefully. My stump was starting to cramp, and I needed to get off my feet.

Or rather, off my foot.

"Will you tell Randy and Amy I went home to shower and change? Please tell him I'm fine, and I'll be really careful. And I'll come back here and meet up with them in a bit." I glanced at the large white-faced utilitarian clock mounted on the wall outside the office. One p.m.

Already? I jolted at the way the day had slipped by.

Miss Blondie chose that moment to lead a beautiful Palomino quarter horse, probably with registration papers out the wazoo, into the indoor arena. "Hey, y'all, like I'm getting ready to ride, so you need to clear the arena," she called out.

Lord, I thought, that girl needed to get a clue. I stood there, realized I appeared indecisive, and thought if I really wanted to get rid of Jeremiah, I needed to appear a lot more in control of things.

"Hey, Miss Mary Joe. Is this yours?" Susan had retraced her steps and now stood beside the table where I had been sitting. She gestured towards something beneath one of the chairs.

Oh. Right. The wooden leg.

I limped across the arena, through the gate. "Yes. I'll take it home with me."

Of course, Jeremiah followed. For the life of me, I couldn't think of a way to get rid of the man.

~ * ~

The earthy aroma of horses, manure, and leather tack reached Patrick Kelly's nostrils as he paused along the trail, then withdrew into the shadows of the trees. The trail opened before him into an equestrian center, probably with boarding stables and riding arenas, although the fog hid them from view. He moved further into the trees, fog swirling him into obscurity, and waited for his breathing to slow.

Someone had witnessed him killing Freddie, and that meant a loose end. He could not afford loose ends. But it had required time to wrap and hide Freddie's body in the trunk of his Camaro, then to obliterate all evidence of the crime, before he could track the horse and rider. His hand rested on the semi-automatic tucked securely in his conceal carry holster, and he retrieved the suppressor from his slacks pocket.

Mulling over the problem, he slowly screwed the suppressor onto the end of his semi-automatic. The horse would have run a distance, would be sweaty. In this fog, he guessed not many riders would be out today. He would reconnoiter the buildings, look for a sweaty, possibly lathered horse with a concerned rider. If he proceeded with care, he ought to identify the witness without much trouble.

And he had to tie up this loose end. His purpose was too important, his plans too valuable to risk interference of any kind.

Chapter Five

Unfortunately, short of inflicting bodily injury, there wasn't much I could do to stop Jeremiah from riding home with me. Fatigue hit me like a cement wall as adrenaline sloughed off, and I decided not to waste what energy I had left arguing with the jerk. Jeremiah didn't try to start up conversation, which was just fine with me.

I pulled into the garage of the house I'd called home for the last eighteen-odd months. He followed me through the door that led into the kitchen, and I motioned with my cane for him to take a seat on one of the counter chairs, then limped to the master bedroom. I closed the door, hobbled into the large bathroom and stripped off my damp clothes. The huge shower stall had been modified for my needs. Railings lined the walls and a wide tiled bench allowed me to sit down. I removed my prosthesis and propped it against the wall beside the shower door, set my cane beside it, then turned the water on as hot as I could stand and eased into the stall using the railings. I sat on the bench and cried as steam swirled from the shower stall into the rest of the room.

I cried because of what I'd done to Twister, I cried because of the awful things I now remembered; I cried because Jeremiah was sitting in the kitchen when I wanted him gone. I cried because I knew I needed to report what I had witnessed on the Parkway between two men, one of whom probably lay dead somewhere on the trail.

I began to tremble at the thought of having to file a report. Conflicting emotions battled between what I should do versus the fact what I should do scared the living daylights out of me. I didn't have any description to offer, no details, only what I had heard. I lived in the middle of the mountains, a rural, isolated part of the country. Gunshots could be heard somewhere almost every day, usually by someone chasing a varmint off their property.

I closed my eyes and wiped my face, which was useless because of the shower water streaming down. Why, oh, why had Jeremiah shown up in the back arena? Real life was indeed stranger than fiction, and I was sick and tired of finding myself in the wrong place at the wrong time. All kinds of wild theories began whirling around in my head, and I concentrated, trying to separate truth from wild imagination.

Jeremiah had shown up at the stables. He had found me despite Stephen's efforts to help me disappear and start a new life.

Well I thought, Jeremiah was going to go away again. Because I was not going to go back to people and places that held nothing but painful memories.

Hawk.

The name generated a debilitating wave of fear. Was Jeremiah still in contact with Hawk? Vague recall hinted Hawk had an accent, but I could not pull it out of my subconscious.

Stephen Campbell had gone to great lengths to erase everything that had happened to me, had taken great care to help me start with a clean slate.

I thought again about the need to file a report with the police, wished with all my heart I could convince myself I had imagined the whole incident. I really loathed the idea of being the target of yet another killer because I had been in the wrong place at the wrong time.

Just like Oklahoma and Colorado.

The water finally ran cold, forcing me to get out. I sat on a bench and toweled off. I had a wheelchair I used when I was tired or my stump cramped, but I didn't want to be in a frickin' wheelchair around Jeremiah, especially now that I remembered the wheelchair I'd been in when a whole bunch of killers had come after me. My crutches leaned in a corner, but I nixed the idea of using them, too.

I put on underclothes, worked my prosthesis through a clean pair of wide-leg jeans, then slid into them and settled my stump into the socket. I pulled on a navy long-sleeve T-shirt followed by a white sweatshirt, pulled my wet hair into a clip knowing it would take forever to dry in the humid conditions.

Pride made me leave the cane in the bedroom. I limped out to the aroma of garlic, onions, and beef. I straightened my spine, tried to stalk over to the kitchen counter. Wasn't very successful because of the limp, and I figured even with the cane I wouldn't have been able to alter my gait sufficiently to send Jeremiah a message.

"Before you throw me out, I wanted to make sure you got something to eat," Jeremiah cut in before I could open my mouth. "I found steaks in the fridge. There is salad on the counter if you want."

I slid onto the nearest barstool and brushed back strands of wet hair that escaped the clip. "I've got housemates. For your information, those aren't mine."

Jeremiah paused in the act of removing the steaks from the oven, then set the sizzling broiler on the stovetop and turned to me. "My apologies. Though I think whoever owns these would not mind, given your appearance and recent scare."

I sighed and admitted, "Aiden would be doing the same thing you are. And he'd probably force feed me if I tried to turn him down."

Before I ate, I retrieved the handset and tried Kinsey's cell but got her voicemail.

"Hey, Kinsey. I'm at the house, so please contact me on my landline." I recited the number and hung up. I didn't think I could be hungry, but aromas of food teased my insides. "Thank you," I said, and took a bite of really good steak. "I remember you always being good at this."

A sly expression flickered across Jeremiah's face and he opened his mouth, then snapped it shut. I watched his expression close and knew exactly what he'd been about to say. And I thought that, before this whole mess, he would've slid in his comment about certain other things he was good at.

"Who is Aiden?" he asked instead.

I shook my head, working through my steak. "If we're going to ask each other questions, then I have a few for you to answer before you start in on me."

Jeremiah forked in a large mouthful, and I noticed with a start he'd already finished his steak and most of his salad. I glanced at him. He looked quite a bit thinner than I remembered. His high cheekbones, naturally prominent, jutted sharply from beneath hollow eye sockets. I turned my attention away before he noticed my frown and reminded myself that whatever his current condition, physical or emotional, it was no longer my concern. "What exactly were all those trips you took to the Rez over the seven-odd years of our marriage?" I asked.

Jeremiah pushed away his empty plate, stacked his empty salad bowl, placed his dinnerware carefully across the top.

"Some of them were legit. I took Mud Rain to the Rez to visit family or to take part in ceremonies, especially the Bear Dance in the Spring. I tried really hard to get you to go with us." Crossing his arms, he leaned onto the countertop and met my eyes. "But several trips were assignments."

"In other words, you told me you were heading to the Rez when in reality you were heading someplace else. You lied to me. A lot." I broke eye contact and stared at my plate. Somehow food didn't look as appealing now as it had when I sat down.

"That is correct."

His frank admission startled me, and it took effort not to jerk my eyes up to his. I toyed with the rest of my salad, then abandoned it and tried to swallow the sudden lump in my throat.

"So, these assignments. What were they?" I managed to choke out.

Jeremiah inhaled before answering. "The kinds of assignments given to government operatives."

A long, heavy silence followed.

"Why in hell did you not tell me you were an operative?" I swore, my voice barely a whisper.

Jeremiah did not move. "I wanted to keep you out of it. Keep you safe."

Another silence, longer this time.

"Have you killed people?" I murmured, mostly to myself. I didn't want to know the answer.

Jeremiah sat on the barstool, his forearms resting on the counter, his eyes drilling through the side of my head, his black T-shirt contrasting sharply with the faded, worn blue denim jacket he wore.

"Yes." His reply boomed despite his whisper.

"How many?" I couldn't help asking, still avoiding eye contact.

From my peripheral vision, I saw him shake his head and lean back. "No."

"No what?" I snapped, stirring my fork around my salad with such violence that a large amount flipped onto the counter.

"No, you do not need those kinds of details," he declared, his words spaced, deliberate.

I glared at him. "Oh, yes I do."

Jeremiah watched me. "I mostly conducted research and reconnaissance. I occasionally was a spotter with a sniper."

I dropped the fork and looked up at him. "Where were you when you went on these assignments?"

Jeremiah shook his head again. "That is classified information."

"I never knew you were in the military." I folded my arms in front of my half-eaten meal. I was talking more to myself than to him. "Looking back on it, I can't believe I was so blind. I don't remember receiving any military type of mail or email or phone calls. Nothing." I leaned back, my hands on the counter, and stared through the window over the sink. "That's really scary, actually. That you could hide something like that so well." I snapped my head to look at him. "Or was I that gullible?"

Jeremiah remained quiet, watching me.

"Why? Why lie to me about what you were doing?" I asked, knowing I was barging into territory that would make me feel stupid and blind.

"I told you. I wanted to keep you out of danger. I wanted to keep you safe."

I stiffened. "But I was your *wife*. How could you possibly believe your job wouldn't impact me someday?"

He ran a hand over his long hair, pulled at his shoulder length ponytail. "It was based on need to know. The less you knew, the safer you were."

I shifted on the wooden chair and folded my arms across my chest. "Did you become an operative before or after we got married?"

He rested his arms on the counter again, his shoulders hunched. "Before. I was approached while I was still with the Navy." He looked defensive, his neck and shoulder muscles tense, his jaw clenched.

"And you decided it was okay not to tell me any of this? At all?" My arms tightened across my chest as anger surged through every muscle.

Jeremiah regarded me in silence for a lot longer than I thought necessary. He didn't move, didn't even twitch with his next statement.

"It gets worse."

I slid off the seat, collected the dirty dishes, limped with them to the sink. After setting them down I turned around, my back against the counter, and braced my palms against the edge of the porcelain basin.

"How much worse?" I asked.

He inhaled, rubbed his temples with his fingers, then leaned back. "Our marriage was…arranged. A way to get me undercover and off the radar. At least that was the initial plan."

I gaped at him. I didn't know what to say, how to respond. For seven years, I'd been married to a man who had married me for a whole slew of reasons, and I was now finding out none of his reasons included the primary motive propelling two people to marry.

But I had loved him. For more than seven years I had loved him, and I had loved and helped care for his younger brother Mud Rain, who had been born with Downs Syndrome. Hearing the truth compounded painful memories now flooding my brain.

"What do you mean, arranged?" I asked, my voice hardly above a whisper.

Jeremiah looked away and stared out the large bay window that normally gave a panoramic view of the Blue Ridge Mountains. Currently, all it revealed was thick gray fog. It took a while before he turned his head and met my eyes again.

"I needed someone who was clean, so to speak. No record with law enforcement, no behavior that might attract attention. Senior brass initially thought a large city would offer the best invisibility, especially since it represented something in stark contrast to my roots on the Rez." His gaze drifted over my shoulder to stare through the window behind me. "But I did not want to be that far from Mud Rain. I debated the possibility of disappearing into another Reservation when I came across your family. Your profile fit the requirements. Senior brass thought my suggestion so perfect they immediately tackled the issue of getting us introduced. It did not take much to get you assigned to the O.U. Weather Center." His eyes locked onto mine.

From the time he'd introduced himself at the weather station on the Oklahoma University campus, my heart had flipped all over my chest every time I'd seen him. I remembered he had not been an aggressive suitor, and for the first few months we had been friends. When things became intimate, he proposed, I accepted, and we'd married a couple of months later. Not a long engagement, now that I thought back on things, but I had been dead sure I was making the right choice. And not that it would have influenced my decision, but Mom and Dad both really liked Jeremiah. The only person who had not liked the turn of events had been my sister, Angela, but I figured it was jealousy because I now had Jeremiah to confide in, which impacted Angela's and my relationship.

Angela. I felt my eyes water and forced down a surge of pain and sadness. It would have been better if I had never regained my memory. The pain of the events after Mom and Dad's death overwhelmed my fragile emotional stability. I thought about Angela's husband, Gary Tacque, the man who had methodically killed every member of my family, whose team members descended on me to avenge his death and destroyed every remaining physical keepsake. I wondered whether Gary Tacque had been connected to any of the assignments Jeremiah was involved with.

I watched Jeremiah watching me, knew he was probably seeing clearly every thought that slid through my head. I turned my back on him and stared through the kitchen window.

I didn't want to know whether the whole mess around Angela's husband had been linked to Jeremiah's work with the government. I didn't want to go down that road because I might find out his efforts to drop off the radar had created the reason my family became targets.

The incredibly loud ticking of the battery run clock on the wall filled my ears. I tilted my head around and glanced at the time. "I need to get back to the stables. Kinsey hasn't called, and I want to be there when she gets back."

But I didn't move. My eyes returned to the dense fog beyond the window, how well it hid everything from view. The lateness of the afternoon brought early gray twilight to the already obscured landscape. I thought it might start raining soon. I really needed for the sun to come out and brighten things up, bring some warmth and light to my insides. I closed my eyes.

"Mattie." Jeremiah sounded close. In fact, he sounded like he was standing right behind me. I visibly jumped but did not turn around.

"I need you to know I did not marry you just to drop off the radar." He sighed. "Okay," he amended quietly. "I admit I did at first. The original plan with Senior Brass was that I marry for two years, long enough to gain invisibility. Eighteen months after our marriage,

I was given orders to file for divorce."

"Well, you're late following orders, but divorce is definitely what you'll get, as soon as I contact Stephen and sign the papers." I left the dirty dishes soaking, something I didn't normally do, angled around him to grab my purse off the counter, and headed for the garage. Jeremiah followed, folded himself into the passenger seat of the Explorer as I swung behind the wheel. I backed out, turned on my fog lights, and crept down the winding gravel driveway until I hit the dirt road bordering my property. I cut across another gravel road to access the paved two-lane mountain road. Twenty minutes later I reached the Interstate and my phone dinged several times. Cell coverage at my house was sporadic, inclement weather interfered with signals.

"Want me to check your messages?" Jeremiah asked.

"Yes, please. See if any of those are from Kinsey or the vet." I handed my phone to him. Interstate traffic bogged down to a snail's pace, and I tapped the steering wheel with an impatient forefinger. We approached a large cluster of flashing emergency lights and vehicles, crept around flares that separated traffic from a pile of crashed cars, no doubt due to poor visibility.

Jeremiah grunted. "Twister is no worse. The vet wants to keep an eye on him for a day or two, though, just in case he tries to colic."

The ensuing wave of relief hit me with such intensity that my eyes teared up and I choked back a sob.

Now if I could just rewind every painful memory and Jeremiah's revelations, I might start feeling better. Silence fell between us as we gained speed along the highway, finally approaching the exit to the stables. It had taken twice as long as normal, and I frowned and wondered why people couldn't exercise simple common sense when visibility conditions were this bad.

"Will you postpone signing the divorce papers for a couple of months?" Jeremiah asked as I swung onto the exit ramp that led to another twisting mountain road and to the stables.

"No." My flat rejection felt good, and the emotional pain began slowly sliding away from my heart towards a deep, vague recess. I had another conversation to work on, and I thought again about Randy and the ring box.

I expected the stables to appear ghost-like, deserted and empty in the damp foggy conditions. I expected Kinsey to be in her office waiting for me to give her an explanation of why I had brought my horse back in such bad shape.

What I didn't expect to see was two town squad cars and a county sheriff's cruiser angled in the parking area.

For a wild moment, I thought they were there for me, to arrest me for animal abuse or something like that. Right on top of that I realized before Kinsey called the cops, she would need to know what had happened. As I squeezed the Explorer between the two town cop cars and parked, my next thought was someone had found the body on the trail and the cops were here to ask me questions.

Jeremiah followed close on my heels as I limped across the graveled parking lot to the indoor arena. I entered through the front doors, then limped around the corner into Kinsey's office.

Amy sat at the desk, facing the computer screen. She turned when we came through the door, and I stopped abruptly at the sight of her face. Tears stained her cheeks, her eyes red and swollen, her color pale as death.

"Amy?" I crossed to a chair and sat down beside her. "What's wrong?"

The young girl slumped into my arms and began to tremble violently, but she did not utter a word. At that moment Susan entered the office, her expression as devastated as Amy's. I swallowed when her bloodshot eyes stared at mine.

"What's happened?" I asked her.

Susan pressed her hands to her face, then collapsed into a chair and looked at me with strangled disbelief. "I…I found Mr. Wittmore a little while ago. In the…in the back arena." She curled her knees into her chest, her feet tucked tightly on the chair she occupied. She stared at the back of Amy's head, opened her mouth, shut it, then opened it again and visibly forced the words out. "He's …he's…dead," she whispered.

"Oh, my god." I covered my mouth with a hand, felt shock grip me with vicious cold talons, and hugged Amy tightly against me. "Randy? Randy Wittmore?" I breathed. "Are you sure?"

Susan nodded, and I tightened my grip around Amy. Her small thin body trembled violently against mine as mine began to tremble against hers.

"No," I whispered. "This can't be true. It can't be true." I forced back questions that would challenge what Susan had just told me, but I didn't believe her. I couldn't believe her, because if what she said was true....

From the corner of my eye, I watched Jeremiah remove his jacket and drape it around Susan's shoulders.

"Stay here." He left, and I clung to the little girl silent and shaking, stared at the teenager who needed someone to be hugging her, too, felt small and vulnerable and needed Randy's strong, protective arms around me.

"Who all is here besides the cops?" I whispered. "Where was Amy when this happened?"

Susan shook her head. "No one, yet. I can't leave until one of the officers talks to me." She motioned towards the child. "Her aunt is on her way."

"Did...did she say whether she saw what happened?" I murmured.

"I found her huddled in the trees outside the arena. She hasn't uttered a sound." Susan was shaking badly, and I wished Kinsey would arrive soon, or Susan's mom, or someone to help console all of us.

Most of all I wished for Randy to walk through the door and prove he was alive and well.

"I found him. I was here by myself, watching things until Miss Kinsey got back." Susan's voice was low, monotone. She pulled Jeremiah's jacket close around her throat. I didn't want her to continue, didn't want to listen to her confirm the horrible truth. "Norseman came racing through the arena doors. He was wet and all lathered up." She paused, rubbed her face with her hands. "He had a saddle on, and his lead was trailing from his halter. He wouldn't let me catch him." She stopped. "I thought maybe Mr. Wittmore had tripped or something, or maybe Norseman just got away from him when he opened the gate. I checked the arenas out front and didn't see him. So, I walked to the back arena." She paused and I silently begged her not to finish.

Susan choked back a sob. "That's when I saw him. His was lying on his back in the middle of the arena. He wasn't moving. I got scared because I thought he had an accident, maybe like the kind that killed his wife. I ran over to help, and that's when I saw his eyes." She stopped and squeezed her eyes shut, her body trembling violently with the memory. "And there was blood around his head."

Amy buried her head deeper against my chest as Susan's words hit me like a giant boulder. My blood ran cold, and the room began to spin. I squeezed my eyes shut and forced out my question, trying to focus on the words so I wouldn't pass out. "What did you do next?"

I opened my eyes, watched Susan rock back and forth, her fingers clutching the edges of Jeremiah's jacket. "I didn't touch him. I was afraid. I didn't want to believe he was dead. And then I heard a noise and looked around. That's when I saw Amy."

"And that's when you called the police?"

Susan clarified. "I called 911. The ambulance already came and went again after they saw him."

"Is Kinsey back yet?" I asked, trying to break my vision of Randy lying dead on the ground.

Susan shook her head. "No. She's on her way."

I was shaking as badly as the two girls. "W-what about your mom?"

Susan wiped her eyes, huddled further into the warm thickness of Jeremiah's jacket. "I called her, too. The officers said to let them know when she gets here. They're all back with…where…."

I turned when a woman appeared, followed closely by Jeremiah.

It was Randy's sister, Jilly. She was older by several years, trim, wore a business suit. Somewhere in my muddled brain I remembered Randy mentioning she was a partner in a local law firm. She knelt and stroked Amy's hair. "Amy, you need to come with me now." Very gently she coaxed Amy from my lap. She gave me a cold, hostile glare before leading the child out of the office.

Jeremiah nodded towards me. "Can I talk to you? Out here?" he motioned for me to follow him and disappeared around the corner.

I wondered seriously whether I could stand up. "I'll be right back, Susan."

Susan nodded. I stood, wavered, reached a hand to grab the various furniture and objects in the office to steady myself, and limped from the office. Jeremiah stood beside the arena out of earshot. I looked across the dirt enclosure and saw the Arab pacing the far end of the indoor arena. Someone had shut the rear doors. Probably Susan.

"The man was shot. Probably back of the head, from the distorted look of his face." Jeremiah murmured when I turned my attention to him.

"How would you know?" I challenged, struggling to keep my voice down. "The cops aren't going to let you just waltz into a crime scene!"

"True," he conceded. "But small-town crime scene protocol is marginally easier to circumvent. What I tell you are the facts."

I squeezed my eyes shut and leaned against the wall so I wouldn't sway into Jeremiah.

Randy had been shot just like that man up on the Parkway. The killer must have followed the trail to the stables. Randy had been using the back arena. The killer had no doubt seen how sweaty the Arab was and jumped to the wrong conclusion.

"This can't be happening," I murmured against my hand. I'm sure Jeremiah didn't understand a word I said.

Jeremiah leaned in close. "You are white as a ghost. Just like when you rode in with Twister. Would this have anything to do with what scared you and your horse earlier today?"

Chapter Six

I stared at Jeremiah. "I don't know what you're talking about," I answered, aware I've never been a good liar.

"You need to tell the investigating officers what you know," he said, confirming that he saw straight through my poorly attempted diversion.

Time to change subjects.

"I need to take care of Norseman." I crossed the concrete pavilion to the gate, then limped across the uneven dirt floor to the sweaty horse. The Arab skittered at my approach, his graceful dish-shaped head tossing nervously as I closed the distance. He was a young horse, gray with dark muzzle, mane and tail, and registration papers probably a mile long. Sweat soaked his chest, neck, and flanks, and I recalled Randy's comments about how nervous the young horse had been on arrival to the stables. I stopped in the center of the arena when Norseman trotted away.

"I need grain," I muttered, feeling useless and vulnerable. Hampered by my artificial leg, it would not be wise for me to try to handle a horse as high strung as Norseman.

"Where do I find some?" Jeremiah asked.

As upset as I was about having him around, the cold truth was I really wanted to settle the horse before Kinsey got back. Dealing with the Arab pushed the truth about Randy from the front of my thoughts.

"There's a grain bin between this building and the nearest tack room," I told him.

Jeremiah nodded and strode away. I limped slowly across the expanse, found a large rubber feed dish, and waited. Norseman pranced around the far end of the arena, his head high and his tail arched, his dark eyes rimmed with white as he watched me. When Jeremiah returned, I noisily poured the grain into the feed dish, then watched the Arab's ears perk forwards. I backed several steps and waited.

"I should handle him," Jeremiah observed quietly when the Arab took a few tentative steps forward. I backed another couple of steps.

"Yeah. Probably," I admitted.

"Should we unsaddle and blanket him?"

I looked at the horse and tried to think what I should do. Though it was chilly inside the arena, the Arab didn't seem uncomfortable, just stressed. But I didn't want him to get chilled as he cooled off and his winter coat dried. "Probably, but not right now," I shook my head.

Norseman's taste for grain outweighed his fear of us, and he gradually closed the distance. When he reached the feed dish, the Arab bent his beautiful gray head and Jeremiah slowly walked towards him. The Arab shied, then seemed to decide the grain was worth being caught. Murmuring softly, Jeremiah retrieved the trailing lead rope, then began stroking the nervous animal. My thoughts shifted to the squad cars outside and the reason for their presence.

The town police force consisted of two squad cars for each shift. The Virginia State Troopers and County Sheriff's department covered everything beyond the town limits. Two town squad cars parked outside meant Aiden and Riley were here.

They both knew Randy.

Sure enough, thirty minutes later Riley marched through the front entrance and joined me.

"Hey, M.J." She kept her voice low. "How are you holding up?"

I inhaled deeply, tried unsuccessfully to keep my voice steady. "Trying not to think about it, Riley. If I start thinking about what's happened, I'm going to lose it."

"I need to talk with the teenager, then to Amy," she said carefully. "You know where they are?"

"Amy is home with her lawyer aunt, so I don't think you'll get a chance to ask her anything. She was too upset to talk anyway." I nodded towards the office. "Susan's in there."

Riley glanced towards the office, then swung her attention to Jeremiah and the Arab. "Do you know if her mom's here yet?" she asked me, frowning as she stared at Jeremiah.

I brushed a hand across my face and tried to bottle up welling emotions. If I started to cry, I wouldn't be able to stop. "Yes, she got here a little while ago."

Riley swung her attention to me, her brown eyes intense. "You've been staying in here with the horse." Hers was a statement with a whole lot of unspoken acknowledgement about why I had not made the trek to the back arena.

I looked at her, unable to hide the devastation washing over me. "I…I can't h-handle what I'm g-going to s-see." I turned to limp to the office when Riley's strong hand gripped my arm, her attention on Jeremiah.

"Is that who I think it is?" she muttered. I shrugged off her hand and followed her gaze towards Jeremiah, still holding the Arab's lead as the animal finished his treat.

"Yes," I grumbled.

She threw me a surprised look. "You've got your memory back?"

"Thanks to him," I waved at Jeremiah. "And how in the hell would you know who he is?"

Riley threw me a look that bordered on disbelief. "Hello, M.J. Stephen Campbell filled Aiden and me in on your past, including pictures of whom to keep our eyes peeled out for."

"Oh." I felt like an idiot. Of course, Stephen would have given them information about my past.

Riley stood rigidly still on the concrete pavilion and scowled so fiercely I thought her expression might permanently freeze.

"How long has he been here?" Hers sounded like an interrogation question. I sighed, debated about trying to lie, knew I wouldn't be able to convince her any better than I had Jeremiah earlier.

I waved an arm in his direction. "Since this morning." I didn't make eye contact with him across the distance that separated the three of us, but I figured he was more than aware of Riley's death stare.

Riley muttered an oath that jerked my head to stare at her. She glanced at me. "Sorry," she muttered, though she didn't look penitent. Her left hand moved towards her holstered weapon.

I caught her arm. "Cool it, Riley. He hasn't posed any sort of threat."

"Like hell he hasn't." With a smooth defensive move she freed her arm. "That dirt bag has a restraining order against him. He's prohibited from having any contact or interaction with you, and he knows it." She stepped away from me and opened her mouth.

"*Riley*," I pleaded in an undertone, aware Norseman would feel our tension and might spook. "He's not the priority. You need to interview Susan." I caught her arm again. "Jeremiah can wait."

The rumble of a diesel engine signaled Kinsey's return.

Riley never broke eye contact with Jeremiah. "I'm Officer Butler," she announced and despite the even tone of her voice, the Arab's head jerked up to full height, his ears pricked forward. "Jeremiah Tyler, there's a restraining order forbidding your presence here. You need to be leaving. *Now*."

"Okay, okay," I pulled at her arm until she reluctantly turned around. "You've told him. Now you need to focus on the interview." As Riley cast a glance over her shoulder at Jeremiah, who had not so much as twitched an eyelash, I added, "If he's still here when you're done, you can arrest him."

"You're damn right I will," she snapped.

"Yeah, and after you do that, you can explain why you and your brother have been lying to me for the last two years," I snapped back, suddenly aware that out of everyone I seemed to know, no one was telling me the truth. Riley shot a startled look at me, then spun on her heel and headed for the office.

Susan sat in the same chair, still had Jeremiah's denim jacket pulled close around her shoulders. Her mother, a plump woman in her fifties with short gray hair, wore jeans and a heavy hooded sweatshirt like everyone else at the stables. She sat beside Susan and held her daughter close. Riley pulled out a small notepad and a pencil.

"Can I listen in?" I asked. Riley nodded and I took the last empty chair.

Riley leaned casually against the wall. I wondered whether Jeremiah would be smart enough to follow her order to leave.

Probably not, I thought. Which meant he would be occupying a jail cell by this evening. Or more probably a hospital bed, if Riley had her way.

Riley looked at the teenager and her mother. "Hi, Susan," she turned her head to the mother, "Mrs. Downs."

Susan glanced at Riley. "Hello…um…Officer…."

"Naw, you know me," Riley interrupted. "Call me Riley. I need to go over the events of this afternoon with you."

Susan nodded, lifting a thin hand to brush tears from her wet face.

"Let me start with the simple stuff like your name and age. For the official report, you know." She looked at Susan's mother. "I'll need the same information from you as well, Mrs. Downs."

"Susan Downs. I just turned seventeen," the teenager replied in a shaky voice.

"I'm Martha Downs. I'm forty-eight." She wrapped an arm around her daughter's shoulders, then gripped both of her shaking hands. Riley asked for other basic information on where they lived, what year of school Susan currently attended, how long they had been in town.

"Now for the tough part." Riley paused, allowing Susan to prepare herself to relive the ordeal. "I need you to slowly go through what happened today, starting from the time you arrived."

Susan closed her eyes and drew a deep, steadying breath. Her mother leaned in and hugged her shoulders. I caught myself leaning forward in my chair, tried to relax back. Tears threatened again, and I blinked rapidly to clear my vision.

"I was in here making calls to cancel Mr. Wittmore's horsemanship classes." Susan stopped and covered her face with her hands. Soft sobbing emanated from her.

Riley bent forward, her eyes soft, comforting. "Susan, please believe me, I understand how difficult this is for you. Take your time, think things over, and tell me what happened." Her brown eyes cut in my direction, no doubt saw the wetness and emotional strain in mine.

I did not want to believe Randy was dead. I did not want to sit and listen to Susan. Jeremiah's words filtered into my thoughts, but I refused to believe him. The whole tragedy reflected yet another horrible equestrian accident. It had to be. Anything else meant I was directly responsible because of events I'd witnessed on the Blue Ridge Parkway.

Before Susan could continue, Kinsey strode through the office door, followed by Jeremiah.

"I can't believe this is happening." Her voice shook, her face as white as the fog outside. She began pacing the crowded room. "I walked back to the arena. Randy's been...."

Riley interrupted Kinsey before she could finish. "A-h-h-h, I was just asking Susan here a few questions."

Kinsey and Riley stared at each other for a very silent few moments, then Kinsey nodded. "Okay. Do you need me here?"

Riley shook her head. "No, ma'am."

"Then I'll go check on Norseman and put him away." She retrieved one of the horse blankets hanging on a rack and disappeared through the office door. Jeremiah leaned against the doorway. Riley ignored him and glanced at her notes.

"I think I was asking you about what happened when you were in here canceling lessons," she said, turning back to Susan.

The teenager nodded, tears trickling down her cheeks. "Linda and I got here this morning, and I saw Miss Kinsey with Twister in the arena. That's Mary Joe's horse. They had an emergency with him, and Miss Kinsey told me to come in here and call the students who were supposed to come today and tell them the horsemanship classes were cancelled."

"So, you were here in the office making calls," Riley jotted more notes.

Susan nodded.

Riley flipped pages. "Where was Mr. Wittmore while you were doing this?"

The teenager sighed again and wiped the tears from her face. "Well, he was in here helping with Twister and keeping Mary Joe company until Kinsey left for the vet clinic with Twister. He and Amy left the indoor arena, probably so he could work Norseman. I remember Linda coming in with Golden Boy and wanting to use the indoor arena. After she was done, she sat in here with me for a while, but then she said she was getting bored, so she left."

"Linda's new in town, isn't she? Moved here a few weeks ago from Oklahoma?"

Susan nodded.

"Had she met Mr. Wittmore?"

Susan shook her head. "No, I don't think so."

"Do you know where she went when she left here?" Riley asked.

Susan released a shaky sigh. "She called one of the guys she met at school, and he came and picked her up."

I stirred. "Randy helped Kinsey and Jen with Twister, then offered to give me a ride home. But I told him I was fine and for him to go work Norseman...." I broke off. *Oh, dear Lord.* I squeezed my eyes shut and forced out the rest. "Amy really wanted to stay with me, but I insisted she should stay with her Dad."

"Is it possible the child witnessed what happened?" Riley

asked me carefully.

"More than probable, based on her emotional state," I acknowledged.

Amy had almost certainly watched her father being shot. How long would it take before she opened enough to give the police valuable information only she possessed?

Jeremiah remained silent as a ghost. Riley shot another laser look at him, and I expected her to pull out her cuffs, or worse, her handgun, although her bare hands posed an equal if not greater threat.

"He rode home with me," I told her, "I…I was still shaky from the whole thing with Twister…." *Careful, don't let it slip what happened up there on the ridge,* I thought frantically. *Not in front of Susan and her mom.* I inhaled. "Randy and Amy left to work the Arab after Kinsey left with Twister for the vet clinic," I clarified. "Linda came in with Golden Boy about the time I…we left to go home."

Riley wrote some more, then turned her attention back to Susan. "Did Mr. Wittmore come in any time while you were here in the office?"

Susan shook her head. "No, he never came back. She stopped and a strange look of comprehension mixed with horror crossed her face.

"What?" Riley prompted.

"Well," Susan began twisting her hands together. Her mother tried to hold them, but Susan jerked them away. "I should've gone out and told Mr. Wittmore the indoor arena was open. I bet the Arab spooked and…and Mr. Wittmore fell…."

Susan covered her face with her hands and leaned over. Her mother knelt close and rubbed her back. I looked at Riley, expecting her to correct the teenager, to tell her Randy had been shot. When Riley didn't say anything, I glanced at Jeremiah who gave me a slight warning shake of his head.

"Susan," Riley spoke gently, coaxing the teenager to look up at her. "Do you remember seeing anyone else here between the time you arrived and the time you found Mr. Wittmore in the back arena?"

Susan shook her head. "Only Mary Joe and this person," she motioned towards Jeremiah. "And Dr. Jen and Miss Kinsey." She paused and frowned, her eyebrows almost touching. "There was someone who walked through. I heard the front doors open and expected whoever it was to come into the office. I thought it might be a student or another volunteer. But no one came in here, so I got up and went to the office door. There was a man crossing the arena. He went through the rear doors, and I figured he must be a friend of one of the boarders. He seemed to know where he was going. He never stopped by the office to ask directions or anything like that."

"Can you describe him?" Riley asked.

Susan shook her head. "No. I'm not even sure it was a man. I just got a glimpse of his back. I can't remember what he was wearing, except a big hat."

"Like a cowboy hat?" Riley pressed.

"No," Susan shook her head. "More like one of those big rain hats. It might have been part of his coat."

Riley scribbled. "Do you think it might have been someone you've seen around here?"

"No," Susan paused, thinking. "At least I don't think so. "Whoever it was, he wasn't a volunteer because he would've come into the office. And I know all the boarders, and it definitely wasn't one of them. If he'd been looking for Miss Kinsey, he still would've come into the office. And he walked straight out the back doors."

"He wasn't wandering around, like he was looking for someone?"

Susan shook her head. "No. He seemed like he knew where he was going."

Riley studied the teenager closely. "Could it have been one of the farriers?"

"No," Susan shook her head. "He wasn't dressed right."

"What do you mean?" Riley flipped the pages in her notepad.

Susan straightened, then rubbed her face with her hands before she continued. "He wouldn't be wearing a big fancy coat like that. He wasn't dressed like the farriers who work here."

"You keep referring to this person as a man," Riley observed. "Something about this person struck you as male."

I thought Susan amazingly observant for a teenager, but that Riley might be pushing too hard and expecting too much. To my surprise, Susan's expression cleared as she concentrated, and her next comments proved how much I'd underestimated her.

"He was sort of average height, but he didn't walk like a girl, and his shoulders were wide. But not fat," she amended. "He had a strong walk, if you know what I mean. Like he knew what he was looking for."

Or *whom* I thought as a chill raised every hair on the back of my neck.

What if Susan had been in the same building with a cold-blooded killer?

"Do you remember whether he was carrying anything?" Riley asked, fortunately her attention on Susan and not on me. My expression would have told her everything.

Susan closed her eyes in concentration. "He had black gloves on. The kind that hug your hand, not big winter gloves." She opened her eyes and looked at her mom who gave her a reassuring smile.

Riley's head snapped up. "Did it rain here at all while you were here today?"

Susan shook her head. "No…." Her voice trailed off and her eyes grew unfocused. "You know, I remember thinking it was odd the way he was dressed. His coat wasn't made for riding. It didn't have a split up the back, like a riding slick would. I remember thinking the way his coat billowed and his hat was so big and wide he might spook some of the horses." She broke off again, her expression showing plainly she remembered something else. "Black. His coat and hat and gloves were black. Black leather."

Riley leaned against the wall and turned her head to stare through the interior office window that gave an uninterrupted view of the indoor arena. Silence fell over our tiny group. I followed her gaze. The arena was empty now. Kinsey had returned the Arab to his outdoor run. I sensed Jeremiah behind me, hoped he wouldn't try any physical contact.

"Here." Susan's mom reached for a Kleenex box and gave several to her daughter. Susan blew her nose, which sounded incredibly loud in the intense stillness.

"Has it been quiet like this all day?" Riley murmured, almost too low to be heard.

Susan wiped her eyes, threw away the used tissues, took more from her mom and blew her nose again as she nodded. "There hasn't been anyone out here at all."

Riley turned her attention back to the teenager. "No sudden noises? What about the horses? Have they been quiet?"

Susan fell silent again, thinking. "They were mostly quiet, but I remember them getting riled up, especially the horses in the back, a while ago."

"In the back. Do you mean the horses near the back arena?" Riley asked.

Susan nodded. "I remember thinking it must've been because Norseman was running loose around the place. Before he ran into the indoor arena." Susan rubbed her face again and managed a weak smile at her mom.

I frowned. Why didn't Riley just ask Susan if she'd heard a gunshot? I thought she was beating around the bush an awful lot when she could just ask straight out whether Susan had heard the gunshot that killed Randy.

Then it hit me. Susan didn't *know* about the gunshot. Which meant she hadn't heard a gunshot.

Which meant the killer had used a suppressor, just like the murder Twister and I witnessed. My suspicions about the stranger Susan saw crossing the indoor arena increased. I felt the blood drain from my face.

Riley turned her brown eyes to me. "M.J., you've gone all pale. Are you okay?"

I nodded, not trusting my voice enough to answer.

"You don't look okay to me." She frowned. "Is there something about what's happened that maybe you should tell me about?" She raised her eyes towards Jeremiah.

I needed to tell Riley what had happened, but I didn't want to tell her with other people present, especially in front of Jeremiah.

"After…after you finish with Susan, maybe I can talk to you…and Aiden…alone?" I felt like a criminal. Randy's death was my fault. Amy had just lost her father, and it was *my* fault.

Riley wrapped things up, and Susan left with her mom. She stood silent for a long time and studied her notes, flipping pages, jotting additions. Finally, she turned to me. "I'm guessing that seeing your soon-to-be ex-husband triggered your memory?"

I nodded.

"Well, at least now I can call you Mattie. I had to use M.J. because I kept mixing up the two names. Stephen should've used a name like Karen or something. At least a name that didn't start with the same frickin' letter." She tilted her head to the radio clipped to the shoulder of her uniform. "Hey, Bro. You still out back?"

A low voice mumbled an unintelligible response.

"Can you break away and meet me in the office? Now? I need assistance." Riley's voice was all business, a tone I'd never heard her use with Aiden. Not thirty seconds later Aiden rounded the corner and stopped short, then looked Jeremiah up and down.

"Jeremiah Black Bear Tyler?" he asked.

Jeremiah nodded. A long, pregnant pause followed.

"I believe there's a restraining order against you." Aiden declared calmly. "If I remember correctly, Stephen Campbell filed one against you, and was present when you were served. Which begs the question why you are here?"

Jeremiah straightened, slowly withdrew his hands from his pockets and dropped them to his sides. "I wanted to talk to my wife."

"You mean your soon-to-be ex-wife," Riley clarified. Her voice matched Aiden's. I noticed Aiden and Jeremiah stood roughly the same height, although Aiden was thicker through the chest and more muscular in his arms and legs. Riley stood significantly shorter than the two men, her aura definitely the more dangerous at the moment.

Riley continued. "I advise you to leave these premises now and avoid any further contact with Mattie Lamont Tyler."

Jeremiah's eyes cut to mine, then back to the two cops. Without a word he nodded, reached over to retrieve his jacket from the chair Susan had used, then walked out of the office. A few minutes later the three of us heard a car engine turn over and tires crunch on the gravel parking area.

Riley turned to me. "We need to talk. You know something about what's happened to Randy, and I want to know when that dirt bag showed up and what he had to say."

"You'd better believe we need to talk," I shot back. "I want to know why the two of you have been lying to me for the past two years."

Aiden looked at his sister. "I'll call Stephen, let him know Tyler's in town, find out whether Tyler talked to him before coming out here. Although I can't imagine he would've told Tyler her location."

"Is VSP taking the lead on the case?" Riley asked.

Aiden nodded. "We're done here, at least for now. If Mattie

has anything to add, she needs to talk to Rivers."

I inhaled deeply, then blurted, "I know why Randy was killed."

Aiden bent over and placed his hands gently on my shoulders, our eyes scant inches apart. "You do?"

I plunged on. "I witnessed a murder on the Blue Ridge Parkway, and a man shot and killed another man named Freddie, and then he shot at Twister and me, and Twister spooked, and that's why he ran all the way back to the stables." I sucked in a lungful of air and tried to quit panting.

There followed a minute of stunned silence.

"I told Randy, and he told me to call the police. I should have listened to him and called it in then and there." I started shaking, my left knee buckled. Aiden gripped my shoulders and guided me to an empty chair.

Riley stared at me. "Kinsey phoned earlier to fill me in about you and Twister. It was foggy down here. It would have been worse up on the Parkway. Anything could have spooked Twister."

Aiden squatted in front of me. "Maybe it was the Hunchback?"

I looked at him, then at Riley standing behind him. They studied me like a bug under a microscope.

"I know I was in bad shape when I got back with Twister, but I know what I heard. It wasn't the tree stump. And I saw the flame of a gunshot," I insisted, staring at each of them in turn.

"You *saw* a gunshot?" Riley asked from behind her brother.

I nodded my head. "I saw the gun flash and heard a muffled shot."

"Suppressed," Aiden muttered.

"Like the one that killed Wittmore," Riley slid in.

"It would be foggier up there than down here, M.J. ..." Aiden started to say, but I cut him off.

"It's Mattie now. Call me Mattie, damn it. And yes, it was foggy, but I know what I saw. And heard."

But the expression on their faces revealed their doubt.

"Randy believed me when I told him," I went on. "In fact, I had to argue with him about *not* calling the police. Why are the two of you looking at me like I've lost my mind?"

Riley and Aiden exchanged guilty looks. "Chalk it up to our experience with the general public," Riley apologized. "You must admit you wouldn't make a good witness. You've been suffering from traumatic amnesia for almost two years."

"Add to that the shock of seeing your ex-husband and regaining your memory, and then the trauma around Twister," Aiden added.

"Well, unlike everyone I seem to be friends with," I gave the two siblings a scathing look. "I'm in the habit of telling the frickin' truth."

Chapter Seven

Aiden and Riley stood in front of me like a couple of statues. Based on their reaction so far, I decided to omit the conversation I'd overheard and focus on the gunshots and the probable body lying dead somewhere at the top of the ridge. I clasped my hands together and swallowed.

"Someone shot a man when Twister and I were on the trail that goes up to the road at the top of the ridge." I tried to keep my voice steady.

"What did they look like?" Riley had her notepad and pencil out again. Aiden's brown eyes scanned my face.

"I...I couldn't see them because of the fog. So they couldn't see me, either," I explained.

"But he shot at you?" Aiden asked.

I nodded. "And Twister spooked and took off."

"Why would someone be shooting at you?" Riley's tone was all business, seeking information rather than consoling a friend.

I pulled my wayward thoughts together. I needed to tell them with as much accuracy as possible what happened up on the Parkway. The trouble was all I could think of was Randy lying dead in the back arena.

"Well," I squeezed my eyes shut and tried to think.

"And you're sure it was a gun shot?" Aiden interrupted, squatting in front of me again. "C'mon, Mattie. You've been through an awful lot in the last couple of hours."

"Yes, I'm sure," I snapped, then inhaled and tried to calm down. "And the creep killed somebody up there. A man, I think. I saw the gun flash twice, and I heard a muffled sound each time that sort of sounded like a shot."

Uncomfortable silence followed.

"A muffled sound that *sort of* sounded like a shot," Riley repeated back to me.

I shook my head. "No, I'm *sure* it was. I heard voices and they were arguing. And then a muffled sound and I saw the flash of a gun."

"If you couldn't see them...." Aiden trailed off, his implication

73

plain. I felt like they were teaming up against me. I tried not to feel intimidated.

"The voices I heard were both male," I insisted. "And then I saw a red flash and a muffled sound, and I heard one of them gasp like he had been shot. And then another flash and the same muffled sound."

"Then what happened?" Riley interjected.

"He heard Twister startle when he fired the first shot. He fired a couple in our direction. Twister spooked and I got him turned around and that's when he galloped all the way back to the stables."

"The killer used a suppressor to shoot Randy." Aiden's comment fell like a lead weight between the three of us.

"Yeah, and I don't believe in coincidences," Riley nodded. "If Mattie is remembering correctly, we may have a connection between the two shootings."

"Are you thinking the killer used a suppressor here because Susan didn't hear a gunshot?" I asked.

"Yes," Riley answered. "The sound of the suppressor startled the horses but would not have been loud enough for Susan to hear. Which is why she thinks Randy died from a fall." She turned to her brother. "We need to tell VSP there may be another shooting in the vicinity. They can take molds of all tire tracks around here and any shoeprints they find. It's not much, but we might get lucky."

Aiden patted my knee. "We'll keep you safe." He straightened and strode from the office.

Riley sat on one of the empty chairs. "Tell me everything that happened, starting from the time you arrived here at the stables."

I took her through the morning events, when Jeremiah showed up at the arena, the resulting jolt of returning memory, our ensuing argument.

"When I took off along the trail, I was upset. I was moving Twister pretty fast because I didn't want Jeremiah to follow us. Between that and the fog, I can't tell you exactly where I heard the two men," I admitted. "But it was after we gained the top of the hill and before the trail intersects the highway. I remember because I was worried about accidentally getting on it in the fog and getting hit by a car."

"Did you hear any vehicle noise?" Riley asked.

I shook my head.

She shut her notebook, slipped it into the front right breast pocket of her uniform, and studied me in silence. "You know, the best thing to do would be to ride up the trail and see if there's a body."

I nodded vigorously. "My thoughts exactly."

"Stay here while I go talk to Kinsey and VSP." Riley strode from the office. I sat in the chair and tried to mentally recreate my ride up the ridge to the Parkway. I understood her haste. The weather would deteriorate soon, rain would wash away any evidence. Local wildlife presented another problem. And while maps of the trails might help locate the general vicinity of the incident, chances would be greater of finding something if we went via the trail.

I knew we would find a body, and the thought sent a jolt of fear through me. But Randy was dead because of what I'd overheard, and I would do anything and everything in my power to bring the killer to justice.

As I waited for Riley, I thought about the time lapse, the distance the killer would have covered on foot down the trail to the stables. Susan's words came to mind and I frowned.

The stranger she had seen walking through the indoor arena, if indeed he was the killer, would have entered the building from the parking area in front of the stables.

Had the killer wanted to check the indoor arena for riders? Had he seen Susan and for whatever reason did not approach her?

No doubt Norseman had become sweaty in the back arena with Randy. And he had been saddled. And since the trail stretched alongside the arena and the killer would have been following the trail, he would have easily found Randy and Norseman.

So why walk all the way to the indoor arena? He would have assumed Randy and Norseman had been on the trail, and were the horse and rider he had shot at.

He killed Randy. Norseman had somehow escaped the outdoor arena and galloped to the indoor enclosure.

I frowned. The timing didn't make sense. According to Susan, the stranger had walked through the indoor arena before Norseman came galloping in. But the killer would have been on the trail behind the stables and that was nowhere near the indoor arena.

The stranger Susan saw crossing the arena didn't seem to fit into a scenario that made him the killer.

So, who the hell was he and why had he been wearing a long black raincoat?

Aiden and Riley strode through the office door and I jerked my head up, swiping away tears on my face.

"She'll ride with me, minion. You fall off the Walmart kiddie horse," Aiden snorted.

"You're making that crap up and you know it. I ride as well as you do," Riley shot back.

Aiden turned to me. He hesitated a fraction when he saw my distress. "You and I are on Tiny. Minion here will be riding one of the lesson horses. Trooper Rivers will meet us on the Parkway in his cruiser. I think Kinsey might be going with us, too."

I inhaled a deep, fortifying breath and stood.

"Are you up for this?" he asked, acknowledging my emotional state.

I nodded. I didn't trust my voice enough to speak.

His brown eyes narrowed. "You look like you'd rather be any-where but here right now."

"She's tougher than she looks," Riley declared. "I still think she should ride with me. You'll take off like a bat out of hell and bump her off and never notice."

"Will not." Aiden jerked his head at me. "Come on. It's going to rain soon, and I don't like getting the horses wet."

"HA," Riley barked, following us through the office door. "It's you that you don't like getting wet. Admit it."

Aiden adjusted his stride to match mine as we walked along the outside pens. A saddling area opened between the back of the indoor arena and one of the tack rooms. Three horses stood patient-ly as Kinsey worked on getting them tacked up.

"Tiny" was a gentle black draft horse, a middle-aged gelding that stood well over eighteen hands, weighed literally close to a ton, and presented an impressive girth and an even more impressive head size. Kinsey had a custom saddle and bridle, and even Aiden needed the mounting block to get on. I climbed the two steps, and Kinsey helped me remove my prosthesis. Then I grabbed Aiden's out-stretched hand and with Kinsey's help swung up behind him. I wrig-gled until I got centered behind the saddle. Sitting on the huge draft horse was like straddling the top of a minivan. With two legs, I would have felt like I was riding in an armchair. Without the equal weight and without something to hang on to, I would slide right off when Tiny starting walking.

"Wrap your arms around me," Aiden said, pulling my arms around his chest.

"I can hold onto the back of the saddle," I objected, but lost the argument when he shook his head.

"I'll handcuff you around me rather than risk you falling off. I'll never hear the end of it from the minion. We're going to be moving fast to try to beat the weather," he admitted, confirming Riley's earlier accusation.

"Fine," I wrapped my arms around him. "And I don't need frickin' handcuffs."

Riley swung onto a sorrel quarter horse I didn't know, and Kinsey climbed onto a brown mare named Hershey. The three of us headed for the trail behind the back arena. Tiny's trot proved a lot smoother than I anticipated, although it was still bouncy enough to make me wish I were on Twister.

"About how far did you go when you rode out?" Aiden asked as we moved into the trees. The fog swirled and eddied around us, hiding everything in a thick gray blanket. Rain was on the way. We'd be lucky not to end up soaking wet before we were done.

"It was past the top of the ridge, but before the trail meets the pavement," I answered, Tiny's gait making my voice bounce.

"We've got a ways to go." Aiden glanced upwards despite the fact he couldn't see a thing, then pressed Tiny into a faster trot.

The steep incline led us upward. Riley and Aiden both rode well and handled horses as though they'd been born on one. They were familiar with the trails and had shown me the easier routes as my own riding improved.

Tiny's long, bouncy trot ate up the distance. Riley rode behind us, Kinsey drew up the rear.

"Hey! Dork Brain! Slow down before you lose your passenger!" Riley called out, breaking the utter stillness.

"You mean before you fall off!" Aiden threw over his shoulder, then pushed Tiny into a slow, ground-pounding canter.

"You're doing this just to piss her off," I yelled in his ear.

Aiden twisted his head and grinned at me. "You bet I am."

He slowed as we neared the steepest section, pulled Tiny into a walk to negotiate the incline. Conversation was minimal except for an occasional question from Aiden. I figured Riley was going to give him an earful when we reached our destination.

Aiden slowed Tiny and leaned over to study the ground. "Not much to see with all the ground cover," he muttered. He walked Tiny, his concentration on the trail.

"Aiden, pull up. Let me in front since I'm closer to the ground than you are," Riley called from behind us.

"Yeah, but my eyes are better than yours. You're blind as a bat." Despite his retort, Aiden guided Tiny to one side to give Riley room to pass. Trees crowded close. Fog crowded closer. I began feeling nervous we might run into the man with the gun.

"Relax," Aiden murmured, patting my hands. "I can't breathe."

I loosened my death grip around his chest and tried not to think about the sound of gunshots.

"Over here, Bro. Looks like this is where Twister spun around." Riley dismounted and squatted down to the ground. Aiden moved Tiny to the part of the trail Riley studied. "Kinsey? What do you think?"

Kinsey dismounted and led her horse around Tiny until she reached Riley.

"Yep," she confirmed crouching for a closer look. "Even with the leaf cover, you can see where his shoes dug gashes into the turf."

Aiden twisted in his saddle to look at me. "Where from here did you see the gunshots?"

I leaned around him and pointed directly in front of us. "Straight ahead. It seemed like they were on the same trail."

"Are you okay up here if I get off and help Riley?" he asked.

I nodded, and he swung his right leg over Tiny's neck and dropped to the ground. I noticed he had his gun in his hand.

"Precaution," he reassured me when he noticed the direction of my stare. I wriggled into the saddle and grabbed the horn when Aiden guided Tiny along the trail towards the place where I'd seen the gun flash. Riley and Kinsey studied the trail and the surrounding tree trunks.

"What I wouldn't give to find a nice bullet slash in one of these," Riley called out, the thick fog reducing her to a dark shadow. "This is like hunting for needle in a haystack. Mattie, you sure we're in the right place?"

"Of course, she's not sure. It's foggy. She was on horseback and upset. But we've found where Twister spun around. Quit asking stupid questions," Aiden called over his shoulder as he led Tiny along the trail.

I glanced back but couldn't make out what they were doing, so I turned my attention to the fog in front of me and thought about asking Aiden to leave Tiny with the others so I wouldn't have to look at a dead body.

We walked slowly along the trail, me on Tiny, Aiden in front of us.

"About how far would you say the muzzle flash was when you saw it?" Aiden asked.

I closed my eyes and tried to think back. "I'm really not sure." I opened my eyes. "But it had to be close. What is the visibility do you think? And then add some more distance because I couldn't make out any shadows. Just voices."

"Good." He fell silent, Tiny's reins gripped in his left hand, his weapon in his right. We continued along the trail until I could neither see nor hear Riley and Kinsey or their horses.

"I think we've gone too far," I suggested after a bit.

"I agree," Aiden said, holstering his weapon and turning to me. "I don't see anything that looks like a body."

"Maybe tire tracks from their car?" I ventured.

Aiden lifted his face and grinned at me. "Ever consider going into the detective business?"

Blue State Patrol lights flashed eerily through the fog to our right. Aiden shook his head and steadied Tiny when he shifted sideways.

"There's no way Rivers is going to see us in this. Can you manage Tiny long enough for me to go flag him down?"

"Yeah," I said, even though there would be no way in hell I could control a horse this big with one leg.

Aiden's brown eyes narrowed. "You sure? I'll never hear the end of it from Whiz Kid back there if you fall off."

I waved at him to give me the reins, and he slipped them over Tiny's huge head. I grabbed a handful of incredibly thick mane and used my other hand to hold the reins and wrap a couple of fingers around the horn, just in case. Aiden disappeared into the fog. The police cruiser's light bar blinked out and a few minutes later a Virginia State Patrol officer appeared with Aiden.

"We've found evidence of Mattie's horse, but no body and, so far, nothing else," Aiden informed him when they reached us. He rested a hand along one of Tiny's reins, turned him around, and we walked back to where Riley and Kinsey continued to inspect the area. I wondered why we hadn't come across a body and began to doubt whether we were in the right location.

"I haven't found anything except Twister's tracks," Riley told us when we reached them.

"Okay," Trooper Rivers nodded. "I'll get help out here and rope off the area. If you can stay, I can use the extra manpower."

"I'll take Mary Joe back to the stables," Kinsey said, walking over to stand with the officers.

"That's probably best," Riley agreed. "We're going to be here for a while, and it feels like it's going to start pouring any minute."

Kinsey moved beside Tiny, and Aiden lifted her enough for her to slip her boot into the left stirrup. She wriggled her right leg over slowly, taking care not to dislodge me, and then gathered the reins. I wrapped my hands around her waist, and we headed for the stables.

"Since there's not much to do except look at white fog, why don't you tell me who that man was who showed up this morning looking for you?" Kinsey asked once we were out of earshot of the others.

I swallowed. "That was Jeremiah. My husband. Soon to be ex-husband," I amended, mostly to myself. "When I saw him, I started remembering who I was."

"You mean you didn't know who you were?" Kinsey asked, her thick blonde ponytail brushing against my face.

"Yeah. There's a lot I'm not sure about. But I remember the basics. Like who I am, who my family was."

"Mary Joe isn't your real name?"

"No, it's Mattie. Mattie Tyler." I paused. "Actually, soon it will be Mattie Lamont."

"Did seeing him trigger it?"

"Yeah." I loosened my grip on her long enough to wipe blonde hair out of my mouth. Lord, the woman had a lot of hair.

"Wow," Kinsey whistled softly.

"You can still call me Mary Joe if that makes things easier for you."

Kinsey laughed. "Thanks. You know me and names. I remember horses' names, no problem. Can't ever remember owners' names until I've asked them a hundred times."

The dense fog turned to thick mist when we reached the ridge, and Tiny's huge hooves sank deep into the damp earth as Kinsey guided him carefully down the steep incline.

"Twister took this at a full gallop," I told her as we worked our way down the hill.

Kinsey twisted in the saddle to stare at me, her blue eyes incredibly clear. "And you didn't fall off? That's impressive." She turned back around. "Your riding skills have come a long way."

The mist turned into a gentle rain, soaking us and our horse by the time we reached the back arena. Figures in rain slicks and hats milled about the area, and I spotted yellow police tape fluttering as we rode by. Kinsey guided Tiny along the alley between the tack rooms, through the rear double doors of the indoor arena, and over to the mounting block. I gripped her forearm and slid off. She dismounted and focused on unsaddling Tiny, then retrieved my prosthesis from the outside mounting block. I worked it into my wet empty jeans leg until I felt the socket grip my stump.

"Go into the office and get something hot," Kinsey instructed as she led Tiny through the rear doors.

Getting something hot into me sounded like a great idea, so I followed her advice and soon had a cup of steaming hot chocolate in front of me. My clothes were once again cold and wet, and I thought about the large fireplace at my house. Officers and other official-looking personnel moseyed in to get out of the rain. I asked whether Randy's body had been taken away yet, and one of them shook his head, saying the county coroner was stuck in Interstate traffic, which meant no one was going anywhere for a long while. Kinsey appeared after a bit, got herself some coffee, and sat down beside me.

"First, I want to let you know Twister is stable," she explained, blowing on her coffee, then taking a careful sip. Her long blonde ponytail hung down her back in a solid wet mass. She set her coffee down and removed the tie from her hair, then hung her hair over one shoulder and began braiding. "Jen's running some tests and took x-rays, which came back negative. She suggested I could bring him home, but I thought it best to leave him there for the night, especially since it's raining."

"Is there any danger of something going wrong?" I asked, picking up on her unspoken hesitation.

"He was really dehydrated, really exhausted," she admitted. "His heart rate was still elevated, and he hadn't started eating yet." She turned to stare through the office window at the indoor arena. "Given the circumstances, it's best I don't have to worry about keeping an eye on him. I still can't believe what happened to Randy." She shook her head, brushed her braided ponytail back, and picked up her coffee. She squinted at me through the steam rising from her cup. "How are you holding up? The two of you were pretty close."

I swallowed a boulder, couldn't keep the tremble from my voice. "He…showed me a ring box this morning. Amy wanted him to kneel and propose right there, but I told him to wait until this evening, and the three of us…." I set my cup down as reality hit. "What is this going to do to Amy?"

Kinsey gripped my arm with strong fingers. "She has her aunt Jilly. Don't worry about her just now, even though I know the two of you have grown close. I'm more worried about what this is going to do to you."

I buried my face in my hands, tried to control the sudden sobbing. "I can't believe it's true. This is a nightmare. And it's all because of what I saw up there on the trail this morning." I paused, thinking about what Susan had told Riley. I looked around and noticed that, for the moment anyway, we were the only ones in the office. "I keep wondering if that stranger Susan saw was the killer. And if he's still around."

"What did he look like?" Kinsey asked. I repeated the description Susan told Riley, and she shook her head. "He doesn't sound like anyone I know," she admitted slowly. "No one around here has a coat like that."

Rain drummed steadily against the tin roof of the building, mimicking the tears that streamed down my face. Early twilight darkened the office. Kinsey stood and flipped the wall switch, throwing bright fluorescent lights on. Riley and Aiden appeared from outside.

"Wow. I didn't think you two would make it back this soon," I told them.

"We needed to get the horses home. We'll be heading back to the Parkway scene. Besides, the Coroner's here. Hopefully the rest of these guys will be out of your hair soon," Riley said, pouring the last of the coffee into a clean paper cup. Kinsey crossed to the cabinets that lined the wall behind us, then went through the motions of making a fresh pot. With a tired sigh Aiden collapsed in Kinsey's empty chair.

"Do you know if anyone else was present besides the killer and the man he shot?" he asked. Kinsey got the coffee machine gurgling and brought Aiden a steaming cup, then pulled over another empty chair and rejoined us.

Riley scowled at her brother. "Save the questions 'til later. We need to get back outside in case Sandy needs help with the body." She threw her empty cup away. "And Rivers is still on the Parkway."

"Sandy's got things under control. So does Rivers. Quit fidgeting and sit down, Sis." Aiden settled into his chair and sipped his coffee.

"You're just avoiding getting wet," she chided.

"I'm following up on an active investigation," he countered.

"Dork Brain," Riley muttered before disappearing through the office door.

"Back to my question." Aiden watched me.

I pondered for a while. "I didn't hear anyone else," I finally answered.

Aiden and Kinsey stared at me. "That doesn't mean there wasn't someone else with him," he ventured after a while.

"Why are you asking?" I wanted to know.

"Trying to get a handle on the man the teenager saw walk through the indoor arena." He finished his coffee and threw away the cup.

"You think he might have been an accomplice?" Kinsey asked him.

Aiden shrugged. "There are two sets of shoeprints in the dirt around the gate and inside the back arena."

"Jeremiah's will be one of them." I told him about the conversation with my husband.

Aiden shook his head. "I'm pretty sure we know which ones are his. These are around the body. But I'm not sure about the timeline. It's not matching up to the events."

I heaved another sigh. "How did he know to come to the stables?"

Aiden sighed. "He would have followed the trail."

Chapter Eight

I stayed at the stables, hoping Riley and Aiden would finish up in time for one of them to ride home with me. As cowardly as it sounded, I did not want to be alone. But neither of them appeared, and the rain continued through the evening hours. I drank the last of the hot chocolate packets, and then drank more (doctored) coffee than I normally drink in a week and drummed up the courage to drive home, watching the rearview mirror for someone following me. Yes, I was paranoid, both from Randy's death and Jeremiah's unexpected appearance. And now that my memory was intact, blurred images of unfriendly faces crowded my thoughts. Traffic was thin along the Interstate. The wipers thumped with calming rhythm as rain drummed the top of the Explorer. I pulled into the garage, limped through the kitchen into the great room, and started a fire in the massive stone fireplace. I used dry wood the siblings stacked along one wall of the garage, then limped through the rain and retrieved some wet wood, which I left in the garage to dry out. Then I limped to my master bedroom. As I pulled off my sweatshirt, something fell from one of the pockets and bounced onto the floor. I looked down, froze, then felt myself sway.

The blue velvet ring box.

In slow motion, I bent down and picked up the box. Thoughts whirled through my head in a crazy clash of silent cacophony.

How in the world had the ring box ended up in one of my pockets?

I tried to think back, to remember who had the ring box, but my thoughts seized, and I couldn't remember the sequence of the day's events. I hugged the box close to my heart, then carefully placed it on the top of my dresser. Limping into the bathroom, I stared at the shower stall, shivered, wondered how many showers a person could take in one day.

To hell with it, I decided, reaching for the control knob. So what if I ended up looking like a prune? Maybe the water would wash away the awful feeling consuming me. I sat on the bench and ran the water as hot as I could stand it, but when I finally got out, I was still shivering. I dressed in a pair of heavy gray sweats, then stared at the wheelchair beside the bed and the crutches propped in the corner. My stump hurt, and I felt like I'd aged a hundred years in the last sixteen hours. I slumped into the metal chair but didn't move. Instead, my eyes rested on the blue velvet ring box on my dresser.

I sat there for a long, long time.

Gentle crackling and hissing gradually penetrated my mind, and I remembered starting the fire. Slowly wheeling into the great room, I stood on my leg and squinted through the semi-darkness at the kitchen clock, but of course couldn't see a damned thing.

It had to be closing in on midnight. I wheeled across the room to the kitchen, turned the lights to low, thought about making some food for Riley and Aiden. My eyes fell to a folded piece of paper and envelope on the countertop.

Jeremiah's hand-writing.

My first impulse was to toss both into the fire. But that meant sitting down in the wheelchair and rolling said chair across the huge room to the fireplace. I opened it instead.

I left steaks in the fridge. Extend my thanks to the owner of the ones we ate earlier. It was good to see you. Hope you use the tickets.

Jeremiah.

I stared at the second envelope. Inside was a computer receipt for a chartered jet flight to Oklahoma City with a number to call for reservations.

I tapped the envelope on the counter and felt anger eat at my insides. The note and the envelope told me Jeremiah had gained entrance into my home while no one was here. I sat down in the wheelchair and thought about that for a while.

Had the garage doors been closed when I got home this evening?

I had not bothered to check the entry doors when Jeremiah and I left this afternoon. The siblings, especially Aiden, got on my case all the time about not locking up. But we were in the middle of the mountains in the middle of nowhere, and I tended to forget about flipping deadbolts. I tried at least to remember to lock the doorknob to the connecting door into the kitchen, but half the time I came home to find I'd forgotten to do even that. To make things worse, a toddler could pick any of the current door locks. Riley and Aiden had been on my case about that, too. In fact, Riley recently bought enough heavy-duty locks to refit all the exterior doors. She and Aiden had been too busy to install them.

I leaned against the back of the chair and tapped the note and envelope I held against the padded arm. Though Jeremiah was not in the house now, he could be in the vicinity. And by gaining entrance into my house, he obviously was choosing to ignore the restraining order.

I rolled around the counter, retrieved the handset, and dialed Stephen Campbell's number. Yes, it was close to midnight, which meant it was nearing eleven in Oklahoma. No, I didn't care that it was too late for polite calling etiquette.

"Hello?" Stephen's voice answered on the fourth ring. He sounded awake at any rate.

"Stephen, it's Mattie." I was too tired and too frazzled to think of a way to start a call made too late to be polite. I opted to go straight to the point. "Jeremiah showed up today."

A lifetime of silence filled the other end. "He found you." Anger gave his voice an edge.

I put the phone on speaker. "Yes." Dropping the handset in my lap, I wheeled slowly to the fire and stared at flames curling around hissing logs. Sparks popped, sending a shower against the screen and crackling into the chimney. "Seeing him brought my memory back. Did he come to see you?"

Stephen sighed through the line. "Yes," he admitted. "I told him to leave you alone. I reminded him none too gently about the restraining order I filed shortly after I relocated you to Virginia." He fell silent. "But he found you anyway."

His words helped me feel better. "Riley and Aiden both said you would not have given him any information." I placed the handset on the arm of the chair, stood on my leg, and took a poker from the stand on the hearth. Bracing my free hand on the mantle, I pulled open the screen, prodded the logs, sent more sparks up the chimney. New flames burst forth, gobbling up the logs in cheery crackling chorus.

"I was afraid he would find you," he said after a long silence.

I replaced the screen and the poker and sat down, picked up the handset. "I understand now why you handled things the way you did. And why Riley and Aiden have been with me since I moved out here."

"Are they there now?" he asked.

"No." I mulled over whether to tell him they were not home because they were occupied with Randy's death, and that said death directly involved me.

Not a good idea to share that information, I decided, not after telling my benefactor about Jeremiah's violation of his restraining order.

I thought again about the ring box sitting on my dresser. Emotions were too raw, too overwrought to bring up Randy.

"Did they intercept him?" His question jolted me out of my thoughts.

"Him?" I echoed, scrambling to remember our conversation. My brain really was fried.

"Jeremiah," Stephen prompted.

Anger ballooned in my chest. "Yes," I admitted. "Today, at the stables. He left without any trouble when Riley reminded him of the restraining order."

"I'll contact Riley and Aiden. I want one of them at your side twenty-four-seven until I clarify with Mr. Tyler that he is to leave you alone." Yep, he was angry.

"Riley should be home soon, and I'll relay your message. They've had a busy shift." I paused. I should at least tell him about the incident from this morning.

"Is…there something else on your mind, my dear?" Stephen prompted through the line.

I released a long, tired sigh. "I'm not sure right now what is real memory and what is not," I hedged.

"Can you be more specific?" he pressed. I told him about the scene I heard on the Parkway, the lack of evidence, Aiden and Riley's doubt.

"I'd like to think I know what I heard, but with everything coming back all at once, I'm not sure whether I may have mixed up memories from the past with events that happened today. I expected us to find a body when we took horses and I showed them the location. When we didn't find anything, I have to admit it made me wonder whether I might have had some type of flashback after my argument with Jeremiah."

"That is more than possible," he consoled.

I continued slowly. "Aiden and Riley were…doubtful," I confessed, "even though they were trying to hide their opinions."

"How much do you remember?" he inquired gently.

"There are a lot of gaps, Stephen," I admitted. "Gaps I'm not sure I want to fill in."

"Why don't you fly out and visit?" he suggested. "This conversation will be much easier if we're face to face. I'll transfer funds into your local account."

I agreed. We said goodbye and I cut the call, then dropped the handset into my lap. Exhaustion rolled over me in humongous, heavy waves, yet I knew if I tried to sleep my eyes would never stay closed. I thought about fixing something for the siblings to eat when they got home. Feeling guilty, I retrieved two more large logs from the wood bin beside the hearth and added them to the fire, then wheeled to the large brown leather couch. I pulled a thick quilted comforter from the back and curled up.

Sitting in the semi-darkness, I stared at the flames throwing undulating shadows across the room, listened to rain drumming gently on the roof. I couldn't get Randy out of my mind, nor could I dampen the vivid image those gun flashes had imprinted on my brain.

Had they been real? Or had I imagined the entire event?

But if I had imagined the whole scene, why had someone killed Randy in the back arena?

And Amy. I choked back sobs. She had lost her father, was now an orphan.

And I had lost the man I would have spent my life with, someone who would have helped make me whole, someone to build a family and a future with.

Emotion flooded through me as memories of my past swept through my mind. I saw Angela in the hospital, my parents' house reduced to a pile of rubble. I recalled Jeremiah's picture on the Oklahoma television news station, the funeral for my parents, the funeral for my sister.

And now I would have to attend another funeral. Randy's. How long would the investigation last? Would Randy's lawyer sister be able to bend rules and get his body released?

I couldn't handle the pain of those thoughts, so I forced my mind back to my regained memory. I could not remember the faces of the men who had kidnapped me. I had only a vague idea of

Angela's husband, even though I did remember his name. I thought there was something about the mountains around Wolf Creek Pass, or maybe it had been Monarch Pass. Somewhere in the southwest part of the Colorado Rockies something had happened that was now fuzzy and unclear.

Jeremiah and his lies. There existed all kinds of movies about husbands who hid behind secret identities, who were operatives, spies, government agents. There were spoofs about the spooks, comedies about the miscommunication between husband and wife, love scenes hot enough to melt the plasma off television screens.

What none of them addressed was the pain and disillusionment of finding out someone whom I'd trusted with my life and my heart had lied to me the entire time we'd been together. Our marriage had been a sham, though I found it interesting how Jeremiah slid in the fact while his orders were to stay married for two years, we had remained together for over seven. But his admission blew serious holes in my confidence and left me pissed as hell. And I was not willing to tolerate that kind of treatment even if it was supposed to be in the name of God and Country.

I forced my thoughts away from Jeremiah and tried to recall the conversation I overheard this morning before the man with the lilt shot his accomplice. Imagined or not, I needed to report anything I remembered to Riley and Aiden. There was a spiral notebook and pen on the table beside the couch. I picked both up, flipped to a blank page at the back of the book and in the dim, flickering light thrown by the fire started jotting down thoughts.

Richmond.

Hot as a jacket potato.

I closed my eyes and allowed the scene to scroll through my head.

I appreciate your efforts, Freddie.

Freddie. I felt my heart jolt. I wrote down the name, then closed my eyes and thought some more.

Sixty-four and ninety-five.

References to Interstates, maybe? I needed a map. Grumbling at my sudden curiosity, I heaved myself from the couch and into my chair, wheeled to the office and retrieved a Rand McNally United States atlas. When I was back under the blanket on the couch, I flipped to Virginia and squinted in the dim light.

Interstates sixty-four and ninety-five ran along the eastern side of the state, and both were close to Richmond. That seemed to substantiate that what I witnessed was real rather than imagined. I closed my eyes again and let my thoughts drift back to the foggy scene. The details seemed to be real, and I could not convince myself I would have imagined a flashback with so much clarity.

Double eagles.

I had no clue what that meant and could only remember the conversation being about a small kind of coin. I wrote down the term and decided I was not moving from the couch again. Googling would have to wait.

The familiar sound of the Jeep rolling into the garage perked up my ears, and I shut the notebook and set it, the pen, and the atlas on the table, then tried squinting through the darkness at the clock on the kitchen wall. I couldn't see what time it was, but I was snuggled too deep beneath the comforter to get up, pull myself into my chair, and wheel all the way across the room to find out.

"Remind me in the morning to smack you upside the head," came Riley's voice as the kitchen door banged open. "It's too late, or rather too damned early, to deal with your stupidity now." She turned up the kitchen lights. "And be quiet, or you'll wake up Mattie."

"I'm not the one making all the damned noise." Aiden sounded exhausted.

"I'm over here," I spoke from the couch. "I have a fire going, but that's all I've done since I got back."

Riley glided across the hardwood floor in her sock feet. She sure seemed to have a lot of energy for it being so early.

"What are you still doing up?" she asked as she slid to a halt in front of the hearth and turned her back to the flames.

I shrugged. "Sleep ain't happening tonight. Not after what happened today."

"Hey, someone left some really nice steaks in the fridge," Aiden said, his voice muffled no doubt because his head was stuck in the appliance. "Who's hungry?"

"Are you serious?" I asked. "What time is it?"

Riley glanced at her wristwatch. "A little after two a.m."

"You can't be hungry at this hour," I objected, then felt my stomach rumble and thought all three of us crazy.

"Hey, it's dinnertime somewhere in the world," Aiden argued, making enough racket to wake the dead as he pulled out pans and cooking utensils. "Riley, get your butt over here and get started on some pasta."

"Needing something to take your mind off the fact you almost wiped out on the way home?" Riley executed good cross-country ski form as she glided over the oak flooring and took the large cooking pot Aiden handed her.

"Did not."

Riley twisted so she could face me as she filled the pot with water from the kitchen faucet. "I heard the most creative language come from him. Never would've believed he could actually pronounce some of them."

"What happened?" I asked, leaving the warmth of the comforter, maneuvering myself into my chair, and wheeling over.

"Nothing," Aiden tried to derail Riley when she opened her mouth. She ignored him.

"He was going too fast along the Interstate and hydroplaned. I tried to tell him to slow down, but n-o-o-o. We almost ended up wrapped around one of the exit signs."

I stood and climbed onto the nearest barstool, then leaned my elbows on the counter and decided it best not to reprimand either of them. No doubt they had been in the middle of one of their arguments, which meant Riley was at least partly at fault for their near miss. "What can I do to help?" I asked instead.

"Sit there and make sure dimwit here doesn't fry my steak to a charred piece of leather," Riley said as she set the pot on the stove and turned on the burner. "I'm going upstairs to shower and change."

"I thought you liked your meat burnt to a crisp," Aiden shot at her.

"That's your problem," Riley retorted. "Thinking."

I rolled my eyes. "You know, the two of you sound like an old married couple."

The water boiled before Riley made it back downstairs, so I used the counter for support and hopped over to help. I dumped two boxes of Mac'n'Cheese into the pot. Aiden seasoned the steaks, then heated up the oven broiler. The place soon smelled wonderful.

"What's this?" Riley asked, smelling of soap and shampoo as she reappeared from upstairs. She picked up Jeremiah's note and the envelope as the three of us sat down. I cringed. I had inadvertently brought them with me and left them on the counter when I hopped over to help with the cooking.

"Something Jeremiah left for me." I stared at the food in front of me and held my breath.

"He was here?" Aiden asked, setting down his utensils.

"The dirt bag found out where you live," Riley said, setting her utensils down exactly the same way.

I rolled my eyes. "No, guys. I brought him here, remember? After the incident this morning, he wasn't willing to leave me alone, and I couldn't think fast enough to figure out how to get rid of him."

"You could've shot him if you'd taken those lessons I was talking about," Aiden scolded, picking up his fork and steak knife. He stabbed the meat with such uncharacteristic violence I figured he was envisioning Jeremiah.

I looked at them and tried to smile. "Anyway, he's gone now. Problem solved, right?"

Riley opened the envelope and removed the computer receipt. "You plan on using this?" she asked, handing it to her brother to read. Aiden forked in a mouthful of steak, then set his knife down and took the paper. His brown eyes scanned the receipt, then jerked up to glare at me.

I shook my head. "I'm a freakin' heiress. If I want to go anywhere, I can damn well buy my own ticket." I paused just long enough for my statement to sink in, then added, "And both of you damn well know it."

"Okay, okay," Riley waved a hand at me. "We're both guilty. But we were under orders, and it was for your safety and protection. You have to take that into consideration."

"You know, I'm really sick and tired of finding out how much people have been lying to me," I groused, stabbing the last of my steak. "And everyone's excuse about how they were trying to protect me. A fat lot of good it did."

"Are you planning a trip?" Riley gestured towards the ticket voucher.

"Maybe," I hedged.

"Probably not to a warm beach in the South Pacific," Aiden stated flatly, pushing his plate away.

I avoided his eyes and stared at the food on my plate. Jeremiah had fixed steaks this morning. The meal tonight tasted better and the company certainly was an improvement.

"What else happened after Dirt Bag showed up?" Riley pushed her uneaten plate away.

My eyes met hers. "Nothing, Riley. I was not friendly, and Jeremiah was very careful not to piss me off any more than I already was."

"But you looked scared enough at the stables for him to decide not to leave you alone," Aiden mused, standing and taking his empty plate to the sink. The man could eat anytime, anywhere, under any circumstances. He returned to his seat at the counter. "Did you tell him what happened this morning?"

I shook my head emphatically. "No, I did not. And believe me, he tried several times to get it out of me." I looked at them. Several minutes of silence passed between us. The rain on the roof blended with the soft crackling of the fire. Time stood still.

"How much did Stephen fill you in on my background when he hired the two of you to protect me?" I inquired after a while.

To their credit, neither of them squirmed or blinked an eye.

"Everything," Riley answered. She looked at the plate in front of her and picked up her fork. She played with the pasta for longer than necessary before she answered. "He provided pictures of Jeremiah, your parents' house…."

"What was left of it," Aiden inserted.

Riley nodded, took a mouthful, and continued. "As well as all the police reports he could get his hands on." She chewed a couple of times and swallowed. "He mentioned something about an assassination network but didn't give us names or descriptions. Which is why he located you clear out here. Weak cell service means no GPS. In case you haven't noticed, both vehicles are older models, which means no GPS on either of them. And your cell is under your alias, which in effect hides your identity."

"So, you're on his payroll?" I asked, picking up my fork and toying with my half-eaten pasta.

"Yes," Riley acknowledged. "As private security. Though both of us volunteered and told him pay wasn't necessary."

"Eat your steak," I admonished, pointing towards her plate. She grimaced and stuffed a large piece into her mouth. "Dork Brain here scorched mine. Or sprinkled strychnine all over it."

"Wouldn't hurt you even if I did," Aiden retorted. Silence fell again as Aiden watched us eat. Riley worked through about half of hers, while I finished my pasta before pushing my plate away. Riley stood and took our plates to the sink, then found containers to store the leftovers.

"What bothers me," she said as she transferred the food into plastic containers, "is how Dirt Bag found your location."

"He's an operative," I blurted before thinking. Both siblings jerked their heads to me. "You didn't know?" I asked them.

Aiden shook his head slowly. "No. We didn't. But it answers a lot of questions. Stephen's efforts to hide you were good, but not good enough to fool someone with that kind of background."

"He would have access to all kinds of records and inside knowledge," Riley agreed, joining us at the counter again.

"There wasn't much more he could do to hide you." Aiden stood and stretched. He still wore his uniform which was damp from being out in the weather.

"You'd better go shower and change into dry clothes before you catch a cold," I admonished.

"Yes, Mommy." He grinned at me.

"I'm being practical," I snapped.

"Practical is too big a word for him," Riley slid in. "He's not smart enough to know the meaning of anything with more than four letters in it."

"Which gives me a much larger vocabulary than you," Aiden smirked.

I rolled my eyes. "Thanks for dinner. Or breakfast. Or whatever food is called at this hour." I slid off the stool and sat down in my chair. Neither of them offered to help which was fine with me. I wheeled myself over to the couch.

"Think you can get some sleep now?" Riley asked. Aiden tromped up the stairs, no doubt to shower and change, then fall into bed.

I shook my head. "Maybe in a while. I'm not sleepy."

"Well, sorry not to keep you company, but I'm dead on my feet," she admitted, releasing a yawn big enough to dislocate her jaw.

"Go to bed." I made shooing motions with a hand. "I need to stay up until the fire dies down anyway."

Riley climbed the stairs much more quietly than her brother.

Instead of swinging myself onto the couch, I snatched the notebook and wheeled over to the small recess that held a rolltop oak desk and several oak shelves. I had Internet service through the local cable company, and I had a sudden, overwhelming urge to look up information on what I overheard this morning. I did not want to ask either of the siblings for information because then they would badger me into telling them everything I remembered from the conversation between the killer and his victim. I wanted to be sure of my facts before I divulged details.

I opened the notebook, flipped to what I'd written down, and started Googling.

The fire died to embers by the time I made it back to the couch. The information I'd written filled pages in the notebook and boggled my mind.

The Harry Bass, Jr., Gold Coin Collection. The special American Numismatic Association Coin Show and Exhibit last week in Richmond, Virginia.

The unique 1870-S three-dollar gold coin, the centerpiece of the exhibit, the unexplained sudden loss of power prompting early closure of the show.

And the location of the American Numismatic Association Coin Museum, home for the Harry Bass Gold Coin Collection and the unique 1870-S three-dollar gold coin.

I curled beneath the comforter and stared out the window at the darkness. I had no idea what time it was, but thought it had to be close to sunrise. The gentle rain and trickling water should have put me to sleep. Instead, I thought over the information I now knew, the loss of life because of human greed, and a little ten-year-old girl who was now an orphan.

Chapter Nine

"Sounds like those two cops don't like you much. Ignoring a restraining order isn't going to improve things." Joe Healing Water sat on a log bench at the rough-hewn log table he used for everything inside his one room adobe. A hurricane lantern threw soft light around the old Ute's abode. High altitude desert Southeastern Colorado air chilled corners beyond the warmth of an ancient cast iron stovepipe wood stove squatting in the center of the room. Late Saturday afternoon October sun shone weakly through the single west window creating more shadows than light. Joe wore his usual attire of red plaid flannel shirt and jeans. His long gray braided hair hung down his back. In the lamplight, his eyes looked more like two celestial black holes than anything human.

"I had to see her," Jeremiah argued, his jaw clenched. He sat across the table and was likewise a native of the Southern Ute Indian Reservation located in the southwest corner of Colorado, having known Joe Healing Water since childhood. He wore his same black shirt, jeans jacket, and jeans, though he had washed everything when he got back to Joe's place. His hair hung loose around his shoulders.

"You ought to have snatched her up, brought her here," Hawk inserted, his British accent jarringly out of place. He stood over the wood stove and kept his attention on the sizzling venison in the cast iron frying pan. His dark hair brushed the nape of his neck, the white streaks along his temples gave him a look of sophistication. His deep-set light gray eyes looked iridescent against the black that ringed each iris. He was dressed in a heavy gray wool sweater and black cargo pants and mirrored Jeremiah in height and age, which was middle thirties.

"Not an option," Jeremiah shook his head. "I left a note and the receipt for a chartered flight to Oklahoma, hoping her curiosity will win over her reluctance to see my side of things."

"Rubbish. You ought to have nicked her, hauled her out here. It took the three of us to locate her in the first place." Hawk carried the pan over and set it on the table, then retrieved cans of corn and potatoes from the top of the stove.

"Careful with the cans. They're hot as jacket potatoes," Hawk warned as Jeremiah and Joe Healing Water forked large venison steaks onto their plates, then reached for the steaming cans.

Joe Healing Water frowned at him. "You and your British colloquialisms." He pulled out a large pocketknife, flipped open a wicked-looking blade, and began carving. "Good food," he mumbled around a bite. "You're hired."

"Right. I've done the bloody cooking for the last eighteen-odd months," Hawk retorted, taking a seat beside the old Indian.

"Beer, anyone?" Jeremiah asked, ignoring Hawk.

"No," Joe snapped.

"Yes," Hawk answered at the same time.

Jeremiah stood. "I'll get them."

Joe lifted his eyes towards the younger Indian. "No. The Brit here will get them. If you go, you won't leave any in the store for customers."

Hawk's black eyebrows almost touched. "I'm not your sodding butler."

Joe continued sawing through his meat. "No, you're not. You're still crawling out of that hole you dug yourself into with Mattie. Be careful, or I just might find a way for you to meet up with another skunk."

"You and those bloody striped rodents aren't the worst of it," Hawk complained, climbing over the log bench. "I'm convinced you damned Yanks spent post-war years creating those mutant eight-legged monsters you call spiders."

"They'll be out in numbers this time of day, so watch your step," Joe called out as Hawk disappeared through the front door towards the gas station.

"Did you really put a skunk in the outhouse with him?" Jeremiah asked after Hawk left.

Joe's lips spread wide, exposing a set of straight white teeth. "Naw. The fella wandered in all by himself. That British clown didn't heed my warning about checking the corners first before he shut the door and took a seat."

"And the tarantula?" Jeremiah added after a moment of silence.

Joe shrugged. "Lots of nooks and crannies. It's an old outhouse. What can I say?"

"He seems set on installing indoor plumbing in the spring."

Jeremiah looked up when Hawk reappeared with three beers.

Joe quirked his eyebrows. "That didn't take long."

"Dodged over and back." Hawk swung his attention to Jeremiah. "Too right I am," he declared, referring to Jeremiah's earlier comment. "I've enough of that bloody box out back." He set the cans on the table and resumed his seat beside Joe.

"You're just too foreign to appreciate our indigenous animals." Joe popped the can tab and took a swallow.

Hawk snorted, unable to suppress a shudder. "You chaps and your alien creatures in the middle of nowhere. I ought to have left after the skunk incident."

"So why are you still here?" Jeremiah asked. He practically inhaled his beer in one swallow.

Joe frowned from across the table. The man's drinking had improved, but he was still a long way from stopping all together. Jeremiah had not been a drinker prior to Mattie's near-death experience and loss of her leg.

"I'm not leaving until I've convinced Mr. Outdoor Man here about a bloody indoor loo," Hawk mumbled through a large bite of food.

"Save that argument for another day," Jeremiah inserted when Joe scowled and opened his mouth. "What do I do about Mattie?"

"You mean, what do *we* do," Joe corrected, wrapping a callused hand around his beer can. He took a swig, set the can down, forked the last of his steak into his mouth. He looked at Jeremiah's untouched plate. "Eat, son. Starving yourself won't give you any ideas."

Jeremiah pushed his plate away and drained his beer. He crushed the can with his hand, the sudden noise sharp in the silence of the room.

"You've no idea what scared her?" Hawk asked, watching Jeremiah, then sliding his eyes towards Joe.

Jeremiah tapped the crumpled can against the table. "Yes. I drove the car down the drive, then hotfooted it back and listened outside the door."

"She didn't tell you herself?" Healing Water mused.

Jeremiah shook his head. "No. She would not tell me."

"Not surprising," Joe grunted. He stacked his cleaned plate onto Hawk's equally empty one.

"She witnessed a murder, then got shot at. Her two cop friends did not seem to believe her," Jeremiah admitted, leaning his forearms on the rough surface of the table. His eyes drifted towards the front door and the direction of the gas station.

Hawk grunted. "That woman. She's rather good at attracting trouble."

Jeremiah slid his eyes in the man's direction. "Watch it."

"You can't blame them for not immediately believing her," Joe inserted, picking up Jeremiah's thread. "Mattie's coming off two years of amnesia, was upset about her horse, had just seen Jeremiah here and regained a slew of very bad memories. She would be considered unreliable at best." He watched the younger Ute for a bit. "Did you hear what she described?"

"She did not see anything. Too foggy, which probably saved the lives of both herself and her horse." Jeremiah explained.

"Are the cops thinking the dead man at the stables is linked to the incident Mattie overheard?" Joe asked, resting his forearms on the rough surface.

Jeremiah rubbed his face with a hand. "Her cop friends decided to ride up the trail, see whether Mattie could locate the scene."

"And did you follow?" Hawk slid in.

"Of course."

A long silence followed.

"They found tracks where her horse spooked, but nothing else," Jeremiah finally told them.

"Which does not support her account of things," Hawk grumbled as he took another swallow of his beer. He scowled. "You Yanks have no idea how to properly age your bitters." He looked at Jeremiah. "You should've nicked her and brought her here. For safety," he added when both Indians glowered at him.

"You kidnapped her twice. Isn't that enough?" Joe retorted. He took the half-full can Hawk set down and moved it beyond Jeremiah's reach. He met the younger Ute's eyes. "If Mattie said she doesn't want anything to do with you, I reckon those two cops aren't going to give you a chance to straighten things out. Not without filling you with bullet holes first," he commented with a thin smile.

"Right," Hawk agreed. "Those coppers do rather complicate things."

Jeremiah thumped his fist against the table. "She may be in

danger. I will not stand by and watch. Not this time."

"Well, do you have anything in mind?" Joe wanted to know.

Jeremiah nodded. "Yes. I do."

Hawk leaned the side of his head against his fist. "Does it include illegal and nefarious activity?"

"It includes ignoring the restraining order," Jeremiah muttered.

Hawk clapped his hands together. "Definitely nefarious. When do we start?" He eyed Jeremiah's full plate.

Jeremiah pushed his food in the Brit's direction. "I am not hungry."

The Brit cast a sideways glance at the old Indian, whose expression remained bland.

"I bloody fixed it," he muttered, picking up his fork and hunting knife.

Joe's eyes glinted with sly humor, but pressed his lips closed and nodded at the Brit with unspoken consent. He shifted to Jeremiah. "With your track record, it might be prudent to talk to Campbell first, find a way to get him on your side."

Jeremiah shook his head. "He would not let me in the door." His fingers toyed with the crumpled beer can as his eyes returned to the front door.

"How about your handler?" Joe asked.

"I have been thinking over an idea that would bring in Bill."

"Reckon she'll use the ticket you left?" Hawk asked. He reached across Joe and retrieved his beer, took a swallow to wash down his second meal. His face scrunched. "My god, this tastes awful."

Jeremiah sighed. "I doubt it," he admitted. "She was upset with me. Upset she recognized me. Upset with me all together. And those two cop friends of hers mean business. Campbell put a real kink in things by assigning those two as security. You are right, Joe. If I show up, they will shoot first, ask questions later."

"Well, you made progress with her if seeing you helped her get her memory back," Joe observed.

Jeremiah shook his head. "Not really. She remembers who she is, who I am. But she has confused events. She thinks Mud Rain and the Parsons are dead. She remembers Hawk here as Charlie and paled to the point of passing out at the mention of his name. And she did not mention you at all."

Joe's neutral expression did not change with his next question. "So, when do you fly back east?"

Jeremiah gazed through the open front entrance. "I planted a couple of listening devices at her house. I am waiting to see what she decides to do."

"Bring her back with you this time," Hawk repeated, stacking the third empty plate on the other two.

Jeremiah shook his head. "That would mean kidnapping. Which certainly will not improve our relationship."

"I'd lay odds she'll fly to Oklahoma to talk to her solicitor friend," Hawk mused, setting his beer down in front of Jeremiah. "Here. You seem to lack taste buds. Drink this." Joe scowled at him, but Hawk ignored the unspoken reprimand and continued. "One of us should relocate there."

"That presents a problem," Jeremiah frowned. "The Pottawatomie County Sheriffs are still looking for both of us."

"What of the underground bunker?" Hawk asked, referring to an elaborate underground setup beneath the Lamont estate in Shawnee, Oklahoma. The original owners had built it as a bomb shelter during the Cold War years.

Jeremiah picked up the beer and drained it in a few swallows. Joe's frown deepened. "That would work," he said, answering Hawk's question while keeping his attention on the young Ute.

"Isn't Mattie's solicitor chap in Norman?" Hawk countered.

"Yes," Joe nodded, "but Shawnee's less than an hour away, so that shouldn't be a problem."

Hawk looked at Joe. "If she flies to Colorado, you pick up the watch."

Joe shook his head. "I'm not running around playing tag with anyone. And I don't think she'll have a reason to come this way unless she starts chasing memories. Besides, I have a gas station to run."

"Ha," Hawk scoffed. "You're pissed she's not remembering you."

Jeremiah stood and stretched, then climbed over the bench. "I think she will. Chase memories that is. Eventually anyway. Her photography equipment, photos, albums, are still in our Colorado Springs apartment." He crossed the room and disappeared through the front door, no doubt heading towards the gas station and more beer.

"Why'd you go and give him your beer?" Joe grumbled after Jeremiah left.

"Because there's not sufficient alcohol in it to make a difference," Hawk retorted. He remained seated when the old Indian rose and headed through the door after Jeremiah.

Hawk thought over Jeremiah's news. Mattie's memory had returned, which meant she would eventually visit Oklahoma and that Campbell chap for answers.

Second, her memory was incomplete, and she was confusing his identity with the assassination network, which bothered him more than he wanted to admit.

His eyes wandered around the one room adobe, the single bed the old Indian used, then to his own sleeping bag and blankets on the floor along the opposite wall.

His prolonged stay at Joe's place did not make practical sense. He should be heading across the waves, or going underground, or connecting with the brass for new assignments.

Well, he mused with a slight quirk of his lips, staying at Joe's place effectively got him off the radar and out of sight, so technically he had disappeared again. Only this time it wasn't through work. No one knew where he was, and that meant a lot of worried and anxious heads in upper management. He knew too much to be on the loose like this, especially after the encounter with the Charlie Network. He should be in meetings, filling his superiors in on details surrounding Mary Eagle Feather and the network she established and maintained for more than a decade. They would be tremendously relieved to know that, at least for now, the assassination team known as the Charlie Network had been effectively dismantled.

He leaned his elbows on the table and rubbed his temples with his fingers. The Charlie Network, his knowledge of their assassinations and personnel, the valuable information he accumulated through his incidental association with Mattie and her brother-in-law, Gary Tacque. All of it paled against the issues surrounding Mattie. He had inadvertently gotten her involved with the Charlie Network, and she had lost her leg because of him. He did not like the guilt accompanying that thought. He needed to square things with her, find a way to return some of what she had lost. He owed her that much at least.

He released a cautious sigh. Though physical objects could never replace loved ones, it was just possible what he managed to acquire during all the chaos might sway Mattie into considering a truce, if not complete absolution.

He could live with a truce.

He could not live with the guilt over what he inadvertently had done, all because of a misinterpretation of what he now realized had indeed been a string of incredible coincidences.

Hawk stared beyond the front doorway, but there was no sign of either Jeremiah or Joe Healing Water. Jeremiah continued to exhibit classic signs of grief. Mattie wasn't dead, but the young Indian might soon be if he didn't get his sodding head back on straight.

No argument, Fate had been bloody unfair to Mattie. He had the means to help with her recovery. He might help get Jeremiah back on his feet, too.

That is, if he survived Healing Water's dangerously wicked mischievous streak.

~ * ~

Joe Healing Water crossed the wide field between his adobe and the small gas station, the setting sun throwing long shadows around him. Evening air chilled rapidly as last rays of light lingered in the expansive, darkening sky. A coyote howled in the distance, taken up by several others in an eerily recurring echo across the high desert plains. Stars shone crystal in the stark clearness, the Milky Way slashing across the night sky like a studded diamond cloth.

He found Jeremiah sitting on a cinderblock and plank bench in front of the store, two six-packs of beer on the ground at his feet. He took a seat beside him.

"I have forgotten how clear the night sky is out here," Jeremiah murmured.

"You haven't been noticing much of anything lately." Joe Healing Water sighed and leaned his head against the wall of the small building. "You need to get your focus back."

Jeremiah crumpled the empty beer can in his hand and dropped it onto the growing pile. "Are you getting ready to wax infinite native wisdom?"

Joe stared at the brilliant night sky. "No. I'm fighting the urge to give you a swift kick in the ass."

Jeremiah grunted, a rue smile touching the corners of his mouth. "It would be well deserved."

Joe Healing Water rolled his eyes and squirmed on the bench. "Get off the self-pity train."

Jeremiah reached for one of the three remaining beers from a six-pack. His words were beginning to slur. "What happened, Joe? Where did things go wrong?"

"You mean between you and Mattie? Or between Mattie and her family? Or between the man you were and the spineless wimp you've turned into?" Joe's caustic words floated across the empty prairie.

Jeremiah jerked his head to glare at the man beside him. "That is not true, old man."

"Answer my question, Black Bear," Joe snapped, using Jeremiah's Native name.

Jeremiah sighed. "You know what I mean. When did things go wrong between Mattie and me?"

"I'd say it started when you pretended to be in love with her," Joe grumbled.

"I thought I was making the right decision at the time," Jeremiah groaned, drinking the beer in his hand with long, desperate swallows. "I thought I would not hurt her if I did not encourage closeness. That by the end of two years she would be ready to make the split."

Joe picked up the remaining beers, then stood and walked into the middle of the graveled parking area. He raised the beers towards the sky. When he spoke, his voice came out low, rhythmic. "Beer. The way to the spirit of wisdom is through the spirit of hops." He dropped his hands to his sides and walked to the gasoline pumps in the middle of the broad graveled area, threw the beer cans into the large trash receptacle. Turning, he ambled back to Jeremiah and took a seat.

Jeremiah stared at the old Indian. "That…has to be the…strangest thing I have ever heard…come out of your mouth." It took effort to get his words out.

"Not as strange as what's coming out of yours. You wanted native wisdom, remember?" Joe grunted. "You must think Mattie's too weak and now too disfigured to be worth fighting for," he accused. "Here you sit, drinking yourself into oblivion. You really don't want her back, do you?"

Jeremiah tried to straighten but swayed instead and almost fell off the crude bench. "Back off, Healing Water. You may be too old to hit, but you are treading on thin ice."

Joe waved his hand at the pumps. "You're packing a load of bullshit, Jeremiah. Just like the bullshit I said out there."

Jeremiah nodded his head and waved a hand at the empty lot in front of them. "I agree. That was a load of shit."

Joe's hand dropped. "Just like that bull shit about going along with the government's cockamamie idea of marrying her so you could drop off the radar. It sure looks like you treated her like some dumb broad and assumed she would never become suspicious of your absences, wouldn't have enough brains to put two and two together." He shook his head. "And you assumed she wouldn't fall in love with you, either. But she did."

Jeremiah leaned forward and held his head between his hands. Joe stared at the night sky. "She put her faith and trust in you. You betrayed that faith and trust from day one. And you wonder where things went wrong?"

Jeremiah rubbed his face. "I did not expect to fall in love with her." His words barely made it out of his mouth.

Joe's eyes flashed. "Yeah, but you didn't mind at all when she fell in love with you."

"She gave me strength, focus. I could not have succeeded in all those assignments otherwise." Jeremiah muttered. "The strength she gave me has created the weakness I feel now. I am not whole anymore."

Joe grunted. "Neither is she."

Jeremiah leaned back. "I am a ghost. A wandering spirit without a purpose." His eyes closed and he mused whether he was steady enough to stand and walk away. Joe's company was giving him a headache.

"Oh, get over yourself," Joe snorted. "You're sounding like a B-rated movie. Much more of this and I'm going to hurl that steak Hawk cooked earlier. Damned good, too. Better than the ones you torched the other night."

Jeremiah shook his head. "I do not see a way to heal the split between Mattie and me."

"Well, you think drinking yourself to an early death will help?

It's not going to be easy." Joe waved a hand at the night sky. "You think it'll just drop down with heavenly brilliance and give you the answer?" He turned his head. "You've been lying to her for close to a decade. That's going to take a lot of unraveling. You need to decide whether you have it in you to go after her for real this time."

Joe turned when Hawk appeared from the darkness. "Any decisions?" he asked, leaning against the side of the station doorway.

Joe grinned at the Brit. "Yeah. Black Bear here is a wandering spirit who has been around a beer can once too many times. I'm expecting him to vaporize any minute now."

"Too bad you are not forty years younger," Jeremiah growled at the old Indian.

"I'd rather like to avoid taking a turn at one another." Hawk crossed his arms and took a deep breath. "There's three of us. There are three locations Mattie might end up. And Jeremiah thoughtfully left some listening devices. I still opt she'll track back to Oklahoma and Colorado to clear up gaps in her memory." He paused. "I also believe we three offer better protection than a couple of half-believing local coppers with too much on their plate."

"The police are still looking for you concerning explosions at the Lamont house and the Parsons' place," Joe observed.

Hawk shrugged. "I wouldn't mind a few days in the bunker. They've not got sufficient description. I can tuck myself away and be quite cozy."

Jeremiah jerked his head towards Hawk. "You were supposed to keep us informed when the Charlie team showed up."

Ignoring his comment, Hawk leaned forward until his nose almost touched Jeremiah's. "What say you? Ready to crawl out of your self-pity pot?"

Joe pressed his eyes close to Jeremiah's. "Because if you've decided to give up, I'll go get the rest of the beer from inside the store. Drink it fast so Hawk and I can get you buried before sunrise."

Chapter Ten

That miserable horse had run him right over, Kelly fumed. He'd never seen the brute coming. It had appeared from within the fog like some banshee from the moors.

Patrick Kelly's Irish accent created a lilt in his speech his parishioners just couldn't seem to get enough of. He'd stood at the pulpit on many a Sunday morning and read from the book of Numbers, and congregations hung on every word.

He cast his eyes nervously towards the overhead clouds, then retrieved a white cotton cloth and began wiping over every inch of the white Camaro. Such a pity, having to sacrifice the car, but necessary.

Kelly had met Freddie Little in the church parking lot after watching the man case various cars, testing for ones unlocked, retrieving registration forms and later burglarizing homes while the occupants attended church service. It had been a neat trick, especially since no security cameras monitored the small parking lot. Kelly had watched him, invited him in for coffee then coaxed him to stay for the service.

Kelly had kept his knowledge to himself, kept a list of burglaries among his parishioners, helped soothe those distraught upon the discovery that their dear possessions had been whisked away. When time came and he needed Freddie's loyalty he'd confronted the stupid little man.

Freddie had been persuasive in his pleas for forgiveness, and Kelly allowed him enough symbolic rope to metaphorically hang himself.

He'd needed an accomplice to take to Richmond, Virginia. Someone expendable but necessary to carry out his plans for swapping the 1870-S three-dollar gold coin with a substitute. And Freddie's electrical background proved quite useful in staging a power outage long enough for him to swap coins.

Kelly's thin smile did not reach his blue-green eyes. He was in his late forties, his small compact Irish body athletically fit. Kinky red hair clung close to his scalp, had started to thin along the top, something Kelly reluctantly accepted as the fate of an Irishman. Subconsciously he raised his hands and carefully smoothed out what hair he had left, feeling the soft tight curls beneath his fingers, then continued wiping the car down inside and out.

He was in a parking lot along a sparsely populated section of Lake Eufaula in northeastern Oklahoma. The sharply cooler temperatures had emptied the surface of boaters and other water enthusiasts.

Kelly walked around his car again. His pre-occupation with the vehicle went beyond obsession. He had to make sure no clues remained to link him to the body in the trunk.

And he needed to dispose of both body and vehicle before heading to Shawnee, then back to Virginia.

His original plan had been to bury the body in the church cemetery, but the body bag leaked all over the trunk, and he could not risk someone becoming suspicious. So that meant getting rid of the car, too.

Kelly opened the trunk only to slam it shut again against the rank odor. He opened the passenger door and retrieved an expensive road bike, wheel, and backpack from the behind the front seats. He wiped down the car yet again and thought back to the chain of events on the Blue Ridge Parkway.

He had heard a low-pitched exclamation from within the heavy blanket of fog after his first shot, heard frantic thumps of excited hooves against soft earth. He'd fired two shots in the general direction after he'd killed Freddie, then followed the trail and found obvious tracks where hooves had dug deeply into the ground cover. It had taken time to dispose Freddie's body in the trunk and to clean up the area before he could track horse and rider along the trail to the stables. Cautiously, he'd come upon the arena, spotted the vague form of a man, seen the sweaty, saddled, agitated animal moving in and out of the fog. He'd smiled at his 'Luck of the Irish', finding his target with such ease. The Arab was beautiful, his grey coloring matching the surrounding conditions so perfectly as to create a ghost-like appearance. And still saddled. No wonder he'd been invisible, that Kelly had not detected their presence when until he fired his gun. Obviously, the rider was trying to cool him off after their hectic run along the trail.

Kelly had kept his weapon hidden at his side when he entered the arena, sauntered to the man in the center. Shooting the rider had been a neat trick. The man had never demonstrated the slightest hint of unease or nervousness, which struck Kelly as odd at the time, but not sufficiently enough to force a change in plans.

When he shot the man, Kelly thought the horse would keep his distance. But the Arab had come out of nowhere, knocked him head over heels, then disappeared through the open gate Kelly had neglected to shut. Dazed, he retraced his steps along the trail, up the steep ridge and to the Camaro. After making sure no one had followed him, Kelly had driven non-stop to Oklahoma.

He had missed the coin almost immediately but thought it had fallen from his pocket onto the floor of the car. Not wanting to arouse suspicion, Kelly had controlled his impatience to recover the coin until he was west of the Mississippi.

A frantic search of the car had proven fruitless.

He dared not turn around and retrace his travel to Virginia. He had a dead body in the trunk he needed to dispose of before addressing the loss of the coin.

Strong prairie winds buffeted his black slacks, black long-sleeved Polo shirt and gray nylon windbreaker, whipped surrounding hardwoods, sent leaves scurrying along the ground. Afraid the cold wind would bring raindrops that would leave tell-tale spots, Kelly pulled the cloth from his pocket and began polishing the rich finish of the Camaro again. Oklahoma was known for its mud rain that left cars covered in red clay. He glanced skyward and scowled at the clouds racing low over the surrounding trees. The longer he lingered the more apt he would be discovered by some passerby.

He cursed over the lost coin. He had swapped it from the numismatic slab to a small round plastic air-tight case which was easier to transport and very easily concealed.

Kelly grunted. The coin had to be in the arena. It must have dropped from his pocket when the horse knocked him head over heels.

Maybe he should not have followed the trail to the stables. He would still have the coin and his collection would be complete. The fog had been too thick for anyone to see anything. He could hardly see Freddie when he shot him, and the man had been standing a scant two meters away.

If he had not followed the trail to find the horse and rider, he would not have lost the bloody coin.

Kelly pulled a pair of latex gloves from a pocket and put them on, then dug the keys from his pocket and inserted them into the ignition. He slammed the door shut and pulled another object from a pocket.

An elementary control Freddie had created to remotely start and drive the car. Kelly pressed the ignition button then used the small hand control to shift the car into drive.

"Goodbye, Freddie," he murmured as he shoved the control forward. With a powerful roar the car leaped, gaining momentum as it traveled several yards towards a small overhang. The car sailed from the embankment, hung impressively in the air a few yards, then dove into the muddy choppy water.

Kelly carefully inspected the ground, saw the deep imprints of custom tires leaving pavement and leading straight off the embankment. He nodded his head in satisfaction. The police shouldn't have a problem locating the tracks, and if they found tracks along the Parkway an investigation would lead away from him.

He jogged to the professional racing bike and his nearby backpack. Quickly changing into riding gear, he bunched his pants and shirt into the backpack to burn later. He slipped into the nylon windbreaker, fitted the front wheel onto the bike, tested the tires to make sure they were aired properly, then propped the bike against a tree. He checked the two full bottles in holders and the full Camelback that was part of the backpack.

He shucked off his wet socks and donned fresh ones, Shimano road shoes, Bell helmet, Oakley sunglasses. Peeling off the latex gloves, he stuffed everything into the backpack, then slipped his hands into long-fingered riding gloves. He mounted his bike, clipped in, and set off down the road to put distance between himself and the scene.

Forty minutes later he was on a service road when three Oklahoma State Patrol cars and two fire engines, sirens screaming and lights flashing, roared past on Interstate forty. He suspected an accident over discovery of the Camaro and smiled a grim, satisfied smile as he rode onward, fighting the vicious headwind, taking breaks when his legs threatened to cramp.

Traffic was light on the service road and eventually he turned onto a two-lane state highway to Shawnee. During one of his breaks he pulled the remote control from his pocket, used his cleat to smash it beyond recognition, then threw the remains into the bordering woods.

Autumn darkness fell earlier than Kelly would have liked, and his progress slowed because he pulled over whenever vehicles approached. He did not use nightlights or safety gear. His black gear rendered him invisible to approaching motorists.

It was well after midnight before he reached Shawnee. He coasted into the driveway of the single-story rancher he had called home for the last twenty-odd years. It was an older house, needed a new roof and some appliance upgrades. He dismounted and walked his bike to the garage door, punched in the code, slipped inside, closed the door. His thighs burned from the long ride, and physical exhaustion washed over him. But whatever fatigue he felt could not dampen his satisfaction as he opened the connecting door and entered the kitchen.

Loose ends were gone. There remained no evidence linking him to either murders or the disappearance of the coin from the exhibit.

The connection between Freddie Little and himself might present a challenge when the Camaro was eventually discovered, but he had been careful to limit his association with the man to church activities. If the police did question him about the man's death, Kelly would be truthful about his membership with the parish, his suspicions Freddie was a thief, how he had prayed daily for guidance to help Freddie change his ways. And the car was registered in Freddie's name.

He parked his bike in the living room beside an indoor bike trainer he used when the weather did not allow him to ride outside. He could not have made the ride today if he had not been in top physical condition. Removing his road shoes and socks, he padded across the carpet to his bedroom, stripped and stood in the shower. Then he put on a pair of blue sweatpants and hooded sweatshirt and made his way to the kitchen for something to eat.

The home décor was that of a bachelor, with brown shades and mahogany the prominent colors, everything clean and tidy. He glanced at the wall clock in the kitchen. Just after one in the morning. He heated a can of vegetable soup, ate it while leaning against the counter, feeling his thighs trying to tighten and knowing he needed to get up early and do a recovery ride on the indoor trainer to prevent lactic acid build up.

But he was too agitated to sleep. He rinsed out the empty bowl and set it in the dish drain, then walked along the hallway to the bedroom that served as his home office. Going to the closet, he opened the double doors to reveal a large cast iron safe. Carefully he twirled the combination lock, gripped the three-barred handle, and opened the heavy door. A couple of rifles and handguns occupied the interior, but his hands went for the heavy leather briefcase on the top shelf. Holding the case, he walked over and took a seat in the mahogany leather desk chair. He turned on a green glass and brass desk lamp, fingered the combinations on either side of the case, and opened the lid. Inside lay his pride and joy, an almost complete collection of US three-dollar gold coins.

An incredible gift from God Himself, Kelly felt sure.

One by one he laid the coins out on the desk surface. Each coin was protected by a clear two-and-half by three-and-a-half inch clear, airtight, sealed plastic case, or slab. He used a large magnifying glass to study the coins as he laid them out.

U.S. gold coins, already valuable for their gold content, even more so for their numismatic value. A gift from a sweet elderly lady after her husband passed away unexpectedly.

Helped along by the hands of Reverend Patrick Kelly, of course.

Kelly learned early on his Destiny was to help souls from this world buy their way to the next, and he had been gifted with unique intelligence in subtle, undetectable ways of bringing about death.

Most parishioners on his special list were modestly well off, a few had only their Social Security checks to offer. Kelly knew God did not mind the varying amounts; rather, it was the percentage of each person's financial wealth that mattered.

Kelly did not keep any for himself, not until the gift of the three-dollar gold coin collection. His need for balance forced him to search for the one coin the collection did not contain.

The 1870-S three-dollar gold coin.

When he discovered the uniqueness of the coin, he had to have it. A complete collection represented his complete commitment to God's purpose for him on this ugly planet.

And God had appeared in the form of Freddie Little. The entire quest for the gold coin had been driven by a divine hand, and acquisition of said coin had gone without a hitch.

Until the presence of that horse and rider on the trail precisely at the moment he killed Freddie. An incredible, unbelievable coincidence, one he could not understand why God created.

An Irishman by birth, Kelly immigrated to the States, discovered his purpose in life, and started his first parish in a small town deep in the Tennessee hills. Admittedly, his first targets had not represented his best work, and suspicions had been aroused, forcing him to flee the area and re-invent his identity.

He'd gone through two more parishes before beginning the one in Shawnee, Oklahoma. By then he had learned the art of patience. He had also gleaned valuable knowledge concerning the human psyche, their need for assurance beautiful life beyond their current one could be guaranteed with generous donations and complete trust in his abilities as their Reverend.

He had also stumbled upon the extensive numismatic enthusiasm surrounding US coinage and especially gold coins, had dabbled a little in buying and selling gold and silver bullion.

But nothing so monumental as the collection that lay before him now. He felt like a proper leprechaun as he gazed with awe at the gold in front of him.

This collection would not belong to the parish. The sweet widow had brought it directly to him during a private luncheon after her husband's funeral. She had been fearful of the value, afraid of someone attacking her, so she had not wanted to show it at the church. Curious, he Googled the three-dollar gold coin and immediately fell in love with the curious story behind that particular mintage.

Patrick Kelly sat back and studied his collection. A coin representing every year between 1854 and 1889 lay before him on the desk. He carefully picked up an object and opened a small compartment. He would keep the iconic coin with him when he finally found it. His hands shook with anxiety, anger, and disbelief.

He had held the coin in his hands. He had owned the famous 1870 three-dollar gold coin for a brief interval.

Where had he lost it? He had searched the car, his clothes, even the body bag and Freddie's corpse, but to no avail. The only other possible location would be along the trail he jogged when he followed the horse and rider to the stables.

Or when that lousy Arab bowled him over.

With shaking fingers, he held up the empty compartment, envisioning the coin in place. His only course of action meant retracing every step, going over every inch of ground along the Parkway, combing every grain of dirt at the stables, especially the arena. He feared someone would find the coin, not understand its historic place in the American numismatic world.

The 1870-S three-dollar gold coin was arguably the most famous of all US gold mintage. By 1907 word was out concerning the singularity of the coin, and by 1909 the coin was legendary. Over the next seventy-odd years it passed through the hands of various numismatic collectors. In 1982 Bowers and Ruddy Galleries auctioned off the coin as part of the United States Coin Collection, also known as the Eliasberg Collection. Harry W. Bass, Jr., had bought the coin for a little under seven hundred thousand dollars.

The coin was now considered priceless. And if some country bumpkin happened upon it in the dirt somewhere, the coin might get thrown into an old coffee can and become lost forever.

Kelly stared at his collection for a long time, then reluctantly stowed the case back in the safe.

Despite the wee hours, he logged onto his computer and Googled the Internet for reports of the coin theft, but nothing came up. He relaxed against the soft comfort of his chair. Either the theft had not been discovered, or the numismatic community did not want to make it known.

He rubbed his eyes, looked at the desk clock. He needed to get some sleep. He would be giving sermons before long and he really needed to fit in a recovery ride before the first service, which meant getting up before sunrise.

Kelly's bedside phone rang, jarring him from a deeper sleep than he had anticipated when he finally went to bed. Bright sunlight streamed through cracks in the heavy curtains of his bedroom. He glanced at his alarm clock and bolted from bed. The first church service started in less than an hour.

"A very good morning. Reverend Kelly speaking," he answered on the third ring.

"Preacher Pat, good morning," Stephen Campbell's rich voice resonated through the line. "I wanted to catch you before you got to the church and got inundated with greeting the congregation. I need your advice about a very close friend who is going through a tough time. I've mentioned her before. Her name is Mattie Tyler."

Kelly rubbed his eyes and blinked, trying to clear lingering haziness. "Yes, of course. George and Ginnie Lamont's eldest daughter. They've been parish members for years." He paused to recall facts. "Didn't she lose her family a couple of years ago? And then she seemed to disappear, I believe. At least she hasn't been to a service in quite a while."

"My doing," Stephen admitted. "She suffered severe trauma and amnesia. And now her memory has returned, and she's upset and not thinking clearly, and she seems to be having some issues with being able to tell fact from fiction."

"How can I help?" Kelly asked.

"I'd like to take you to lunch at the club after the last service today and talk things over, get your opinion," Stephen suggested.

"Let me check my calendar." Kelly padded to his desk, flipped through an old-fashioned event calendar. He used a phone app but retained the habit of having his schedule written down.

"Yes, that works. Shall I meet you there?"

He hung up and hurried to get ready for his first service.

Stephen Campbell, dressed elegantly as usual, waited for the Reverend on the steps of the local country club. He smiled with relief when he saw the small man approach.

"Preacher Pat, thank you so much for making time." He shook hands with the Reverend and led the way inside. He asked for a table in a corner, waited until water and menus had been served before addressing the subject on his mind.

"I believe Mattie Tyler is having emotional issues with the recent return of her memory and I need advice on how to best help her," he started. "Your extensive knowledge in psychology and emotional trauma, and your connection with her family through the church, seems in my mind to make you the perfect resource."

"Well, old friend, I'm all ears," Kelly smiled.

Stephen took a long drink from his water glass before continuing. "Mattie believes she witnessed a shooting in Virginia. No evidence has been found, but she is distressed and upset, and I'm at a loss how to support her."

Kelly leaned against the back of his chair, his expression shocked.

"A *shooting?*" he gasped. "How terrible!"

Stephen nodded. "She almost rode her horse to death getting away from the scene. If that alone wasn't enough, her husband, Jeremiah, chose that same day to visit her. Against my wishes I might add. He's responsible for much of the emotional trauma that caused her amnesia."

The Reverend held up a hand. "I'm afraid you've lost me, boy-oh. Please fill me in from the beginning."

Kelly listened with growing agitation as the man across the table gave him the details. Two glaringly obvious disasters became clear. First, he had shot the wrong person in the arena, which explained the man's complete lack of suspicion when Kelly approached him.

Second, Mattie Tyler presented a dangerous witness because she would recognize his voice. After all she and her family had attended his church services for decades.

Their lunch orders arrived, and Kelly took the ensuing silence to collect his thoughts. According to Campbell, local law enforcement had not found evidence of a shooting, which cast doubt upon Mattie's report and reassured him his cleanup had been effective. But he struggled to cover his anger and frustration over killing the wrong rider. He should have known it was too easy. He should have checked buildings and other horses before making his decision.

He should have made sure the Arab was the only horse showing distress from recent activity.

"She contacted me to say she's flying to Oklahoma," Stephen continued after a long break. "I know I'm asking a lot because you are a very busy person. Do you reckon you could set aside some time to help her sort through some of this emotional turmoil?"

"I most certainly will," Kelly consoled. "Please let me know when she arrives, and the three of us can have lunch."

Stephen agreed, and they finished dessert and coffee before going their separate ways.

Kelly drove home, changed into riding gear, turned on an afternoon football game, then donned his riding shoes and clipped into the indoor trainer. His thighs were tight but loosened with the easy cadence, and the steady rhythm calmed his nerves.

Mattie and Jeremiah Tyler. He had met the husband a few times, and just those casual conversations had alerted his instincts.

He'd worried a bit whether the man was there to investigate him. His demeanor screamed investigator or someone of that ilk. Dear Mattie had demonstrated innocent bliss concerning her husband. Women were so typically blind when it came to love.

But Mattie would no doubt recognize his voice. She had grown up listening to him preach every Sunday. Such testimony might not stand up in a courtroom, but any media coverage might be seen by a law enforcement officer investigating his early failures.

He had to get to her before she told anyone else what she'd overheard. Before Freddie's body and the Camaro were discovered in the lake. Because if Freddie's body came to light, that might provide enough of a link for authorities to listen to her story.

And Mattie Tyler could tie him to the body.

He finished his ride and strode down the hallway to his office, opened the safe, and removed a small wooden box. Checking the contents, he noted what items needed replenishing then carefully replaced the box and locked the safe.

He had used the last of his concoction recently on dear old Mrs. Agatha Smithers, a very wealthy widow whom he had convinced to leave the bulk of her estate to the parish. She had quietly passed away the night after a dinner with him at a local restaurant.

First order of business would be to restock his supplies.

And then he would get rid of Mattie Tyler.

Chapter Eleven

Saturday and Sunday merged together, rain and fog socking in the entire area. I tried several times to talk with Amy but got voicemail. Unfortunately, when her Aunt Jilly finally answered the phone, I got an earful rather than a conversation.

"I told the police Amy needs time. She's not talking to anyone right now, and in my opinion, talking to you will only worsen her emotional state," she ranted through the line, the pain of her own loss clearly in her voice. "She's brittle, and she's lost her father under conditions that could have been avoided if he had stopped working with those stupid creatures and found a regular job."

I explained to Riley and Aiden the bits of information I'd overheard on the Parkway between the two men, and both promised to follow up with the numismatic museum and inquire whether there had been a report of a lost or stolen coin from the Richmond exhibit.

When I crawled from bed into my wheelchair on Monday morning, the view through my bedroom windows revealed another day of foggy gray dampness. Faint sounds of television drifted up from downstairs, which meant at least one of the siblings was home. No bets on whether Stephen had contacted them with orders to stick to me like glue.

I dressed in gray sweats that matched my gray mood and the gray day, then wheeled into the kitchen. As if on cue, Riley poked her head through the door that led to the downstairs.

"You finally up?" She nodded in answer to her own question and joined me. She wore dark green sweats and sported an impressive bed head.

"Where's Aiden?" I asked as I transferred myself onto one of the barstools and reached for the phone handset.

"At work." Riley went through the motions of making coffee, and soon the cozy aroma filled the kitchen.

I dialed Kinsey's cell, and she answered on the second ring.

"How's Twister?" I asked her. He had returned to the stables last evening.

"He's fine, back to his old self," she answered, although I

heard hesitation in her voice.

I leaned my forehead against the palm of my free hand. "What's up, Kinsey?"

"He's a bit off his feed, that's all," she admitted. "What's really screwed up is my schedule. I've had to cancel all riding activity around here until the police are done with their investigation."

There wasn't anything I could say that would help her feel better, but I voiced my regrets and understanding, told her I'd be out to check on Twister and hung up.

"Stephen filled us in on what the two of you discussed." Riley set two steaming cups down and took a seat. I reached along the counter and retrieved creamer and sugar.

"Wimp." Riley drank hers black and never missed an opportunity to harass Aiden and me on having what I considered normal taste buds.

"So why aren't you at work with Aiden?" I asked, ignoring her jab.

Riley blew on her coffee and took a sip. "Because Stephen left explicit instructions not to let you out of our sight." She held up a hand when I jerked my eyes to hers. "His words, not mine. I'm just quoting the man."

"I'm flying to Oklahoma City this afternoon," I told her, hoping my admission wouldn't lead to an outburst.

Riley shrugged. "Want company?"

My first reaction was to tell her no, that I didn't want company on the memory trail I planned to chase down. I set down my cup.

"I hadn't given it much thought," I answered truthfully.

"You've been through an awful lot over the last couple of days. And I won't lie. I'd feel a lot more at ease if someone accompanied you."

"Can you get the time off with this short of a notice?" I asked her.

Riley sighed and plunked down her own coffee cup. "I'm on temporary leave, thanks to my damned brother."

"Oh?" I wasn't sure whether to pursue the conversation and ask for details.

"Yeah," she scowled. "Aiden and his typical male chauvinist attitude. Makes me want to puke."

"O-kay." I could imagine the ensuing argument between them.

"Stephen wanted someone with me all the time, and Aiden pulled rank on you," I guessed.

"You got it." To her credit, Riley kept the subsequent string of oaths under her breath.

"So, you're free to fly to Oklahoma with me?"

"Like I asked earlier, do you want company?"

"Stephen's worried about me," I guessed.

Riley eyed me over the rim of her cup. "Well, duh, Mattie. Aiden and I are, too. Neither of us liked the way that scumbag husband of yours showed up at the stables like he belonged there." She tapped a forefinger on the counter, emphasizing each word. "He. Knew. About. That. Restraining. Order."

"I told him in no uncertain terms I didn't want him around," I told her.

Riley snorted. "Like that did any good. He went and left a note and tickets on the counter, for crying out loud!" She ran a hand through her bed head. "All the way home, Aiden and I argued over whether we should've arrested him. Dork Brain didn't agree when I pointed out we should have nailed the son of a bitch and thrown him in a jail cell. He thought we did the right thing by letting him off with a warning." She snorted again, sounding a lot like an angry bull.

I grinned at my comparison.

"What?" she demanded.

I waved a hand at her. "Nothing. A non sequitur moment, that's all."

She continued. "That's why he hydroplaned and almost ran off the road. Because we were arguing."

"Again," I interjected. I released a frustrated sigh and opened my mouth to read her the riot act, realized it wouldn't do a bit of good, and clamped my lips shut. I pushed my coffee away. "So, are you going to tell your brother you're flying out with me?"

Riley's lips pressed into a thin line. "I shouldn't, after the way he treated me. He could easily have taken time off, but n-o-o-o, he told the chief it made more sense for me to go on leave, me being a woman and all."

"Excuse me for creating the problem," I snapped.

Riley ignored my outburst. "But he and I need to stay in contact in case anything breaks in Randy's murder. And I can tell him to contact the Pottawatomie County Sheriff's office, put a bug in their ear about keeping an eye out for your soon-to-be ex-husband."

I folded my arms and stared at the two slips of paper Jeremiah left on the counter. Riley picked up the one containing the charter information and eyed it with distaste. "I'll bet my bottom dollar he did this to keep track of you." She waved the paper in front of my nose. "You know he left this little present so it would be a piece of cake following your movements. Right?"

She had a point.

"Maybe he was offering an olive branch. Trying to make up."

Riley's Olympic eye roll should've lost her eyeballs somewhere in the back of her head. Somehow, they made it back to glare at me again. "You have *got* to be kidding me. That's bullshit, and you know it."

"Yes, I do know it, Riley. For crying out loud, give me a little credit!" I blew out an aggravated huff. "That's why I made my own arrangements." I grinned at her. "Please tell me you don't think I'm stupid enough to take him up on the chartered flight?"

Riley wasn't convinced. "Yeah, well, he still has all the contacts he needs to track your every move, especially now that he's got your alias." She dropped the paper onto the counter. "He also might be stupid enough to show up at the Oklahoma City airport and try to intercept you. And since Dork Brain won't be with us, I would love to see that son of a bitch thrown into a jail cell."

I slid off the stool and moved my cup along the counter as I hopped to the sink. "I can handle him if he shows up. I was married to him for seven years, remember?"

Riley's next words stopped me dead in my tracks. "Yeah, the perfect blind, floozy wife."

I jolted, almost lost my balance, and used the counter to steady myself as I whipped around to gape at her. "That was uncalled for and you know it," I accused, my voice shaking with anger.

"But it's the truth, and *you* know it," she shot back. "During those seven odd years, you never once asked him about all those trips he made, whether he was having an affair. For Pete's sake, Mattie, any woman in her right mind would've become suspicious after seven years!"

"Back off, Riley!" My voice echoed against the walls. I inhaled, fought to regain control over my temper. "Back off," I repeated, my tone lower but still seething. I spun away to glare through the kitchen window at the grayness outside.

"Sorry to be so blunt about it." Riley didn't sound the least bit contrite.

I rinsed out my cup, replaced it in the cupboard, then avoided eye contact as I hopped back to my chair. "I need to get out and see Twister before I head down to the airport."

I wheeled into my bedroom and closed the door so Riley wouldn't follow. I packed haphazardly, not really paying attention to what I threw into a large suitcase. I figured if I filled it full enough, then I should have something to wear in Oklahoma. I tucked the ring box into a corner. Keeping it with me helped me feel as though Randy were close, hovering over my shoulder, protecting me.

An hour later Riley and I were in my Explorer on the Interstate heading to the stables. Our suitcases were in the back, and I had my mud boots with me so I wouldn't ruin my good shoes. The police cars were gone as I crept up the hill to the parking area, but the image of their flashing lights permeated my memory. While Riley waited in the car, I slid into the rain and picked my way among the puddles to Twister's run. He stood beneath the shelter and nickered when I reached the gate.

"You're a smart boy, you know that?" I murmured, sliding between two poles set just wide enough to allow passage, then limping carefully along his pen to the lean-to. I had left my cane in the car. "Here you are, tucked away snug as a bug in here, while I get all wet." He lowered his head and nuzzled my chest. I ran my hands carefully over his hindquarters and legs, along his neck, finally rubbing his muzzle. In soft words, I told him about Randy, and he dipped his head low as though saddened by the news. Tears leaked down my cheeks again, and I spent long minutes with my arms around his neck and my face buried against his warm hide.

"I've got to attend to some business in Oklahoma, but I'll be back," I told him, wiping the wetness on my face. "You take care of yourself. And start eating your breakfast and dinner like a good boy." Despite the drizzle, he followed me to the gate, and I limped to the tack room and retrieved a couple of treats for him. Then I squelched my way back to the car. Riley had moved to the driver's seat, which was for the best because my eyesight blurred from emotions too raw to control. I changed my footwear, crawled into the passenger side. Riley manipulated the hand controls. Soon we were on our way south towards the Tri-Cities Regional Airport in Tennessee. Rain drummed the car and the pavement against the steady thumping of windshield wipers. Ragged wisps of clouds hung between the mountains. We hit patches of fog, but fortunately nothing that impaired visibility.

"Riding that puddle jumper to Atlanta will be interesting in this weather," Riley muttered as we pulled into the small parking lot of the airport.

"Hey, you're the one who volunteered to come along." I climbed from the car and pulled the hood of my raincoat over my head. Clouds crowded close to the earth, and I got a bad feeling in the pit of my stomach that we might not be going anywhere today. Riley hauled our suitcases from the back, and we headed for the small terminal.

"I don't see any planes on the tarmac," Riley muttered when we reached the entrance.

"Think positive," I admonished, limping into the building with the aid of my cane.

"Okay," she retorted, "I'm *positive* I don't see any frickin' planes on the tarmac."

I ignored her and walked to the lone woman manning the counter of our airline. The other airline counters were likewise minimally staffed. The few passengers milling around didn't seem to be heading towards the security gates, which was a bad omen.

"May I help you?" the desk attendant asked. She was young, overweight, her smile forced. She looked thoroughly disgusted at the prospect of dealing with another potentially irate passenger. The pit in my stomach dropped a couple of floors.

"Hi," I smiled as I handed her my ticket information. Riley set our suitcases on the metal scales beside the counter, then handed her information over as well.

The young woman swallowed, brushed a hand across the dyed black bangs against her forehead, and looked at me with blue eyes accented by neon blue eye shadow and petroleum black mascara. Her short sleeve blue airport uniform shirt and black slacks appeared wrinkled, and I wondered whether she was pulling extra hours due to the weather. "I am so sorry, but all our flights have been cancelled for the rest of the day."

Riley turned to me. "Told you so." She glared at the attendant.

"Great. Now what do we do? Drive back home?"

"Riley. Please. Let me handle this." I forced a smile and directed my attention to the girl behind the counter. "What about other airlines?"

The woman sighed and turned to her computer. "Let me see," she muttered as she began typing. I saw by her expression her actions were wasted. She already knew the answer but was going through the motions of looking helpful. "I'm sorry, but there are no other flights in or out today."

I leaned my arms on the counter. "What's the earliest flight tomorrow?"

"What's your destination?" she squinted at the screen.

"Oklahoma City."

"Tomorrow?" Riley interjected. "I think we should check weather reports before we start asking about flights out. We ain't going nowhere if conditions don't improve."

I ignored her. The desk attendant acknowledged Riley's comment with a nod, then turned to me.

"Assuming the weather improves, we have a flight to Atlanta with connections to Will Rogers in Oklahoma City at six a.m."

Riley groaned. "Mattie, make it later. Please. You know me and mornings. You, too, for that matter," she added. "You didn't crawl out of bed until almost noon today."

The attendant nodded. "You might have a better chance of improved weather if you wait until tomorrow afternoon," she suggested. "If you're not on a schedule, I can get you into Oklahoma City by eight tomorrow evening if you take the noon flight out of here."

I debated longer than I really needed to, but finally consented. "Okay." Riley and I waited while she made changes.

"Since our flight is cancelled, will the airline put us up for the night?" Riley asked when the woman handed us new tickets.

"I'm really sorry," she said, shaking her head. "When flights are cancelled because of the weather, we're not responsible for providing overnight accommodations."

"Well, that sucks." Riley hauled the suitcases off the scales and turned to me. "You'd better not be thinking about camping out in this place."

I took in the sparse terminal. No restaurants, no venders. We'd be lucky to find a snack machine. I turned back to the desk attendant. "Where's the nearest overnight accommodations?"

She produced a sheet with a few black lines. "We're here," she pointed to a red dot. "There's a string of places about two miles down this road." Her finger trailed along one of the lines. "There are a couple of cheaper places further along, closer to town."

I took the crude map. "Thanks."

Riley retrieved our suitcases and the two of us left the terminal. We stepped outside into premature twilight as clouds dropped lower and rain fell harder.

"I still think we ought to head home," Riley muttered as we made our way through rain and puddles to the Explorer.

"Let me drive." I wiggled my fingers for her to hand over the keys.

Riley shook her head. "I'm good. Get in."

Grumbling, I climbed into the vehicle, rested my cane against the door. Riley studied the crude map for a few minutes, then maneuvered us through the terminal exit and along a two-lane paved highway. A green hotel sign appeared on our left through the heavy rain, Riley turned into the parking area, and we pulled under the covered entrance.

"Stay here while I get us a room." Riley left the engine running and opened the driver's door. "Lock the car when I get out, okay?"

I rolled my eyes. "You're nuts. No one's going to be out in this mess."

Riley scowled. "Humor me and lock the doors." She got out and I rested my head against the back of the seat. Riley knocked on the window and pointed to the car locks.

"Go get us a room," I waved her off. "I'll be fine."

Riley spun towards the entrance. I watched her pass through the automatic doors of the hotel and failed to see a shadowed figure approach the driver's side of the Explorer.

The car door opened, and Jeremiah slid behind the wheel.

"Hello again." He glanced at the various hand controls, shifted, and had the car moving before I could snap my mouth shut. He turned onto the two-lane highway in the direction towards the airport. The hotel sign disappeared around a curve, and Jeremiah slowed.

"Where in the hell did you come from?" I finally managed to

croak. Riley was going to go apoplectic.

"Outside," he answered as he drove through the downpour.

I couldn't believe he was sitting behind the wheel. "I should've locked the damned doors like Riley told me to," I spluttered.

"Lady Luck was with me," he shrugged. "Spotted you in the terminal, overheard your conversation."

"Riley will know in a heartbeat what you've done," I accused. "She'll have a BOLO out in no time, and she won't bother with a verbal warning when she catches up with us."

"No doubt." His attitude flamed my anger.

"How did you know where I was?" I demanded. "No way this stunt of yours is by accident!"

"I planted a couple of listening devices when I left the steaks and flight information," he admitted.

I thumped my head against the car seat. "I should've known. *Damn it.*"

Why hadn't I thought of that? He'd admitted he was an operative. Only a moron would've ignored the probability he'd left behind a few bugs when he left the note and ticket information. Riley would be spitting nails. His timing was impeccable.

Jeremiah turned into an empty lot and pulled alongside a light gray Toyota four-door sedan.

"Riley is going to kill you," I ranted. "And don't expect me to try to stop her."

He ignored me. "Time to change vehicles." He jumped out, opened the back of the Explorer, and grabbed both suitcases. "Come on. Your bodyguard will already be on the horn about this, so we need to get moving."

I sat in the Explorer. Jeremiah opened the passenger and leaned in. "Would you like me to carry you?"

I knew by his expression I was not going to win this argument. Grasping my cane, I stood in the pouring rain, thought again about Riley and wondered whether she was already in pursuit.

She'd better be, I winced. Otherwise, Jeremiah would get us under the radar and make it impossible to find us. I glanced at the Explorer, then with a growl reached in to retrieve my purse.

"Leave it," Jeremiah shook his head.

"Not likely," I retorted. Before I could react, Jeremiah twisted my purse from my grasp, tossed it into the Explorer, and slammed the door. Stunned by the speed of his actions, I clamped my lips shut, limped to the Toyota, opened the passenger door, and angled into the seat. Jeremiah slid behind the wheel, and we were on the road faster than I could blink. I realized with a sinking feeling we were headed towards the hotel again. Jeremiah was backtracking his movements in case Riley had seen what direction the Explorer had taken.

As we whizzed by the hotel sign the seatbelt alarm began to ding with dainty, polite insistence.

"Fasten your seatbelt," he instructed.

"Go to hell," I snapped.

"The roads are slick," he pressed, glancing frequently in the rearview mirror.

"Yeah, well, I want the option of jumping out." I stared through the window at the rapidly darkening surroundings. The dinging doubled, still dainty, still polite.

"I suppose the place you parked this car doesn't have any type of surveillance equipment?" I observed after a while.

"Correct." Jeremiah reached for the dash controls and turned on the heater. His clothes were soaking wet, and I couldn't help but marvel that he had accurately predicted which hotel we would choose. He must've jogged from where he parked the Toyota to the hotel entrance.

The dinging abruptly stopped. Silence filled the space between us.

I frowned.

"What are you thinking?" Jeremiah asked through the darkness.

"Whether Riley can backtrack your movements fast enough to get someone on your tail." I admitted.

Jeremiah shook his head. "No."

"I don't believe this is happening," I groaned, throwing up my hands. "How did you manage to get into the airport? All flights were cancelled!"

Jeremiah drove through the downpour, his movements efficient, his control impeccable. "I flew in yesterday, before the weather turned sour. From there it was a simple case of surveillance." He paused and glanced in my direction. "Why did you not book a private plane?"

"I wasn't about to use the arrangements you so conveniently left for me," I snapped.

"Lucky for me your flight was cancelled," he observed.

"Well, this whole thing isn't going to work. You'll be caught before morning." I was wet and shivering, and the hot air from the heater felt good. I reached over and turned the fan on high.

Jeremiah released a suspiciously contented sigh. "Not likely."

I turned my head and studied the man who had been my husband for the last seven-odd years. "You sound awfully sure of yourself."

He glanced in my direction, then in the rearview mirror again. "Yes."

I shook my head. "Well, I still think Riley's going to catch up, and you're going to find yourself up a creek without a paddle." I glared at him. "And I won't help you."

"You have already made that quite clear," he stated.

"Yeah, well, I mean every word," I growled. I uncrossed my arms and ran my hands through my wet hair. Surely Riley would be onto us before long. The car we were in had to be a rental from the airport when Jeremiah flew in. She would have the description on the police radio. It was only a matter of time before a state trooper pulled us over.

As if reading my thoughts, Jeremiah slowed when we approached the outskirts of a small town. "Time to change vehicles again."

I gaped at him. "You're kidding. Do you have another car stashed somewhere? Or are you just going to steal one this time?"

His answer felt like a kick in my chest. "The latter. Unfortunate, but necessary." He rolled along the narrow streets, passing tiny houses, until he came to a mobile home park. "Ah. Here we go," he muttered as he angled the Toyota into a space beside an old two-door Honda Civic parked in front of a decrepit single-track mobile home.

"Sit tight," he instructed, cutting the engine and opening the car door.

"No." I was already halfway out of the car. "I can use these folk's phone and call Riley." I started for the trailer door.

"If they're home." Instead of trying to stop me, he walked with me to the rusted door of the structure and rapped on the aluminum side. Ratty curtains hung across the dark windows. No lights came on despite Jeremiah's noisy banging. He turned to me.

"Time to decide, Mattie. Choose to stay here, stranded, without money, ID, or transportation. Or put your faith in me. My destination is the Parsons' house in Norman." He paused, his eyes black as flint in the dim light, his wet hair hanging in limp strings around his shoulders.

By the time I sorted through what to do Jeremiah had the Honda started. He transferred the suitcases from the Toyota to the trunk of the Honda.

I confess that by now I wasn't quite sure whether Jeremiah had all his marbles. I had never pegged him as a thief, yet he was at this moment committing grand theft auto. I felt like we were in an altered reality.

Jeremiah left the Toyota unlocked with the keys in the ignition, then slid behind the wheel of the Honda. He rolled down the window. "Well?"

I limped over and slid into the passenger side. I had to put my cane on the back seat because there wasn't enough room in the front. "Won't the owner of this car report it stolen?" I asked as he shifted the manual into gear and retraced his route to the highway.

He shrugged. "Possibly. Though by the look of their trailer, my guess is they will opt to use the Toyota and delay reporting the theft."

"Wow. And to think I was married to you for seven years." I turned my head away to hide my shock.

He went on. "By the time this car makes the hot sheet we will be two states away and most likely at our destination."

"Really." I tried to hide the shake in my voice. "Pray tell me how you know so much about stealing cars?"

Jeremiah kept his voice neutral. "A necessary skill in my line of work. Not one I use much, but it does have advantages. If the owner decides not to take the Toyota and notifies the cops, it will cut into our time a little. If he chooses the Toyota, we have at least twenty-four hours before a report is filed. And like it or not, stolen cars rate down the list."

"How did you know the owner wouldn't be home?" I asked.

"Experience. I have been doing this for a while. I know the signs." Jeremiah wove through the small town.

"Riley will report this as a kidnapping," I observed.

"Yes, and that will be to our advantage," Jeremiah explained.

"*Your* advantage," I corrected him.

"My advantage, then," he acquiesced. "While kidnapping rates higher than a stolen car, the local guys will have to notify FBI, and relaying information will eat up time."

I stared at Jeremiah in the darkness between us. "Wow," I breathed after a long silence.

He sighed. "There is whole different me that you do not know."

I stared through the windshield. "Do you mean we're driving to Oklahoma? In this…this…cracker box of a car?"

"Could be worse," he paused. "I could have stolen a Smart Car."

I shifted, uncomfortable in the low cramped space, my prosthesis at an awkward angle. "Why Oklahoma?" I asked after another long silence.

"You and I both have business to conduct there." Jeremiah slowed and turned onto another two-lane highway.

"You could use the Interstate," I observed. "It would make the drive faster."

He shook his head. "It would also increase the probably of being spotted by law enforcement."

We drove in silence for a couple of hours. Jeremiah pulled into a small gas station to fill up. I spotted a pay phone at the corner of the old building and wasted precious minutes arguing with myself whether I could get a call through to Riley.

Except that I didn't have her number memorized. Damn it.

Jeremiah finished fueling the car, then escorted me to the bathroom facilities located around the corner of the building.

"Hungry?" he asked when I exited from what had to be the dirtiest bathroom on the face of the planet.

"No," I growled. "I feel like I should be steam cleaned."

He opened the door for me, and as I slid back into the Honda, I wondered how in the world Riley would be able to track me down.

Chapter Twelve

Riley reached the check-in counter when movement in her peripheral vision made her spin around in time to see the Explorer accelerate out of sight.

"Now where does she think she's going?" Riley muttered, walking through the front entrance. "She could've waited for me before she parked." Her stomach dropped when the vehicle swung onto the highway towards the airport. Two facts belatedly presented themselves.

First, there was no way Mattie could have exited the passenger's side and walked to the driver's side without catching Riley's attention. And second, there was no way Mattie could have crawled over to the driver's side, not with her prosthesis.

Which meant some asshole had just carjacked the Explorer and kidnapped Mattie. Riley spun around and ran into the lobby.

"Hey! Call the cops! My car has just been stolen and my friend has been kidnapped!" she yelled at the front desk clerk. The twenties-something kid behind the counter picked up the phone, a look of disbelief on his face.

"Let me talk to them," Riley held out her hand. The kid handed over the receiver.

"I need to report a carjacking and a kidnapping." Riley couldn't pace because of the corded phone. These people seriously needed to upgrade to the twenty-first century. She gave the license number, make and model of Mattie's car, then a detailed description of Mattie.

"Did you leave the car running when you went in to make reservations?" asked the dispatcher.

"I did, but I told Mattie to lock the doors. She was wet and I wanted to keep the heater going," Riley admitted, thinking the lady was asking questions that really needed to be asked by responding officers. "When can you get a unit out here?"

"Well, ma'am," the woman on the other end drawled. "Probably forty-five minutes or so."

Riley clenched her fist and barely controlled the urge to pound the counter. "Can't you get someone out here sooner?"

"I'm sorry, ma'am, but all our units are out on calls. We've had some nasty vehicle collisions in this weather."

Riley felt her face heat and glanced at the desk clerk who backed up until he stood ramrod straight against the wall. He looked like he was facing a firing squad. Riley took several deep breaths and managed to control the urge to start throwing things.

"I understand," she choked out. "Please get someone out here ASAP." She handed the receiver to the clerk.

"Hi, Wanda," he spoke into the phone. His wide brown eyes glanced at Riley then away again. His thin brown hair brushed the collar of his white hotel Polo shirt. Wanda must have said something less than complimentary about Riley because his already red face turned a deep crimson. "Aw, Wanda, knock it off. Just tell the Sergeant to get himself out here as soon as he can." He hung up and turned to Riley. "Ma'am, I can offer you a free room for the night if that would help things."

"Has this happened before?" Riley forced her voice to a normal level, while her insides felt like molten lava.

"Well, most of what we get are cars broken into or stolen from the lot," he confessed.

"Where's your security personnel?" Riley barely avoided spitting the words out. "I want a car. At least I could go after them."

"Um, well, he went into town to get take-out." His face turned scarlet again.

Riley stared at the kid. "I don't believe this," she spat, whipping from the counter and pacing the lobby. Her cell phone rang, and she dug it out of her jeans pocket. It was Aiden.

"Hey, Bro, we've got a problem," Riley answered as she paced back and forth.

"What's up, Little One?" Aiden reserved the term for tense situations. He knew something was wrong.

"Got my vibes, did you?" Riley walked through the front entrance and stood in the cool night air. Rain drummed steadily on the covered entryway.

"If that's what you want to call it," Aiden replied.

They had been connected since grade school. Aiden scoffed at the term telepathic whenever she mentioned it but had never actually argued the point. While what they experienced was not true telepathy, both of them demonstrated a unique ability to sense when the other was in distress. Riley felt his calm through the cell and inhaled deeply before continuing.

"Someone carjacked Mattie's Explorer and took off with her in it. Right in front of the hotel when I went in to get a room." Briefly she told him about the cancelled flight and their decision to spend the night locally.

"How long before local cops get there?" he asked.

"Probably an hour," Riley groaned. "We're talking Tennessee hills out here. I feel like I've been dropped into *Deliverance.*"

"Well, if you hear banjo picking, get the hell out of there," Aiden advised. "Have you talked to hotel security?"

"He's out getting dinner." Riley slumped onto one of the hotel benches. The cold and dampness seeped through her layers and she shivered.

"What about surveillance cameras?"

Riley jerked her head up to the ceiling of the covered entryway and spotted a security camera in the far corner.

"Damn. I should've thought of that." She jumped up and ran through the doors to the check-in counter.

"Any news from Wanda on how far away the cops are?" she asked the clerk, keeping her cell phone clamped against her ear.

The kid's face turned red again. "She said they're on another accident call. Big interstate pile-up. It's going to be a while."

Riley felt frustration winning over her control. "For a frickin' carjacking and kidnapping?"

He backed away from the counter. "It always takes them forever to get out here."

"Surveillance cameras," Aiden repeated, hearing his sister's agitation and figuring he needed to intervene before blood started gushing. Normally she was rock solid during a crisis. Hearing her almost frantic told him a lot.

Riley heaved a deep, calming breath, and pulled her badge from her hip pocket. "I'm a Virginia cop. I need to see the footage from the front entrance security camera."

The desk clerk nodded.

"Hey, Little One. Pull in your fangs and ask him his name. Mauling the help isn't going to get Mattie back any faster," Aiden suggested.

"It would make me feel better," Riley growled as she followed the clerk to a small room behind the counter. "These guys belong on America's Most Inept."

"I imagine they have a huge amount of territory to cover and a very small man count to handle it," Aiden observed. "Active calls are going to take priority over ours, regardless of how we feel about it. You haven't asked the kid his name. Put on your happy face and be nice."

The room held several security screens with poor resolution black-and-white images.

"It would be this one," the kid said, pointing to the bottom row of screens, the furthest screen to the left.

Riley swallowed her irritation. "Uh, thanks, um…."

"Jimmy." The kid sat down in the empty seat. Riley fumed over the absent security guard.

"No one in the security room to monitor the screens," Riley told Aiden.

"Not to say having someone there would've sped things up," her brother countered.

"You're not helping, Bro," she seethed.

"Yes, I am, Little One," he soothed.

"Security personnel would've seen the activity on the screen and would've been on the horn." Riley watched Jimmy rewind the VHS machine. "Lord, Aiden, these people are stuck in the dinosaur age. Corded phones. VHS security machines. What next? We need speed and modern equipment here."

"Remember, don't maul the help," Aiden repeated.

"Every minute counts and you know it," she snapped.

"And you know the number of calls we've answered where the security guard on duty was either snoring or stinking drunk," Aiden reminded her.

Riley growled again and watched the images moving in reverse.

"Hold it!" she ordered when the Explorer backed into the screen and a lone figure backtracked into the surrounding darkness. Jimmy reset the video, and Riley watched as Jeremiah Tyler appeared from the rain, looked straight into the camera, then slipped into the driver's side of the Explorer.

"Damn. Damn, damn, damn." Her stomach clenched as she cursed into her phone. "It was Tyler." She gripped the cell until her fingers hurt.

"Doesn't surprise me," Aiden sighed on the other end.

Riley wanted to spit nails. "Looked straight into the camera before he hopped in and took off with Mattie."

"What direction did he go?" Aiden asked as Riley stalked into the front lobby and began pacing again.

"Towards the airport. And I'm stuck here unless I call a cab or wait for the frickin' local cops to show up. Either way is allowing Tyler to put a lot of miles between me and him right now." Riley stopped mid-stride and turned to Jimmy, who was behind the desk again.

"Hey, Jimmy. Do you guys have shuttle service to the airport?"

"Good thinking," Aiden told her.

Jimmy nodded. "But the driver's gone home for the night."

"Okay. But what about the keys?"

"Hold on." He started opening drawers. "I think there's a spare set of keys around here somewhere."

"I'm on the Interstate heading your way. Don't leave town without me," Aiden advised as Riley strode to the front desk and drummed her fingers on the counter.

"Okay, well hurry up. I'm not promising anything." Riley held her hand out when the desk clerk kid came up with a key. He dropped it into her palm, and she spun towards the front entrance.

"We'll get her back in one piece, Little One." Aiden's voice held confidence.

"I'm first in line to kick Tyler's ass to hell and back," Riley snapped. She cut the call and ran through the doors. Spotting a hotel shuttle bus to her left, she jogged through the rain and pointed the fob at the van. The lights blinked, and she jerked open the driver's door and jumped in, started the van, and headed for the highway.

As she drove to the airport, Riley tried to put herself into Tyler's shoes. How would he have followed them? How had he known which hotel they chose? Why had he taken off towards the airport? She punched Aiden's number and put her phone on speaker.

"Hey," she said when he picked up. "Are you close to a computer?"

"I'm on the Interstate," he reminded her.

"Damn. I need to find out whether Tyler was on one of the flights that got to Tri-Cities before they shut things down."

"Does that matter?" her brother asked.

"Of course it matters, Dork Head," she retorted as she turned the wipers to high. The rain fell in heavy sheets, obliterating visibility. "If he flew in, he needed ground transportation. If he didn't fly in, that means he had his own transportation and possibly followed us from town."

"Check the car rental building," Aiden told her. "We might get lucky."

"Do you think he bugged the house?" Riley asked. She spotted the airport sign and turned.

"You and I both checked the house. If he left some kind of device, we both missed it."

Riley heard her brother's unspoken thoughts. "He's good," she muttered.

"Yes, he is," Aiden agreed with reluctance.

Riley cut the call when she spotted a small building to one side of the terminal. She parked, then jogged through the rain to the entrance. The front desk was reluctant to offer assistance until she flashed her badge. The supervisor, a man in his fifties, wore a red Polo shirt and tan slacks.

"Russ," he said as an introduction, extending his hand. Riley shook it and noticed his sweaty palm.

"I need to look at your security camera footage," she told him.

"What's this all about?" he asked, not moving.

"We've had a kidnapping at the hotel a couple of miles down the road. We caught the suspect's image on the hotel security, and now I'm assisting local law enforcement with running down any possible leads, including whether he might have followed her from the airport. I need to see your security footage and every rental agreement you've processed today."

Russ nodded. "Follow me." He waved her around the desk and into a back room.

"What time was the kidnapping?" he asked as the security guy began reviewing the digital footage of that afternoon.

Ignoring his question, Riley stared at the images, then shook her head. "Is that all of the footage from today? Including early this morning?" The security guy punched the computer keyboard. Riley felt her heart sink when no image of Tyler appeared. "What about yesterday?" she suggested. The security guy complied, and she stared at the screen, willing for Tyler to appear. She practically jumped when his image popped up. "That's him!" She turned to Russ. "I need the paperwork and description of the car he rented."

"Sure thing," he answered. "Want anything while you wait? Some coffee maybe?" He looked at Riley's wet clothes. "It's been pouring all day."

"Thanks, but no." Riley shook her head.

The time spent running down the car Tyler rented meant more miles between herself and Mattie. Riley fought the urge to bite her nails when she climbed into the shuttle and pointed it towards the hotel. She phoned her brother again.

"How far away are you?" she asked when he answered.

"About thirty minutes. Do you want to meet me at the airport or at the hotel?" he responded.

"The hotel. It's a couple of miles past the turn off into the airport," Riley said as she drove through the rain. "Be careful, Bro. Don't wrap yourself around a tree."

An unmarked police cruiser parked beneath the covered hotel entrance when she arrived. She eased the shuttle into its original slot, then sprinted through the rain to the entryway. Two officers waited in the hotel lobby. They were about the same height and weight, looked middle-aged, and had military haircuts. One was blonde with brown eyes, the other had brown hair and eyes. Riley strode across the tiled floor.

"Hi, I'm Officer Riley Butler," she said pulling out her badge.

"Officer Doug Jones," the blonde officer greeted. "And this is Officer Gary Miller." He squinted at her credentials.

"Virginia, eh?" He glanced at her, his eyes scanning her face, then doing a once over assessment of the rest of her. "What brings you to these parts?" He had no notepad, did not seem in a hurry to start running down the issue at hand.

"Jimmy said you used the shuttle to backtrack to the airport car rental," Miller interjected, extending his hand. A notepad and pen occupied his other. "We've contacted the local FBI office, and they're sending someone over. Jimmy said you recognized the suspect?"

Riley gripped his hand and knew from a glance at his eyes that Miller didn't miss much. He would be the brains behind the questions. "Yeah. Jeremiah Tyler, her soon-to-be ex-husband. He's wanted in Oklahoma in connection with possible terrorist activity and several murders. And he's got a restraining order against him, which he ignored when he showed up Friday at her house."

"We've located the stolen vehicle," he continued, referencing his notepad. "Looks like he dumped it about a mile north of here, which means he probably had another car waiting."

"He rented a car at the airport. Tyler probably switched vehicles." Riley gave him the description. Miller tilted his head to the radio clipped to his uniform and relayed the information to dispatch. Riley felt herself relax a tiny bit. At least now there were eyes all over the area looking for the rental car.

"Did you say husband?" Jones interrupted.

Riley nodded. "Soon to be ex-husband, but yes."

"So how do we know his wife isn't in on this? She could have agreed to go with him." He looked at his partner, then Riley.

Riley stared back. "Are you being serious?"

Miller paused in jotting notes. "It's a possibility we must consider. You know that."

Riley blew out a slow breath. "Yes, I realize in some cases that might be a possibility. I can assure you it's not in this case."

Jones wasn't ready to concede. "She's an adult. It could be a joint plan they cooked up between them." He inhaled, his chest expanding. "You said yourself he rented a car at the airport. They may have taken off on a trip to try to patch things up."

"We found a purse with a wallet and cell phone," Miller continued after a long hesitation. Obviously, something was bothering him.

Riley winced. "What about the luggage in the back of the car?"

Miller shook his head. "No luggage."

She frowned. "That's not good. Taking our luggage and leaving her purse means she now has no ID and no way for us to track her via GPS." She inhaled and shifted her feet. "It also means we have another problem."

Miller looked up from his notes.

Riley's expression was grim. "I packed my off-duty weapon in a locked hard case in my luggage. If he's taken all the luggage, that means he now has a Glock and more than enough ammunition to put lots of holes into anyone who tries to confront him."

"Taking all the luggage?" Jones interjected. "If he was kidnapping the woman, he wouldn't want to be bogged down with luggage." He shook his head. "This is looking less like a kidnapping and more like an anniversary elopement."

Miller looked from Riley to Jones and back again. "My partner has a point. If the suspect is the woman's husband, maybe this isn't a kidnapping."

Riley swallowed her agitation. "He's her husband." She paused, waited until both cops looked at her, then added, "And there's a restraining order against him. He's part of the reason why she's missing her right leg."

Miller's eyes dropped back to his notes. "Any idea what direction the suspect might have taken?"

Riley frowned. "No," she admitted. "Since you found the Explorer between here and the airport, I've no idea."

Miller nodded. "We've got three Interstates and a mess of state highways to try to cover."

"And he's gotten a great head start," Riley turned when her brother strode through the automatic front doors. Aiden had changed into jeans, T-shirt, and a black leather jacket. Riley waved him over and made introductions. "My brother, Officer Aiden Butler."

The three men shook hands, then Riley brought him up to date on the information they had.

"Any idea when the Feds will show up?" Aiden asked.

Jones shook his head. "We're having homeland security issues in the area, in addition to a slew of collisions on the interstate. I'll put the call in, but no telling when they'll send an agent over." He looked at them. "It would be helpful if you could stay in the area overnight for an interview."

"It's too messy to drive home anyway," Aiden agreed.

"We'll keep you updated on anything that develops," Miller said. The two local cops turned and left through the automatic doors. A few minutes later their police cruiser disappeared into the darkness.

Riley slumped into an upholstered lobby chair and ran a hand over her damp hair. "I can't believe I let this happen."

"Park it there, Sis. I'll get us a room." Aiden walked to the check-in counter.

Jimmy, still behind the desk, attempted a smile that looked more like a pained grimace. "I've got a suite," he said, looking at the computer screen. "On the house. I feel really bad about what's happened. Our security guy isn't back yet, but I'll tell him. I'll take it up with management, too. See if I can get better security coverage out of this."

"Did you hear that?" Aiden asked his sister after making the arrangements and walking back to a lobby chair.

"Yeah. Makes me feel oh so much better." She rolled her eyes. "Hey. Any update on the investigation into Randy's death?" She checked her watch. "Wow, it's ten p.m. How time flies when disaster strikes."

"Got some interesting developments I'll tell you about later." Aiden sighed and relaxed into the cushioned upholstery, stretching his long legs in front of him.

"I'm waiting," Riley frowned.

Aiden shook his head. "Not now."

"Why don't we just go up to the room where we can talk?" Riley drummed her fingers on the arms of the chair.

Aiden heaved a sigh and slowly got to his feet. "God, you're a pain in the ass."

They rode the elevator to the third floor, found their room. A spacious sitting room with heavily padded chairs, a small sofa, coffee table and a work station greeted them. Doors led to two bedrooms with matching baths.

Aiden slid out of his shoes and collapsed into a deep armchair. "Ballistics showed it was probably a forty-caliber round. The guy used a hollow point, so there wasn't enough bullet left to do anything with."

"Well, that's just peachy." Riley felt her mood sink down around her ankles as she slumped into an armchair.

"In other news," Aiden continued, "CSI found tire tracks off the road in the vicinity where Mattie's horse left tracks on the trail."

"And...?" Riley prompted.

He grinned. "And, they matched a set found in the dirt turn in at the stables before the gravel starts."

Riley straightened. "Really?"

Aiden nodded, a tired expression on his face.

"That's a lot of coincidence," Riley mused, her expression

thoughtful.

"Maybe," her brother yawned. "We might get a break with the tire tracks. Lab called me when I was on my way down to meet you. The tires are specialty."

"Which narrows things down," Riley muttered.

"Yeah, well, I wouldn't put too much hope on finding them signed with a note saying, 'I went this way'. Then again, you never know what might turn up." Aiden stopped. An unsettled silence fell between them.

"What else?" Riley prompted.

Aiden inhaled. "Jilly's refusing to let us talk to Amy."

Riley felt her insides coil. "Well, that's not surprising. Both are devastated over Randy's death."

Aiden brown eyes studied his sister. "And how are you holding up?"

"Riley straightened in her seat. "I'm fine."

Aiden nodded. "Like hell you are. I've never seen you lose your cool like you did tonight."

"I told you I'm fine," Riley repeated, her expression closed.

"Remember the meaning of 'F.I.N.E.'? I can't remember the movie, but it describes you right now. 'Freaked out, Insecure, Neurotic, and Emotional.' I think that was it."

"You're quoting *Italian Job*? At a time like this?" Riley ran a hand roughly through her short hair. "Lot of help you are, Dork Head."

Aiden shrugged out of his wet jacket, took off his socks, and wiggled his toes. "You like Mattie. A lot."

Riley sniffed. "That goes for both of us."

"True. But you really wanted her and Randy to connect."

Ignoring his comment, Riley stood and began pacing the room. "Do you think Tyler's involved with Randy's murder?"

"I don't know," he sighed, rubbing a hand over his face. Riley noticed the deep circles beneath his eyes.

"What I'd give to go back in time. I'll never leave keys in a car ever again." She resumed pacing.

Aiden tried but failed to suppress another yawn. "I don't believe in coincidence."

Riley stopped and regarded him. "Yeah, me neither. You're exhausted. I'm exhausted. Let's get some sleep. Things will look better in the morning."

Aiden's eyes opened wide. "Is this common sense I'm hearing coming out of your mouth? Who are you, and what have you done with Riley?"

"Oh, go to hell." Riley wriggled her feet from her boots and then padded sock-footed to one of the bedrooms.

Chapter Thirteen

By midafternoon Tuesday my butt felt permanently glued to the car seat, my stump hurt from the cramped conditions, and my mood resembled the wall cloud of an EF-five tornado.

"Tell me again why you are so bent on making it to the Parsons' house in Norman?" I asked him, though we'd been through this conversation already.

"Bill Parsons has been my handler since my move to Oklahoma." Jeremiah squirmed in his seat, obviously uncomfortable with having to repeat yet another facet of his life which he had lied about for the duration of our marriage.

"And this was before or after we got married?" I pressed, enjoying his discomfort.

Jeremiah frowned. "Before."

"And now you're heading to his house so you can dump this cracker box into his lap?" I waved a hand at the crappy inside of the Honda.

"He will be able to…dispose of this vehicle and provide me with a new set of wheels." Jeremiah's eyes darted between the rearview mirror and the two-lane highway in front of us. We had crossed the Oklahoma/Arkansas border. Lines of fatigue creased his face, but I felt no sympathy.

"I still can't believe they're not dead," I admitted. "I thought they died when their house exploded."

"Hawk got them to safety before the house blew," Jeremiah told me as the little car ate up the miles. His words triggered a deep memory and a face almost surfaced through the fog in my brain.

"Hawk," I murmured to myself. I frowned at Jeremiah. "Doesn't he have some sort of accent?"

Jeremiah's eyebrows quirked. "You do not remember Hawk?"

"No." I shook my head, but a part of my subconscious did because a surge of raw terror shuddered through me. I thought again about the voice I overheard on the Parkway.

"Hawk is British." Jeremiah flicked his eyes at me, then back to the road.

British. I corralled my wandering thoughts, closed my eyes, and focused on what I remembered. The accent I had heard was European for sure. I just couldn't recall the sounds of the words clearly enough to decide whether the killer's accent had been British. Another irrepressible tremor rocked through me.

"Some part of you remembers him," Jeremiah murmured when I crossed my arms to control my sudden shivering.

"I'm glad Bill and Becky are alive," I said, changing subjects, "and Mud Rain." I thought over Jeremiah's earlier comments. "So, Bill is your…." I stopped.

"Handler," he supplied.

"Does Becky know what he does? And is Mud Rain still with them?" My train of thought jumped tracks faster than I could keep up. I wasn't sure I was making any sense.

Jeremiah wriggled around in his seat again and ran a hand through his hair, which he had tied into a ponytail. "Yes," he finally acknowledged.

"Yes, what?" I pressed.

Jeremiah clarified. "Yes, Mud Rain still lives with the Parsons. And yes, Becky is aware of what Bill does."

"And yet you didn't think it appropriate to let me in on this side of your life?" I challenged.

Jeremiah's eyes narrowed, his jaw clenched, and the corners of his mouth tightened. "What I omitted telling you I did because I was trying to protect you from harm."

I jumped on his admission. "If ignorance is so safe, why did Bill tell his wife about his ulterior lifestyle?"

"That would be between Bill and Becky."

I was treading potentially dangerous ground but jumped in with my next comment anyway. "Is that why you dumped Mud Rain on my parents, then on the Parsons? Because you never knew when you'd be off doing something for God and Country?"

A faint flush tinged Jeremiah's prominent cheekbones. "I did not dump my younger brother off and you know it."

"What I *know*," I retorted, emphasizing the last word, "is a far cry from the truth, and *you* know it."

Jeremiah's jaw clenched again. "Your parents and the Parsons had access to interventions and programs that have helped my brother enormously in his progress." His eyes locked with mine before turning his attention back to the road. "Our lives were in too much turmoil when I moved him off the Rez. You were working on establishing a photojournalist career, I was trying to get my foot in the door at the Boulder Forecast Office."

"And running around on missions I knew nothing about." I snapped my head to stare out the window. Silence fell between us, as gentle rolling hills of eastern Oklahoma slid by and warm autumn afternoon sun bathed the inside of the car. Silence fell as our conversation lapsed. I stared through the window and watched rolling hills gradually succumb to flat mid-western prairie.

Insight dawned and I turned back to him. "Did Bill help you track me down?"

Jeremiah's eyes flickered in my direction before answering. "Yes."

"Did he know about the restraining order against you?" I frowned.

"Yes."

I glared at him. "Stop it with the monosyllabic answers. You did more than enough of that during our seven-odd years of marriage."

Jeremiah sighed. "Bill has impressive connections with all sides of government and various law enforcement agencies, which helped him track you down. And when I explained the murder at the stables, he agreed I should get you out of there as soon as possible. We both have more resources than local law enforcement to keep you safe." His eyes cut to mine. "Including those two assigned to you."

"You're only saying that because you want to control me." I swung my eyes to stare through the passenger window again. "Everyone is trying to control me, even Riley. None of you seem to believe I can take care of myself."

"Your disadvantage…." The minute the words left his mouth, Jeremiah's mouth snapped shut.

I clenched my teeth so hard I felt my jaw pop. "A disadvantage I've managed not only to cope with but has not stopped me from doing whatever I want to," I seethed. "And I would not have broken any laws in the process, while you've managed to break a restraining order and commit two felonies, all in one day. I wouldn't call that exactly *protecting* me." I felt like our conversation bordered on something from the Twilight Zone. "And now you're heading to friends I'm finding out are a lot more than *friends*." I ran a hand through my hair. "Did Mom and Dad know Bill Parsons was your...handler?"

The corners of Jeremiah's mouth tightened. "No."

"So, you lied to them, too." I rubbed my forehead with my thumb and forefinger and felt the beginnings of a headache. "I don't believe this," I muttered. I thought about Bill and Becky Parsons, friends of my family as far back as I could remember. Our families had gone to church together every Sunday, sat and listened to Preacher Pat's stories about his Irish upbringing. Bill and my Dad discussed music, sermons, and O.U. athletics with irrepressible fervor.

I vaguely remembered Stephen being present during some of those visits with my Dad and the Parsons. Bill and Becky had a son who had grown up in his mother's footsteps and now worked in the Norman O.U. campus weather center. I remembered Angela and me running around our backyard with Dale. I hadn't cared what Bill did then, and as the years passed, I assumed he was somehow involved with the national weather station the same as his wife and son.

"Bill and Becky rebuilt," I mused aloud, seeking a change in subject to something less bizarre.

"Yes." Jeremiah inhaled and his face relaxed, no doubt relieved, because he elaborated. "They rebuilt on their property, and Bill got the large entertainment room he always wanted, complete with more O.U. paraphernalia than you can imagine."

"I remember he always had some O.U. sport on whenever we visited their house," I smiled. Bill was a small, rotund little man approaching his sixties with a shiny bald scalp and a jolly laugh like Santa. I remembered Becky as petite with snow-white short, wavy hair, a soft southern accent, and genteel manners.

"How is Mud Rain?" I asked, thinking of Jeremiah's younger brother. He would be around sixteen now, although he had never grown beyond the size of a middle-school youth. His facial features resembled Jeremiah strongly despite the effects of the Downs Syndrome.

"He is finishing sixth grade level material and still is in the therapeutic riding program." Jeremiah reached the outskirts of Oklahoma City and turned south onto a broad, mostly straight boulevard. The man had managed to negotiate an impressive number of back highways without once consulting a map.

"I wonder if that's why Stephen insisted I start a therapeutic riding program after I moved to Virginia." I stared out the window at buildings and businesses that looked strangely familiar.

Jeremiah nodded, then glanced at me again. "You are aware Stephen refused to allow anyone to visit you in the hospital or during your rehab?"

I shrugged. "I asked him about that, about why no one ever came to visit me. He said my family was killed in the crash that caused me to lose my leg. He evaded the question when I asked him about friends."

Jeremiah continued. "He feared we might still be under surveillance. Bill and Becky both desperately wanted to be a part of your recovery. They kept current with your progress through Stephen."

I sighed. "Which is probably how Bill told you where I was."

To his credit, Jeremiah winced. "Yes. Stephen was not pleased."

My lips curled. "I bet he wasn't."

Memory cleared and I recalled the small black pony Mud Rain rode every week. "Does Mud Rain still ride?" I asked. "Twister, I think. Was that his favorite pony's name?"

Jeremiah's expression relaxed. "Yes. Mud Rain will be happy to see you. He has asked about you constantly since you have been away."

The afternoon sun lengthened into golden rays as we reached the outskirts of the college town. Fall colors dressed foliage in magnificent reds, oranges, yellows, rich browns and greens—a brilliant show of beauty before winter prairie winds wiped branches clean. Streets looked pristine; the passing residential neighborhoods could have been scenes from a Kincaid painting.

"This is almost as pretty as the Blue Ridge Mountains this time of year," I murmured, staring out the window as we drove through town. Thoughts of what I considered home now spurred a pang of regret. "I miss my Twister. And he's going to be missing me." Thoughts of my horse triggered other memories, painful realities. "I wonder how Amy is doing." My eyes watered and I stared blankly at the passing scenery. "And if they've made any progress with…with…."

…with Randy's death.

I squeezed my eyes shut as a heavy, painful weight crushed my chest.

Randy. The ring box. If only I hadn't ridden out on that stupid trail.

Jeremiah turned down a broad boulevard, then slowed and took a right that brought us to a gated community. Impressive houses on acre sized lots filed by. He pulled into a wide tarmac driveway and rolled to a gentle stop in front of a garage the size of a three-bedroom home.

"Stay put." Angling out of the Honda, he walked over to the garage door and punched a code into the keypad. The door rose, revealing an empty bay big enough to store an eighteen-wheeler or one of those recreational busses. Maybe even a small plane.

Jeremiah slid behind the wheel again and pulled the Honda into the garage.

"I don't remember their house looking like this," I frowned.

"I told you. They rebuilt after the explosion." Motioning for me to get out, Jeremiah stood and stretched. A door at the far end of the garage swung inward and a small rotund bald middle-aged man appeared. He wore jeans and an O.U. sweatshirt. A smile threatened to split his face.

"Mattie. Oh, my goodness, it's good to see you." Bill Parsons scurried across the bay, helped me from the Honda, then wrapped me in a hug that squeezed the breath right out of my lungs. He ran around the Honda to Jeremiah, and despite the fact he barely reached the taller man's chest, wrapped his arms around him in the same ferocious hug. He stepped back and waved at the Honda. I watched him, and regardless of the numerous reassurances from Jeremiah during the drive, felt shock and disbelief he was obviously alive and well, which meant Becky and Mud Rain were alive and well, too.

"Another one of your under-the-table acquisitions?" he grinned at Jeremiah.

Jeremiah nodded. "Not sure how hot it is. I left a rental, hoping the owner will take the swap and delay reporting the theft."

Bill walked around the Honda, his light blue eyes scrutinizing every rusty detail. "I'll run it down, find out whether it's on any lists, then decide what to do."

I gaped at the two men. Jeremiah strode to the controls beside the garage door, and the colossal door slid quietly down. Bill motioned for me to precede him through the side door. I retrieved my cane from the back seat of the car but didn't move.

"From your expression, I gather Jeremiah has filled you in," he smiled. "You're exhausted, hungry, and no doubt overwhelmed by a lot of new and probably shocking information."

I shook my head in disbelief. "How in the world are you still alive?" I pressed my free hand to the side of my head. "I saw your house blow up!"

Bill walked over and patted my shoulder affectionately. "I told Becky Jeremiah and you were on your way. She came home early so she would be here when the two of you arrived."

"Jeremiah told you his plans?" I waved a hand at the Honda. "And does this mean you knew Jeremiah was going to…to…."

"To violate a restraining order, abscond with you, and hot foot it out here in a stolen car?" Bill smiled, finishing my thoughts. "Well, yes. He contacted me late Sunday night." He sidled over to the side door and rested a hand on the knob. "We'll be more comfortable if we take this conversation inside," he suggested, looking slightly embarrassed.

I shook my head. "You helped him track down my location knowing full well about the restraining order." I rubbed my forehead and felt my headache getting worse. Life would be so much simpler if I had not regained my memory.

"Mattie, you're exhausted. Let's go inside where it's warm, get something to eat, and talk all of this over," Bill repeated, throwing a worried look at Jeremiah.

I scowled at the two men. "I want answers before the FBI shows up on your doorstep, which I'm sure is going to happen sooner than later."

Bill's round cherub face assumed an expression of mischievous innocence. "They already have."

I felt my jaw drop. "The FBI have been here?" I looked at Jeremiah, who remained motionless beside the closed garage door, an unreadable expression on his face. I snapped my mouth closed and glared at Bill. "No wonder you're looking like the cat who just ate the canary." I rubbed my forehead again. "I wish someone would start talking sense."

Jeremiah walked over to stand between Bill and me. "Did they follow their usual surveillance routine?"

"Of course," Bill nodded. "And I followed my usual routine of interference with said surveillance when I knew you were close." He looked at me with his wide, clear blue eyes. The overhead lights reflected off his shiny white scalp. "According to their camera views, no cars have come or gone except Becky's, and there are at least four agents currently heading towards the Southern Ute Reservation, where I told them the two of you were probably going."

"Did they talk to Mud Rain?" Jeremiah asked.

Bill nodded again. "But he couldn't tell them much." He turned to me. "Becky is dying to see both of you. She's been worried sick ever since Stephen relocated you to Virginia. Would you mind terribly if we continue this conversation inside?"

Without waiting for an answer this time, he turned and led the way through the side door. Jeremiah followed.

I was feeling more than a little stupid. Over the years most of my interactions had been with Becky, Jeremiah, and Mud Rain. I had taken everyone at face value. Bill and Becky lived in an upper-class neighborhood, they went to church on Sundays, they had been friends with my parents for decades. Jeremiah worked at the O.U. campus weather station, had been polite and supportive, had never shown any inkling of ever having done anything underhanded or suspicious.

"It seems like I really don't know any of you," I muttered as we entered the main house. We passed through a large mud room into a massive recreation room joining the kitchen. Comfortable crimson and cream, overstuffed furniture faced a theater-sized flat screen television mounted on the wall opposite the open kitchen. Pictures of O.U. football and basketball players lined the brown stone walls, O.U. blankets and throws lay on every chair, O.U. trashcans occupied corners. Floor-to-ceiling picture windows at one end offered a view of the surrounding trees on the large grounds.

Becky, dressed in a red O.U. sweatshirt and blue jeans, scurried around the corner of the large cooking island and ran to me.

"Oh, Mattie, you're here." Though I stood significantly taller, she stood on tiptoe, threw her arms around my neck, and hugged me so hard I leaned heavily on my cane to keep from toppling backwards. Her short white hair and clear blue eyes brought a surge of emotion so intense tears slipped down my cheeks, and I hugged her back. I could not remember the last time I had seen either Bill or her, but I did remember them being with me after my parents' funeral.

Before I could ask her anything about what Bill and Jeremiah had been explaining in the garage, a small dark-haired boy ambled slowly from one of the hallways. He dressed in basketball shorts and a red short sleeved O.U. T-shirt. His bare feet padded across the hardwood floor.

"Miah! Miah!" He rushed over to Jeremiah, who knelt down, wrapped his arms around the boy, and swept him up despite his size.

"Missed me?" he asked, ruffling the youth's hair. Mud Rain threw his arms around Jeremiah's neck and hugged him. When Jeremiah set him down, Mud Rain walked to where Becky stood and looked at me.

"Maddie?" His voice sounded tentative, and he stopped several paces away. Becky turned around.

"Mud Rain, do you remember Mattie?" She held her hand to towards the boy, and he took a hesitant step forward.

The sight of Mud Rain slammed another avalanche of memories into my vision. Memories of trips with him and Jeremiah to the Southern Ute Reservation, his uncontrollable enjoyment at the annual Bear Dance Ceremony each spring. The look on his face the first time he sat on one of the therapeutic riding horses at a local stable. With a hard twist of my gut I remembered how horribly weak he had been when he first started riding. I even remembered the small brown pony he became attached to. I dragged my eyes from Mud Rain and stared at Becky. "Did you know I was in a therapeutic riding program in Virginia?"

She nodded, hugging Mud Rain close to her side.

"Did…did you tell Stephen about Mud Rain's therapeutic riding?" I pressed.

Becky nodded again, tears dampening her face. "Yes. We talked a lot while you were in the hospital and in rehab."

I lifted my hands. "I really wish Stephen had let you and Bill come to visit. I might have gotten over my amnesia sooner. Seeing the two of you and seeing Mud Rain would have helped my recovery. I know he was trying to protect me; Jeremiah keeps telling me that, but I feel like I've lost so much time because I was kept in the dark."

Bill joined his wife and slid an arm around her waist. I looked around for Jeremiah, but he had left the room.

"We tried, Mattie," he explained, his light blue eyes damp. "Please believe me when I say we tried to become involved with your recovery. But Stephen was afraid of who might still be after you. He and I both worried our activity might be under surveillance, and our priority was to get you out of harm's way. As difficult a decision as it was, Becky and I agreed to stay away. We've been getting updates on your progress and hoped when you regained your memory you would come back to us."

My eyes drifted to Mud Rain. His T-shirt triggered another memory, this time of a dark cave, a small gurgling stream, gunshots, and terror beyond anything I had ever known. I shuddered and allowed the images to fade back into mental shadows.

"Hi, Mud Rain," I smiled into the silence. "I know I probably look different than the last time you saw me." For years, I wore my black curly hair short. Now it fell shoulder length and was almost completely gray. I figured I also looked thinner, not to mention the limp that would never go away.

He looked me up and down, then watched when I limped to the large couch and sat down. Bill and Becky disappeared into the kitchen.

"You have owie?" he asked, following and taking a seat at the opposite end. He clasped his small chubby hands together. His features displayed the classic characteristics of a Down Syndrome child. I remembered his mental capabilities significantly improved once Jeremiah relocated him to Norman and got him into several special-needs programs.

"I do," I nodded as I watched him. "It's my leg."

"I kiss it. Make it better." Mud Rain slid from the couch and walked over until he stood next to me. He leaned down and carefully kissed the knee of my prosthesis.

"Better now?" he asked, his eyes searching mine, his collar length black hair, nose and high cheekbones making his Ute heritage prominent despite the effects of his condition.

I nodded, too choked up to say anything.

"Do you still go to therapeutic riding?" I asked, groping for something familiar between us and struggling with the impact of so much recall in a way too short amount of time.

Mud Rain gave me a puzzled look and walked back to the far end of the couch. He scooted onto the crimson and cream cushions and clasped his hands together again, then looked at me.

"Do you still ride that brown pony?" I repeated, re-wording my question.

He grinned, lifted his arms and sat straight, then wiggled his hands and feet as though he was riding. "Giddy-yup," he laughed.

I smiled back, my mood lightening as I watched him. "What's your pony's name?"

Becky walked from the kitchen and sat in the armchair beside the couch. Her face looked wet, and I realized she had been crying. Mud Rain looked at her, his eyebrows furrowed as he struggled to put the words together. Becky nodded encouragingly. "Go ahead. Tell her, Mud Rain. Think about how the letters sound."

"Thisser…thwiss…thwi…Thwisser…" he worked through the word.

"Twister," Becky clarified.

I smiled and wiped at the tears that dampened my own face. "Well, guess what, Mud Rain? I've been riding a horse, too. And his name is Twister. He's all black, with a black mane and tail."

How ironic I had named my horse the same as Mud Rain's. Sub-conscious influence could be powerful indeed.

Mud Rain made riding motions again. "Giddy-yup, Th-thwisser." He looked at me and frowned, then shook his head. "No, not Thwisser."

"Not Twister?" I asked, trying to follow what he wanted to tell me.

Mud Rain scooted across the couch until he sat beside me. "Bwackie. Hiss name Bwackie." He grinned again, and I could see similarities between him and Jeremiah.

"Oh," I said, realizing what he meant. "I should call him 'Blackie'?" I chuckled when Mud Rain nodded. "Because he's black, right?"

"Are you hungry?" Becky asked. "It seems Jeremiah's gone straight to bed. I've made a casserole and fruit salad if you'd like to eat."

Mud Rain followed us to the kitchen, and I took a seat on a barstool along an expansive marble island. He wiggled onto the stool next to me and seemed content with the company.

"Where did Bill go?" I asked as Becky made a plate that disappeared beneath a mountain of food enough to feed Yeti himself. I caught a whiff of the aroma and thought my stomach would growl its way right through my abdomen. I dug in when she set the plate in front of me, along with a glass of ice water.

"Oh, he's in his office, probably making some calls." She took a seat beside me and took a sip from the glass of water she held.

"Is he really a…a handler?" I asked through a mouthful of food.

Becky's snow-white hair glinted in the overhead lighting. It took some time before she answered. "He's worked with Jeremiah for a long time." Sounding apologetic, she added, "Jeremiah's the only operative he works with now."

I saw the words coming from her mouth but could not reconcile their meaning.

Becky saw my confusion. "I know all of this sounds really strange, especially on top of regaining your memory. Try not to worry about it too much, at least for now," she said, leaning over and patting my hand. "I am so glad you and Jeremiah are back together, and I'm sure you'll want to talk to Stephen as soon as possible. I heard Bill on the phone with him earlier today, catching him up on where the two of you were."

I resisted the urge to tell Becky that Jeremiah and I were not back together and instead finished my plate and wondered whether I had strength enough to make it off the stool and into bed. I looked around for a clock, spotted one on the kitchen wall above the double oven. Seven p.m. It felt more like midnight.

"Mud Rain, you need to get ready for bed," Becky told him. "You have school tomorrow."

The boy scooted off his stool and disappeared down one of the many hallways. I stared after him and drummed up the courage for my next question. Turning and meeting Becky's clear blue eyes, I inhaled and took the plunge.

"Can I have my own room?" I hoped she wouldn't start asking questions I didn't want to answer.

Becky hesitated, her blue eyes locked with my green ones. After a long silence, she nodded.

"This way." She led the way along the hallway Mud Rain used earlier, then up a flight of stairs. "Take any of the rooms up here." She hesitated again, then pointed, "Jeremiah's in the one on the end."

"Thanks." I said goodnight, then slipped into the nearest bedroom. I didn't even bother to undress. Removing my prosthesis, I collapsed onto the soft down comforter and lost contact with the conscious world.

Chapter Fourteen

I crawled out of bed late Wednesday morning after a rare night of uninterrupted sleep. I fit my prosthesis on and limped into the adjoining bathroom, passing my suitcase which someone had left on a chair, a new pair of O.U. sweats draped across the closed top. After attending to Nature, I moved the sweats to the bed, opened my suitcase, and rummaged around for some clean underclothes, then opted for a bath so I wouldn't have to stand on one leg. I came out of the bathroom so wrinkled I could have passed as an overgrown prune, but I felt better than I had in days. I left my wet hair loose, wished for my wheelchair but realized the limitations Bill and Becky's house imposed, and coaxed my stump into the prosthesis after I put on the pair of freshly washed, crimson O.U. sweatpants and matching hooded sweatshirt Becky had no doubt bought for me late last night, probably from Walmart or another twenty-four-hour super-store. I grinned at hers and Bill's irrepressible Sooner spirit. Retrieving my cane, I ventured into the hallway.

The house felt cool, and I wondered what the weather was doing outside. Despite Oklahoma being significantly less humid and quite a bit warmer than Virginia, wind chill created by prairie winds drove desolate cold straight through one's bones.

I limped down the stairs and found Jeremiah at the kitchen counter, a large mug of black coffee in front of him. I glanced through floor-to-ceiling windows at trees thrashing about in a typical prairie windstorm. Clouds scuttled across the sky like so many fleeing ghosts.

"What happened to the sunshine we had yesterday?" I complained, looking around and spotting the coffeepot, which was empty and clean. I searched cabinets and found filters, then searched some more and found coffee.

"A low-pressure system from the Rockies," Jeremiah answered, watching me. "Those new?" He asked, referring to the sweats I wore.

I nodded. "No doubt a gift from Becky."

"You look good in them." He watched me over his cup as he drank.

A memory drifted through my inner eye, one of my mom and

Dad, their crimson and cream décor scattered around their estate, including their cars. I smiled wistfully, felt tears threaten, allowed the memory to slip back into my subconscious.

Jeremiah's next words spoiled the moment.

"I hoped we would sleep in the same bedroom. At least keep up appearances. Did you not know which room I was in?"

I retrieved a mug from one of the cherry wood cabinets and waited while the coffee brewed, filling the air with its earthy, comforting aroma. I poured some for myself, spotted cream and sugar nearby, and haphazardly doctored my coffee. Then I shuffled to the far end of the counter.

"Mattie…?" Jeremiah pressed.

"Becky told me which room you were in." I met his eyes, then reached over and retrieved creamer and sugar again, poured creamer in until my coffee looked like milk, then added an equally ridiculous amount of sugar. I needed the comfort of dairy fat and sweetness to get me through what I knew was going to be a tense conversation.

Jeremiah set his mug down and regarded me, his eyes expressionless. "We are still legally married."

I met his eyes, my expression honest and (I hoped) civil. "We might be according to the law, but we're not according to me. And in the end, that's what really counts." I drank my lukewarm concoction of creamer-slash-sugar-slash-coffee.

I'd spent a lot of the morning in bed thinking about Randy and the stupid reasons I had avoided intimacy. Imagining anyone seeing me naked completely turned me off, and in my heart of hearts I knew if anyone could get me over my self-image issue Randy could. I wanted to be in Virginia with his arms around me, hugging me close, filling me with warmth and safety. No one else would be able to replace him, and if Jeremiah didn't back off the whole *we're-still-married* mindset, I would have a serious melt-down.

I thought about the ring box tucked in the corner of my suitcase. I should open the damned thing and put on the ring. Maybe that would send a message strong enough to penetrate Jeremiah's thick skull.

I scowled. Despite my efforts, through the night memories of Jeremiah had crept to mind, creating a soul-shriveling aversion because I had been a whole person, at least physically, during our seven years together. Mind's eye did not create a viable image, and I shuddered to think what any man's expression might unintentionally reveal, despite claims of acceptance.

"You did not want me to see you without your prosthesis." Jeremiah stared at me, seeing straight into my thoughts.

I slapped my mug down on the counter. His bluntness shocked me, and I decided abruptly I'd had enough of his company. "Where are Becky and Bill?" I asked, hoping he would follow the change in subject.

"Mattie, do not feel self-conscious..." he started.

"Just drop it, okay?" I stood and took my still full cup to the sink, dumped the contents, then rinsed out my cup and set in down.

"Becky is running errands, Bill is in his office down that hallway," Jeremiah indicated with a nod of his head. "But I should warn you..."

"You don't need to warn me about anything," I barked and limped with my cane from the kitchen to the hallway Jeremiah indicated. I heard voices coming from the other side of a closed door, and without bothering to knock, I opened the door and stepped in.

"Mornin', Bill."

That was as far as I got.

The room was full of faces, but the face that froze my attention belonged to a man standing furthest from the doorway. His presence generated such an explosive surge of pure unadulterated hatred that I stumbled. The man's gray eyes locked on mine.

"I wanted to warn you that Hawk is here," Jeremiah muttered into my ear.

To this day I cannot explain my next actions. I don't even remember the course of events. But according to every other person in that room, I calmly walked across the space separating myself from the man I knew as Hawk...

...and abruptly whipped my cane up with both hands, catching him squarely between his legs with such force that he collapsed like a deflated balloon.

And then I walked out.

I found myself back in the kitchen, trembling so badly I thought I would fall right off the barstool I sat on. I hugged my chest with both arms and rested my forehead on the cold marble counter.

How dare they bring that man into this house! How dare they!

I wanted to run all the way back to Virginia. Right now. Screw the divorce papers. I would have Stephen fax them to me. Or mail them by FedEx.

"Mattie...?" a tentative voice whispered behind me. I rolled my forehead enough to glimpse Bill standing at my side.

"I can't believe you let that man in your house," I choked, turning away from him.

An older gentleman stepped beside me.

"Stand down, Warrior Woman." Humor laced his words. I blinked and lifted my head. The old man's gray braid trailed down his back, and he wore a long-sleeved red plaid shirt and jeans. He looked American Indian, but he did not look familiar. His words breathed calmness through me.

"Who are you?" I asked him.

"Just an old fart," he answered mildly. "You've got quite a swing. You should pick up golfing."

"Yeah, right." I lowered my forehead to the counter again. "Why don't the two of you just leave me alone."

The men did not move.

Sighing, I straightened and shook my head. "I suppose I have to go back to your office," I glared at Bill.

"I must insist," he murmured apologetically.

I slid off the stool, gripped my cane, and followed the two men. Limping through the door, I carefully avoided eye contact with the other occupants in the room. I spotted a couch along the wall furthest from the others and sat down.

"No one is looking for trouble, Mattie." Bill stood behind his desk, his voice calm, his expression neutral.

"Then why congregate the people who are responsible for what happened to me?" I challenged.

Bill shook his head. "You're misinterpreting things. I invited everyone here this morning because I want to get to the bottom of the murder that occurred at the stables where you ride. You've been off radar for almost two years. I don't like that someone's been killed right under your nose." He leaned his knuckles on the smooth top of the enormous oak desk. "It's too odd to be coincidence."

"Well, why don't you ask him?" I shot back, pointing an accusing finger at Jeremiah. "He's the one who led him to where I was!"

"Led who?" Jeremiah stared at me.

My hand shook badly as my finger drifted to the man now seated in a chair across the room.

"H-him," I stammered. "I h-heard him on the ridge. W-when he k-killed that man."

Silence dropped like a thick curtain.

Lowering my hand, I glared at Jeremiah, then at the other occupants in the room. "I was safe and secure until Jeremiah showed up. And the man on the ridge had an English accent. And two hours later, R-Randy..." I stopped, drew a deep breath to steady my voice, then continued. "Randy is found dead at the stables. Too damned much coincidence, if you ask me." My whole body stiffened with sudden resolve. "I'm going back to Virginia. I have a new life there, new memories."

With slow, deliberate motions Bill sat down behind his desk, his light blue eyes on me.

The ensuing conversation morphed into a buzz. Anger morphed into terror that scorched through me as I stared at the man with the gray eyes, and I gripped the cushions of the couch as I struggled to mentally talk myself off the emotional ledge.

The horrible man slowly turned his attention to Bill. "We've the same priority. We wish to protect Mattie." His voice sounded rough and abnormally high, and I imagined he was sitting because he could not yet stand. His gray eyes flickered towards me. "I expect you've been updated by the progress of the investigation?" He wheezed.

"Which is none of your business," I cut in, hearing my voice shake. "Especially since you're going to end up at the bottom of it."

Okay, not that I was making much sense, but I needed to keep the anger from being snuffed out by my fear.

The man shook his head. "It would be of benefit if we agree to work together, share information." His eyes locked on mine and I felt he could see every thought in my head. His British accent sent a fresh wave of hysteria surging through me with such force I began seeing stars and figured it was only a matter of time before I ended up in a puddle on the floor.

"Breathe, Mattie." The old Indian's voice broke the silence. "Bill, you got any brandy? That would go a long way to helping her feel better. If nothing else, it'll put color back into her cheeks. She looks about ready to join the spirit world."

"In there." Bill motioned towards a corner cabinet. The old man ambled over, found what he was looking for and poured some into a glass. He crossed the room, his black eyes on me. He nudged my arm with his elbow.

"Get a grip, Warrior Woman." His words cut through the fog in my brain. "No one's going to come near you except for me, and I'm just an old man."

He pressed my hands around a crystal tumbler half full of rich brown liquid. "And the name's Joe Healing Water, since from the look on your face you don't remember me," he muttered as an introduction. "Drink that before you fall over in a dead faint."

I took a tentative swallow.

"You need to drink more than that for the damned stuff to work," Joe admonished. I looked at him again, trying to remember whether I should know the man.

"Yeah, you should know me," he declared, acknowledging my confused expression. "But for now, I'll settle for anonymity if you'll drink more of that."

I tilted the glass and choked down more than I wanted but soon felt the effect loosening muscles, relaxing paralyzed limbs.

Bill raised his hands, palms outward. "Mattie, please listen to me. You're upset, your memory has clouded details concerning Hawk. Please believe me when I say he saved my life, my wife's life, and Mud Rain's life. He's on our side, no matter what you remember. I've only met Joe Healing Water this morning. And I tried to explain last night my connection with Jeremiah and the circumstances that drove his actions."

"And I'm sure your explanation sounded very logical and academic," Stephen Campbell's voice interrupted. I started at the sound of his voice. I was not aware he was in the room. I glanced around and spotted him in a corner.

He continued. "You and Tyler have lied to this woman," he pointed to me, "for almost a decade. Somehow that doesn't instill confidence in accepting your word as Gospel. When you consider Mattie's amnesia and loss of her leg are both direct results of your lies, I feel more than justified to tell you that you can sit here and revel in your explanations until the cows come home. In the meantime, I'm taking Mattie back to Virginia and hopefully help her get her life back together." Stephen stepped forward and glared at each of the occupants. "If I had my way all of you would be under arrest." He spun on his heel and glowered at Jeremiah. "Especially you."

My eyes jerked up when Stephen crossed the room to the couch where I sat. He leaned down and gave me a gentle kiss on the cheek. I hoisted myself awkwardly to my feet and buried my face into his chest. His arms wrapped around me in a supportive, caring hug. "I am so sorry for the shock. I had no idea who would be present when Bill called me over this morning," He murmured into my ear.

"Why didn't you call me?" I mumbled against his tweed suit, realized he wouldn't understand a word I said, and lifted my face. "Why didn't you call me?" I repeated.

"I tried. You didn't answer or call back," Stephen replied.

Oh. That would be because my cell phone was in the back of the Explorer. In Virginia. I shot an annoyed glare at Jeremiah.

"Never mind," I muttered. "I don't have my phone with me." My eyes slid again to Hawk, who watched me from across the room. I resumed my seat on the couch, groped for the tumbler, my hands shaking badly as I managed to down another hefty swallow. It was more than possible I might pass out from the amount of liquor I'd just consumed on an empty stomach.

"I asked everyone here..." Bill paused and glanced at a wall clock. "...this afternoon to reintroduce Mattie to those involved with the whole mess roughly two years ago, both to help clarify her memory, and to discuss whether the recent killing at the stables is connected in any way with past events." Bill motioned for everyone to take seats. Stephen took a seat beside me on the couch. Jeremiah stood near the door, his arms crossed, and his legs braced, anger and frustration radiating from him in almost palpable waves. Joe Healing Water crossed the room and sat down in an empty chair near the desk.

Bill went on. "Hawk, Joe Healing Water, and I have been reviewing events, trying to determine whether Mattie is in danger again from men with connections to those who went after her two years ago."

Stephen turned to me. "Do you want to stay and listen to this? Because we can leave. I have a spare room at my house."

"I'd rather call a cab to the airport. I want to go home. To Virginia," I admitted. I looked around the room, met each man's eyes except Hawk's. I shuddered, took another swallow of the brandy. "But I've been here this long, so I'll stay."

Stephen clenched his jaw. "Okay, let's hear what you have to say," he told Bill.

He sighed. "In a nutshell, two years ago a team from a group known as the Charlie Network kidnapped Mattie, blew up the Lamont estate, then our house to avenge the death of her brother-in-law, who had been one of their leaders. It is vital to know whether the Wittmore death is somehow connected to these past events." He turned to me. "But to determine that we need to hear what information you have concerning the investigation."

I straightened. "I already told you the connection." I pointed at Hawk again. "It's him."

Jeremiah cleared his throat. "Mattie, I hate to break it to you, but Hawk was not the man you heard on the ridge. The accent may be similar, but Hawk was in Colorado the day you witnessed the murder on the ridge. And when Randy Wittmore was killed."

"You witnessed a killing?" Hawk interjected, his eyes on me. I swallowed, avoided looking at him and bobbed my head. Beside me Stephen inhaled, but Hawk continued before he could speak.

"You were seen?" he pressed, remaining motionless in his chair.

I shook my head.

"It was foggy," Jeremiah explained. "Visibility was down to a few yards. Under such conditions there was no way the killer saw Mattie. That also means Mattie did not see the killer or his victim."

"But your horse was heard." Hawk stated.

I nodded.

Bill looked at his notepad. "There lies the connection between Mattie and the killer."

"We don't know that," Stephen interrupted. "Mattie has been through several serious shocks."

"Mattie and her horse were in poor shape when they returned to the stables," Jeremiah inserted quietly.

"And under those conditions, anything could have spooked her horse," Stephen declared carefully. "I've spoken to someone with experience working with victims of severe emotional trauma such as Mattie has suffered. What she feels she experienced may well have been a flashback of something from her past."

His words created a heavy, uneasy silence.

"Are you trying to tell us that Mattie *imagined* the incident?" Bill's expression looked shocked as he regarded Stephen.

Stephen cleared his throat. "I'm saying there has been no evidence found to support what she claims she saw, and that this meeting was unnecessary and harmful to her emotional and psychological recovery."

Tension filled the room.

"Why a murder at the stables shortly after Mattie rides in?" Hawk asked into the uncomfortable hush.

I avoided eye contact but cut in before Stephen could reply. "Because Randy was working an Arab in the back arena, and the horse is young and nervous and was all sweaty. I'm sure the killer thought Randy was the one who had just ridden in from the trail. He was using the arena right beside the trail I took when I rode up to the Parkway." I drained the rest of the glass and gripped it with shaking fingers, then turned to Stephen. "Sorry, I know you mean well, but facts are facts. I did witness something on the ridge, and Randy was killed because of what I heard." I paused, drew a breath. "There's something else. I know why he killed whoever it was up on the Parkway." I went through the scene, including the fact the killer's voice sounded familiar. I glanced in Hawk's direction, carefully avoiding eye contact. "The killer had a European accent of some kind. Not German or French. Maybe…English or something similar."

Hawk didn't move, didn't blink.

"Can you tell me what his exact words were?" Bill interrupted, jotting notes like crazy.

I shook my head. "No. Not anymore. Only fragments like 'hot as a jacket potato', and something about a rare coin and a coin show in Richmond. The man who got shot on the Parkway, his name was Freddie."

"*Jacket potato* is a colloquialism particular to Brits and the Irish. It's a baked potato wrapped in foil," Hawk inserted quietly, his gray eyes on me.

I crossed my arms over my chest. "I did some research on the computer over the weekend. There was a rare coin expo in Richmond, Virginia, and some of the Harry Bass Collection from Colorado Springs was on display." I closed my eyes, felt my head swim with the effects of the strong liquor. "The killer mentioned something about a unique coin. A one-of-a-kind. Gold coin, I think, and the date was 1870-something."

"Would it be the 1870-S three-dollar gold coin?" Stephen interjected, looking down at me, his eyes wide with surprise.

I stared at him. "Yeah, that sounds right."

Stephen leaned into the deep cushions. "Your father was quite interested in coins. I wonder if you're remembering snippets of conversations he and I had together."

I frowned. "I don't think so."

Stephen refused to relent. "There is no way someone could forge a coin to replace something like that. And the display would have all kinds of high security, alarms, and precautionary measures. Don't you see what you think you heard and saw couldn't have actually happened?"

"The news report I read mentioned a power outage that caused the event to be shut down early," I ventured.

Stephen persisted. "Well, it's still an impossible feat. I don't think anyone could be good enough to forge a coin that would pass long enough for someone to steal the real one."

Obviously, he was convinced I had imagined the entire thing. As if reading my thoughts, he swung his attention to Bill. "In the reports you've received, has there been any evidence at all that supports what Mattie is claiming?"

Jeremiah cut in. "They did not find a body when they followed the trail to search the location where her horse spooked."

I glared at him. "And just how would you know that?"

Jeremiah eyed me with a bland expression. "Because I followed you."

Stephen looked satisfied. "See? That was within a few hours of what Mattie claimed she saw and heard. *But there was no physical evidence.*"

I stiffened. "The killer could've covered his tracks."

Stephen pressed. "That would take time. And then you are suggesting he knew which trail to follow, and that he followed it all the way back to the stables. After he supposedly killed someone and then cleaned up the mess? Do you realize how absurd that sounds?" He was sounding like a lawyer instead of a friend. I bristled but clamped my lips together.

"You know something about coins?" Bill asked, changing subjects.

Stephen nodded. "I've been a numismatic nut since I was a kid." He turned his attention to me. "That's the other point I'm trying to make. I just don't see how someone could pull off stealing a rare coin, especially one as rare as the 1870-S three-dollar coin."

I refused to concede. "Maybe they didn't use a forgery. Could they swap coins?"

All eyes in the room fell on Stephen, who tapped a forefinger against his lips as he appeared to consider my question. I got the feeling he was humoring me. "Not likely. It would have to be an inside job, most likely one of the security personnel. The coins are usually displayed face-up. If a coin was swapped, it might not be noticed until they were putting things away for the night."

"Would the thief try to sell the coin?" Bill asked, leaning against the back of his chair.

Stephen shook his head. "Impossible. Stealing something like the 1870-S three-dollar coin would be a personal acquisition. He wouldn't even show it to close acquaintances. The coin is unique. He would risk exposure if he tried to sell it or show it to anyone." He turned to me. "Which is why I find all of this...well...." To his credit, he hesitated before voicing his thought. "Quite frankly, I find the whole thing ludicrous."

"Do you know what kind of value we're talking about?" Bill inquired.

"The 1870-S three-dollar gold coin is priceless." Stephen's answer hung in the air.

"A black-market sale of a coin of that magnitude would attract attention no matter how hush-hush they tried to keep it," Jeremiah interjected.

"Exactly my point," Stephen nodded. "There just isn't enough motive for someone to steal something that iconic."

"Well, just to cover our tracks, someone should contact the company that provided security for the coin expo, find out whether any of their employees have gone missing," Bill suggested, then looked at me. "What day was it again you thought you heard voices and gunshots?"

I stiffened. "I know what I heard. And I saw the muzzle flash.

Twice." I inhaled to calm my insides. "The incident occurred last Friday. I told two local officers the conversation I overheard, and they agreed to contact the numismatic museum where the rare coin collection is kept, find out whether anything went missing during the expo."

"And what did they find out?" Stephen wanted to know.

I hesitated. "I called my house number this morning and talked briefly with Riley. According to her, Aiden followed up on the coin angle. He said the museum claims no coins are missing." I carefully omitted informing current company of Riley's reaction when I told her where Jeremiah had taken me.

Stephen's expression rankled me.

"Do you really think they would admit losing a one-of-a-kind coin? They've probably got their own investigation going and are wanting to keep the theft from going public," I argued.

Stephen's expression did not change.

"Well, we can still look into things ourselves," Bill sighed. But his expression mirrored Stephen's, and I thought of the irony that out of all the occupants of the room, I was the only one telling the truth.

Yet, I was the one nobody believed.

Chapter Fifteen

"I'd better check on Becky," Bill said, rising. He disappeared through the office door.

Joe Healing Water and Hawk exchanged surreptitious glances. "We'll leave, let you all decide what needs to be done," Healing Water muttered as the two slipped across the room and through the doorway. Stephen remained seated beside me and didn't appear in a hurry to go anywhere. Jeremiah stood by the doorway and sent the two of us a hooded expression.

"I advised you to stay away from her," Stephen commented, breaking the silence.

"That was not a decision for you to make," Jeremiah countered, his voice cool. "Neither were the divorce papers."

The front doorbell rang. A satisfied smile flickered across Stephen's face.

"So," I turned my attention to Jeremiah. "Did Bill get rid of the car you stole?"

"As of this morning, it has not been reported stolen," he replied.

I squirmed. He had been right about the owners. They were no doubt enjoying the rental for several days. I glared at him. "Seriously? No one has reported that piece of crap stolen?"

"Possibly because it is a piece of crap." Jeremiah leaned against the doorframe and folded his arms across his chest.

His observation made sense, probably represented the reason he made off with it to begin with.

Damn.

Stephen stood as voices echoed along the hallway. "But the Feds don't have anything to do with the restraining order you so conveniently disobeyed."

As if on cue, two Norman police officers appeared in the doorway. Stephen smiled. "And now you have an escort to a place I believe you're familiar with."

"Mr. Jeremiah Tyler?" one of the officers asked as they both stepped into the office.

Jeremiah sent me a look curiously devoid of emotion. "Yes."

He turned around and placed his hands behind his back.

"You are being arrested for violating a restraining order regarding Matilda Lamont Tyler." The first officer stepped forward and retrieved a pair of handcuffs from his belt. He snapped the cuffs on and opened his mouth to continue, but Jeremiah cut him off.

"I am aware of my rights."

The officer nodded and they escorted Jeremiah out of the office. I heard the front door open and close, then silence.

Stephen turned to me. "He won't be in long, I expect. Bill will have him out by the afternoon."

"Did you call the police?" I asked.

He shrugged. "Yes, I did. Aiden and Riley approved; in case you're wondering."

"Why do you not believe me about what I saw and heard on the ridge?" I asked abruptly.

"Because I have it on professional authority that you have a very high chance of experiencing flashbacks that will seem to you to be real events," he answered calmly.

"Riley and Aiden both believed me," I countered, hedging on the truth. In fact, they had initially expressed similar doubts. Even I doubted the reality of the event, especially so close to the shock of seeing Jeremiah and getting my memory back.

Until Randy was killed. How ironic that the killer, in an attempt get rid of the witness, had in fact proven what I experienced had been real.

I continued. "And they're the ones who've been closest during my recovery over the last two years. I haven't had anything like this happen before. Why would it happen now?"

"Because Jeremiah contacted you, and your memory came back."

I stood and limped over to Bill's desk. "You realize how ironic it is that, here I am telling the truth, and no one wants to believe me?"

Rather than waiting for an answer, I picked up Bill's office phone and dialed my home number. Riley picked up on the third ring.

"Hey, there, it's me again," I told her.

"About time you called back. Where are you now? Has that dirt bag husband of yours been arrested yet? Are you okay?" Riley sounded understandably pissed. I'd been curt with her during our call earlier this morning.

"In Oklahoma, yes he has, and yes, I'm fine," I reported. "How's Twister, and do you have anything new on the investigation?"

She paused for longer than I thought necessary. "Twister seems okay, though Kinsey called today to say he's still not eating much. I talked to Aiden about what progress they've made, including a more thorough investigation of the scene where your horse spooked."

Ah. Where my horse spooked. *Not* where I had been shot at. A bad feeling began creeping along my spine. "C'mon, Riley. Spit it out," I demanded, leaning forward in my chair.

Riley heaved a frustrated sigh through the line. "Mattie, we haven't found *anything* that supports what you think you heard and saw."

"What do you mean, what I *think* I heard?" I retorted, anger filling my chest. I glared at Stephen, who kept his expression neutral. "You think I made all of that up?"

"Mattie, I want to believe you. So does Aiden. But we haven't found anything besides prints where Twister spooked. We haven't found casings, bullet holes in tree trunks, much less blood or a body. All we found were tire tracks, and those have led us to squat. We can't follow up on something we have nothing on. I told you this morning what Aiden learned from the numismatic museum. And Stephen…" She broke off.

"You've talked with Stephen?" I swung an accusatory stare towards him.

Riley rushed on. "He thinks you experienced a hallucination, or a short in your memory, or that you mixed up what happened two years ago with what actually happened up there on the ridge."

I stared at the lawyer, then leaned my forehead against my palm. "Is that what you really think?" I asked her.

Riley took a long time to answer. "Yes, Mattie. That is what I think. It fits the facts."

"Any theories why Randy was killed?" I choked the words out. Silence.

"C'mon, Riley. Out with it," I demanded.

"Aiden told me they're thinking it's drug related. Or that one of Randy's clients had a beef about the way he was training their horse. They're interviewing all the owners of horses he's trained since he moved here."

"How are they coming up with a drug theory?" I demanded, limping around the corner of Bill's desk and slumping into his deeply cushioned leather office chair.

Riley hesitated a long time before answering. "Look, Mattie. You don't know everything about Randy. He…well, he sort of went off the deep end after he lost his wife, and he got hooked on some pretty nasty stuff for a while. His sister tried to win custody of Amy, but Randy straightened himself out and managed to beat her on that. But he has a history of substance abuse and he got arrested for several DUIs. He would've done jail time if the judge hadn't known him so well and what happened to his wife. He ended up doing a slew of community service hours, mostly at the stables."

Silence filled the room. "Why didn't any of you tell me?" I shook my head, not wanting to believe anything less than perfection about Randy.

Riley's voice sounded strained. "Because none of us wanted to burst your bubble. You've been through enough."

I jerked my head up. "Oh, for crying out loud. Would you people quit treating me like I'm made of glass! Everyone has secrets they don't want to share," I blurted. "And he never drank or looked like he was on anything after I met him!"

Just like Jeremiah had secrets he did not share.

The thought sizzled through my head. *Well*, I argued, *Randy hadn't lied to me for seven years.*

You only knew him for two.

Oh, shut up, I mentally scolded.

Meanwhile, Riley continued. "Meeting you did him a whole lot of good. You got his life on track and working with horses gave him the physical outlet he needed."

I bristled. "Now wait just a damn minute…"

Riley cut in. "I'm not implying anything, Mattie. I'm just stating facts."

Bill wandered into the office. "Have you seen Becky?" he asked. "She was supposed to bring dinner." The words barely left his mouth when a slamming door echoed through the house.

"I'll bet that's her now, probably bending double under a load of groceries." He disappeared down the hallway.

Stephen watched me. "I've invited a close friend to talk to you," he told me after a long pause. "Just to give you someone with background in handling the kind of emotional trauma you've been through."

Great. Everyone seemed to be chalking me up as a head case. I ended the conversation with Riley, hung up the phone, then stood and headed for the door. "If we've got guests coming, then I want to help Becky with dinner."

Becky smiled when I limped into the kitchen. "How are your cooking skills?"

"Lousy, unless it's from a can," I admitted, relieved I could avoid talking to Stephen. He and Riley both had dropped down a good deal on my list of people I wanted to be around. "I'm good at cleaning up, though." I pointed to my sweats.

"Perfect fit," I grinned at her. "Thanks."

Twilight fell early under a cloudy sky, the wind thrashed tree branches and filled currents with scurrying leaves. Becky made chili and barbecued ribs and I washed pots and pans. Aromas filled the house, stirring childhood memories of Mom's cooking.

"You look sad." Becky came over and gave me a hug.

"Where's Mud Rain?" I asked, not wanting to admit what was on my mind and simultaneously realizing I hadn't seen him all day.

"He should be home any minute," Becky answered, picking up a spoon. She lifted the lid off the chili pot, dipped the spoon in, took a taste. "That's about right," she nodded, turning to me. "He's been in class, then to therapeutic riding. He gets home around five thirty. The Special Needs bus drops him off. That's been a Godsend with my work schedule and Bill always away on some project."

"You've known all along Bill was a handler?" I asked, reviving our conversation from yesterday.

"Yes," she said, checking the time on the baking ribs. "I thought you knew, too, since he and Jeremiah worked so closely together."

I shook my head and sat on one of the kitchen stools. I looked around for Stephen, but he had disappeared. Probably giving me space and time to cool down. I leaned my elbows on the counter to ease the discomfort shooting up what was left of my right thigh.

"No, I didn't. What about my parents? Did they know?"

Becky leaned against the counter, her clear blue eyes locking on my green ones. "You know, I don't think so. Bill kept a lid on it. Sometimes it was hard for me to remember not to accidentally say something when we were with friends."

The sound of the front door caught my attention and Mud Rain wandered into the kitchen. He was dressed in jeans, an O.U. sweatshirt, and sneakers.

I laughed. "Boy, you and Bill really have Mud Rain brainwashed when it comes to the Sooners."

"Maddie!" Mud Rain ran over, wrapped his arms around my waist, almost pulling me off the stool. I hugged him back.

"How was your day?" I asked. He squirmed onto a stool, unable to contain his energy and excitement.

"Giddy-yup, Thwisser!" He waved his arms wildly over his head and bounced until I thought he would topple onto the floor.

Becky smiled at the youth. "That's his favorite thing to do," she said, watching him with loving fondness.

"Does he ride every day?" I asked.

"Whenever the weather permits." Becky pulled out plates. "Will you start setting the dining room table, please?"

"Sure." I grinned at Mud Rain. "Want to help?"

Mud Rain nodded and I handed him plates. The two of us followed the hallway to another large room with a massive oak sideboard and a matching table large enough to seat twenty people. I seriously hoped Becky and Bill were not planning a large gathering to celebrate Jeremiah's and my arrival, especially since Jeremiah was now sitting in a jail cell.

I wondered whether Stephen had told Bill about Jeremiah's arrest.

As Mud Rain and I returned to the kitchen, Bill and Stephen ambled into the great room and Bill switched on the massive screen. "It'll be a little while before dinner, right?" he called to his wife.

Becky threw him a frown. "Are you boys getting ready to watch another recorded O.U. game?"

Bill laughed. "Of course. I need to brainwash Stephen here whenever I get the chance. He still claims to be an O.S.U. fan."

Becky shook her head, unable to hide her laughter. "Lord, you boys are hopeless."

Bill grinned and turned to Stephen. "I want you to see our

new All-Star running back. His moves remind me of Barry Sanders."

"Barry Sanders was from O.S.U.," Stephen slid in, his blue eyes twinkling.

"Yeah, well, nobody's perfect." Bill laughed, then called out to me. "You and Jeremiah need to come over here and get comfortable. You have a lot of catching up to do on O.U. games."

I debated whether to ruin the festive atmosphere.

Oh, what the hell.

"It's going to be a little difficult for Jeremiah to join us," I informed them.

Bill turned to face me. "Why is that?"

Stephen's face reddened.

I waited a beat. "Because he was arrested a little while ago and is probably sitting in a jail cell now."

A pan clattered to the floor, and my eyes jerked to Becky. She was white.

"Arrested?" she echoed faintly. "Is that what the two officers were here about? I thought they were here to get more information about what happened two years ago."

"He violated a restraining order," Stephen answered, his voice curt.

Bill hit the pause button, freezing the players on the screen. "When did this happen?" he demanded, his joviality evaporating.

"After you and the others left," Stephen told him. "I'm sure you'll have him out before dinner, now that I've told you."

Bill looked at me, his distress obvious. I turned to Stephen.

"By the way, I need the divorce papers so I can sign them." If I was going to spoil the festivity, might as well do it in style.

Becky gasped. "Oh, Mattie, oh, no. Please don't tell me you and Jeremiah are splitting up. You can work things out."

"I'm not working anything out with someone who lied to me for seven years." The minute the words left my mouth I regretted saying them. Leaning heavily against the kitchen counter, Becky looked frail and vulnerable, Mud Rain looked at me with confusion, while Bill appeared incredulous.

I decided changing the subject was an infinitely better idea than trying to get any of these people to understand my view of the situation.

"Stephen," I plunged on, "would you elaborate more about

the gold coins you and my father used to talk about? Since that seems to be what I experienced instead of an actual theft?"

Boy, my bluntness was digging a hole deep enough to reach China.

Stephen opened his mouth, then shut it again. I felt marginally victorious that I had actually left a lawyer speechless.

"Excuse me." Bill dropped the remote and strode down the hallway. The door of his office banged shut.

Becky stood motionless at the sink. "Please tell me you and Jeremiah aren't splitting up, that you'll try to work things out," she pleaded in a choked whisper.

I succumbed. Even though I had no intention of trying to patch things with Jeremiah, I could not handle the devastation on Becky's face.

"Okay. I'll wait on signing the papers," I told her.

Yes, I lied. Just like everyone else. Might as well join them.

Stephen wandered over and took a seat at the breakfast table in a small nook of the kitchen. I followed.

"Between the two of us, we've managed to foul up what was supposed to be a celebratory gathering," he muttered.

"Yeah, we did," I agreed. "So, tell me about the coin I imagined."

He threw me a mildly irritated scowl but acquiesced. "The three-dollar gold coin proved one of the worst ideas the US Mint came up with, and now one of the most sought-after coins in the entire numismatic community."

"Why?" I asked. Becky ignored us and busied herself with cleaning dishes at the sink.

"A three-dollar coin seems an odd thing to make," he shrugged. Through the windows, I watched the howling wind toss surrounding trees. I shuddered suddenly with the feeling that someone was watching us.

"Numismatic nuts like me love the three-dollar gold coin," Stephen explained. "It was a US Mint anomaly. Every other gold coin was a division of ten, five, two-and-a-half, and one-dollar. The man who designed it had to come up with something unique enough that wouldn't be confused with the two-point-five coin already in circulation."

"Why did the US Mint decide to make it?" I asked him.

"It was authorized by the Act of February 21st, 1853," he explained. "Most collectors believe the government decided to create the three-dollar gold coin because it would buy one-hundred-subject sheets of the three-cent stamp."

"That seems odd." I frowned.

Stephen nodded. "It really wasn't a popular coin and very soon fell out of circulation, especially along the East Coast. It was used a little more on the West Coast. It lasted from 1854 to 1889, I believe."

Bill appeared suddenly from around the corner. He sank into one of the deep cushions.

"Getting Tyler out of jail?" Stephen inquired mildly.

"None of your business." Bill's cool tone matched his expression. Stephen and I had definitely thrown a wrench into the afternoon.

"Bill," Becky walked over and squeezed his hand. His bright blue eyes met hers. "Don't worry, Sweetie. Everything will be okay." He turned back to us.

"In the conversation I *thought* I heard, one of the men said he didn't understand why the coin was so valuable. He said there were bigger coins that were worth more," I told Stephen.

"Well, that depends on which 1870 three-dollar coin you're talking about. The 1870-S three-dollar coin is the only one in existence," Stephen clarified.

"Why would anyone steal something like that?" Bill countered. "Someone earlier made the point the thief would never be able to sell the thing, even on a covert black market. It would attract instant attention."

"That's absolutely right," Stephen agreed, turning to me. "Which is why it's so hard to believe what you think you witnessed actually happened. If the coin was indeed somehow stolen, it would be by a coin collector. Why would a collector run that kind of risk? He would never be able to even show it, much less sell it. And collectors love to show off their collections, especially of rare coins."

"Yeah, you've said that already." I folded my arms across my chest.

Stephen studied me with an apologetic expression. "Mattie, I actually called the Numismatic Museum in Colorado Springs, where the Harry Bass Collection is kept. No one has reported the 1870-S three-dollar coin missing."

I met his gaze levelly. "That's what Aiden told me. Neither of you are considering the fact that maybe they don't want to admit they've lost it."

Silence fell between us.

I leaned forward. "Do you really think I could make up something about a subject that is so totally foreign to me?" I argued. "Where in the world would my subconscious come up with stealing some gold coin I know nothing about?"

"Exactly why I want you to talk to my friend who's coming for dinner," Stephen sighed. "I don't understand, either. But there is absolutely nothing concrete to support what you think you heard."

"Can you give us some history on the coin and why there's only one?" Bill interjected.

"It came about from a government mistake, actually," Stephen smiled. "Dyes similar to the Philadelphia Mint coin were sent to the San Francisco Mint. But whoever made the dyes forgot to include the "S" to denote which mint would be stamping the coins."

"Does that mean there are no 1870 three-dollar coins at all?" I asked him as I rubbed my right thigh where the muscles were threatening to cramp.

Stephen tilted his head. "The Philadelphia mint made 1870 three-dollar coins. The San Francisco mint made other coins that year. Just not the three-dollar gold coin."

"What makes this coin so special it's considered priceless?" Bill asked.

Stephen settled his long frame deeper into the chair and brought the tips of his fingers together. "The 1870-S three-dollar gold coin is the only unique coin in the whole regular issue of US gold coins. The chief coiner at the San Francisco mint in 1870 was a man by the name of J.B. Harmstead. According to notes he left behind, he scratched out an "S" in the plates and stamped two coins. He kept one of them as a watch fob. Again, according to his notes, the other one was supposedly put into the cornerstone of the new San Francisco Mint that was built to replace the old building, but that coin has never been recovered. He later sold his coin, and it passed through several collectors before Harry Bass bought it at auction in 1982. At that time, he bought it at the Eliasberg Sale for somewhere around six hundred thousand dollars. I want to say six twenty-five, but I'd need to look it up to be sure.

Despite some scratching and the fact that it's not in mint or proof condition, it's been the centerpiece of the Harry Bass Collection ever since."

"Just how big is this guy's coin collection?" I pressed.

Stephen sighed. "The Harry Bass US gold coin collection is the only complete collection in existence because of the 1870-S three-dollar gold coin. A lot of numismatic enthusiasts," he paused for emphasis, "and I meant a *lot* of them acutely regret now not bidding for that coin. It should have sold for over a million. Harry got it for a steal."

"Are any of the other dates as rare as this one?" I asked.

Stephen nodded, his wide, bright blue eyes on me. "All of the three-dollar coins, especially ones made in the later years, are rare. The fact the Harry Bass Collection had a complete set of them is quite remarkable."

The front doorbell chimed into the silence.

"Here I've been talking your ears off and we have guests coming," Stephen apologized.

Bill rose. I followed him.

"Must be the guest Stephen invited," I told him.

"Yes, he said he invited Preacher Pat over for dinner. Becky and I have been wanting to do that for a while."

I fervently hoped Hawk and Joe Healing Water were not coming back, although Becky had given me enough plates to set the entire table. I tried but could not recall other friends who might be arriving. I stood behind Bill when he opened the door.

"Hello, hello, Preacher Pat," Bill grinned, standing aside to allow the man on the doorstep to enter.

The man's blue eyes met Bill's as he enthusiastically shook hands. "My, my, it is grand to see you." His eyes swung over and met mine.

I froze.

"Why, if it isn't Mattie Tyler! What a pleasant surprise!" Reverend Patrick Kelly beamed at me, his Irish lilt bringing back childhood memories of sitting in church with Mom and Dad...

...and warping me to the top of the trail along the Blue Ridge Parkway.

Chapter Sixteen

"Mattie Tyler." He grinned, his lips stretching across his straight white teeth like a tiger ready to pounce.

I almost fell over. My vision fogged and I panicked for a moment, thinking he had teleported us to Virginia and he was going to pull a gun out of his coat pocket and shoot me right then and there.

"I haven't seen you, lass, since your parents' funeral." His clerical collar peeked out from the black shirt he wore underneath a brown wool sweater.

"Preacher Pat," Becky greeted from behind me. "Come in, come in. When Stephen phoned about asking you over for dinner, I told him it was a wonderful idea. Bill and I haven't seen you in ages."

"And you've not been to church, my lovely lady." The Reverend stepped past Bill and gave Becky a smooth peck on her cheek. Becky smiled and started to lead him through the foyer. She glanced over her shoulder at me. "Come on, Mattie. Join us in the den. It'll be more comfortable than the formal sitting room."

"Might I have the pleasure of seeing your husband, Jeremiah?" the Reverend turned to me, his light blue eyes intense with something a long way from friendship.

"It has been a long time, Reverend." Jeremiah's voice sounded from behind me. I visibly jumped, felt Jeremiah's strong fingers grip my arms as he pulled my back briefly against his chest. His action saved my balance.

Revelations raced through my brain, and I realized Jeremiah must have entered through the garage...

...that Bill and Becky were completely oblivious to the type of maniac they had just invited into their home...

...and that my blood ran so cold as to freeze my insides when I realized Preacher Pat represented the "professional opinion" Stephen referenced during our earlier conversation.

The reverend followed Bill and Becky through the front entryway. I grabbed Jeremiah's hand and whispered a frantic warning.

"That's him."

Jeremiah acknowledged with a barely discernible nod, then

gently took my elbow and supported me as I limped after the Parsons and their lethal guest.

Stephen left the kitchen nook and joined us in the massive entertainment area.

"Thank you for making time for a visit," he greeted, shaking the reverend's hand.

"Pleasure is all mine, I assure you," Preacher Pat cooed. He turned to me. "Stephen has filled me in on your woes, lassie. I am most anxious to be of assistance."

Spots began to dance before my eyes, and I knew I had to leave the room, or I would end up in a dead faint.

"P-please excuse me, everyone," I managed in what sounded like a normal voice. "I need to go upstairs. M-m-my leg is really bothering me." Without waiting for an answer, I turned and did not need to fake the heavy, painful limp I used to get to the stairs. Jeremiah's hand never left my elbow as he supported me along the hallway, then up the stairs. I clung to the railing and trudged up the stairs like a doomed prisoner climbing the gallows. I got to my room, Jeremiah right behind me, and shut the door.

"What has Stephen done?" I whispered frantically.

Jeremiah steered me to a chair, sat me down, gently guided my head between my knees. Cold sweat streamed down my face, soaked my clothes. I thought I was breathing but couldn't be sure.

"Mattie, close your mouth. It will help slow down your breathing," he instructed softly. I did as he instructed, and slowly the room quit spinning, and the roaring in my ears diminished.

"Please tell me you believe me," I croaked out.

"Yes." Jeremiah squeezed my shoulder. "I remember hearing him say 'hot as a jacket potato' numerous times from the pulpit. Usually in reference to where we all would be going if we did not dig deeper into our financial pockets."

"And Stephen has told him everything about me and what happened on the Parkway because he thinks I imagined it all, and that...*that man knows it's all true!*" I felt the room start to spin again. Jeremiah tightened his grip on my shoulder.

"Which we will turn to our advantage," he reassured quietly.

The calm confidence in his voice derailed my panic attack. I squeezed my eyes shut, lifted my head, then opened them and stared at him.

"Can we really do that?" I asked, but I already knew the answer.

"Yes."

"That man is a long-time preacher, well known and obviously well liked. How will we convince Bill and Becky? And Stephen? All three of them think I'm a nut case!"

"Sleight of hand," Jeremiah murmured. "Smoke and mirrors."

I stared at him. "I'm not following."

"I do not mean for you to." He straightened and disappeared into the adjoining bathroom. The faucet ran, and he reappeared with a damp cloth, which he handed to me. I wiped my face and neck and tried to pull my splintered wits into something recognizable.

A soft knock almost made me jump out of my skin. The door opened and Becky peered around the edge.

"Are you feeling well enough to join us? We're moving to the dining room. Preacher Pat would really like to talk to you."

"We will be down momentarily," Jeremiah told her with a smile.

I clenched my teeth and nodded, and Becky closed the door.

"There's no way I can fake my way through this," I told him, hearing the panic in my voice.

"Do not try to hide any emotion," he advised. "If he asks you questions, be truthful with your answers. I will be with you and will interject if he asks something dangerous."

Voices and laughter filled the hallway when I finally opened the door and started limping down the stairs. Jeremiah followed.

"Get a bowl and plate. The food is in the kitchen. Please, help yourself," Becky instructed when we entered the dining room. We retrieved the dinnerware from the table, then headed to the kitchen.

To my dismay, Preacher Pat came up behind me. "Mattie Tyler, it is such a pleasure to see you."

I prayed frantic, silent pleas any comment I made would come across as crazy as a Looney Tune. I turned and motioned him to step in front of me.

"After you," I suggested.

"Oh, no, love, after *you*." Preacher Pat gently pushed me ahead of him. With no other choice, I dished chili into a bowl, then stared at the barbecued ribs and the salad. My stomach gave a couple of sickening rolls, and I opted to leave it to chili for now, until my digestion improved.

Preacher Pat deftly plucked my bowl from my hands. "Please, lassie, allow me," he said, holding both our servings of chili, and balancing his plate of salad. Nodding, I turned and limped to the dining room.

"Sit beside me, lass, and perhaps I can help with your memory a wee bit." He smiled again, looking more like a hyena than a human, as he set our servings side by side. My heart practically pounded through my chest.

"My apologies, Reverend," Jeremiah spoke up from across the table, "but I would like Mattie here, beside me." Jeremiah gestured to the seat beside him.

"Of course, of course." Preacher Pat's smile broadened. He picked up my bowl and practically glided around the room. With a flourish, he set my bowl next to Jeremiah's.

"I do so want to catch up on how you've been these past two years," he leaned close, his head cuddling against mine, his hands strong when he squeezed my shoulders. I thought I might pass out right then and there.

So why a murder at the stables shortly after Mattie rides in? Hawk's question popped into my brain as I fought a sudden bout of dizziness.

Hawk and Jeremiah both had challenged Stephen over his doubts concerning my recount of events I witnessed on the ridge. At the time, I was too shocked to think things through, but now, abruptly, Hawk's and Jeremiah's expressions filled my mind.

Both Hawk and Jeremiah were operatives. Both told me on separate occasions about following their gut instincts.

Neither Hawk nor Jeremiah expressed any doubt over my statements.

"A penny for your thoughts?" Preacher Pat's voice spoke close to my ear. I shuddered, shaking my head to bring my thoughts back into the room.

"I…I'm sorry, my leg is still cramping. I'm not totally with it tonight," I managed to say.

"Well, no matter." The man patted my arms. "A little of dear Becky's wonderful cooking should brighten you up."

Jeremiah, who had been standing behind me, grasped me gently by the arm and guided me into the chair beside him. He held his serving of chili and threw a slightly embarrassed glance towards Becky. "I forgot to add a bit of hot sauce."

Becky started to rise, but Jeremiah waved her down. "I know where it is. I will bring it, in case someone else wants to use it." He disappeared into the kitchen, returning a moment later. Mud Rain sat between Stephen and the reverend on one side, Jeremiah and I occupied the places directly across from them, Bill and Becky sat at either end. Conversation lapsed after the blessing, as everyone dug into wonderful southern cooking. I picked up my spoon and managed to choke down what should have been really good chili. The spices breathed fire into my mouth and along my throat, and I thought how good my mother's chili had been. Savory, without so much bite. I wondered whether it would be rude to ask for some ketchup but decided not to bother Becky about it. I spooned down some more.

Stephen opened his mouth and promptly sealed my fate. "Mattie here has been having issues with flashbacks. In my opinion, she's confusing fact with fiction. Mattie, why don't you tell Preacher Pat what you think you heard and saw during your ride? He has several degrees in psychology and counseling. Maybe he can help you sort through what's real and what your imagination has created."

Jeremiah quietly cut in. "Stephen, as a lawyer, you know Mattie cannot discuss anything about an on-going murder investigation."

I almost fell out of my chair. If Jeremiah's blatant statement was how he intended to help, then Preacher Pat might as well pull out his gun and shoot me now.

Preacher Pat gazed at me through crystal blue eyes. His short, curly red hair clung close to his scalp, and he had a habit of gently patting it into place with his hands.

"What investigation?" he asked, his voice full of innocent curiosity.

Stephen opened his mouth, but again Jeremiah cut in. "Someone has died under suspicious circumstances near the stables where Mattie rides."

"Oh, my. What a shock." Preacher Pat leaned across his half-eaten meal. "I'm certainly glad you are here where you can be properly cared for."

I dropped my eyes to my chili and felt sweat bead along my forehead. A wave of dizziness washed through me.

Stephen, oblivious to his perilous mistake, barged on. "I've talked with the investigating officer, Jeremiah. They are looking at a link with drugs concerning the Wittmore death. So there really isn't any reason Mattie can't describe the incident on the ridge."

I shook my head. "The details are blurry, and I'm not remembering much of anything other than Jeremiah's visit." From the corner of my eye, I saw Jeremiah give a miniscule nod of approval.

Bill swallowed, set down his spoon, and leaned forward. "Preacher Pat has been a family friend for years, both our family and yours, Mattie. If anyone can help you, he can."

"Stephen, I remember your visits with George Lamont. A lot of them included discussions about coins, I believe," Jeremiah prompted, smoothly switching subjects.

Follow the prompt, I silently begged. I tried to drink some water, but that aggravated rather than appeased the burning in my mouth and throat.

Stephen glanced at Jeremiah, then at me. "Yes," he nodded. "George liked coins, enjoyed learning the history behind them. I brought over my collection on several occasions. He was quite enthusiastic."

Jeremiah glanced at me, must have noticed the sweat on my brow. "The chili is somewhat spicy," he murmured. "Let me get some ketchup. You always liked that on your stews anyway." He rose from the table. "Be right back."

"I'll go with you," I said, a strange sensation making my stomach turn sour. Jeremiah caught my eye and smiled.

"You are fine, Mattie. Stay seated and rest."

I got the strong feeling he wanted me to do something. No, not do something, say something.

Say what? I groped for an answer.

Continue the conversation.

I turned to Stephen. "I don't remember Dad being interested in coins. He never talked about any of that to me, or to Angela," I told him. "He and Mom were always interested in restoring old churches."

Preacher Pat's eyes locked on mine. His expression appeared downright gleeful. "And listing them as historical landmarks. Quite a remarkable man, was your father."

Stephen continued. "George loved anything that represented

history. I'm sure that's where your imagination came up with what you think you saw." He leaned back and raised his water glass to his lips, drank deeply, moistening his mouth before continuing. I prayed hard he would choke and end up on the floor in a heap. Anything to shut him up.

Stephen cleared his throat. "Churches were their priority, but they rescued several other buildings from being torn down." He paused, his expression thoughtful. "I wonder whether he ever started a coin collection of his own."

Jeremiah returned with a bottle of ketchup, which he set down beside me. He resumed his seat and began to eat. Stephen addressed him.

"Jeremiah, do you remember whether Mattie's father started collecting coins?"

Jeremiah's comment sounded casual, almost disinterested. "His financial accumulation represented a gold mine in itself."

"Gold coins, eh?" The reverend ventured.

Stephen smiled. "I have a small collection of numismatic gold coins. I'm sure that's where Mattie's imagination picked up the image."

I retrieved the ketchup and squirted a generous amount on my meal, then choked down some more of the chili.

"I'm a bit of a coin nut," Preacher Pat released a hearty laugh. "Must be the leprechaun in me." He turned to Bill, who had remained silent during the entire conversation. "What about yourself, my good man? Ever been interested in coins?"

Bill shook his head. "Don't know a thing about them."

Preacher Pat leaned back and pushed away his empty plate and bowl. "My goodness, that was good." His eyes locked on mine. "Worth a three-dollar gold piece, if I had one." He glanced at my half-eaten meal. "My dear lass, it's quite obvious the emotional upheaval has taken a toll. You've hardly touched your supper. Please, eat."

Becky rose and waved for everyone to remain seated as she gathered empty dishes. "Anyone up for dessert?" she asked.

"I would love some, but am stuffed to my gills," Preacher Pat replied with a broad, satisfied smile.

"Me! Me!" Mud Rain waved his hand enthusiastically. Preacher Pat leaned over and grinned at him.

"Now that's what I most enjoy," he said to the youth. "A lad with a robust appetite." He turned back to me.

"Tomorrow is Thursday and the parish will be quiet. I would be happy to spend time with you, help you sort things out." His voice dripped with compassion.

"That is very accommodating of you," Jeremiah nodded.

The walls were closing in. I glanced around the table again, saw nothing but earnest expressions wanting to help me with my recovery. Involuntarily, I winced as my stomach cramped.

"I-I'm not feeling well." I pushed back my chair and stood. "Please excuse me."

A look of pure malice flashed across the reverend's eyes before being replaced by sympathetic kindness. He stood when I got up. "I do hope you feel better soon, lass. I hope to see you tomorrow." He glanced at his watch. "Well, time is getting on, and I need to be bidding you fine people a good evening."

Bill and Becky appeared as I started up the stairs.

"Are you feeling okay, honey?" Becky leaned towards me. "You look awfully pale."

"M-my leg is cramping again," I lied, and ascended the stairs before any of them could follow me. At the top, I glanced back in time to see Reverend Kelly at the front door.

"Thank you for a fine meal, lovely company, and for being such a wonderfully genteel woman to change your schedule to aid a friend in need."

Jeremiah headed for the stairs, and I turned and entered my bedroom.

"That was very informative." Jeremiah declared with satisfaction, closing the door behind him. I sat on the edge of the bed and shivered.

"Easy for you to say," I muttered.

"Are you feeling all right?" He asked, squatting in front of me. "You are pale."

"No, I'm not feeling all right," I snapped. "I had to stare death in the face throughout the entire meal."

~ * ~

Patrick Kelly entered his home from the garage, dropped his keys into the dish he kept handy on the kitchen counter, then retrieved his cell phone and plugged it in to re-charge. Then he wandered into his office and sat down behind his desk. He pumped his fist enthusiastically.

The bloody woman would be dead by morning. Instead of a visit, the Parsons would be calling him about funeral arrangements. The evening could not have gone better. Stephen's invitation had been a perfect opportunity to slip her a lethal dose in plain sight. No one would suspect him because she would die sometime in the early hours. He had used that concoction on several occasions with absolute success. He whistled as he stood and ambled into his bedroom to change clothes.

The final loose end gone, nice and tidy. Now, he needed to locate the coin.

Had someone found it already? Had it been returned to the museum in Colorado Springs?

There was only one way to find out. It made sense to ascertain whether the coin was in the collection before he took the risk of searching for it in that bloody arena. He rummaged through an old but still useful Rolodex, found the name of a minister who could sub for him over the upcoming weekend.

He would fly to Colorado Springs, see for himself whether the real 1870-S three-dollar gold coin was on display. If not, his next move would be to fly post haste to that small town in Southwest Virginia with a metal detector equipped to locate gold. He tapped nervous fingers against the surface of his desk. His coin might still be lost somewhere in that arena, but it might also be locked away in an evidence box and beyond his reach. They would be combing the arena for a bullet casing, would not know there was a connection between the murder and a gold coin.

If authorities came across a gold coin at a crime scene, would they lock it away as evidence?

Of course they would.

How to find out? Was there any way to determine whether the gold coin had been found?

He worried over the sticky wicket for most of the night. In the end he decided that before working out how to get information he needed from the local police force, he first needed to confirm whether the 1870-S three-dollar coin was still missing.

Chapter Seventeen

A light knock on the door, and Becky entered the bedroom.

"There's a phone call for you." She held out the handset. I wondered whom it might be.

"Hello?"

Riley's voice came through the land line. "Are you sitting down?"

"Yes." My heart started pounding. Riley sounded serious.

"Twister has colicked."

Oh, my god. I felt the blood drain from my face. Jeremiah gently took the handset and put it on speaker.

"Say again, please," he told Riley. I heard her hesitate, knew she wanted to tell Jeremiah to go to hell, but her professionalism and concern over-rode her personal feelings.

"Twister has colicked. The vet's on the way. Kinsey is walking him. She gave him some Bute, but he still wants to lie down, which isn't a good sign."

I wrapped my arms around my body and started to rock. 'Bute' was short for phenylbutazone, a powerful painkiller used sparingly, usually in emergency situations. "I need to fly out there. Right now."

"Not a good idea," Riley's voice countered.

"I agree," concurred Jeremiah. "How long has this been going on?"

Riley sighed. "I've been keeping an eye on him. Ever since he got back from the vet clinic he's been off his feed. Kinsey's been walking him every day, offering him to graze. He's done a little of that. Hold on. The vet's here." Commotion and voices drifted through the line, then Riley's voice again.

"I'll call you back. Stay close to the phone."

I closed my eyes and curled into a fetal position on the bed. "I can't lose him," I whispered, "Not him, too."

Jeremiah rubbed my back. "He is in good hands. Stay positive."

Suddenly, I wanted Randy. I wanted him close, enveloping me in one of his strong, comforting hugs. The image of the ring box

188

came to mind, and I sat up. Jeremiah dropped his hand when I crawled off the bed and limped to my suitcase. Rummaging through the clothes, I located the royal blue velvet box and clutched it against my chest.

"What is that?" Jeremiah inquired softly.

I unfolded my arms and showed it to him.

"Randy. He was going to…he was going to give it to me," I stammered, my voice cracking. "It's a ring, I think. I found it in my pocket the day he died."

Jeremiah reached out and gently grasped my arm. I followed and sat back down on the bed.

"Have you opened it?" he asked.

I shook my head.

"Open it now. It will bring him close to you." Carefully, he took the small box from my hand and lifted the lid. "This is quite beautiful," he murmured. Removing the ring, he grasped my left hand, and slipped it onto my fourth finger. Through tear-filled eyes, I gazed at my hand.

The ring was white gold, in the shape of a horse shoe. Two beautiful diamonds winked at me from the ends of the horseshoe, a third from the base of the curve. Three diamonds representing Randy, Amy, and me. I swiped the tears rolling down my face. Jeremiah studied me.

"You found it in your pocket?" He prompted carefully.

I nodded.

"How did it get there? Did Randy give it to you?" He seemed to be asking his questions very slowly, as though to a child.

The thought generated a memory. I lifted my eyes.

"No. He showed it to me. At the stables. Amy, his daughter, was with us." I paused, thinking. "Amy. She took it from his hand and put it in her jacket pocket." I frowned. "How did it end up in my pocket?" I mused aloud, staring down at the ring again.

"Amy was in your lap for a while. When we heard the news regarding Randy," Jeremiah prompted.

Comprehension dawned. "She must've slipped it into my pocket while I was holding her."

Jeremiah handed me the open box. I stared at it for a long time.

"My God," I finally managed to choke out.

The phone rang, and Jeremiah put it on speaker.

"I'm here," I said. I gripped Jeremiah's hand in preparation for the worst.

Riley kept her voice even. "The vet tubed him. There's no odor of rot. She gave him a dose of oil, and they're walking him around again. His temperature and heart rate are normal. Do you want to talk to her?"

"Yes," I answered immediately.

"Okay. Let me get her on the line."

Jen's voice came on after a brief pause. "He has perked up, but that may be from the Bute he got earlier. The most positive thing is that I didn't smell anything when I tubed him."

"And that's good news, right?" I asked her.

"Very good news."

Riley came back on the line. "I have some news I think you should hear concerning the investigation. Can you shoo your dirt bag ex-husband out of the room long enough for me to fill you in?"

I sighed. "No, Riley. I need him with me right now. There's some things I need to tell you that happened here."

"Well, shit. Please don't tell me you've decided to make up." She sounded more than disgusted.

"No. It's not about him and me. Now, what were you going to tell me?" I stared at the ring as she went on.

"Jillian allowed Aiden to see Amy. Amy wanted to know where you were, if you were okay. Then she told Aiden she saw something round and shiny in the dirt when she ran over to her father. She saw the person with the gun but could not give a reliable description because of the foggy conditions. She did say the Arab ran the person over and knocked off the hat he was wearing, but it was too foggy for her to see what the person looked like. She wasn't even sure whether it was a man or a woman."

I opened my mouth, but Jeremiah cut in. "Do you think she saw a casing?"

Riley's voice answered in a flat, professional tone. "No. She knows what a bullet casing looks like. What she described sounded like a gold coin." After a pause, she added, "There's more. Aiden said they followed up with the security service that covered the coin Expo in Richmond last week. The head of the company said one of their guards left and didn't come back."

"So, he might have been the one that got killed up on the ridge," I guessed.

Riley's next words got our attention. "Care to guess the name of the missing guard?"

"Freddie something," I breathed. Jeremiah stood and leaned against the dresser.

"You got it. Freddie Little. From Shawnee, Oklahoma."

"Same town where Reverend Patrick Kelly lives. Too much coincidence," Jeremiah spoke up.

"Damn right. According to the head of the security firm, the missing guard's car was gone, no body has been found, and there is no sign of foul play. Which means there still is nothing concrete to back up your statement. All we have is circumstantial."

Jeremiah picked up the conversation.

"Reverend Patrick Kelly paid us a visit tonight, courtesy of Stephen Campbell. The good reverend is a long-time friend and confidant of both Bill and Becky Parsons, and Mattie and her family. In fact, he has known both families since before their children were born."

"Okay, and this relates to our investigation in what way, exactly?" Riley asked.

Jeremiah's next words dropped a bombshell.

"The good reverend tried to poison Mattie during dinner."

Silence filled the room. I gaped at Jeremiah. On the line, no sound at all.

"You're shitting me," Riley accused. "He wouldn't be that stupid. Not in front of everyone."

"Not only did he," Jeremiah countered, "but he enjoyed himself thoroughly during the attempt."

I stared at him. A tiny smile of satisfaction flickered across his lips. "Sleight of hand. Smoke and mirrors. Remember?" He murmured to me.

I raised my hand and covered my mouth.

"So, are you telling me that this reverend is the one Mattie heard on the ridge?" Riley sounded aghast.

"That, and he is most likely the one who shot and killed Randy Wittmore," Jeremiah confirmed.

"Why am I not dead?" I choked out, feeling my stomach cramp again.

"So, how the hell are we going to prove it?" Riley demanded through the phone.

"I swapped bowls," Jeremiah smiled at me, then continued with Riley. "Mattie and I have an appointment with him in the morning, which I am sure he anticipates will not happen. He will no doubt be expecting a call about her funeral arrangements."

"Surely, you're not going to show up?" Riley challenged.

"We will not only show up, but we be able to subtly dictate his moves from here on."

Silence came across the line, then an audible sigh of disgust. "Aiden's right. You're damn good."

"Thank you."

"He's sharp." Riley grunted. "You'd better watch your ass. If anything happens to Mattie, my brother and I both will come after you."

"I would expect nothing less," Jeremiah acknowledged.

"My off-duty weapon is in my suitcase," she said abruptly. "Is my suitcase still with Mattie?"

"Yes," I told her, eyeing the second piece of luggage, unopened, standing beside the chair.

"At the risk of me getting fired for saying this, use it if you have to. Although I'll deny any knowledge."

"I will keep that in mind," Jeremiah mused, eyeing the closed suitcase.

"What? Me getting fired?"

The corners of Jeremiah's mouth twitched.

"There's more," Riley continued. "I might as well tell you while I've got you on the phone. There's been another murder, and investigators think the two cases might be related. Same caliber handgun."

"Where?" I asked.

"Outside of town. The body was found beside a dumpster. The gun was found in the dumpster. Hollow-point bullets, so we can't run ballistics, but that makes two in close vicinity with the same caliber. Too much coincidence."

"Kelly must have gotten rid of his weapon before he left the area," Jeremiah mused.

"My thoughts exactly. Without ballistics or fingerprints, we can't tie the weapon to him."

"What about registration?" Jeremiah asked.

"The numbers have been filed off. Probably a black-market weapon. Too many variables to follow that route anyway."

Silence fell again on the Virginia end of the call.

Riley finally said. "Twister is perking up. Kinsey is keeping him indoors and will stay with him through the night."

I started trembling uncontrollably.

"Hey, Mattie, you there? Did you hear what I said?"

"Yes, she did," Jeremiah answered for me.

"My advice to you would be to fly out here tomorrow. Forget the meeting with Kelly. Don't go anywhere near that man," Riley urged.

"We will take that under consideration," Jeremiah hedged.

"You'll follow my advice, dirt bag, or I'll fly out there and arrest your ass," Riley snapped.

"We've got an appointment with Preacher Pat in the morning," I declared carefully, my brain starting to crank into motion.

"I'm telling you, don't go anywhere near that man." Riley's voice sounded like she might appear through the handset.

"Please keep me posted on Twister," I told her.

"Don't you go and change subjects on me. Promise me you're not going anywhere near that maniac." Riley sounded desperate.

"I'll keep the phone close. Good-bye, Riley."

"Promise me you won't do anything stupid," Riley pleaded.

"I promise that I won't go alone, and that I'll be very, very careful."

Riley was growling through the line when I cut the call. I rose and replaced the beautiful velvet ring box in the corner of my suitcase.

"Are Hawk and Joe Healing Water nearby?" I asked Jeremiah.

He nodded, studying me with a closed expression. His eyes dropped to the ring on my left hand.

"I want help," I declared flatly.

"I agree."

"And I don't want to be kept in the dark." I released a frustrated sigh. "You and your smoke and mirrors."

~ * ~

Jeremiah guided Bill's sedan along the gently winding drive

that led to the destroyed Lamont estate. Midnight had come and gone, but I was not tired. He pulled to a stop near the mound of rubble now overgrown with weeds and other plant life. As I exited the passenger's side, I caught sight of a large white moving van parked on the property. The sight stirred a memory, but I could not bring it to the surface.

"I should have known." I followed Jeremiah, who carried a small knapsack in one hand. The wind had died to a gentle prairie breeze, the night sky was clear with a slight chill. Winter was coming, and soon ice storms and vicious winter winds would strip the surrounding trees of their colors.

He led the way across the broad front lawn to a small garden shed tucked into the corner of the property next to the trees surrounding the estate. He tested the door, found it unlocked. "They must be expecting us," I mused as we stepped inside. Without a light, we felt our way to the shelf along the back wall. Jeremiah leveraged the shelves outwards.

"This isn't going to work," I grumbled, realizing I could not crawl with my prosthesis on.

"I'll carry it," Jeremiah slipped the knapsack onto a shoulder and held out his hand. Reluctant, I pulled my prosthesis through the O.U. sweats I still wore, leaned against the wall, and handed it to him. Then I sat down on the concrete floor, wriggled my way into the tunnel. Pitch black darkness filled the interior, but I knew it was straight and not terribly long. A soft light appeared and grew steadily larger. Someone had opened the door at the far end. I reached the opening, and strong fingers grasped my arms, pulling me gently upwards to my foot.

Joe Healing Water's hands steadied me, then Jeremiah appeared and stood. The two of them helped me work my prosthesis back into place. Jeremiah stepped away, and I glanced around the room.

It was as I remembered it, roomy yet compact, with a ceiling much lower than my childhood self recalled. Bunk beds lined one wall. Storage shelves and supplies lined the rest.

"Hello again," Joe Healing Water extended his hand. I shook it. Hawk stood the furthest away, next to the bunk beds. Joe took a seat at a desk that held computer and surveillance equipment.

"Ah, so that's how you knew we were coming." I inclined my

head towards the camera screens that scanned the entire property. "I forgot Dad installed all of that."

"Naw, we're telepathic. Knew what you were thinking." Joe's stony expression belied his humor.

Jeremiah slung the knapsack off his shoulder. "I bring gifts." He unzipped the canvas pack and removed two handguns, which he placed on the large table situated in the middle of the room.

Joe Healing Water studied me. "A white flag?" Jeremiah retrieved one of the weapons then handed the other to Hawk.

"Very dirty and at half mast," I grumbled. "But yes. I'm here to...to discuss a situation with you." I threw a glance in Hawk's direction. "All of you." I motioned towards the and benches. "Can we sit down?"

The others complied, and I sat the farthest away from Hawk I could. I went through the events of the day, including Preacher Pat's visit and the fact it was his voice I heard on the Parkway. I recounted Stephen's conversation about the gold coin and telling the Reverend what I had seen and heard. When I paused to breathe, Jeremiah picked up the thread.

"He tried to poison Mattie at dinner."

"A serial killer hiding in plain sight," Hawk inserted slowly. "He could use any number of options. A wily sleight-of-hand to slip a lethal dose into her meal. A fine needle or stiletto to cause a slowly fatal hemorrhage."

I found myself being scrutinized by three pairs of very serious eyes.

"What?" I objected. "I feel fine, if that's what you all are wondering."

Hawk turned his attention to Jeremiah. "Anything else of note during the Reverend's visit?"

Jeremiah grinned. "He appeared secretly pleased, too much like a cat who has eaten the canary."

Hawk swung his attention to me, his gray eyes so intense I physically leaned away despite the fact we were at opposite ends of the table. "The Reverend made physical contact with you during his visit? Handled your plate of food?"

I ducked my head to avoid his stare. "Yes, he did both," I nodded slowly. "He gave me a hug around the shoulders and carried my dinner into the dining room. He was wanting me to sit beside him, but Jeremiah nixed that."

"I switched the bowls, carried the doctored meal to the kitchen," Jeremiah explained. He turned to me. "Bill tested the contents. He said to extend his apologies about not believing you."

"Is there enough evidence to go after him?" I ventured.

Joe shook his head, his expression grim. "Won't do us any good pursuing that lead. Nothing concrete to tie to the bastard."

"He's a bloody wily weasel, I dare say," Hawk muttered.

"He is also on a mission," Jeremiah observed. "He will not give up trying to get rid of Mattie until she is dead. Or we give him a very good reason to leave her alone." He looked around the table. "We have a meeting with him in the morning, which he will no doubt be expecting us to cancel, since he is under the impression he was successful in his attempt to poison Mattie. We now find ourselves in a position to be able to dictate his moves."

I chose my next words carefully. "I'm the one he's after. So that makes me the best person to set things up."

"What are you talking about?" Joe demanded.

I studied all three men. "Let's just say Jeremiah and I have a pretty good idea what Kelly is going to do next. But since he knows both of us, we need some…discreet help."

Hawk's gray eyes locked on mine. "And you are willing to put yourself in the center of peril? Again?"

"I won't plan on being alone this time," I countered, trying to sound more confident than I felt. "Preacher Pat is expecting a phone call about my funeral, not for Jeremiah and me to show up at his doorstep."

"What is your plan for the meeting with Kelly?" Joe asked.

Jeremiah leaned his elbows on the table. "The visit will give you time to set things up to follow his movements." His eyes slid towards my left hand, then to my face.

"Right," Hawk nodded. "Time to make arrangements to stop that bloody git in his tracks."

~ * ~

Mid-morning Thursday Jeremiah parked Bill's sedan in the short flat driveway of the parish house. I stared at the closed front door of the residence. The house was styled in the typical single-story rancher common in this area because of the high winds, tornadoes, and the fact that most of Oklahoma lay below sea level which did not make it advisable to dig a basement. The day was overcast with a typical prairie wind blowing, though in benign gusts as clouds scurried across the huge sky.

"This seemed such an easy plan last night," I muttered as my watch practically flew to the top of the hour.

"Answer questions honestly," Jeremiah advised softly beside me. "Allow him to lead the conversation. There is nothing you need to hide, since he is already aware of what you saw and heard, thanks to Stephen Campbell."

"And he's not expecting us to even show up, especially me. That should give us a little bit of an advantage," I added, trying to bolster my courage.

"We have considerable advantage. And the information Officer Butler relayed strengthens our position." Jeremiah's reference to Riley brought a thin smile to my lips.

"You don't like Riley," I observed.

"She has provided much needed protection for you over the last two years. I value her intelligence and her observations," Jeremiah replied evenly.

My smile broadened. "Yep. You don't like her." My eyes fell to the ring on my left hand. The three diamonds glittered with a spectrum of color despite the overcast conditions.

"That is a very nice ring," Jeremiah complimented, noting my distraction.

"You were right," I murmured. "It's keeping Randy's spirit close. It's like I can feel him nearby." I narrowed my eyes on the parish house. "Let's get this over with. I want to nail that dirt bag and put him behind bars."

We exited the car and strolled slowly along the winding front walk, climbed the two steps to the small concrete stoop, and rang the bell.

Preacher Pat answered almost immediately. He must have seen us from inside the house, because he did not show surprise to find both of us on his doorstep.

"By the mark, Jeremiah Tyler." His face warmed into a smile as he extended a hand. Jeremiah shook it. The reverend waved us into his home. The small entryway opened into a living room with brown and green furniture. I wondered whether the green tones reflected his Irish background.

"Have a seat. I'll make tea." He gestured for us to sit on the couch, then turned and disappeared around a corner, no doubt to the kitchen.

"Do not eat or drink anything," Jeremiah whispered urgently into my ear.

We waited. I kept my eyes down, not wanting to look around in case my behavior might appear suspicious. I'm sure Jeremiah's sharp observation skills reconnoitered our surroundings in under a minute. A kettle whistled softly, and Preacher Pat reappeared carrying a tray with a ceramic blue patterned teapot and matching cups. He set everything down and made a show of pouring tea into three cups, then setting cups in front of Jeremiah and me. He added sugar and cream to his, stirred, then tapped the spoon gently against the rim and set it carefully in the saucer. He blew across his cup and took a sip.

"Please, help yourself," he encouraged, relaxing into a deep armchair, his blue eyes watching us with what I thought poorly suppressed predatory anticipation.

Jeremiah picked up a saucer and cup and settled against the cushions. He blew across the top, then returned the cup to the saucer. I leaned back as well but avoided picking up the steaming cup of tea in front of me.

"Well, then," Preacher Pat started, gazing intently at me. "Tell me all about your…episode, shall we call it? And the recent recovery from your amnesia."

I nodded slowly. "For basically two years I haven't known anything about my past. Or what happened to my family. Or the men who kidnapped me and blew up my house, then the Parsons' house." I felt my eyes water and blinked the moisture away.

"Quite an ordeal, my dear lass," Preacher Pat soothed. "What do you think might have caused this rather imaginative episode?"

I shrugged. "I honestly don't know. At the time, I thought it was real. My horse almost died running all the way back to the stables." I took Jeremiah's absolute stillness as a silent affirmative to continue. "Jeremiah showed up suddenly, and it was really foggy, and my horse was nervous. And then *wham*. All my memory, or at least a lot of it, came slamming back. It was…," I faltered, not sure how to describe the feeling.

"Overwhelming?" Preacher Pat offered gently. He seemed so innocuous, so genuine, so…*normal*…that I found myself doubting it had been his voice up on the ridge.

"Yes," I agreed with a shaky sigh.

"Drink some tea, dear," he urged, motioning with his cup towards my own. I reached to retrieve the cup and saucer, but my fingers shook so badly that I tucked both of my hands between my knees.

"M-maybe in a bit," I stammered, nerves getting the better of me in spite of my efforts. "M-my stomach was upset last night, and it's still queasy."

"And then, a murder at the stables. A terrible tragedy," the Reverend continued, shifting his attention to Jeremiah. "Were you there?"

Jeremiah casually crossed his left foot across his right knee. "I was. Mattie was terribly shocked, as was the small daughter of the man who was killed."

"Any more news concerning the investigation?" Preacher Pat asked, and it seemed to me his focus became more intense.

With an undetectable movement, Jeremiah's hiking boot gently nudged my knee.

I shook my head. "Only what Riley said yesterday about Amy seeing something round and shiny in the arena when she ran in to check on her father."

"Authorities have found naught?" the Reverend pressed.

Again, I shook my head. "No. Nothing that fits the description of what she saw." I paused, then half-shrugged. "I wish I knew whether what I saw and heard was real. Stephen said he even followed up with the numismatic museum in Colorado Springs, but they said no gold coins were missing from the Harry Bass Collection. So, I must have imagined the whole thing." I stared at my hands, afraid to make eye contact because I didn't want the man reading my expression.

Beside me, Jeremiah stirred his tea. "Unfortunately, there seems to be absolutely nothing to verify what Mattie thought she witnessed. No missing coin, and Officer Butler did tell us later there is no one missing in Virginia that fits the type of person Mattie thought she heard being shot. What a shame." His voice trailed off.

"Beg pardon?" the Reverend said after two seconds too long

of silence.

Jeremiah leaned forward and set his cup and saucer on the table. "Well, if there were anything to support what Mattie thought she saw and heard, then it would connect the man she heard on the Parkway to the death in the arena."

I drew a deep breath, steeled the sudden nerves in my gut, looked the Reverend straight in the eyes, and revealed the ace up my sleeve. "And then Stephen would have to believe my story about the shooting, the gold coin, all of it. And the police could start looking for a missing gold coin, instead of a lost brass casing."

Chapter Eighteen

Reverend Patrick Kelly strolled through the sliding doors of the Colorado Springs Airport into the crisp, arid high-altitude desert air of an October afternoon. Directly west the Front Range rose with imposing rugged magnificence, the green slopes running north until interrupted by an ugly bald brown section torched to a crisp by the Waldo Canyon Fire of 2012. Slightly behind and towering over the Front Range rose Pikes Peak, the brown summit generously sprinkled with recent snowfall at fourteen thousand-plus feet. The azure sky stretched wide, reminding him of Oklahoma. A light breeze touched his face and despite the milder temperatures he felt the dry, intense heat as sun beat through significantly thinner atmosphere. Hailing a cab, he gave instructions to the Colorado Springs Numismatic Museum, then leaned against the durable plastic imitation leather and watched the city slide by.

Colorado Springs proper was not nearly so dense as Oklahoma City, though significantly larger than Shawnee. Boulevards followed rolling plateau terrain, surprisingly flatter than he had anticipated. Desert plains emphasized the grandeur of steep mountain slopes, and he marveled a bit over the dichotomy between two such opposing topographies.

Cottonwood and elm trees dominated downtown avenues; their branches already barren of leaves. Remnants of recent snow clung to the north side of lawns and pavement despite the afternoon warmth.

The taxi pulled into a tiny parking area beside a small, nondescript tan building with a sloped ramp. Kelly paid the driver, then followed the ramp to the double front doors. A receptionist sat behind a counter.

"Good afternoon, sir," she greeted him. "How can I help you?" She was an older woman, probably in her mid-sixties, on the heavy side, and wore a printed long-sleeved blouse. Her short white hair framed a cherub face with slightly pink cheeks as though she pinched them often. Large glasses magnified her brown eyes.

Reverend Kelly's smile oozed with bonhomie. "And a bonnie day to you, my sweet dear." He noted with hidden pleasure the way her smile widened, and her expression brightened at the sound of his accent. "I'm here on a wee visit and was told you have a most unique museum." He thought belatedly whether he should have hidden his accent to remain as unmemorable as possible. He glanced surreptitiously at security cameras and carefully kept his head bent enough to avoid a clear image of his face.

"Are you visiting from overseas?" the woman inquired as she motioned towards a sign-in registry.

"I am," Kelly replied. "And I must say your delightful Broadmoor Hotel is quite an impressive little chalet." He whisked out an unreadable signature, then smiled at her. "Is there a fee, love?"

The woman's cheeks flushed. "Yes, sir."

He paid, and she proffered a couple of flyers. "Here's information about the world of coin collecting, including our pride and joy, the famous Harry Bass, Junior gold coin collection. And our gift shop."

Kelly thanked her and wandered into the museum proper. To his left were displays of area history, including several exhibits of the Ute Indian culture, weapons, and clothing. To his right stood a massive circular vault door. Feeling his heart rate rise several notches, he stepped into the display area of the famous and unique gold coin collection.

The exhibit lined the walls, with additional freestanding display cases in the center of the large room. He started to his left, following the display of various gold coins, reading the background of each. With a wry smile he noticed the heavily reinforced bullet-proof glass and the subtle alarm system embedded in each case, but soon found himself completely absorbed by the enormity and utter exhilaration of being surrounded by such an extensive collection of United States gold coins.

The collection represented coins minted between 1795 and 1834 and included the two-dollar-fifty-cent coin, dubbed the "quarter-eagle"; the five-dollar coin, otherwise known as the "half-eagle"; and the ten-dollar coin, known as the "gold eagle". He knew from his own research the three-dollar gold coins had been minted from 1854 until 1889. In addition, on display were gold coins minted from 1834 to 1933 ranging from one-dollar gold coins of various types to the twenty-dollar gold coin, otherwise known as the "double-eagle." Information plaques explained that after 1933 the United States ceased minting gold coins until 1986. There were also displays of rare currency including the series of 1896 bills.

Though he had familiarized himself extensively with the three-dollar gold coin, Kelly had not familiarized himself with Harry Bass, Jr. His eyebrows quirked in surprise when he read Harry Bass had been instrumental in improving the grading process of coins. Reading further, Kelly learned Harry Bass, after purchasing a ten-dollar 1803 gold piece in May of 1966, discovered a fourteenth star embedded in the rightmost cloud above the eagle on the reverse side. His minute and exact notations of each coin he purchased became the standard by which all coins were graded and rated.

Kelly made his way slowly around the room, anticipating yet dreading arrival to the display of three-dollar gold coins. He knew he would instantly recognize whether the 1870-S three-dollar coin on display was the genuine item. He feared someone had found the coin in the arena and had quietly returned it to the museum. As he reached the case, he closed his eyes and inhaled deeply, then opened them and bent close to study each three-dollar coin beneath the glass.

The gold coin on display glinted at him, and Kelly felt his heart sink to the soles of his feet. Someone had found the coin, his coin, and had returned it. He glanced at the photos above the coin that presented images of both sides. From the display case, the obverse side of his coin shone up at him.

Time slowed. With a frown Kelly studied the picture of the obverse side, commonly known as 'heads', then bent until his nose touched the glass to peer closely at the obverse on display. With a pounding heart, he straightened and glanced around to see whether anyone else was present. He was alone in the vault of gold coins, so he allowed himself a brief, flashing grin of triumph.

The picture of the obverse did not match the coin in the display case.

And that meant the real 1870-S three-dollar gold coin was missing. To hide the theft the museum had substituted a similar coin. After all, the mint mark was imprinted on the *reverse* side of the coin. With the obverse face-up, the museum could easily hide the switch. Kelly doubted whether the museum had even alerted the Bass family about the theft.

Hardly believing his luck, Kelly bent again and carefully studied the face of the coin. Sure enough, the minting was too clean, the surface of the coin too free of scratches and other signs of wear to be the genuine 1870-S version of the coin. The real 1870-S three-dollar gold coin had been used as part of a key fob until the owner decided to sell the coin, and therefore the coin was not in mint condition, unlike the coin glinting at him through the glass case.

Which meant the real 1870-S three-dollar gold coin was either somewhere in that damned arena or locked up in the town police station.

Kelly worried over the conundrum of locating the gold coin. How should he approach a small-town police force concerning a gold coin he should know nothing about?

And if they had indeed found the coin, how in the world could he possibly regain possession?

"That thar seems a senseless waste of good ore," a deep voice drawled behind him, startling Kelly so badly he physically jumped. He snapped his head around as a man appeared beside him.

"Personally, I don't reckon I'd trust nothin' that weren't pumped from the ground or standing on four legs, if you get my meanin'," the man continued. He stood significantly taller than Kelly. A scruffy brown beard covered his face, long brown hair hung in oily strings past his shoulders. He wore old jeans and a black T-shirt. Scuffed, muddy cowboy boots peaked from beneath the frayed edges of his jeans.

"You from these parts?" the man continued, his gray eyes sliding across Kelly's without making contact. Clearly, he seemed unimpressed with anyone interested in the coin collection.

"Visiting." Kelly turned his head away, unable to leave the case and the visible proof that in fact the real 1870-S coin might be a phone call (and a bit of impersonation) away.

"You like collectin' stuff like this?" Clearly, the stranger was not picking up on Kelly's nonverbals.

Kelly shrugged. "Interesting history."

The man grunted. "Ain't nothin' interestin' 'bout history 'less thar's money to be made. History's done gone, an' if you ask me, my advice is keep yer eyes on th' future, not th' past. Current history. Like currency," he added with a half laugh, obviously amused by his own humor.

"Sound advice, my good man," Kelly nodded, wondering fleetingly why someone so uninterested in history and coins would be standing in a numismatic museum.

His preoccupation with the 1870-S coin overrode his normally keen instincts. He reached his hands to carefully pat into place the tight curls that clung to his scalp. Before the irritating visitor could continue, he smiled and said, "A very good day to you, sir." He spun on his heel and strode from the vault room.

Kelly left the building and hurried down the ramp before forcing his legs to slow down. He walked along the shaded boulevard and eventually hailed a passing taxi. He didn't waste time touring the many iconic landmarks in Colorado Springs. Instead, he told the driver to take him to the airport. He gave the man a ridiculously generous tip and practically skipped through the terminal doors to find the earliest flight to Southwest Virginia.

Hawk watched the small Irishman leave and scratched his head beneath the wig, then left the museum and pulled his cell phone from his pocket.

"Well?" Healing Water answered.

Hawk grunted. "You might say hello."

"Well?" the old Indian repeated irritably through the satellite connection.

"He seemed quite pleased when he left, which indicates the real coin is indeed missing and the museum is keeping mum," Hawk reported, ambling along the shaded sidewalk. He removed the wig and beard after he slid into his rental car.

"So, how did Mattie know he would visit the museum?" Joe asked.

"Excellent question," Hawk mused, staring at the squat brown building.

"Do you think she knows where the coin is?" Healing Water reflected.

"It certainly appears that way," Hawk ventured. "Which means Mattie knows more than she's admitting," He rubbed a hand across the bristles on his jaw. He did not like the idea of Mattie going off half-cocked, especially with someone as adept at killing as Kelly. A strange, alien sensation filled his chest. He refused to identify the cause.

"Where is she?" He asked, turning the ignition and starting the sedan. He should drive straight to the airport. Instead, he glanced at an address jotted down on a scrap of paper and took a detour.

"Mattie? She's in Norman with the Parsons today, will be back here this evening," Healing Water replied.

"Has she asked about the van?" Hawk inquired, easing through downtown traffic.

"No, she has not," Jeremiah inserted. Hawk grunted. Joe must have his phone on speaker.

"Have you run your errand?" Hawk slowed as a signal light changed from yellow to red. He grumbled. "You Yanks have yet to learn which side of the bloody road to drive along."

"On my way after this call," Jeremiah retorted mildly. "We needed to confirm there was something to look for."

"Especially since Mattie isn't willing to share what she apparently knows," Healing Water complained.

"That copper in Virginia. Think she's confided in that woman?" Hawk pulled into a small lot alongside a park following a broad creek through the middle of the city. He turned off the ignition, heard the low, powerful rumble of diesel engines, and watched a freight train creep along barely thirty yards away.

"Don't know. But that's a good question," Joe fell silent.

Hawk cut the call, sat in the car and casually watched the long train roll by, then directed his attention to the various human traffic on the broad gravel trail as enthusiasts made the most of remaining daylight.

Afternoon waned towards early evening. Clouds took over the western horizon and Hawk wondered whether snow might be on the way. The high-altitude atmosphere cooled sharply as shadows lengthened and the western sun dipped inexorably towards the omnipresent, snow-speckled summit. Twilight came early here, as the city fell beneath the shadow of towering Pikes Peak. The sun slipped, threw long rays with a final burst of intensity, then bowed behind the mountains, back-lighting the summit with gold and rich yellows. As Hawk continued to watch, the surrounding clouds darkened, then suddenly began to glow like embers until the entire cloud cover radiated with a brilliantly rich, fiery orange so intensely beautiful it took his breath away. The colors gradually deepened into an expansive crimson, finally paling to a soft rose before darkening to a muted gray.

Hawk turned the ignition, eased from the now deserted parking area and headed north along one of the main boulevards. Eventually he turned into an apartment complex and pulled into a slot in front of a ground floor unit in the building furthest from the main entrance. He cut the engine and sat in the car for a long time staring at the closed curtains of the unoccupied apartment.

Why was he here? What in bloody hell had gotten into him?

He exited quietly from the car, hunched his shoulders against the sharply colder air, and approached the ground floor apartment door. Slipping on a pair of latex gloves, he picked the lock with professional efficiency, then gently pushed open the door and flicked on the lights.

Foul odors of stale beer and rotted food assaulted his nostrils as he stepped into the small unit. A kitchenette located to his left took only a glance to tell him Jeremiah had not cleaned a dish since the last day Mattie lived here over two years ago. His eyes wandered over walls decorated with framed professional photographs, his attention lingering on a particularly spectacular shot of Pikes Peak, its snow-covered top rosy in the pre-dawn. In another framed picture a swirling, tightly wrapped coil of gray cloud twisted across flat empty prairie landscape, the surrounding low, menacing black clouds obscuring any horizon. He moved down the hall and opened the first door to his left, entered a spare bedroom with a bed frame and mattress devoid of any bed coverings. Pictures and albums lay strewn on the mattress. Crumpled beer cans and cartons littered the carpeted floor.

Hawk sank onto the bed and picked up an open album. A family album, he noted, and began carefully flipping through the pages. Pictures of a teenaged Mattie, her sister, her parents, their vacations, holidays, special events, her parents' musical performances ….

His hands stilled as he stared at a picture of a young Mattie and her sister at Coors Field. They looked to be in their early twenties, and the photographer had zoomed in on their profiles in a candid shot of the two sisters with their heads bent close, their attention on something other than the camera. Mattie's short black hair sprang from beneath the Rockies baseball cap she wore, while her sister's long, silky brown hair appeared carefully styled to perfection. Mattie's strong features and large dark green eyes contrasted sharply with her sibling's more delicate bone structure and brown eyes. It was an intimate shot, one taken by a parent, probably their father, probably before Jeremiah entered their lives. Hawk stared at the image for a long time.

If only he had known then what he knew now. He would not have gone after Mattie, threatened her life, gotten her involved in the Charlie Network.

He glanced up, registered the framed photographs adorning these walls, too, but saw only dark shadows as his attention turned inward.

Had her involvement been his fault...or Jeremiah's? And had Jeremiah's deterioration over the last couple of years been due to what had happened to Mattie, or because Jeremiah realized that by marrying her, he had exposed her and her family to the Network's radar?

Through his conversations with Healing Water, Hawk had learned Jeremiah recognized Mattie's brother-in-law as a killer connected with the Charlie Network, but failed to notify anyone about it.

Had he been ordered to keep quiet? Or had he felt confident he could handle the situation and thought he would efficiently rid the world of Gary Tacque before Gary Tacque rid the world of him?

If Gary Tacque had a hit out on Jeremiah Tyler, he would have had ample resources to locate the man. Discovering Jeremiah had married into wealth must have seemed an incredibly delicious bonus.

So, what drove Jeremiah's actions now? Guilt? Revenge? Loneliness?

Mattie certainly seemed finished with Jeremiah. And it was yet another stroke of bloody bad luck her new beau had ended up with a bullet in his brain.

Now, instead of being the target of mayhem, she was leading the charge. And in doing so she had learned how to keep secrets.

Hawk set the album aside and stood, then carefully picked his way among the debris to the hallway. A quick tour of the rest of the apartment revealed more neglect, and Hawk started to retrace his steps to the front entrance. He paused at the door to the spare bedroom and stared at the album lying on the mattress. After a slight hesitation, he crossed to the album, eased the baseball photograph from its sleeve, and carefully tucked it into the pocket of his shirt. As quietly as he had entered, Hawk closed the front door behind him, locked it, and returned to the rental car.

~ * ~

Dusk created ample shadows without complete darkness, and October twilight lingered across the broad Oklahoma horizon. A mild breeze stirred trees still dressed in their fall colors as Jeremiah casually strolled along the short driveway leading to Reverend Kelly's parish house in Shawnee. Wearing latex gloves, he expertly picked the lock on the front door and slipped inside. He reconnoitered the premises, found no alarm system, several lights on timers, and a large gun safe in the closet of the Reverend's office. The combination lock proved only a minor hindrance, and before long he gently swung the heavy door outward. With the aid of a small flashlight he took inventory of the contents, paused on a leather briefcase, decided to look inside, and carried the briefcase to the Reverend's desk. As he sat down the desk light, with the aid of a timer, conveniently switched on. He worked with the combination locks on the briefcase until they opened with a quiet click. He lifted the lid and studied the treasure within.

Three-dollar gold coins. A lot of them, each one in its own sealed plastic case set into a rectangular felt-covered depression.

Pulling out his cell phone, he took several pictures, then carefully closed the case, spun the combination locks, and replaced the case in the safe. He closed the heavy door, spun the dial, and turned towards the office door. The phone rang and he paused to listen to the answering machine.

"Preacher Pat," a quavering older female voice emitted from the phone set on the desk, "I'm just calling to see whether you're back in town yet. Old Mrs. Jeffery Brown passed away this morning, and her family is asking specifically for you to handle her services. She was such a dear, and she left quite a donation to our parish. I'll try your cell, but I was hoping you'd be back in town by now. Well, since you're not answering your phone, goodbye."

As Jeremiah slipped invisibly from the house, he wondered whether old Mrs. Jeffery Brown had been helped along to the hereafter by the good Reverend Patrick Kelly.

~ * ~

I managed my way through the tunnel to the bunker, lugging my prosthesis along the way and needing to take several breaks. Joe Healing Water's lined face peered through the open end of the passageway; his strong, gnarled hands helped me into the room. I sat on the floor, worked the prosthesis into place, then grabbed his proffered hand and hauled myself up.

"Did Jeremiah catch you in Norman?" Joe asked, ambling to the desk with the computer and security monitors. "He finished up his errand and drove down to meet you."

I shook my head and limped over to stand beside him. "No."

Joe cut his eyes to mine. "You missed him on purpose."

I met his glare evenly. "Yes, I did." I dragged a folding chair over and sat down.

"You should've waited for him," the old Indian admonished, redirecting his attention to the monitors. "He has some interesting news concerning his trip to the Reverend's house."

I ignored his tease. "Where's Hawk?" I asked instead, hoping the man would not suddenly turn up at the bunker.

Joe sighed and leaned back in his chair, his eyes returning to mine. "Hawk's somewhere between Colorado Springs and here. He was supposed to check in hours ago, but I haven't heard squat from him."

"And Preacher Pat? Did he make a trip to the Numismatic Museum?" I asked as I shifted on the chair. The damned thing was more uncomfortable than standing, but my stump was cramping. I really needed to leave the prosthesis off for a couple of days, which meant using a wheelchair or buying a set of crutches.

"He did." Joe's curt answer caught my attention. His eyes narrowed. "And I'm mighty interested in knowing how you knew where he'd go after you and Jeremiah visited him on Thursday. And why you dropped the hint about the coin. How in hell would you know he apparently lost the damned thing?"

Instead of answering, I squinted at the monitors. I wanted to be long gone before either Jeremiah returned from Norman or Hawk returned from Colorado Springs. I was banking on the probability Jeremiah and Bill would have information to exchange before Jeremiah headed for the Interstate.

"What did Jeremiah tell you about what he found?" I asked, changing subjects.

Joe blew out an irritated sigh. "You were right about that theory, too. Kelly does indeed have a very impressive collection of three-dollar gold pieces. Jeremiah took pictures and showed them to me before he took off for Norman."

I met the Ute's keen eyes and inhaled deeply, then took the plunge. "Joe, I need a favor."

"You plan on telling me what you're up to?" Joe asked, folding his arms across his chest.

I shook my head. "No, actually, I'm not."

"Mind explaining all this sudden secrecy?" he persisted.

I scowled at him. "Oh, like you and Jeremiah—and Hawk—haven't been keeping secrets of your own?" I hauled myself out of the chair and leaned against one of the red clay walls. "If I want to keep my business to myself, then that's my prerogative."

"Not very amiable after crawling in here and asking us for help," Joe shot back.

"Okay, forget it. I get the hint." I ran my hand along my ponytail and thought about cutting all my hair off. It had been much easier to care for when I wore it short all those years.

"I didn't say I wouldn't help you." Joe sounded like he was backpedaling. "I'm just bothered by your sudden personality change."

"You mean by my refusal to be put in a corner by the three of you?" I challenged.

"What's your favor?" Joe grumbled.

I regarded him for several silent moments before answering. "It requires a return trip to the parish before Reverend Kelly gets back."

Joe's expression turned stony. "Well, in that case, hand me your leg, and let's get going through that damned tunnel."

Chapter Nineteen

Kelly leaned his bicycle against a tree at the bottom of the gravel drive leading to the indoor arena and the horse pens. Brilliantly discreet inquiries at the stables and the local police department had supplied the information he needed.

No gold coin had been recovered.

Which meant the gold coin was somewhere in the back arena.

He spent all day reconnoitering the stables, watching cars come and go, riding lessons use the outdoor arenas, countless riders embark on surrounding trails only to return later, their horses sweaty from their exertion in the warm afternoon sun.

Afternoon sunlight traveled across a sky hemmed in by the rolling Blue Ridge Mountains. Slanting rays and shadows enhanced rich fall colors as things slowly quieted around the stables. Evening sounds caressed his ears as crickets and other insects began their nightly calls. Temperatures needed to drop soon. A hard freeze would end the mosquito season, as he smacked one on his forearm.

But a hard freeze would make his search more difficult, so Kelly put that thought aside and waited for full dark. He debated whether to pull a pair of night-vision goggles from the backpack he carried, but thanks to a half-moon the night was not pitch black. Besides, he had excellent night vision and the goggles would prove cumbersome and might possibly alarm the horses.

No lights shone as Kelly approached the back arena. The horses remained quiet, though a few nickered when he passed, but he maintained a careful distance from the pens so he would not spook any of the animals and cause the onsite managers to investigate. He carried a special metal detector he could break down and store in his backpack. It had been an expensive purchase but well worth the investment. He had no doubt he would find the missing 1870-S gold coin. Then he would be on his bicycle and leave no trace of his presence here tonight.

The arena gate was closed when he reached the back and he pondered whether to risk squeaky hinges if he tried to open it. He had decided to climb over instead when something fluttering in the evening breeze caught his attention. He stepped in for a closer look.

A sheet of white paper with Duct tape clung to the top railing of the gate. Curious, Kelly caught hold of the loose end. A message printed in large, capital letters with a black marker.

WANT YOUR COIN?
FOLLOW THE TRAIL

The message stunned him. For several minutes, he stood rock still as he tried to sort out the meaning behind the message.

Was the message a trick? Had his inquiries created suspicion among investigating officers? Had the police discovered the coin and were now luring him into a trap?

Hiding the metal detector and his backpack in undergrowth crowding the arena railings, he checked his semi-automatic concealed under his waistband, then retrieved a small flashlight. Using the hem of his shirt to cut down on the glare, he flicked the light on. He found the trailhead beside the arena, a large phosphorescent yellow arrow appearing on the ground in the muted beam of his flashlight. He snapped off the light and made his way along the trail.

Kelly took his time, stopping often to listen to night sounds. Nothing disturbed the steady chirping of the crickets and other insects. Fireflies flitted about, blinking with soft yellow regularity in the dark shadows. The slight breeze calmed.

This isn't a trap, he thought. Law enforcement was not this good at reconnaissance.

A long, steep incline left him breathless, which surprised him until he realized the stress of the situation was taking a toll rather than physical exertion. The trail leveled out and the surrounding forest retreated somewhat, the overhead canopy thinning until large blotches of moonlight lit the trail. Large trunks stood with sentinel poise, hiding their secrets deep within their shadows.

A trick. It had been a trick. Probably Jeremiah Tyler, since the woman would not have the courage to try something like this on him.

Ah, Mattie Tyler. She wouldn't live to greet the next month. Kelly's lips quirked into a cruel smile and he abruptly spun on his heel to retrace his steps.

"Patrick Kelly."

A woman's voice, barely above a whisper, carried clearly in the darkness. Simultaneously, a small light flashed on. Kelly spun and squinted at the form behind the light. She seemed to be crouching just off the trail.

"Why, Mattie, is that you, love….?" He started to coo.

"The 1870-S three-dollar gold coin, the one you murdered at least two people for, is not in the arena," the woman interrupted.

"Murder? Me?" Kelly countered softly, taking a step forward, his flashlight in his hand. The woman appeared to be trying to minimize herself as a target behind the bright light. "Why, I think you must be mistaken, lass. There is absolutely nothing to suggest I have done anything so…so vile."

"You know full well what happened up here," the woman's voice echoed among the trees. "You killed a man in cold blood, then killed an innocent man in the arena at the riding stables."

"Strong words, lass." Malice laced Kelly's words as he took another step forward, tucking his flashlight into a pocket. He wanted both hands free when he pounced.

"And I know where the 1870-S coin is, and you're thinking you can wring the answer from me and then wring my neck." The bluntness of her statement sent a sudden chill along Kelly's spine, and he stopped. The figure with the light had not moved.

"Perhaps you are not alone?" he ventured, backing a step. The woman might also be armed. Surrounding shadows toyed with his senses and he thought he saw movement to his left. He jerked his head but could not see anything because of the effect of the light on his eyesight.

To complicate things, he could not be certain whether the voice belonged to Mattie Tyler. Perhaps this was a trap after all. He quickly reviewed what he had said so far, breathed a silent sigh of relief that nothing he had uttered could be considered incriminating.

"Maybe a dozen police officers are listening to our conversation," the woman countered. "Look around."

"Pray tell why you've lured me to the top of this ridge?" Kelly backed another step, just in case the woman was packing a weapon. His hand eased to the firearm tucked against his waist. She would be an easy target, holding the light like that.

"Before bullets start flying, I should tell you that you no longer own that three-dollar gold coin collection you've accumulated while stealing your parishioners blind."

Kelly froze in the middle of drawing his handgun. "What do

you mean?" he demanded, his raised voice echoing through the trees. "What are you talking about?"

"Furthermore, the 1870-S three-dollar gold coin is beyond your reach and will soon be returned to the Numismatic Museum in Colorado Springs." The woman's voice sounded annoyingly self-satisfied.

Kelly felt his jaw drop.

"So, you have a choice," the shadow continued. "Kill me now and lose forever all those gold coins you've collected over the years. Or leave with instructions on where to find your precious gold coins and the promise you will not go after anyone with intent to harm."

Surely, this was not the copper, Kelly thought malevolently. Law enforcement would not offer this kind of deal. The figure behind the light had to be the Tyler woman. Carefully, with undetectable movements, he drew his weapon, turning ever so slightly to keep his actions concealed.

"I see you have thought this one through," he stalled.

"Which will it be?" the woman demanded.

Kelly shrugged. "My coin collection, if indeed you have stolen it. And I will swear in a court of law those coins were purchased by money earned honestly and cleanly."

"With no evidence to prove otherwise," the woman stated flatly. There seemed to be the slightest hint of disappointment in her voice. "And your promise?"

Inwardly, Kelly laughed and laughed. Stupid woman. Careful to keep his humor hidden, he answered, "Upon my word as a minister and a gentleman."

"Here, then. Catch." The woman tossed what looked like a baseball in his direction. It fell short and rolled off the trail. Leaping from the path, he raised his handgun and pressed close against the trunk of a large tree. Taking careful aim, he squeezed off one, two, then three suppressed rounds at the figure behind the light.

His actions caught the Tyler woman off her guard, and she had no chance to dive for cover or even to voice a protest. Without a sound, she collapsed backwards and vanished. The light she held fell to the ground.

Gun still in hand, Kelly covered the distance quickly, picked up the small outdoor light, shone it around. A sharp precipice appeared, explaining the sudden disappearance of the woman. No sound came from the direction where the she had fallen. He pulled his flashlight from his pocket, flicked on the small, powerful beam, and spent several minutes searching the deep ravine.

Dense ground cover and forest growth hid all evidence of the dead woman.

Snapping off his flashlight and returning it to his pocket, Kelly holstered his weapon, lifted the light, and retraced his steps to find the baseball. He located it almost immediately and ripped the paper wrapped around it. He unfolded the sheet, read the contents, then snapped off the camping light and released a string of curses.

If this paper were to be believed, his beloved coin collection was buried in the back arena.

~ * ~

I held my breath when I saw the flash of Kelly's handgun, watched the Hunchback of the Ridge teeter, then roll over a sharp drop off and fall into a deep ravine.

Kelly had shot a tree stump with a raincoat thrown over it. The same stump that fooled trail horses each year into thinking it was a strange, hunchbacked human.

Fear tingled along my spine as I watched him scan the deep recess with a small flashlight, praying he wouldn't make the effort to negotiate the steep precipice in order to confirm his kill.

Relief washed over me when Kelly used the light to retrieve the baseball. Abruptly darkness fell when he turned off the light, and I listened to his string of curses. I waited, careful not to make a sound, barely even daring to breathe.

Leave, I mentally demanded. *Leave and go look for your precious gold coins.*

Movement beside me practically sent my heart ripping through my chest, and I grabbed for the Taser tucked in the waistband of my black sweatpants.

"Easy, Mattie. It's just an old Ute." Joe's voice spoke barely above a whisper.

I relaxed.

His fingers touched my lips. "Sh-h-h-h-h." And abruptly, he was gone.

Like I've repeatedly said, I'm not a good liar, and I won't lie now. An immense wave of relief washed over me at the presence of

Joe Healing Water. He knew how to handle a character like Reverend Patrick Kelly, and I felt safe knowing he was my backup.

I continued to wait in the thicket, Taser out and ready, just in case. Pale moonlight filtered through the thin overhead foliage, and I listened and watched for unusual sounds or movements.

A hand touched my shoulder, and I practically jumped out of my skin. Again.

"He's gone." Joe spoke in a low voice behind me, and I whipped around so fast I would have lost my balance if he had not gripped my shoulder. I couldn't tell what he wore, but it blended into the shadows so well all I could see were long silver highlights as moonlight reflected off his braided hair. Plus, his white teeth when he grinned at me.

"Not bad, Mattie. Hawk and Jeremiah better watch their backs. You'll end up a better spook than either of them." Joe moved from the bushes and walked over to examine the jagged edges where I had snapped the old rotted stump before propping it precariously on the edge of the ravine. "Where'd you come up with this idea?"

Tucking the Taser into my belt, I followed him. "It dawned on me that if the Hunchback Stump spooked horses, it might fool a person, especially if I dressed it up a bit and used a light to mess with Kelly's ability to see." I held up the remote I had used to switch the light on.

A chuckle rumbled deep in his chest. "Like posting watch. Anyone looking towards a light won't be able to see what's sneaking up on them in the surrounding darkness." He turned to face me. I noticed then he held a compound bow in his left hand and a quiver of arrows slung on his back.

"Hawk and Jeremiah are currently trailing our malevolent reverend," he informed, his voice low and even.

I nodded, though the image of Hawk in the vicinity sent icy fingers crawling up and down my spine. I involuntarily shuddered but managed to control the urge to whip the Taser out.

Joe ambled to a fallen log and took a seat. "Nice op you and Jeremiah cooked up." He patted the log beside him. "Sit down. We need to talk."

I didn't move. "Is Hawk coming back?"

Joe shook his head. "No, they'll be sticking to Kelly like flies on fly paper. It's you and me, and we need to talk," he reiterated.

I sat down beside him.

"What are you going to do about Jeremiah?" he asked without preamble. His bluntness shocked me, and I couldn't come up with an immediate answer. I turned my head away and stared at the spot on the trail where Kelly stood not too long ago.

"I'm…I'm not sure what you're asking," I said after a while. "We're no longer married, if that's what you mean. I stopped by Stephen's house and signed the papers before I flew out here. I don't see where I need to do anything about him, other than tell him to leave me alone."

"You signed the divorce papers?" Joe asked.

"Isn't that what I just said?" I balked.

He grunted. "According to Jeremiah, when he last spoke with Stephen, you hadn't signed the papers."

I threw up my hands. "Fine. No. I haven't had signed them yet. Too much going on. But it's first on my list when I get back to Oklahoma."

"Right." The sarcasm in his voice practically oozed onto the ground.

"Hey, just a minute," I glared at him, which was useless I'm sure because he couldn't see my expression in the dark. "I'm spoken for. I'm wearing the ring Randy was going to give to me."

"Did he ask you to marry him?" Joe challenged.

"He was going to," I argued.

Joe shook his head. "That's not what I asked."

I felt like a schoolgirl being reprimanded by the principal. "You know, none of this is any of your business."

"Did he ask you to marry him?" Joe repeated, ignoring my resistance.

I blew out a sigh. "No." Tears threatened. "He was killed before he had the chance. I should've asked him to kneel right there in the fog and mud and ask me in front of all the horse pens. Like Amy wanted."

Joe shifted on the log. "And you haven't signed papers finalizing the divorce between you and Jeremiah. I'll ask you again. What are you going to do about Jeremiah?"

"What is there left to do but sign the papers, get him out of my life, and start over?" I swiped at tears trickling down my face.

In the pale moonlight, Joe's black eyes glinted. "And why are you divorcing him?"

I rolled my eyes. "Well, duh, Joe. He's basically lied to me for the entire length of our marriage. I had no idea he was an operative, that he worked for the government, that he went on assignments. Or that he's killed people. And he wasn't there when I was in danger and needed him most."

Joe waited a beat before answering. "Yeah, well, you happen to be guilty of every damned thing you're accusing Jeremiah of doing." He shrugged. "Though this secret keeping nonsense of yours started more recently." Joe wriggled on the log. "And you haven't been around the last two years to help Jeremiah when he needed *you* most."

Silence caught us in a giant net, binding me as tightly as though physical cords wrapped my arms against my chest. We sat there in the darkness, the surrounding sentinel trunks like the bars of a cell, the soft night sounds deadened by the ring of Joe's words in my ears.

"So," Joe's voice, barely above a whisper, broke the stillness. "What are you going to do about Jeremiah?"

"I don't know," I blurted. I swiped at tears again. "I don't know." I sniffed, rubbing my face with the front of my sweatshirt. "But I do know I can't go back. Too much has happened."

"I agree," he murmured. "Going back never works. Neither of you are the same person you were before all of this went down."

I hunched my shoulders forward. The ensuing silence lasted a long time.

"In the meantime," Joe stirred again, "are you going to tell me where the gold coin is?"

His question jarred me from morose thoughts. "What?"

"Where's the damned coin?" he repeated. "You told Kelly it wasn't in the arena, that it's out of his reach and will be back in the museum soon. So, you know where it is."

I nodded. "Yes. I do."

Joe shifted on the log. "Where the hell is it?"

"Here," I told him.

He looked like a specter hovering above the ground, white strings of luminescence creating a halo around his skull. I turned my eyes to stare at the trail.

"You need to be more specific." Joe sounded more than a little annoyed.

I reached into the pocket of my jacket, pulled out the blue velvet ring box, held it out. "It's in here. Jeremiah and I haven't told anyone because we don't want Amy to get into trouble."

"Jeremiah knew?" Joe sounded aghast. I grinned in spite of myself.

"Yeah. And kept secrets from Hawk. And *you*. How's that for irony?"

"And just how long have you been carrying it around with you?" Joe took the box and peered at it closely in the dim moonlight.

I leaned forward and rested my forearms on my thigh and prosthesis. "I've had it since the day Randy was killed. But I didn't open the box until a few days ago. Amy must've found it in the arena when she ran in to check on her father. According to what she told Aiden; the Arab ran Kelly down. The coin must've dropped from his pocket. Amy found it, tucked it into the box with Randy's ring, and slipped the box into my pocket while she was curled up on my lap."

Joe carefully opened the lid. "There's an old Indian saying about this unquenchable thirst for gold."

"Yeah, I've read it," I stared at the overhead foliage, trying to remember the exact words. "Something about when the last of the food and water are gone, only then will man realize he can't eat money."

"Close enough." He snapped the lid shut and handed the blue velvet box to me. I zipped it back into my jacket pocket.

"Technically, that's evidence," he noted. "Concrete evidence, possibly with Kelly's prints, depending on who's handled it. It would give the cops a major breakthrough in the case."

I nodded. "I know. But if I turn it over to the police, they'll keep it locked up with other evidence, and I'll bet dollars to donuts the coin will disappear sooner than later never to be found again."

Joe grunted. "So, you intend to return it to the museum." He rubbed his hands against his thighs. "And that means Kelly will never be convicted of Randy's murder."

"There are already complications with the whole case anyway," I admitted, staring at the ground. "Riley told me the investigators think there's a connection between Randy's death and another victim in the county. Same type of weapon, same type of death."

"But not by the same person," Joe murmured into the stillness.

"Exactly," I agreed. "Which means we'll never get a case going against Kelly."

"He's a sneaky son of a bitch," Joe breathed.

I blew out a sigh, watched the warm air from my lungs condense in the rapidly cooling night air. "Yes, he is." I waited a bit, then admitted, "I'm not sure how to return the coin to the museum without them thinking it was me who stole it in the first place."

"That's where Jeremiah might prove useful." Joe's words hung almost visible among the shadows and patches of moonlight.

"I don't know that I want to try to patch things with him," I admitted slowly.

"You're going to end up damned lonely being engaged to a dead guy." Joe observed. "And I'm not advocating trying to patch things."

"You mean start all over." I straightened. I felt Joe's eyes on me as he spoke.

"See if there's anything that sparks between the two of you. You both have learned some pretty scary life lessons over the past couple of years."

I pondered his words until the night chill made me shiver. Or perhaps it was the ghosts of Randy and the guy murdered up here on the Ridge floating up and down my spine.

"No promises," I told him.

~ * ~

Jeremiah stole among the trees as he followed Kelly's retreat along the trail. When Kelly bypassed the arena and headed for the front drive, Jeremiah paused. Time ticked by with soft insect chirps before he felt the presence of another human.

"What is he doing?" Jeremiah murmured into the darkness.

"Calling his cleaning lady to inspect his safe for the coin case." Hawk's voice matched Jeremiah's.

"Confirming Mattie's statement before he starts digging," Jeremiah nodded slightly.

"He's in for a rather nasty surprise." Hawk settled beside the Ute. "If he's thinking she buried the case with the coins inside. Knowing that woman, she's spread those coins from here to yon."

Jeremiah grinned into the darkness. "Indeed."

"Bloody unsporting of her, if you ask me." Humor laced

Hawk's words.

The two men continued their reconnaissance, separating and keeping Kelly between them when he appeared in the stable area again. They watched him retrieve his backpack and the metal detector, watched as he spent hours creeping round the back arena, noted how his movements became increasingly agitated as night approached early morning. The eastern horizon lightened considerably before he finally abandoned his search and retreated down the front drive.

"You thinking what I am thinking?" Jeremiah asked his British companion.

"That we ought not let this chap waltz out of sight?" Hawk nodded, and the two men returned to their rental car. Judiciously they followed Kelly as he cycled through town to the parking lot where he had left his rental car.

"You wired the vehicle?" Jeremiah breathed as he pulled to the curb just out of sight.

Hawk sniffed. "We should expect fireworks any moment now."

"I want a visual of the hit," Jeremiah started to shift the car into gear, but Hawk held up a hand.

"Too risky. The town is too small, too much risk alerting him."

"Then we go on foot." Jeremiah cut the engine and quietly exited the driver's side. Hawk eased from the passenger side, and neither man closed his car door.

Patrick Kelly braked his bicycle to a stop at the trunk of the car he had used to travel from the Tennessee Regional Airport into town. With practiced efficiency, he removed both wheels and tucked them behind the front seats, then stored the frame in the trunk. He slipped behind the steering wheel and quietly shut the car door. He reached to turn the ignition when his ears picked up a faint click. His gut screamed a primal warning. Throwing the door open, he dove from the car and rolled across the tarmac and into a ditch.

KAAA-BOOOOM.

The explosive device must've been on a timer triggered by the car door. The hair on his head singed right off and he felt his exposed skin blister. He cowered in the ditch, seeking to avoid the rolling flames and thick, intensely hot black smoke. Only when sirens pealed above the roaring inferno did he risk moving, crawling on his belly around the corner of a nearby building. He lay there watching emergency crews arriving, feeling relatively secure from detection because he was wedged between the building and a steep embankment. As he watched the emergency crew activity, he thought things over.

The person behind the explosion had to be Jeremiah Tyler, the message he sent plain as day.

Well, he would pick up the metaphorical gauntlet. First on his list was to recover his coins. And then he would get rid of Jeremiah Tyler. There was no way the man could constantly be on alert, and Kelly had countless proven options when it came to ending the life of his targets.

And then he would leave Oklahoma and find a new location, start fresh. He rose to leave his hiding place when the skin on the back of his neck crawled, and his sixth sense warned he was not alone.

He whipped his head around, recognized Death. Anger mingled with disbelief jolted through him.

Before he could utter a sound, retribution descended.

Chapter Twenty

Riley burst into my bedroom Monday morning before even the sun had a chance to wake up.

"What were you thinking?" She shook me roughly, jarring my eyes open. I stared at her nonplussed.

"W-what?" I croaked, trying to orient myself to where I was, who I was, and what Riley was doing in my room at the crack of dawn.

Riley stomped back and forth between my bed and the open doorway. To my dismay, Aiden appeared and leaned against the doorframe. I was too groggy to notice what either of them wore. I barely had enough brain cells awake to recognize them. I sat up, registered I'd slept in my sweatshirt and pants, and rubbed my face with both hands.

"What time is it, and what are you doing in my room?" I managed to ask.

Riley halted abruptly at the foot of my bed. Her brown eyes blazed with so much anger I expected lasers to cut right through me then and there.

"What were you thinking?" she hissed, her words searing with rage that surpassed her expression. Bewildered, I glanced at her brother.

"What made you decide to face down a known killer by yourself in the middle of the night on the top of the Ridge?" Aiden translated.

Oh. Okay, I was in trouble. Riley looked ready to haul me out of bed and into a jail cell.

"Can I wake up a little more? How about some coffee?" I suggested, trying to deflect her anger.

"Not until you give me—us—some answers!" Riley's rough tone started alarm bells clanging around in my head and my heart thumping hard in my chest. She really did look ready to haul my ass out of bed and beat me to a pulp. I shot a look at Aiden to see whether he intended to intervene before Riley started throwing punches. He remained motionless against the doorframe. If anything, his expression reflected Riley's, and I thought I might be pummeled by them both before the sun rose.

"Okay, okay. Please, Riley calm down…." I started.

Riley practically leaped forward and thrust her face so close to mine that our noses bumped.

"Don't you *dare* tell me to calm down! You pulled one of the stupidest moves I have ever witnessed from *anyone*, including the morons I run into on a daily basis! You have *no idea* what that scum bag was capable of, how close you were to disappearing—never to be seen or heard from again!"

With a start, I realized tears filled her eyes. She realized what I'd seen and jerked around to hide her motion of swiping at her eyes. I scooted back to rest against the headboard. "I used a decoy. He didn't actually know where I was."

Riley, her back still turned, fisted her hands on her slender hips and tilted her head to the ceiling. "Did it never dawn on you he might realize the shape was a tree stump and would have started looking for you? That he had more than enough motive to hunt you down, torture you until you begged for mercy, and then enjoy killing you?" Her words came out in a hoarse croak.

"I was banking on his surprise when I told him about his missing coin collection. That he would leave and either check out my story or go digging around the arena for his coins," I admitted. I didn't want to leave the bed because I'd have to use the wheelchair or crutches since I'd left my prosthesis in the bathroom.

Aiden stepped forward suddenly and gripped his sister by the shoulders. "Cool it, Riley. Deep breaths. I know you don't want to hear it, but you need to get hold of yourself. She's safe and like it or not, her husband and that British dude seem to have taken care of Kelly."

I noticed then they both were dressed in sweats.

"You two are going to be late for shift report," I observed, glancing at the clock on my bedside table. I looked beyond the exposed windows of my bedroom. Fog sifted in vague whiffs between trees, and the scent of dampness heralded probable rain today.

Aiden sent me a strained look that sent a different set of alarm bells clanging around in my head.

"The two of you look after each other," he told me, easing his sister to the bed until she plopped down on the foot. "I need to run some errands." He looked at Riley. "You. Behave. Got it?"

Riley swiped at her eyes again. "I won't promise anything until I've wrung what I know from her."

"She's already told you. It's water under the bridge. Taking your worry out on her now won't help things. Figure out how to tell Jilly Wittmore she needs to let Mattie see Amy." He stepped back, and abruptly turned to face me. "And you. No more of this bravado shit. Okay?"

I nodded silent assent like a scolded child.

Aiden disappeared through the doorway and a few minutes later the engine of his Jeep growled to life. I heard the crunch of tires on gravel, then the noise faded into the early morning stillness. I turned my attention to Riley, who had not moved from the foot of the bed.

"Riley. I'm sorry. I know that doesn't help much now, but I do realize what kind of chance I took last night." I hesitated, then added, "Would it help to know Joe Healing Water, Jeremiah, and Hawk all three were with me? I knew I couldn't do it on my own, so I made sure I had back up."

Riley shook her head. "No, that doesn't help. It doesn't change the fact you put yourself in a lethal position."

I ran a shaking hand through my hair. "Okay. I'm sorry."

Riley snorted. "You're damned right."

I felt the walls closing in. She wasn't going to like what I'd decided to do next, either. Might as well admit it now instead of blindsiding her again.

"I've asked Jeremiah to drive me to the Tennessee airport. He's going to help me return the gold coin without me ending up in jail for a theft I didn't commit."

With deliberately slow movements Riley stood, met my eyes briefly, then turned on her heel and stalked from the bedroom, slamming the door so hard the entire house shuddered.

I hauled my butt out of bed and into the bathroom, dressed in a blue turtleneck, jeans, and a dark cardigan. I put on my prosthesis, then went looking for Riley.

I found her on the back porch, still in her sweats. She stared, without seeing, at the damp morning as shreds of fog crept between the mountains, eddied around darkened tree trunks, invited secrets and solitude and the promise of permanent protection from prying eyes. I sat on the porch swing and wrapped my cardigan snuggly around my chest to ward off the damp chill. Silence enveloped us, as impenetrable as the surrounding blanket of clouds.

"I need to talk to Jilly and to Amy," I said breaking the stillness.

Riley released an irritated huff. "Good luck. Jilly is refusing any contact with either Aiden or me, and I wouldn't be surprised if her attitude stretches to include you, too, since the three of us have been living under the same roof for the last two years."

I frowned. "Why her animosity towards the two of you?"

Riley clamped her lips together.

The two of us sat on the porch in silence, watching the weather gradually obscure first the rounded mountain tops, then the valleys. I was shivering violently before I finally stirred. "I'm guessing you're not going to elaborate?" I prompted.

Riley shook her head.

I stood. "Then I'm going to fix you something to eat, and then we need to talk about Jeremiah. Please?"

I took Riley's grunt as a 'yes'.

I fixed comfort food for both of us, which meant country biscuits and gravy, scrambled eggs, bacon, and coffee. Yes, most of it came out of boxes, given my limited talents in the kitchen.

Fog turned into rain, and Riley shuffled indoors. I told her to take a hot shower and change into dry clothes. Surprisingly, she didn't argue. Her color looked better after we finished eating, and I sat at the counter trying to figure a way to bring up the subject without sending her into another tirade.

"So, you and your ex are going to patch things up?" She looked as though she'd just eaten a bushel of lemons. I cringed and to gain time stood and took the dirty dishes to the sink. Rain drummed gently on the roof, water dripped and trickled with rhythmic melody along gutters and eaves. I shivered and limped to the fireplace. Soon flames licked around small logs, adding a soothing crackle to the muted sounds coming from outside. Riley slumped into one of the couches and stared unseeing into the soft fire. I sank into the second couch and pulled the afghan around me.

"I'm not going to patch up what no longer exists," I voiced into the stillness.

"Why pursue it? Why not start over with someone else?" she

challenged.

"I don't have a good answer for you," I admitted, staring into the fire. "But he represents past family, and I'm not sure I want to cut that off."

"Don't Aiden and I represent family?" She shot back.

I nodded. "Yes, Riley, you do. Both of you. Which is why I want to throw out an idea for you to consider." When she didn't answer, I continued. "I've been thinking about rebuilding my parents' estate and turning it into a riding stables and offering therapeutic riding. I would need a lot of help to get it going, and I've been wanting to ask you and Aiden if you would be willing to re-locate with me, but I didn't want to wreck what you guys have here."

"Maybe," Riley murmured after a long pause.

We sat listening to the rain and the gentle crackling of the burning logs.

"I'm not sure I won't still go through with a divorce," I confessed after a while. I glanced at Randy's ring on my left hand. "I don't have any expectations between Jeremiah and me."

"Do you still love him?" Riley's bluntness felt like a shock wave in the ambient atmosphere.

I pondered her question for a long time. "I don't know," I finally admitted.

Our conversation lapsed after that, and eventually Riley disappeared downstairs.

I made a difficult phone call.

"Hello, Jilly, it's Mattie Tyler," I greeted when she answered.

"I know who you are. And I want you to know straight out you will stay away from Amy. Period. Do you understand?" Jilly's voice sounded like she was in a courtroom facing a hostile jury.

"I really wish you would reconsider," I tried. "At least tell me why you don't want me to see Amy?"

Apparently, Jilly had prepared for my request. "It's because of you her father ended up dead in the first place. If you hadn't met Amy at the stables, Randy wouldn't have started working there."

I could have told her Randy could have died from an overdose, drinking and driving, or by a drunk driver. Or in one of the almost daily fatal collisions along Interstates eight-one and seventy-seven. I could have told her it was because of me Amy started opening up socially after her mother's death, that Randy got his act back together, and that all of our lives were moving in positive directions precisely *because* I had met Amy and her father.

But I also knew no amount of talking on my part would convince someone whose mind was already made up. And part of Jilly's hostility towards me came from the pain of losing her brother.

"Can I talk to her? I'd at least like to say goodbye, since I'll be moving out of state soon," I requested carefully.

"Thank goodness for some good news," Jilly retorted, but I heard her call Amy's name and within a few minutes her voice came on the other end.

"Hello, Miss Mary Joe," she greeted, then stopped. "I mean, well, darn. I can't remember what to call you now."

I chuckled. "Mary Joe is just fine, Amy," I told her. "How are you doing?"

"I'm okay, I guess. I can't do much else besides try to be okay, since nothing is going to bring Daddy back," she admitted, then sniffed.

"Are you still riding Fuzzy?" I asked.

More sniffing. "No. Aunt Jilly told Miss Kinsey to sell him, that I'm not going to be riding anymore."

I listened for a moment to see whether Jilly was on an extension. "Do you know where your Aunt Jilly is right now?" I asked her.

"She's at her desk looking at her computer. She's always working," Amy told me.

"Okay, then you listen to me. How old are you?" I limped back and forth in front of the hearth. Warmth radiated from the burning logs.

"Almost eleven," she answered.

"Well, you hang in there. I'm going to start a riding stable in Oklahoma. And I will make sure I buy Fuzzy and keep him out there. And if we're really nice to your aunt, maybe we can talk her into letting you spend the summers with me in Oklahoma. What do you think of that idea?"

The hope in Amy's voice brought tears to my eyes. "Do you really think she might let me do that?"

"I will work as hard as I can to convince her summers in Oklahoma will be really good for both her and for you." And I suddenly thought part of Jilly's attitude stemmed from the fact she was saddled with a kid she didn't really want and didn't know how to raise.

"We'll work something out, I promise," I reiterated. "It's going to be too cold and icky to ride any more this season anyway. So, you won't miss much at all."

"I'll miss going out to say hi and to brush him." Amy's voice shook.

"I'll send you pictures, and I'll keep him and Twister side by side so I can brush both of them and tell them hello for you every day. How's that sound?" I reassured her.

"Okay. I guess so." She didn't have a chance to say anything else because Jilly came back on the line. I repeated to her I would be moving to Oklahoma, and I asked her to consider letting Amy visit once I got settled.

Jilly's abrasive attitude did not relent, but she did not say no.

Riley was asleep when I checked on her, so I left a note saying I was heading to the stables to give Twister a long overdue hug. When I arrived, things were quiet. The weather had nixed lessons and the horses were tucked beneath their shelters. I grabbed brushes and a handful of treats and joined Twister in his pen beneath the generous lean-to. I cooed and doted over him, brushed his increasingly heavy winter coat until his blackness shone. I talked to him about Amy, about buying Fuzzy and about transporting the two of them to Oklahoma when I got things built. He nuzzled me with his soft nose, his intelligent, gentle brown eyes relaying he understood much of what I was telling him, and I felt the strong empathy horses possess and thought things might work out for everyone. Next, I went into Fuzzy's pen and brushed him down. He was much easier, being so much smaller than Twister, and he munched contentedly on his afternoon hay while I worked on him.

I was putting away the brushes when I sensed someone in the tack room with me. I turned to find Jeremiah standing in the doorway.

"Hello," I greeted evenly.

"I called your house. Riley told me where to find you," he explained. He wore a black sweatshirt, jeans, hiking boots, and a heavy jacket. He still looked too thin.

"Wow," I mused. "She actually talked to you? I figured she'd just give you an earful and hang up." I led the way outside and headed to a large open sided barn where hay and alfalfa was stored. I took a seat on a bale. Jeremiah found a seat opposite me. Rain still fell, and the earthy smells of rich loam, horses, and hay mixed with the damp scents of the weather.

"Hawk and I followed Kelly," he replied, watching me.

"And Joe Healing Water spirited himself to the top of the ridge." My statement generated a chuckle and a hint of a smile from him.

"That may well be true," he agreed. "I am not sure how much human he is versus ghost."

"Has he mentioned anything about our conversation?" I asked him.

Jeremiah shook his head.

I inhaled and stared at the gentle rainfall. "I need your help to return the stolen coin to the numismatic museum in Colorado Springs. Otherwise, I'm afraid they'll think I'm the one who stole it."

Jeremiah regarded me with an unreadable expression. "From what I have researched, there are no leads concerning who stole the coin. Surveillance cameras went down when the power went out. Technically, you could claim you found the coin, Googled the background, and found who to contact regarding how to return it." He fell silent for several moments. Light rain rattled the overhead tin roof. "Realistically, you do not need my assistance to return the coin."

I felt my eyebrows raise in slight surprise.

"Okay, let's put that point on a back burner for a minute," I stalled, not quite sure what he was trying to tell me. "Changing subjects. The car that exploded and was all over the local news. Were you and Hawk involved with that?"

Jeremiah nodded. "Yes."

"Who wired the car to explode?" I pressed.

Jeremiah watched me. "Hawk did."

"The news reports said Reverend Kelly's body was discovered behind a nearby building." I picked at the strands of hay poking up from the bale.

"Yes."

My eyes snapped to his. "In this case, your monosyllabic answers are a good thing, because I don't want to know details." I fell silent and listened to the rain. "Well," I ventured after a while, "At least I won't have to worry about running into him digging up the back arena."

Jeremiah nodded, then grinned. "You do have a mischievous streak. You know as well as I do you did not bury those coins in the arena. Those coins are lost in plain sight."

I shot him a surprised look. "You know what I did?"

Jeremiah studied me. "Yes."

"Does Hawk know?" I asked.

Jeremiah's eyes never wavered. "No, he does not."

I inhaled deeply. "Then am I to assume you are always somewhere in the background, keeping an eye on me?"

Jeremiah shrugged.

"Are you planning on keeping me under surveillance for the rest of my life?"

My question caught Jeremiah off guard, and I saw a startled look flicker across his features. I smiled at him. "Yes?"

Jeremiah shifted but didn't answer.

I continued nonchalantly. "So, would it make your reconnaissance easier if we sort of work as a team?"

His eyes met mine, his expression as unreadable as a stone wall. "What do you have in mind?"

I explained my idea to rebuild my parents' estate and construct stables for riding. Jeremiah listened in silence until I finished.

"That way, we could bring Mud Rain to live with us, hire experts to help run the therapeutic part, and hopefully have a place for Amy to spend summers with Fuzzy. Aiden and Riley might even end up joining us."

"You want to fix a lot of people's problems," Jeremiah noted.

"I want to build a new family," I countered bluntly. "Problems will always be there. But I want to work on positive solutions, whether they end up working out for everyone or not."

Jeremiah gazed at me. "I am willing to be part of your life in whatever role you choose for me to be."

I shook my head. "No, I want you to be part of my life and be who you have always been, and I will be who I am now, and if we find common ground, then we build a life together."

Epilogue

Prairie wind buffeted the Explorer as I turned onto the winding drive leading to the destroyed Lamont estate. November had arrived and departed amidst a slew of trips between Virginia and Oklahoma. December had commenced warmer than usual, but that would end this weekend when a cold front brought arctic winds and an ice storm. At least for now, late afternoon temperatures remained mild. I slowed the Explorer to a stop at the bottom of the homeless front staircase leading to nowhere, shifted to park, and cut the engine. I did not unfasten my seatbelt or roll down the window. I stared at the desolation from the protective interior of my vehicle.

Twilight emphasized barren branches surrounding the property of my parents' former estate. A large familiar white moving van occupied the space beneath a canopy of tall sturdy trees, the same van I'd spotted when Jeremiah and I came to the bunker in October. I stared at the vehicle for a long time, trying to work out why it seemed familiar. Maybe some idiot had abandoned it on my parents' property. Vivid memory supplied images of what the estate had looked like, my childhood years spent running through hallways and across the broad manicured lawn, but those images did not include a white moving van.

My parents' estate. Somehow, I could not think of it as my estate, which technically it was now. Had been for over two years. As my parents' home, the place held memories of family. Trying to think of it as my home generated nothing but pain.

I'd argued with Jeremiah about driving out here alone. I wanted him along, didn't want to make the trip by myself when he made the suggestion. I was ready to nix the idea altogether, but Jeremiah insisted. When he gave his reasons, I argued even more vehemently for him to come with me. He remained firm, reassured me that I would be safe, asked me to trust his decision.

I didn't want to. I wanted him to be in the car, sitting beside me, to be with me. The thought of the imminent confrontation terrified me beyond reason, and I debated on calling the cops.

I sighed, feeling morose. I'd made mistakes, and I needed to own up to that fact. I'd been blind and oblivious when I should have been asking questions and working harder to crack the shell around him. His professional training, his past, and his potential future all seriously intimidated me, and I was using the resulting strain as an excuse to run away.

Becky kept trying to intervene, reassuring me I would adjust.

Bill focused on the Sooners' chances of a play-off bid, and I was finally recognizing he had as thick a wall built around him as Jeremiah did.

In the meantime, I felt out of place and homeless and missed my Virginia house, the memories I'd collected over the two years I'd lived there, the close, protective feel of the surrounding mountains, the stables.

Ghosts of lost loved ones haunted me day and night, ridiculing my efforts to put the past in its place and focus on the future. My eyes wandered across the overgrowth and debris, and I doubted the wisdom of my decision to rebuild and add a stable. I debated pulling out my cell phone and calling Riley to tell her I was changing my mind and returning to Virginia.

But ghosts haunted Virginia, too. Memories of Randy, Amy's lessons and her excitement and growing ability as a budding equestrian. I thought about buying Fuzzy and keeping him there, but then no one would ride him because Jilly refused to allow Amy anywhere near the stables.

Ghosts floated everywhere, in the past and in the present. I couldn't help but wonder whether they would haunt my future, too.

Construction would not begin until next summer, after tornado season. I had six months to change my mind and return to Virginia. I glanced at Randy's ring on my right hand and thought I could live with Virginia ghosts more easily than ones floating around out here.

Sighing, I opened the door and slid onto the unkept driveway. William and his wife, Anna, had moved off the property to an assisted living establishment after William suffered a mild stroke. Stephen had given me their address, encouraged me to visit them soon. I knew I needed to see them but kept putting it off. I wandered among the rubble overgrown with weeds so much now that mounds of bricks seemed part of the topography. Only the concrete slab remained, although Mother Nature was beginning to fracture the slab with plants more stubborn than anything man-made. I prayed no one would show up. My thin shred of courage evaporated, and I started to return to my car.

A movement in my peripheral vision caught my attention, and I spun around. Hawk stood about ten yards away, just visible in the rapidly lengthening shadows. Wind ruffled his collar-length black hair, his dark jeans and long-sleeved shirt blending so perfectly with the background shadows I thought he might be a hallucination.

"Yes, I am, in fact, here," he called out softly. "Though you apparently prefer a specter to flesh and bone based on your similar expression to my appearance after your sister's funeral."

His words prompted a memory of the evening he materialized in the music room after guests had left the funeral reception.

I swallowed, nerves making my stomach churn. "That was also the evening a bunch of your friends came and blew up my parents' house," I replied, backing up. I had not been alone with this man since that awful night. "W-where did you come from? H-how'd you know I was here?"

"Underground bunker," he answered, not moving. "Spotted you when you drove in."

Jeremiah's and my argument came back to mind. "Jeremiah told me you would be here." My voice cracked despite my efforts.

Hawk gave a slight nod. "Yes."

"Then whatever your business is that brought you here, you need to discuss it with him."

"My business involves you, not Jeremiah." His statement sent a shiver down my spine.

Damn. Jeremiah had told me the same thing. I tried another tact.

"Y-you need to leave. Now." I gave up trying to sound brave. "Or I'm calling the police." I pulled out my cell phone and backed several more steps.

Hawk waved a hand at the white van. "I've an olive branch, if you're willing."

Insight hit and I swung my attention to the van. "That's why the moving van seems so familiar," I mused aloud. "I remember now. I saw it through the kitchen window. It rolled down the driveway right before those m-men…." I trailed off.

Hawk nodded. "Precisely."

"Why now? Why an olive branch, as you put it?" My voice

sounded muted in the deepening twilight. The wind was not obstructive, just normal prairie breeze.

"A long overdue offer. To make amends." His voice carried despite his low tone. He turned towards the van.

Puzzled, I watched him cross to the vehicle. He retrieved a key from a pocket and released a heavy lock securing the rear doors. With a powerful heave, he lifted the sliding door then stepped back and turned to me.

"The honor is yours." A large flashlight appeared in his hand. "You'll want a torch." He stepped away from the trailer, maintaining distance between us, when I moved forward. I climbed into the back. From outside, Hawk flicked the light on, and the strong beam revealed the contents.

Two large, oblong objects wrapped in heavy quilted blankets and strapped securely to the interior walls quirked my interest. With a sudden surge of astonishment, I realized what lay beneath the protective coverings.

Mom and Dad's two seven-foot grand pianos.

I whirled, dizzy with realization, and felt Hawk's strong fingers grip my upper arm, my heart lurching hard in my chest with the contact. He steered me gently to what I recognized as one of the piano benches, heavily wrapped and secured, and sat me down.

"H-how…?" I stammered, breathless.

He stepped back so he wouldn't tower over me. "Just accept I could not tolerate two beautiful instruments such as these destroyed by those thugs." He walked to the rear of the trailer. When he reappeared, he held an object that took my breath away. My heart imploded inside my chest and I felt the blood drain from my face. I gripped objects nearby to keep from toppling off the bench. I did not reach for what he held because I didn't believe what I saw, couldn't believe, dared not to believe for fear this was some gruesome nightmare. I did not want to wake up to find it all nothing more than a cruel joke generated by my subconscious.

"D-does J-Jeremiah know?" I choked out.

"Yes, he does," he murmured. He knelt before me, hugging the object close to his chest. "The past is the past and I cannot undo what was done," he continued, his voice barely above a whisper. "I hope these will help you embrace the future and allow new memories to replace the old." His voice, his accent, echoed softly through the interior of the trailer.

I met his eyes. His gray eyes stared back, his expression as unreadable as Jeremiah's. Two men alike in so many ways physically, professionally, emotionally.

Two men with a code of honor so rare as to be difficult to recognize. I felt Jeremiah's spirit enclose protectively round my heart as I dragged my eyes from Hawk's and stared again at the object in his arms.

Angela's urn.

I slid off the bench onto the hard metal floor of the van. Hawk carefully, reverently held the urn towards me.

I wrapped my arms around the urn that held my sister's ashes and wept.

About the Author

F.L. Godfriaux (Lynn Godfriaux Maloy) has spent most of her adult life raising her two children and teaching piano. She received both a Bachelors and a Masters in piano from the University of Oklahoma and is an active performer, adjudicator, and presenter. Her writing career began through poetry and culminated in her first book, *The Well-Tempered Poet: 24 Pictures and Poems*, which was published in 2010. She has written articles about dyslexia in the music field in the CSMTA newsletter and *Clavier Companion*. Now that her family has grown, Lynn is focusing on writing, performing, and spending time with her husband and with her horse.

Check out the other books in this thrilling trilogy

BLIND EYE

Mattie Lamont Tyler loses both parents in an apparent car accident, then finds herself estranged from her only sibling when her sister Angela elopes with a new boyfriend. But Mattie, a photojournalist with (ironically) a phobia of guns and violence, is blind to dangers around her until Angela ends up on the critical list in an ICU six hundred miles from home and Mattie's husband, a Southern Ute who appears to be a quiet, unassuming weather forecaster, stops answering his cell.

Before she can figure out what's going on, Mattie is kidnapped by Hawk, a ruthless stranger with accusations Mattie does not understand. Her own survival and the lives of her loved ones depend on whether Mattie can see beyond her "blind eye" into unknown inner strength.

From the plains of Oklahoma to the mountains of Southwest Colorado, Blind Eye sweeps the reader into a frantic race against greed, lies, and pre-meditated murder.

EYE FOR EYE

In the second installment of the Blind Eye series, billionaire heiress Mattie Tyler is abducted by a team of mercenaries sent to avenge the death of their leader, whom Mattie shot while defending herself and her family in the southwest Colorado Rocky Mountains.

Crippled by a recent gunshot wound and unable to defend herself, Mattie helplessly watches the killers destroy her family home, then target her closest friends.

As the trail of death and destruction grows, Mattie's husband, Jeremiah "Black Bear" Tyler, must rely on his experience as a covert operative to recruit questionable allies in order to save her. But in a shocking twist of fate he finds himself the prime target of law enforcement when circumstantial evidence convinces investigators he is after Mattie's family wealth.

More mysteries await in these books from WolfSinger Publications

da sticks – Rich Kisielewski

Not long ago, Harry had moved back to the town where his ex-wife and kids reside and was trying to rebuild his life. The "work hard and play hard" attitude that carries Harry through life is balanced by the softness evidenced in his dealings with his children. Once again, he was going to have to be away from them and the new life he had been trying so hard to establish.

Going undercover at MechInsCo, Harry gets exposure to executives within the company including his lifer accounting boss, the psycho senior finance executive and a frantic company president. They all paint the same picture-a company losing money with no idea how, or why. His stint at MechInsCo supplies Harry with some raucous times: large amounts of information, booze and ladies provide him with much more than he signed on for.

da bug – Rich Kisielewski

Harry Mickey Shorts gets a call from M. Randle Trundle, a New York business tycoon, who is in need of Harry's help. Without a thought, Harry drops what he is doing and races off to help his benefactor, and his friend.

Trundle is a part owner in Board Room Farms—a horse racing stable—which is run by his brother, Danny Trundle. He informs Harry the stable's stud breeding stallion was found dead in his stall and Trundle feels something is wrong. Harry agrees to help Trundle with the case and does what he does best by going undercover and begins digging into the world of thoroughbred horse racing. Having bet on more than a few nags before in his lifetime, Harry is comfortable around the track and blends in very smoothly.

During his investigation, Harry forms an alliance with the ranch's female vet—in more ways than one. She agrees to provide needed intelligence on the current and prior goings-on at Board Room farms. Along the way, she becomes a serious love interest in

Harry's life. Unfortunately, that conflicts with Harry's renewed part-time interest in his ex-wife that may prove to be a "pick one" dilemma, sooner, rather than later. His love for, and continued attempt to become part of his two children's lives, remains paramount in Harry's thinking.

da nuts — *Rich Kisielewski*

Harry Mickey Shorts, street wise private detective, gets a call from Max who just happens to be his favorite as well as his only son. Max doesn't ask his dad for much but he and his buddies are in need of Harry's help. Without a thought, Harry drops what he is doing and races off to help his son and his friends.

Max informs Harry he would like him to investigate the untimely events that prohibited Clint, their current cult hero, from participating in a first ever poker tournament. Clint had played over a quarter of a million hands of poker by the time he had reached his eighteenth birthday and, as evidenced by the size of his bank account, he had won a lot more of those hands than he had lost. All of that meant nothing when he turned up unconscious in his hotel room on the morning of the first day of the inaugural "Under 18 World Championship of Poker" tournament.

During his investigation, Harry uses his expertise that sets him apart from other private investigators and goes undercover to explore the world of internet poker. The twist with this version is only kids between the ages of sixteen and eighteen can participate and all winnings may only be paid to higher institutions of learning for the kid's college education. Once he uncovers the wrong-doings of the unscrupulous masterminds behind this scheme he partners with his benefactor M. Randle Trundle, a New York business tycoon, to set things right and preserve the previously dashed hopes of the winning poker teenagers. Harry's renewed part-time interest in his ex-wife and his love for and continued attempt to become part of his two children's lives complicates his own life but remains paramount in Harry's thinking.

da kid — *Rich Kisielewski*

Much to his surprise, Harry Mickey Shorts gets a call from

Mel, his ex-brother-in-law, who needs his help. It is a rare occasion when Mel asks Harry for anything at all never mind his help. When it does happen Harry takes notice and drops what he is doing to see what it is that troubles "Big Mel."

Over a few cool ones Mel tells Harry a long-winded tale from his past involving a kid he had coached. Little Billy Burns had walked out of the gym before the end of a basketball game and soon vanished all together. Mel's belief that he had somehow failed Billy has lingered and he now sees an opportunity to rectify that wrong.

With the help of his friend, Tom, Harry's investigation takes him back to Central Pennsylvania to meet with Billy who currently resides in the Cumberland County jail. Their journey begins with an introduction to Billy's extended con-artist family and ultimately to some Las Vegas hustlers who are looking to continue their venture into golf course swindles. And at long last is Mel's reunion with Billy. At the same time Harry's part-time interest in his ex-wife, his love for his children and his continued attempt to become an integral part of their lives, continues to complicate his own life.

The Dolmen – *Matt Bille*

When attorney Julie Sperling's fiancée is murdered while researching a controversial museum exhibit, she calls on her ex-lover, science writer Greg nightmarish pursuit as very real predators from ancient folktales try to hunt down anyone with knowledge of their existence.

For Greg and Julie, the City of Angels has become the gateway to hell...

Murder Most Howl – *Margaret H. Bonham*

Dog Mushing Can Be Murder

For Stephanie Keyes, noted sled dog racer in Colorado, sled dog racing can be dangerous enough. But when a fellow musher and rival is found murdered and she's a prime suspect, Stephanie races to find the killer before he can strike again.

Missing sled dogs and deadly goals abound in this super sleuth tale—or is it tail?